April 2014

Dear Friends,

Weddings are magical, aren't they? There's such joy, excitement, and anticipation with weddings. The brides are beautiful, and the grooms are nervous and excited. It's a gathering of family and friends for a celebration of love and life. I always tear up at weddings; I simply can't help it. Little wonder I enjoy writing about falling in love as much as I do.

Our daughter was married last summer. So as I was writing *Blossom Street Brides,* I was involved in the planning of Jody and Greg's wedding. I wrote their vows and sniffled through the ceremony, which took place on a beach on a glorious July afternoon.

This story is an invitation for you to attend a wedding, and my wish is that you'll read it with the same anticipation and pleasure you would if you were personally acquainted with the bride and groom.

As always, publishing a book is a team effort, and I want to be sure to acknowledge the talented team of professionals I work with at Random House. To mention each by name would require another book. Jennifer, Shauna, Susan, Kristin, to mention just a few, work tirelessly to publish the best books possible. I want you to know how grateful I am for your talent and dedication. A special note of appreciation to my agent, Theresa Park, and her incredible staff for managing the details of my complicated career. And last, I would be remiss if I didn't mention my own team, who so diligently strive to keep my head above water and me on deadline. So thank you Renate, Adele, Wanda, Heidi, Carol, Katie, and Brittany for giving me the opportunity to do what I love most, and that's write.

Some of my best ideas come from readers. Leighann McInnis wrote to tell me about Street Knits in New Brunswick, Canada. I loved the idea so much I incorporated it into *Blossom Street Brides*. Thanks, Leighann.

So, my friends, roll out your Sunday best; you're about to attend a fun and very special wedding. My wish is that as you read this story you will fall in love all over again yourself.

Warmest regards,

Debbie Macomber

P.S. Getting feedback from my readers is important to me. You've been the guiding light in my entire career. You can reach me via my website, DebbieMacomber.com; on Facebook; or at P.O. Box 1458, Port Orchard, WA 98366.

BLOSSOM STREET
BRIDES

Debbie Macomber

BLOSSOM STREET BRIDES

A Blossom Street Novel

BALLANTINE BOOKS

NEW YORK

Copyright © 2014 by Debbie Macomber

All rights reserved.

Published in the United States by Ballantine Books, an imprint of Random House, a division of Random House LLC, a Penguin Random House Company, New York.

BALLANTINE and the HOUSE colophon are registered trademarks of Random House LLC.

ISBN 978-0-345-52884-1
eBook ISBN 978-0-345-54986-0

Printed in the United States of America on acid-free paper

www.ballantinebooks.com

2 4 6 8 9 7 5 3 1

FIRST EDITION

Book design by Dana Leigh Blanchette
Title-page illustration: © iStockphoto.com

To Jody and Greg Banks:
May your love last a lifetime.

BLOSSOM STREET
BRIDES

Chapter One

*L*auren Elliott had received the most depressing news of her life.

Her sister was pregnant.

Her *younger* sister.

Oh, she was happy and excited for Carol, but mingled in with the joy was an undeniable sense of envy. The fact that Carol was about to become a mother shouldn't have come as a shock—her sister and Jason had been married for two years, after all. Lauren loved her sister, and Jason would make a wonderful father. What bothered her was the fact that at age thirty-four, Lauren was still unmarried.

Single. Oh, how she'd come to hate that word.

Walking down Blossom Street, Lauren buried her hands deep into the pockets of her fawn-colored rain jacket. Tulips and crocuses bloomed in the flowerpots that hung from the streetlights, and the scent of roses, lilacs, and camellias followed her as she walked past Susannah's Garden, the flower shop.

Lauren kept her head down as she mulled over this latest development. This was it. The end of her rope. The line in the sand. She was finished waiting for Todd to give her an engagement ring. A year earlier she'd had the DTR—Defining the Relationship—talk with Todd and he'd assured her that marriage was definitely part of their future. Only he wasn't in a financial position to make the leap just yet. He'd suggested they give it time, and she'd reluctantly agreed. That was twelve months ago, and frankly her patience was shot. She'd dated the popular local television newscaster for three years and it was time to own up to the truth. If Todd was sincere about wanting her for his wife, then she would have had a diamond on her ring finger long before now.

Clearly Todd enjoyed their relationship just the way it was, and in some ways so did she. Todd was fun and smart, and she liked being with him. Because of his job, Lauren frequently accompanied him to high-profile social events. As a result, she was able to mingle with some of the city's elite, and it didn't hurt that many of these socialites came to John Michael Jewelers, where she worked, for their jewelry needs.

Lauren passed A Good Yarn and the window display instantly caught her attention. She stopped to give it a look and shook her head. Wouldn't you know it, the display in the yarn store's window was a baby blanket.

A beautiful baby blanket knit in lovely pastel colors. Lauren wanted to groan. She loved her sister, but there'd always been a friendly rivalry between them. More laid-back of the two, Lauren didn't have big career ambitions, whereas Carol worked as a program designer for a large software company out of California. She'd married her college sweetheart and seemed to have the perfect life.

Lauren had dropped out of college after a couple of years and over time had worked at a number of jobs. She enjoyed sales and seemed to be good at it. The irony was that her specialty was engagement and wedding bands. The couples she dealt with were deeply in love and eager to start their lives together. It gave Lauren a deep sense of satisfaction to help them take one of their first steps toward commitment.

The bottom line, she realized now, was that Todd was completely content to leave matters just as they were. They got along great and talked frequently. Rarely a week passed without them attending some sort of social event. They would like to spend more time together, but Todd was busy with his broadcasting career. He had his sights set on getting an anchor position and focused most of his attention on achieving his professional goals.

"Hello, Lauren," Lydia Goetz said, coming up from behind her.

"Oh, hi." Lauren spun around to greet the owner of the yarn store. Lydia's husband, Brad, had purchased his wife's wedding band at John Michael Jewelers, where Lauren had worked for the past five years.

"Isn't that a beautiful baby blanket?" Lydia asked, apparently noticing that Lauren's gaze was focused on the window display.

"It is." Lauren had no option but to agree.

"I think I've sold more yarn from this display than any I've ever done. There's something about knitting for babies that draws people into the shop. Just yesterday a customer stopped by and bought yarn for the blanket and told me she doesn't know anyone who's having a baby, but she thought she'd knit it anyway."

Lauren faked a smile. "I just got word my sister is pregnant." She didn't elaborate and explain that Carol was a full two years younger than she. "When I saw this blanket I thought I should knit it for her."

"I'm sure she'd treasure it. Anything homemade makes a baby gift all the more special."

Lydia inserted the key to the front door, and while Lauren was tempted to purchase the yarn right then, she needed to get to work herself. "I'll be by later today or tomorrow to pick up the yarn."

"Make it Thursday. I'm sold out, but I have a new shipment due in then. I'll be here if you need any help with the pattern," Lydia assured her.

John Michael Jewelers was one block down from the yarn store. Elisa Lippincott, the original owner's daughter, managed the store now with her husband, Garry. Lauren enjoyed her job immensely and considered Elisa a friend as well as her employer.

"Morning," Lauren said as she came into the store. She locked the door behind her. When the safe was open all the doors leading into the store remained locked.

Elisa stuck her head out of the walk-in safe. "Morning," she returned brightly. She had a pair of jewel cases in her hands, which she set into the display window that looked out onto Blossom Street.

Lauren removed her raincoat and stuck it in the back office along with her purse. Right away she helped Elisa get out the semiprecious stones. Despite the down economy, the store continued to do well. Elisa, Garry, and Lauren—all working full-time, along with a few part-time sales associates—were a good team.

"Garry will be in sometime this afternoon," Elisa explained as she set out the semiprecious stones. "He's got a meeting at the school for one of the boys, and then he's headed to lunch with the Rotary Club."

Garry was the company expert when it came to men's and women's watches. Lauren headed up their diamond sales, and Elisa handled just about everything else.

"I heard from my sister," Lauren said casually as she set the jewels in the display case, locking them inside. "Carol and Jason are pregnant." She made sure she sounded pleased and excited for her *younger* sibling.

"That's great."

"It is," Lauren agreed. "It's just wonderful. Mom and Dad are over the moon. Their first grandchild."

Elisa paused and focused her attention on Lauren. "You sound like you're ready to cry."

"I could break into sobs at the drop of a pin," she admitted, and tried to laugh it off, but the only sound that came out was reminiscent of something one might hear on the Sci-Fi channel. She quickly got hold of herself. "Tell me, Elisa, and please be honest. Is there something wrong with me?" Because Elisa was her friend, she expected the truth.

"Wrong?"

"Am I annoying?"

"Not at all." Elisa sounded shocked that Lauren would suggest such a thing.

"Do I have a domineering or unpleasant personality?"

"No way."

"Do I bore you?"

"No." Her friend shook her head.

"Am I unattractive?"

This question produced a laugh. "Hardly. Have you looked in a mirror lately? You're gorgeous—tall and slim, with your stunning blue eyes and that dark hair. I swear there must be some Scottish blood in you somewhere. Half the men who come in this shop leave half in love with you."

Her friend's words were a balm to her wounded pride. "Then why am I still single?"

Elisa didn't hesitate. "Because Todd Hampton is an idiot." She gently squeezed Lauren's forearm. "You've been much too patient with him. You need to give Todd an ultimatum," she suggested. "He loves you. All he needs now is a gentle shove in the right direction. Tell him it's time; you've been patient to this point, but you aren't willing to continue without a firm commitment."

An ultimatum for Todd—Lauren had reached the same conclusion but then rethought the matter. The fact was, she'd spent the majority of the night tossing and turning, mulling over her options with Todd. She'd teetered back and forth with the relationship, wondering what would be best. She hated the idea of forcing him to set a date, and then wondered why she'd been so willing to let matters drag.

"The thing is . . ." Lauren didn't get the opportunity to finish her sentence when Elisa's cellphone chirped.

"It's Katie." Elisa grabbed it before the second chirp.

Lauren knew the shop owner had been anxiously awaiting a call from her oldest child. Katie was a college freshman, and Elisa had undergone separation anxiety sending her only daughter away to school, which was less than three hundred miles away in Pullman, Washington. Elisa worried incessantly over Katie's diet, studies, partying, alcohol, and dating. If Katie didn't contact her mother at some point during the day, Elisa was convinced her child had fallen victim to any number of dreadful possibilities.

"Katie, why haven't you called?" Elisa demanded. "You didn't answer the text message I sent, and—"

Elisa paused, then let out a loud gasp and hurried into the small office, quickly closing the door. Lauren couldn't help but wonder what that was about. Her friend tended to be something of a drama queen. Even with the office door closed, Lauren could hear Elisa, although she couldn't make out what she was saying.

The possibilities raced through Lauren's mind. More than likely, it was something minor. Katie might have flunked an important test. Or she needed extra money put into her bank account. Quite possibly, she hadn't turned in her library books on time and had allowed the fine to accumulate. Lauren liked Katie and considered the teenager levelheaded and responsible. As a friend and employer, Elisa was great, but as a mother, she was a bit fixated.

Ten minutes later, Elisa reappeared, as white as a sun-bleached sheet.

"Elisa," Lauren asked tentatively. "Is everything all right with Katie?"

Her friend didn't answer and then simply shook her head.

"Do you need to sit down?"

Elisa nodded.

Lauren scooted over a stool, and Elisa sank onto it in slow motion.

"Do you want me to call Garry?"

That got an immediate response that came as a shout: "No . . . no!"

"Can I get you coffee?"

"I need something way stronger than coffee. Way stronger."

Lauren didn't think they kept anything more potent at the store, unless it was for a special sales event. Even then it was champagne, and Lauren suspected Elisa wasn't in the mood to celebrate with a glass of bubbly. "Can you tell me what's wrong?"

"I . . . I don't know." Tears welled in Elisa's eyes.

Apparently, this was something far worse than an overdue library book or a failed test. Disregarding what Elisa had claimed she needed, Lauren brewed her a single cup of coffee, making sure it was extra-strong. She added three cubes of sugar and stirred until it had dissolved before delivering it to her friend.

Elisa held on to the cup with both hands as though it was all that was keeping her from falling off the edge of a ten-story building. "Do you remember Dietrich?"

"Of course." Katie had recently brought the farmer's son home during spring break. His family was from the Walla Walla area in the southeast corner of the state. Dietrich's family farm was one of the largest producers of sweet onions in the country.

"I didn't like him the minute I met him."

Actually, Elisa had disapproved of the young man even before she'd met Dietrich. Because he was a senior and three years older than Katie, Elisa was convinced he was too old for her daughter, which was ridiculous. Garry was three years older than Elisa. That was simply an excuse, Lauren suspected, because Elisa didn't want her daughter getting into a serious relationship.

"Did Katie and Dietrich break up?" Lauren asked, although that wouldn't make sense. That news would have relieved Elisa.

"I wish," she snorted. Then, as if realizing she was holding a mug of hot coffee in her hands, she sipped it. After one taste, she grimaced. "I can't believe this is happening. It's a nightmare." Squeezing her eyes shut, she shook her head and then covered her mouth with her hand.

"Katie isn't . . ."

Elisa nodded. "My daughter is pregnant. She's only nineteen. She's a baby herself, and now she insists that she loves Dietrich and wants to marry him. Tell me, Lauren, do you honestly see Katie married . . ."

"Ah . . ." Lauren hardly knew what to say.

"It's ridiculous. Utterly ridiculous. She's far too young."

Lauren sat down next to her friend. "What did you tell her?" Lauren asked, concerned. There'd been a lot of shouting going on.

"What else? I insisted she come home immediately. There are ways of dealing with situations like this. I never thought I'd say this, but I can't allow my daughter to go through with this pregnancy. A baby now would ruin her life. We've got to think about her future."

"Isn't this Katie's decision?" Lauren asked gently.

Elisa's eyes snapped with anger. "Not you, too."

"Me?"

"That's what Katie said, and she insists she's going to have this baby. She's convinced she's in love with that . . . that farmer."

Now didn't seem a good time to remind Elisa that at age twenty-two Dietrich was an adult and, from what Lauren had seen, a responsible, kindhearted one.

"He took advantage of Katie," Elisa insisted, straightening now.

"Is that what Katie said?"

"Oh, no, she wouldn't admit to anything like that. Instead, she defended him and insisted they were equally responsible."

Personally, Lauren felt that this was a matter between Katie and Dietrich and that Elisa would be well advised to let them decide how best to deal with the situation.

"I insisted Katie come home right away, but she refused." Elisa took another taste of the coffee and made a gulping sound as though it was difficult to swallow.

"I wish I knew what to say," Lauren confessed. She felt at a loss and wasn't certain she had anything of value to contribute.

"This is history repeating itself," Elisa whispered, and wiped away a tear that had spilled out from the corner of her eye. "Garry and I . . . I was pregnant at nineteen, too."

Naturally, Lauren realized Elisa and Garry had married young. They must have, in order to have a daughter in college. Identical twin boys had followed three years later. Tim and Tom were high school sophomores and played varsity on the high school soccer and baseball teams. Lauren had attended their games with Elisa and Garry. Because of their connection, Todd had done a human-interest story on the boys that played on the local evening news.

"It turned out fine between you and Garry," Lauren reminded Elisa.

"Well, yes, but my family always liked Garry. I agree we were young and foolish. Dad wasn't happy with me—Mom, either, for that matter—but Dad took Garry under his wing, taught him the business. Dad saw to it that when it came time for him and Mom to retire, Garry and I were capable of taking over the store." Elisa hung her head. "I can't imagine what my parents will say when they hear about this." Right away she straightened. "They will never know. I'll make sure of that. If Katie won't come to me, then she gives me no other option but to go to her."

Lauren resisted the urge to advise her friend not to act on impulse.

"I'm booking a flight right this minute." With a look of determination, Elisa reached for her cell.

"Do you want me to contact Garry?" Lauren asked.

Elisa looked aghast. "Why would you do that?"

"To cover for you while you're away."

"Oh." Elisa set down her phone and exhaled a long, slow breath. She brushed the hair off her forehead while she thought matters through. "I'd better wait and talk to him about this. I swear, if he knew before me I'll shoot the man for keeping it a secret."

"Did Katie tell you how far along she is?" Lauren asked.

"No. When I asked, she refused to answer."

Lauren suspected Katie might have been pregnant when she was in Seattle for spring break the previous month. No wonder she'd brought Dietrich home with her. Lauren had met the young man only once and had immediately liked him. He was polite and respectful and seemed intelligent. She remembered watching him with Katie and feeling a pinch of envy at the way he couldn't keep his eyes off her.

All at once it hit Lauren. A double whammy. Her younger sister was pregnant, and now her dearest friend, who was only a few years older than Lauren, was about to become a grandmother.

Without weighing the decision, she retrieved her cell and called Todd. Generally, she avoided contacting him during work hours, but he wasn't on the set until right before noon. As best she could figure, he would be sitting in a chair in the makeup room.

He answered on the third ring. "Hey, honey, what's up?" Todd sounded rushed and a bit distracted. She half expected him to remind her that it wasn't good practice to contact him while he was at work.

"Can you meet me tonight?"

"Tonight?" he repeated. "Can't. I'm taping a story for the eleven-o'clock report."

"What about Thursday?" Any night was fine for what she had in mind. Lauren had made her decision.

"Thursday it is," Todd agreed. "Be sure and watch the noon news. And I've got a lead on a great story. I'll tell you about it later. We'll talk more about it on Thursday. Gotta go."

With that, the line was disconnected. It wasn't until she heard the buzz in her ear that she realized she hadn't had time to ask where they should meet or what time.

Chapter Two

Bethanne Hamlin Scranton waltzed into A Good Yarn wearing one of the biggest smiles of her life. This happiness felt as if it would explode right out of her if she didn't share it soon.

"Lydia, oh, Lydia," Bethanne cried, so full of joy it was difficult to hold still. "I've got the most wonderful news."

"Max is coming for the weekend," Lydia guessed.

"No, it's even better than a visit from my husband." Max was living in California, where his wine-distribution business was located, while she lived in Seattle because of her party company. It meant weekend trips from either him or her, which was a ridiculous way to be married, but Bethanne didn't want to think about that now, not when her heart was this full.

"Okay, I give up," Lydia said, laughing. "Tell me."

Bethanne practically skipped to the front of the store near the display window and gestured toward the baby blanket artfully draped over a bassinet.

Lydia's eyes widened and she covered her mouth with both hands. "You're pregnant?"

"Not me. Courtney. I'm going to be a grandmother."

"Oh, Bethanne, that's wonderful news." Lydia laughed and briefly hugged her. "I remember when I first met Courtney and what a shy, withdrawn teenager she was. And now she and Andrew are going to have a baby?"

"Max doesn't know yet, but I guarantee he's going to be as excited as I am." She already suspected what her husband would say. He'd claim she'd be the sexiest grandma he'd ever known. Bethanne nearly blushed at the thought. They'd been married more than a year now, and while it was a strain to live apart, they remained deeply in love. While it sounded like a bit of a stretch for her to be pregnant—an impossibility, since her tubes had been tied—it wasn't from lack of bedroom activity. Fifteen months out and it was as if Max and she were still on their honeymoon.

Love the second time around had come as a surprise to Bethanne. Grant, her first husband, had been her college sweetheart. They'd married, had two children a year apart, and then, after twenty years, without warning, Grant had left her for a younger woman. As a stay-at-home mom, Bethanne had been sent reeling, facing an uncertain future.

She'd needed to reinvent herself, and with trepidation, she had. Not once did she expect to fall in love again. But then life seemed to be filled with surprises, and some of those surprises, mainly Max, were simply wonderful.

"I want the pattern and yarn for that baby blanket," Bethanne told her friend. "I can hardly wait to start knitting." The thought of her first grandchild filled her with excitement and joy. She'd knit the baby blanket, but already she was thinking of two other patterns she wanted to tackle. This child would lack for nothing.

The smile left Lydia's face. "Oh, Bethanne, I'm sorry. I've sold out of that particular yarn, but I have a new shipment coming in on Thursday. I can put five skeins aside for you if you want."

"I do. I'll stop by Thursday afternoon and pick it up. Can I come around five?"

"That would be perfect. The shipment is sure to have arrived by then. Lauren Elliott is stopping by around that time, too."

"Lauren Elliott . . . Lauren Elliott," Bethanne repeated. "Why is her name familiar?" She tapped her index finger against her lips. Generally, she was good at remembering names, a necessity in her party business, with so many repeat customers.

"Lauren works at John Michael Jewelers."

"Oh, yes. I was in the shop not long ago, and she was helpful."

"Buying diamonds, are we?" Lydia teased.

Bethanne sighed. "Max wanted me to pick out something for our first anniversary." It saddened her that he hadn't been with her, but their weekend time together was limited. There were far more important matters that needed attention, mainly each other. From the way they acted, one would think they were twenty-year-olds. Max made her feel loved and cherished.

The shop doorbell jingled as Margaret, Lydia's older sister, came inside. It was hard to picture the two as siblings. Margaret was big-boned and tall, while Lydia was petite and delicate. That wasn't the only difference. Their personalities were polar opposites. Lydia was warm and welcoming, and Margaret was a bit gruff, with ragged edges.

"The weirdest thing just happened," Margaret said, frowning. "When I got off the bus I saw a woman knitting, but then she left the knitting on the bench to get on the bus."

"She left her knitting behind?" Bethanne asked.

"Yeah, so I stopped her and pointed out that she'd forgotten her knitting, and she said it wasn't hers."

"She was knitting on someone else's project?" Lydia asked. "Well, that's odd."

"I thought the same thing," Margaret said. "I mean, really, it's pretty nervy to just pick up another person's project and start knitting, don't you think?"

Bethanne had to agree.

"So what did you do?" Lydia asked. She walked around to the cash register and made a notation on a tablet. Bethanne saw that she was noting the baby blanket yarn for her to collect on Thursday. Lauren Elliott's name was on the list as well.

Margaret fiddled with the large buttons of her light jacket, slipped it off, and hung it over her arm. "It really wasn't any of my business, but I couldn't help myself."

"You looked at the knitting."

"It was in a basket. A really nice one. It sort of reminded me of one Mom had years ago. I'm sure we sent it to some charity when we moved her into the assisted-living complex. Remember the woven basket with the purple stripe?"

Lydia shook her head. "No. Mom had all kinds of baskets."

"True. Well, never mind, that isn't important. I lifted out the yarn and needles, and there was a note inside with big letters that said: KNIT ME."

"Knit me?" Lydia repeated.

"Yes. Apparently, someone left this project there on purpose, wanting people to work on it while they wait for the bus."

"What is it they're supposed to be knitting?" Bethanne asked.

"A scarf. The note said that once it's finished it will be given to a homeless shelter."

Bethanne found this all rather interesting, and, looking at Lydia, asked, "You haven't heard of anyone doing this before now, have you?"

"Not a word," Lydia replied. "But I think it's a great idea. It's a wonderful way to help others, and as a bonus, it might get more people interested in knitting."

"I hadn't heard of it, either," Margaret said, "and here's the thing. While I was looking at the project on the needles, a woman came up to me and said she saw another basket in the park with the same message."

"You mean there's more than one project out there?"

"Apparently so."

"I wonder how many?"

Bethanne was amused. "For all we know, they might be all over the city."

"I wonder who's doing this?" Lydia asked. "I mean, I think it's great, but I'd like to know who came up with this idea."

Margaret nodded her head. "Me, too, and whoever it is shops here."

"What makes you think that?" Lydia asked, smiling now. "Was the yarn a brand we sell?"

"We apparently did at one time," Margaret said, "but it must have been before I came on staff, because I didn't recognize the name."

"Then how did you know it was from A Good Yarn?" Bethanne asked, her curiosity mounting.

"Easy. The price tag had A Good Yarn stamped on it."

"Really?" Lydia's eyes rounded in surprise. "I wonder who put this together."

"Can't tell you," Margaret returned, "but I wish I'd been the one to think of it." She started toward the office and then abruptly turned back. "I nearly forgot. When the yarn runs out, the project is finished and the last person knitting needs to bring the scarf to the shop."

"Here?"

"Here," Margaret answered. "It specifically says to deliver the finished project to A Good Yarn. Kind of fun, isn't it?"

"Kind of. I just wish whoever thought of this would've taken the time to clue me in."

Bethanne glanced at her watch. It'd been a long day at the office and she was ready for her tea break. Besides, she was waiting for Max to return her call. "I better head home. I'll stop by on Thursday for the yarn for the baby blanket."

"Do you mind if I tell Margaret your news?"

"Please do."

Bethanne drove home to the very house where she'd raised her children, the home she loved. At one point, not long ago, Grant had tried to lure her away from the house and from Max. He seemed to think that if they could start over and put the past behind them the world would right itself again.

She loved this colonial-style home with the green shutters and the spacious rooms. It was much too large for her now, but she couldn't bring herself to sell it. After Grant moved out, she'd struggled to hold on to the house. At the time it had seemed an impossibility, but she couldn't let it go. Her children had already lost their father, and she was determined they wouldn't lose the only home they had ever known. It wasn't their fault their father couldn't keep his pants zipped. Bethanne was proud that she'd survived those first torturous months following her divorce. At the same time, she realized she'd never have been able to do it without the encouragement and emotional support she got from her friends.

Once inside the kitchen, she put on water for tea. She'd found that she enjoyed a few minutes' respite at the end of the day. The house was quiet, and she turned on the television for the early news broadcast simply for the noise. When Andrew and Annie, her children, had lived at home, they seemed to be constantly coming and going, music blaring, cellphones ringing. These days there was silence. It was more peaceful, but she missed the chatter of her children. Within a few months she would again hear the noise, only this time it would be from a newborn.

A baby.

It'd been a lot of years since this house had heard a baby's cry. A lump filled her throat as she carried her tea to her preferred spot in the family room off the kitchen. Her favorite chair sat close to the fireplace, and a container with her knitting rested on the Oriental rug next to the overstuffed chair and ottoman. She automatically reached for it. While she currently had two or three projects going, she would put them all aside and immediately start the baby blanket once the yarn arrived.

She hadn't taken more than a sip of tea when her cell rang. Seeing that it was Max, she eagerly grabbed the phone. She'd left a message with Rooster, Max's friend and business partner, for Max to call her as soon as he was available.

"Honey, what is it?"

"Andrew called me this afternoon, and Courtney's pregnant," she blurted out in one quick breath.

"She's pregnant? Well, congratulations to Andrew and Courtney. I imagine you're walking on cloud nine."

"That doesn't even begin to describe how I feel. When I heard the news I wanted to laugh, and at the same time I had to hold back tears. It's been so long since there was a baby in the family."

"You're gonna be one sexy grandma."

"I knew you'd say that." A warm, happy feeling stole over her. "I wish you were here right now."

"So do I." His voice dipped low. "This makes the decision all the more difficult for you, doesn't it?"

Bethanne didn't need clarification. They'd gone round and round about her selling her party business so she could move to California. Over the years it had grown and prospered. Bethanne had a huge emotional investment in it. Still, it went without saying that it would be far easier for her to sell her company than for Max to move his wine-export business to Washington State.

While Washington was the second-largest wine-producing state in the country behind California, it wasn't anywhere close to competing.

"I . . . I don't know." The thought of selling her business was one thing, but to move away from a grandchild was something else entirely.

"Do you regret marrying me?" her husband asked.

"Max! How can you even ask that?"

"You're right. It's a ridiculous question. We belong together. I knew it the minute you climbed on the back of my motorcycle and held on to me so tightly you nearly crushed my ribs.

"You're smiling."

"How can you tell?"

"I know you, my love. You're thinking about the two of us riding down that road in Nevada shortly after we met."

Bethanne laughed, remembering all too well being stuck in the middle of the Nevada desert with a broken-down car.

"I can still see the look on Annie's face when we saw you and Rooster. Both of you in leather vests with tanned muscular arms, looking for all intents and purposes as though Rooster would have liked nothing better than to do away with the lot of us."

"Rooster has that way about him."

"That he does," Bethanne agreed. She'd come to admire and appreciate Max's closest friend. It'd been Rooster who'd held the company together after Max's wife and daughter died. Without him, Max would have lost everything.

Suddenly, the front door flew open and Grant let himself into the house. "Bethanne," he all but shouted her name.

"Hold on a minute, Max," she said.

Wearing a huge grin, Grant came toward her. "I just heard the news."

Bethanne set her cell aside and stood. Grant wrapped his arms around her waist, lifted her off the ground, and swung her around.

Bethanne let out a squeal and, laughing, demanded, "Grant, Grant, put me down this minute."

"We're going to be grandparents."

"Yes, I know. Andrew phoned me this afternoon."

"We need to celebrate."

"Grant, hold on." She reached for her cell. "Max, Grant is here. I'll call you back in a few minutes."

"What does he mean you need to celebrate?"

"I don't know; he just got here." Her husband sounded jealous, which was ridiculous, seeing that the two of them were deeply in love and married. "I won't be long, I promise."

"Call me back when you can."

"Will do. Love you."

"Love you, too."

Bethanne ended the call and turned to face her ex-husband.

"Are you as excited as I am?" Grant asked, his face aglow with happiness.

"More so." Bethanne could barely sit still.

"We can't let this opportunity pass without celebrating. Let me take you to dinner."

Bethanne hesitated but then agreed. Max wasn't the jealous type; he'd understand, and she'd phone him later with plenty of reassurances. But now was a time to celebrate.

Chapter Three

*L*auren knew Elisa was stunned by the news that her daughter was pregnant. Thankfully, Elisa had resisted the urge to rush to Pullman and browbeat Katie into getting an abortion, thanks mostly to Garry, her husband.

On hearing the news, Garry had insisted they give Katie and Dietrich time to sort this situation out themselves, the same way Elisa's parents had done twenty years earlier when they discovered Elisa was pregnant. Although Elisa didn't like it, she'd agreed to give the two young adults breathing room. It was hard for her friend to stay out of it, Lauren realized, and she had to admire Elisa's restraint.

In the morning Elisa was already at the store when Lauren arrived just before ten, and Lauren was determined to distract her from dwelling on the situation with Katie.

"I've made my decision," Lauren announced.

Elisa looked up from the computer screen and blinked as if she didn't have a solitary idea what Lauren was referring to.

"About me and Todd," she elaborated. "It's clear that since he's been riding the fence this long, he's simply not ready to move forward. I can accept that. I don't like it, but it is what it is."

Elisa rolled back her desk chair as she nodded approvingly. "So you're going to take my advice and give Todd an ultimatum."

"No."

Elisa's eyes widened. "No?" she repeated.

"I'm uncomfortable pressuring him to make a bigger commitment when clearly he isn't ready, or more than likely he wants to keep matters the way they are, which tells me he simply doesn't want to *marry* me."

"So what are you going to do?"

As far as Lauren could see, she had no other option. "I think it's best if the two of us make a clean break of it."

This didn't appear to make sense to Elisa. "But, Lauren, you've got all this time invested in the relationship already. It would be foolish to give up on Todd now. What he needs is a bit of incentive."

"I've already given him incentive. As my father would tell me, why put good time after bad, only he'd say money instead of time. My relationship with Todd is stagnant. His focus is on his career, and that's not going to change. I have no option but to own up to the fact that he isn't interested. He doesn't see himself as a husband and father, at least not with me as his wife."

"But—"

Lauren cut her off. "Our relationship is exactly where it was twelve months ago when we had 'the talk.' Todd likes attending social functions with me, and frankly I've enjoyed it as well." And she had. Parties and charity events had become a natural extension of their relationship, but Lauren couldn't remember the last time they'd had a serious conversation. Everything revolved around the places they went, the food and wine they'd tasted, the people they met. Until recently it hadn't struck Lauren how shallow their relationship had become. It bothered her to see how far off she'd wandered from what she'd once considered important. No longer. She had seen the light.

"Todd has helped build up our clientele," Elisa reminded her.

Unwilling to be sidetracked, Lauren didn't argue the point. "I've made a list."

"A list of what? Customers?"

"No, silly. A list of what's important to me in a man. I always thought it was someone like Todd. Handsome, outgoing, ambitious, but those qualities are actually superficial and basically not all that important."

Elisa continued to look at her as if seeing Lauren with fresh eyes. She leaned back and rolled a pencil between her palms. "So tell me, what qualities did you put on your list?"

"I've dated handsome. Handsome is a dime a dozen. Character is far more important."

"Personality?"

"No, character: a man of integrity and honor."

"You want to marry Abraham Lincoln?"

Lauren grinned. "I'd tell him to get rid of the top hat, that's for sure."

Elisa smiled. "What else is on your list?"

"I want him to have a decent sense of humor."

"I agree with you there," Elisa said. "I can laugh with Garry like no one else."

"I know, and I admire that about the two of you."

"I was lucky, you know," Elisa said. "I was still a teenager when Garry and I decided to marry. I didn't have the sense God gave a goose; it was the luck of the draw that he was someone I could love my entire life. Garry's a really good guy."

Lauren agreed. "Basically, that's what I want, too. A good, down-to-earth guy."

"Was it a hard decision?" Elisa asked.

"Not really." That was what had surprised her. Lauren had been ready for this for a long time, only she hadn't known it. "Todd and I are supposed to meet tomorrow night for dinner. I'm stopping off at the yarn store to pick up supplies to knit a blanket for my sister's baby. I suggested we dine across the street at The French Cafe, but I give you odds Todd will be late." It'd happened so often Lauren had come to expect it. "Naturally, he'll have a good excuse; he always does."

"Do you think he suspects you want to break up?"

"Todd? Probably not." One of his biggest flaws was how oblivious he could be when it came to her feelings. "More than likely he won't believe I'm serious."

Lauren felt her best friend's scrutiny. "Will he be able to change your mind?"

After a sleepless night mulling this decision over, Lauren was fairly certain she knew what she wanted. "Not this time."

"Not this time? You mean to say you've tried to break up with Todd before?"

"Just once, about a year ago. If I'd walked away then I would have saved myself twelve months," she said, dealing with regret. Her instincts had been right on, only she hadn't found the resolve needed. Because she wanted to believe Todd, she'd given in and their relationship had continued. For a while it was better, but it wasn't long before they slipped back into the same routine. She wouldn't be so easily persuaded this time around. Since receiving her sister's news, Lauren knew what had to be done.

"What happened a year ago?" Elisa quizzed. "I thought you told me everything."

"I wish I had told you, because you might have talked some sense into me. I needed to know where our relationship was headed."

"And?"

"And," it was fairly humbling to explain, "Todd kept telling me how unfair I was being and that no man wants to have his back pressed against a wall. He claimed he loved me and wanted us to marry, but he had a few financial problems he needed to clear up first. He felt certain everything would right itself once he got the anchor slot for the five-o'clock news. Plus, he had an inheritance from his grandfather coming."

"Oh, Lauren."

"Someday he probably will be offered that position, but as far as I can see, it isn't likely to happen anytime soon."

Lauren's cellphone rang, and she dug it out of her purse. When she read the caller ID, she said, "Speaking of the devil."

"It's Todd?" Elisa asked.

Lauren nodded. "Hi, Todd," she said, and wrapped her free arm around her waist as if to protect herself.

"Hey, sweetie, about dinner—"

"You have to cancel," she finished for him.

"No, not cancel, but I thought I should warn you that I've got a great lead on a story, and—"

"It's fine, don't worry about it," she said, doing her best to hide her irritation. It seemed Todd didn't even have time for her to break up with him.

"I am worried; you know how I hate to disappoint you. You're upset, aren't you? But you have to know I wouldn't put you off if this wasn't important."

"Right. It's fine, it really is." She glanced at Elisa and rolled her eyes.

Elisa covered her mouth to hold back her giggles.

Afraid she might laugh herself, Lauren turned her back on her employer. "Listen Todd, it's probably for the best."

"The best? What's up?"

"My sister's pregnant."

Todd paused as if he needed a moment to translate. "Oh, boy, I know what's coming," he muttered, as if this was the last thing he wanted to discuss. "Are we going to revisit the marriage issue again? Come on, Lauren, you know where I stand on the subject. When I get a few bills paid off and lock in the anchor slot, we'll set the date."

"Dan isn't anywhere close to retiring."

"Not true . . . just the other day I heard a rumor that—"

"I'd rather not do this over the phone," she said, cutting him off. Normally she wasn't this rude, but dragging this out would do neither of them any good.

"Do what?" Todd asked.

"You're leaving me no option."

"What?" he demanded.

"Todd, I think it would be best if we ended it now."

"End it? Is this a joke?"

"No joke."

"You're just upset because your sister is pregnant," he insisted.

"I'm not upset. If anything, I'm disappointed in myself. I hung on to this relationship far longer than I should have."

"You're serious. You actually want to break up with me?" Todd asked, with what sounded like utter disbelief.

"Yes." She couldn't make it any more clear than that. She didn't offer excuses or explanations. She was finished. End of story.

"Let me make sure I've got this straight. This is all about you and your sister?"

"Not entirely."

"But that's what led to your decision?"

"In part, yes."

He sounded exasperated. "This. Is. Ridiculous." Each word was carefully enunciated.

"To you, it probably is. This is my life, Todd, and I want to marry and have children. I'm sure you do, too, but not with me, and it's time I accepted that."

"Hold on, let's talk this out."

She should have realized he wasn't going to make this easy. "I can't talk now, and it's pointless. Besides, I'm at work and I know you are, too. Let's leave matters where they are. Like I said, I'm not upset. Really, I'm not. I would have rather done this face-to-face than over the phone, but you had to cancel our dinner plans."

"That isn't what I said," he argued. "I said I *might* have to cancel. I called because I wanted you to know it was a possibility."

"We've had a lot of fun together over the years, Todd. I'm sorry it didn't work out."

He hesitated, and his voice dipped. "Is there someone else?"

That he would even ask was an insult. "No. At least not yet."

"Not yet?"

"I haven't met the guy yet, or maybe I have and simply don't know it."

Again he paused. "I don't feel good about this."

"I'd rather have done this over dinner. I'm sorry to spring it on you." Lauren did feel bad that she was forced to break up over the phone. It seemed a bit heartless, especially after a three-year relationship. Todd deserved more than a quick call. "Like I said, I would have preferred we did this in person. I've had a couple of days to grow accustomed to the idea and you haven't. But when you've had time to sort through your feelings, you'll realize this is for the best."

"Meet me."

"Todd, no. Talking this over isn't going to change my mind. It's clear to me we aren't meant to be together."

"Keep our dinner date."

"You have a lead on a breaking story, remember? You had to cancel." One would think with all the leads he'd followed he'd have been sought after by a national news outlet by now.

"I said I *might* need to cancel," he snapped. "I'll give the story to someone else. This is more important."

"Todd . . ."

"Come on, Lauren, hear me out. You owe me that." His voice took on a husky, pleading quality.

Lauren vacillated, unsure what was best.

"If I hadn't phoned, you would have followed through with the dinner, right?"

He had a point. She'd fully intended to be at The French Cafe Thursday night. She sighed. "Yes, I would have been there."

"Then just pretend I didn't call. I'll meet you at The French Cafe at six o'clock just the way we planned, and then we can talk. I don't want to lose you, Lauren. I love you."

Lauren was convinced she was going to regret this. "All right," she reluctantly agreed, "but you should know right now, my mind is made up. I'd like for us to remain friends, if possible."

"Of course it's possible, but you should know something, too."

"What's that?" she asked.

"I don't intend to let you go without a fight. You're the best thing that's ever happened to me. See you Thursday."

They ended the call, and Lauren exhaled as she slipped her cell-phone back into her purse.

"Well?" Elisa asked after an awkward moment. "How'd that work for you?"

Lauren snorted softly and shook her head. "He called me a *thing*."

"A thing?"

"He said I was the best *thing* that had ever happened to him. I'm a woman with a heart and with feelings and with dreams, and those dreams don't mesh with his."

"Oh, Lauren." Elisa stood and gently patted her back. "I wish I knew what to say."

"You don't need to say anything. It's been a long time coming. I should have ended it last year."

"Listen," Elisa said, perking up considerably. "I want you to fly to Vegas with me for the gem show next month."

"But I thought you were going with Garry?" Lauren had attended before, and it was an amazing show. For the last couple of years she'd looked after the store while Elisa and Garry were away.

"Garry suggested it might be good for the two of us to have some girl time. Besides, he really isn't all that keen on Vegas."

"I'd love it."

"We both could use a break."

Time away was exactly what she needed. She looked at her friend and laughed. "Let me at that *Wheel of Fortune* slot machine."

"And remember, what happens in Vegas stays in Vegas."

Maybe for others, but Lauren tended to live on the tame side of town. Then again, maybe she should kick up her heels.

Chapter Four

"I'm so sorry I didn't call you back," Bethanne told Max while he clung to the telephone receiver in his Sonoma Valley office. He hated that living apart made this form of communication with his wife a necessity.

"It's just that oh—Max, please don't be upset with me," she said.

Max exhaled, doing his best to hold back his irritation. Bethanne had been with her ex, and while Max hated to sound insecure and jealous, that was exactly how he felt. He didn't trust Grant Hamlin for an inch when it came to Bethanne. The other man had made his intentions clear. Grant wanted Bethanne back in his life. Furthermore, he was willing to do anything necessary to undermine their marriage.

"So apparently Grant was with you for quite some time." Max had waited up half the night to hear back from Bethanne. When she didn't call, it left his mind open to speculation. He could well imagine what Grant had thought up this time to keep Bethanne occupied.

"Max, I am so sorry. I meant to call you first thing this morning, but I had three phone calls before I even got into the office, and then I had one meeting after another all day. A new balloon company is trying to get my business, and their representative was with me a full hour, and then Annie needed help planning a huge party function for the Boeing Company. It's been crazy around here. Before I knew it, the entire day had evaporated and it was after six. I can't tell you how sorry I am." She continued to offer him a litany of excuses.

"You didn't answer the question," Max reminded her.

Bethanne hesitated, and then on a breathless note confessed, "I can't remember the question."

"You and Grant. Just how long was he at the house?"

"Oh . . . that question."

"Yes, that question." Rooster walked into Max's office, and, see-ing that Max was on the phone, started to leave. Max didn't think this conversation would last much longer, not in his current frame of mind, at any rate. He was annoyed and frustrated, so he gestured for Rooster to take a seat, which his friend did. Rooster lounged back in the chair and crossed his long legs, balancing his ankle over his knee.

"Did I hear someone come into your office?" Bethanne asked.

"Rooster. You're avoiding the question, which tells me I'm not going to like the answer."

"You probably won't. Grant and I went out to dinner to celebrate Andrew and Courtney's news."

"Just the two of you?"

"Yes. It didn't mean anything, Max. I was married to Grant for nearly twenty years. We have a long history together."

Max didn't need a reminder. After a disastrous second marriage, Grant had realized what a huge mistake he'd made leaving Bethanne and their family. He'd made no secret that he wanted Bethanne back. When he abandoned her, he didn't have a clue what an incredible woman she was. Her ex-husband had learned a painful lesson.

When Grant realized Max was in the picture, he'd panicked and done everything he could to convince Bethanne to take him back. His ploy hadn't worked, and Bethanne chose Max. Grant's loss was

Max's gain. That, however, wasn't the end of the story. A man who cheated on his wife wouldn't hesitate to do it again. While Max trusted his wife, he had no faith in Grant's sense of honor and fairness. The other man was capable of using whatever means available to destroy Max's relationship with Bethanne.

"Grant has made no secret he wants you."

"I'm married," Bethanne returned, as if that decisively settled the matter. While she might have that mind-set, Max was all too aware that Grant didn't.

Rather than argue the point, he moved on, doing his best to sound as casual as possible. "Where did you go for dinner?" If she told him the little Mexican place that had been their favorite spot early on in their marriage, Max was afraid he might lose it.

"Zapata's."

"I thought so," he said, his jaw tightening. "Are you really so naive that you can't see what Grant is doing?"

"Naive?" she snapped, paused, and took in a deep breath as if she, too, were struggling to control her own impatience. "I resent that."

"What else would you call it? You seem completely oblivious to Grant's manipulations."

"I'm married to you," she reminded him again. "I know Grant far better than you do. You're overreacting, Max. This isn't like you."

Max ignored her comment. "What time did you get home?"

"From Zapata's?" She didn't wait for him to answer. "Just what are you implying?"

"Nothing. You didn't call."

"No, I didn't. It was after ten, and I knew you'd had a busy day, and I didn't want to wake you."

She needn't have worried; he was up well past midnight waiting. He would have phoned Bethanne, but in his frame of mind it wouldn't have been a good idea. The fact that she'd taken nearly twenty-four hours to connect with him had done little to cut the edge off his frustration. He was both annoyed and aggravated, and struggling not to let this conversation break into a full-blown argument.

"Did you have a good time?" he asked, downplaying his displeasure as much as possible.

"As a matter of fact, we did."

Bethanne was unwilling to offer him reassurances, it seemed.

"Grant and I talked about when I learned I was pregnant with Andrew and how excited both sets of our parents were when we told them the news."

"Fine," he muttered. She could have gone all day without mentioning these details. How easy it was to picture the two of them with their heads together, laughing and reminiscing over the early, happy years of their marriage. He clenched his jaw so hard that his back teeth ached.

"Listen, Max, as much as you'd like me to forget the twenty years I was married to Grant, I can't. We have children together. Andrew and Annie will always link me to my ex-husband. That doesn't mean I love you any less or that I'm susceptible to Grant's less-than-subtle attempts to build the very bridge he chose to tear down. What I expect from you is a bit of patience and trust."

Max didn't want to get into these issues with her. What he wanted, what he needed, was reassurance.

"Will you be seeing Grant again anytime soon?" Max asked, as conversationally as he could manage, knowing at this point he wasn't fooling anyone, least of all Bethanne, and most certainly not Rooster. Max caught a glimpse of Rooster rolling his eyes.

"Grant wants to take everyone to dinner this Saturday."

"Everyone."

"Andrew, Courtney, Annie, Harry, and me."

"Harry? I thought Annie was dating some guy named Aiden."

"That was so last month."

"Oh." His stepdaughter went through boyfriends the way some people went through a six pack of soda. "It's hard to keep track of who her current love interest is."

"Well, you're most definitely mine. Now, please, let's put this matter behind us."

Max didn't know if he could, especially in light of this family dinner idea. He didn't like it one bit. He feared Grant had the upper edge this time around. He had proximity and a twenty-year history with Bethanne. And now Grant and Bethanne would share a grandchild.

"About dinner," Bethanne said. "I know this weekend is my turn to come to California."

"Yes, it is," he said, unwilling to bend.

"Could you manage to fly up to Seattle instead? I'd like it if you could join us for this dinner."

"No." He flat-out refused.

"You're acting like a child, Max Scranton. You're going to force me to choose between you and a family function, and that's . . . that's wrong."

"I can't come to Seattle this weekend; I have a dinner with two wine company executives that's been on the schedule for weeks. A dinner during which I'd hoped to be able to introduce my wife."

"I'm sorry, Max . . . I—"

"Don't worry about it," he snapped, cutting her off. "Just be aware that Grant is going to use every excuse he can to drive a wedge between you and me. Do you honestly think the fact that you're married to me means anything to him?"

"I can't speak for Grant, but you should know it means a great deal to me."

Background noise told him someone had stepped into her office.

"Grant?"

Max heard the surprise in Bethanne's voice.

"Hold on a minute," she said to him, and then whispered, "Sorry."

Once again, Max was about to be set aside in order for Bethanne to chat with her ex-husband. This was exactly what he'd warned his wife would happen. Grant was on the prowl. Bethanne knew Grant's games as well as he did, and still she continued to play. She assumed she was immune to her ex-husband. Max, however, wasn't willing to risk losing his wife.

One of the hardest decisions Max had ever made had happened after he'd fallen in love with Bethanne. Grant had been working to win her back then, too, and in order to give her the freedom to make her own decision, Max had stepped aside and allowed Grant time and opportunity to woo Bethanne back. As hard as it was to remain out of the picture, Max had stayed away, unwilling to influence her one way or the other.

In the end, she'd chosen to marry Max. The road hadn't been nearly as smooth as he would have liked. Their main difficulty, besides living in two different states, was his rocky relationship with his stepdaughter. And now this.

Instead of putting him on hold, Max realized Bethanne had laid the phone down on her desk in order for him to overhear the conversation. It was small comfort, but he was grateful.

"What can I do for you?" Bethanne asked stiffly. "As you can see, I'm busy."

"Yes, sorry to interrupt." Grant sounded friendly and apologetic to intrude. "Tell me, did I happen to leave my sunglasses at the house last night?"

"No. I don't believe you were wearing sunglasses."

"You're sure? Maybe I should stop by."

"Not tonight."

"What about tomorrow, then?" Grant asked.

"I'm going to the yarn store, and I'm not sure when I'll be home, but I'll check for your sunglasses again and let you know."

"I appreciate it. They're designer frames."

"Okay, now if you don't mind—"

It was about time, Max mulled. The longer the conversation lasted, the hotter he fumed.

"Goodbye, Grant," Bethanne said pointedly.

"You'll phone if you find my glasses."

"Of course," she promised.

Max would have felt better if she'd told her ex that Annie could deliver the sunglasses. Knowing Grant, he'd purposely left them behind as an excuse to stop by the house yet again.

After a pause, she picked up the phone. "I'm back."

"Do you need any further proof?" he demanded. "Sunglasses?"

She paused, and once again Max heard her set the phone aside. "Yes, Grant," she grumbled impatiently. "What is it now?"

"Let me know about dinner this weekend."

"I will. Would you mind closing the door when you leave the office? Thank you."

Fuming now, Max heard the door close. He didn't wait for Bethanne to reconnect. "That says it all, doesn't it?"

"Max, listen—"

"I think it might be best if we continue this conversation at another time," Max said, afraid their discussion was about to escalate to the point he might say something he'd later regret. "Goodbye, Bethanne." Then, without giving her an opportunity to respond, he disconnected the line.

Silence vibrated through his office while he shuffled through his emotions.

"Well," Rooster said after a moment, "that didn't sound good. Grant again?"

"Who else?"

"Do you trust Bethanne?"

"Of course." And he did. What he wanted was for her to confirm that she was aware of Grant's game plan.

"Then don't you think you're playing right into Grant's hands?"

Max was too unnerved to consider that. "He's planning a family dinner to celebrate Andrew and Courtney's news."

"And Bethanne wanted you to be there?"

"Yes. You know that isn't going to work. We're having dinner with the executives from Kendall-Jackson." It'd already been delayed once, and Max wasn't willing to put it off a second time.

"They'll understand," Rooster insisted. "They are the ones who canceled the dinner the first time, and this is for family."

Max rubbed his hand over his eyes. "Let me sleep on it."

They left the office and walked through the warehouse. Rooster headed for his motorcycle, and Max toward his car. He'd met Bethanne while riding his bike. She'd fallen in love with him on the back of his bike. Maybe what she needed was a reminder of that. He stood outside his vehicle, thinking.

"Something wrong?" Rooster asked.

Max didn't realize he was so readable. This matter with Bethanne had his gut twisted in knots. He loved his wife, and while he had every reassurance she loved him, too, he wanted more.

"You have plans this weekend?" Max asked his friend.

"Dinner with you and the good folks from Kendall-Jackson."

"You up for a ride?"

Rooster chuckled. "To Seattle?"

"Seattle," Max confirmed.

"I'll head back to the house, get my leather jacket and chaps, and pack my saddlebags. We'll hit the road early tomorrow morning." It was a good twelve- to fifteen-hour ride, if not longer. Naturally, they'd need occasional stops along the way, which would add additional time to the trip.

"How soon can you be ready?" Max asked.

"Any time you say."

"Thanks." Max was sincere. He appreciated what a good friend Rooster was. Before he left, he'd connect with the winery and rearrange dinner. Then he'd eat and get a few hours' rest. He was eager to hit the road. He would be available for Bethanne, show her that she and her children were important to him. If nothing else, this would prove he was willing to bend.

"You going to let Bethanne know you're on your way?" Rooster asked.

"No. I want to surprise her." He would make sure their reunion was one neither of them would soon forget.

Chapter Five

When knitting for a loved one, put a kiss in every stitch!

—Nicky Epstein,
designer and author

*T*hursday afternoon, Lauren arrived a few minutes after five at A Good Yarn. She was anxious to get started on the baby blanket for her sister and for this final dinner with Todd to be over. Breaking up was never easy, and this was sure to be hard on Todd's ego. The truth was, this wasn't something she wanted, either, but she was convinced it was necessary.

Ambition was one of the qualities she'd put down on her husband list, but Todd's insistence that he become the prime-time anchor went beyond ambition and bordered on obsession. As far as Lauren could tell, Todd linked his self-worth to his ability to step into the lead newscaster slot. Everything hinged on that. It was as if the rest of his life was on hold until he got what he wanted most. And unfortunately, that wasn't building a life with her. Todd was a great catch, but she was releasing him.

Lauren was looking for more than ambition in a husband. Much, much more. Her list wasn't long, though. She had a few basic prerequisites—qualities she should be able to identify within short order. One thing was certain. She was completely unwilling to wait for the perfect match to come along. She was on the prowl.

The yarn store was busy when Lauren came in. Margaret was helping one customer while several mulled around, checking out the knitted samples. Lydia was at the cash register, helping another woman purchase the same yarn Lauren intended to buy. The other woman looked vaguely familiar. It took Lauren a moment to remember. This was Bethanne Scranton. She'd been by John Michael Jewelers recently.

"Hello," Lauren said, coming up behind Bethanne.

"Lauren." Bethanne surprised her by remembering who she was. "Lydia told me you were coming in this afternoon."

That explained it.

"I'm glad you're both here at the same time," Lydia said, handing Bethanne the credit card slip for her signature. "Do you have a few minutes to sit down? I learned a new cast-on method that is very clever, and it works beautifully for the blanket. If you'd like, I'd be happy to demonstrate."

"That would be great." Lauren had an hour to kill before she was scheduled to meet Todd. Besides, it'd been a while since she'd picked up a pair of knitting needles. With Lydia's help, she collected the variegated pastel yarn, knitting needles, and stitch markers. By the time she finished, Bethanne was already seated at the table in the back of the shop.

"We're offering a class for different methods of casting on and off a week from this Saturday, if either of you are interested," Lydia said. "J. C. Briar is teaching it, and she's such a good teacher. I believe there are a couple of spaces left."

"I . . . I don't know what I'll be doing next weekend," Bethanne murmured, keeping her gaze lowered.

"Will you be seeing Max?" Lydia asked. "Silly question. Of course you will."

Bethanne managed a weak smile.

"Sounds like something I'd like to learn." Lauren could use a bit of encouragement to sharpen her skills. She had the basic knit and purl stitches down, but it'd been a long time. Knitting was a craft that had long interested her. Even now, she wasn't sure why she'd stopped.

They both cast on per Lydia's instructions, using a long-tail method but also employing both ends of the skein. Lydia was right. This was a clever technique. Lauren picked up on it right away, but Bethanne needed a bit of extra help. Then Bethanne miscounted the number of stitches and appeared irritated with herself and started over again, jerking the stitches off the needle.

"Is everything all right?" Lydia asked gently.

Bethanne nodded weakly. "It's fine . . . Max and I had a bit of a falling-out over something silly."

"I'm sorry," Lydia said in that same caring tone.

Bethanne sighed. "I felt terrible about it this morning, but I haven't been able to get ahold of him all day. It isn't like Max not to answer his cellphone."

"Did you call his office?" Lydia asked.

Bethanne nodded. "His assistant called in sick, and the woman answering the phone said that the only information she has is that he's out of the office."

"Men," Lauren muttered under her breath. She braced her elbows against the tabletop and kept the yarn in her lap as she read over the pattern. The first eight rows were knit in garter stitch, knitting every row to form an even border that would prevent the blanket from curling.

"Are you having man problems, too?" Lydia asked Lauren.

"After this evening I won't," she said with determination. "I've been dating the same guy for three years and I'm calling it quits." She purposely didn't mention Todd's name because that invariably led to a discussion about him and his job with the local television station.

"You sound like you've made up your mind," Bethanne said, looking up from her own knitting. Lauren noticed that she hadn't progressed far.

"I have," she concurred. "It's embarrassing to admit how easily influenced I've been by good looks, charm, and prestige. Right now I'm more interested in intelligent, funny, hardworking, and kind."

"You aren't alone in prejudging a man by his looks," Bethanne assured her.

"I'm not looking to marry the Hunchback of Notre Dame. But I refuse to overlook a potential husband because he doesn't fit the tidy, neat picture formed in my mind as a college student. Back then I thought I knew what I wanted in a man. I assumed I'd found that, but unfortunately he turned out to be a . . . disappointment."

Lydia chuckled. "Brad would be miserable in the corporate world. My husband's a blue-collar worker, and I couldn't ask for a better man. I thank God every day for bringing him into my life."

The back door opened, and in walked a short teenage girl, hauling a heavy backpack. She tossed it on the table next to Lydia. "I had the worst day ever."

"Hello, Casey," Lydia greeted, sending apologetic looks to both Bethanne and Lauren. "What happened?" She wrapped her arm around her daughter's shoulders and gave her a hug.

"Jack asked Hadley to the dance."

Lydia was instantly sympathetic. "I'm sorry, honey."

"Oh, it gets worse. I flunked my algebra test."

Lydia seemed surprised. "But you studied, and your dad said you had the equations down pat."

"I did, but Mr. Hazel didn't test us on that."

"Oh, sweetie."

"And then I dropped my purse and everything spilled out and it's my time of the month and, well, you can guess what happened when the guys saw my stuff."

"It sounds like you had a perfectly dreadful day."

"I need to see Grandma," Casey pleaded. "Can you drop me off after work and then pick me up later?"

"Yes, but what about—"

"Mom, please, it's important. Grandma always makes me feel better."

"Grandmothers have a way of doing that," Bethanne chimed in.

Casey looked at the other woman. "Oh, Bethanne, Mom told me Courtney's having a baby. This is so cool. Are you knitting the baby blanket for her?"

Bethanne said that she was. "Tell me what it is your grandmother does that makes you feel better so that when Andrew and Courtney's child needs me to help him or her, then I'll know what to say."

"Okay." Eager to explain, Casey pulled out a chair and slumped forward, leaning against the table, elbows on top. "First of all, Grandma calls it *grousing* instead of complaining. When I asked her what the word meant, she had me look it up in the dictionary."

"She probably needed a reminder herself," Lydia supplied. "Mom has memory issues."

"I like the word *grouse*," Casey said, "and now all my friends say it, too."

"So what does she do so you don't grouse?" Bethanne asked.

Lauren was curious, too. It seemed the teenager and her grandmother shared a special relationship.

"It's sort of a takeoff on the Glad game," Casey explained, "you know, from the book *Pollyanna*?"

"Right," Bethanne said.

"At first I thought it would be stupid, but Grandma says it works every time."

"What's the game?" Lydia asked.

"Well, when I start grousing, she insists there must have been something good that happened that day."

"And is she right?" Lauren asked.

"Almost always I insist there isn't anything, but then Grandma starts asking me questions, and before I know it I can hardly remember the bad stuff because I've got so many good things to remember."

"Was there something positive that happened today?" Lydia asked.

Casey shrugged. "I suppose. One thing. I had macaroni and cheese for lunch. It's one of my favorites."

"I packed you a lunch this morning," Lydia reminded her.

"I traded it with Charlie for his macaroni and cheese." She paused and frowned.

"What?" Lydia asked, apparently reading her daughter.

"He said mac and cheese was his favorite, too, so it makes no sense that he would trade with me. And he sat with me at second lunch. He's never done that before."

"Do you think he might have wanted to ask if you'd go to the dance with him?" Lydia asked, and cocked her head to one side with the question.

"He didn't."

"Was it because you complained about Jack and Hadley the entire time you were with him?"

Again Casey shrugged and an absent look came over her as she appeared to be mentally reviewing her lunchtime conversation with Charlie. "Well, maybe. Come to think of it, he did ask me if I'd be at the dance tomorrow night."

"Maybe it wasn't such a horrible, awful day after all," Lydia suggested.

"I still want to visit Grandma. Can I?"

"Okay. I'll drop you off after I close the shop, and then your father can come get you when he picks up your brother from softball practice."

"Great." Casey appeared to be in better spirits already. She left the table, but Lauren saw that Lydia looked worried. Bethanne noticed it, too.

"Something wrong with your mother?" Bethanne asked.

"Casey and my mother are close. We adopted Casey when she was twelve," Lydia explained, apparently for Lauren's benefit.

"Twelve?"

"She's only been with us three years. Until she came into our lives she was in the foster-care program. She never knew her grandparents, and she's gotten to be tight with my mother. Mom often repeats things three and four times, but while Margaret and I grow impatient, it never seems to bother Casey. She listens to Mom's stories as if they are new every time. The funny part is, Mom will sometimes confuse me with my sister. She'll call me Margaret, but she's never once forgotten who Casey is."

"Mom," Casey called from the far side of the store. "Can I bring Grandma some yarn?"

"No," Lydia replied right away. "My mother already has more yarn than she knows what to do with."

"Are you sure?" Casey pleaded. "This fancy stuff is so pretty, and I know Grandma would love it."

"Not today, honey."

"Okay." The lone word was heavy with disappointment. "Saturday?" she asked again, more hopeful this time.

"I'll think about it."

Reluctantly, Casey returned the skein to the shelf. "That means no."

Lauren smiled, and remembered that her own teenage interactions with her mother were much the same.

Lydia continued explaining her concerns, her voice low so only the two of them could hear: "I'm worried how Casey will react when my mother dies."

"Is it imminent?" Bethanne asked, her eyes sympathetic.

Lydia shrugged. "Truth is, I'm surprised Mom has hung on as long as she has. We moved her into the assisted-living complex a few years back. The move was hard on her. Mom didn't want to leave the house, and I was sure we would lose her then. But I was wrong. It seemed she got better after Casey came into our lives. Margaret tells me she believes it's Casey who's given Mom the will to live."

"That's so great." Lauren had fleeting memories of both sets of her grandparents, who lived on the other side of the country. When she was a kid they visited at least once a year, but as their health failed the visits became less frequent. She could recall only a handful of trips east. The expense of flying the entire family to the east coast was more than her parents could afford.

"Casey's always thinking of things to do with my mom," Lydia went on to say. She was about to add something more when Lauren heard the irritating sound of motorcycles roaring down the street. She grimaced and glanced out the window but couldn't see the riders.

Blossom Street tended to be a more reserved neighborhood, so the piercing sound of the motorcycle engines took her by surprise.

Half rising out of her chair, Bethanne set down her knitting and craned her neck, looking out the window. Apparently disappointed, she sat back down. "For just a minute I thought that might have been Max."

The sound faded into the distance.

"My head is playing games with me. Even if Max was in town, he wouldn't know I was at the yarn store." Bethanne's mind wasn't on her knitting. She looked completely miserable. "I guess it's just wishful thinking on my part." She reached for her cell, grabbing it out of the side pocket on her purse. "I told myself I wasn't going to call him again. As it is, I've left him five messages. That's enough. When Max is ready to sort this out, he'll contact me." While her words were strong, Lauren noticed Bethanne's hand trembling as she replaced her phone. She released a slow breath. "I can remember my mother telling me never to go to bed without resolving an argument. That was good advice. I don't ever want to go through another day like this one."

Casey walked up to Bethanne. "Did you have a truly terrible day, too?"

Bethanne nodded. "I want to talk to my husband."

The bell above the shop door made a jingling sound, and two men walked into the shop.

"I think that could be arranged," the taller of the two men said.

"Max." Bethanne was out of her chair so fast it nearly toppled backward. She hurried across the space separating them and threw herself into her husband's arms. Then they were kissing and hugging and clinging to each other as if the world had suddenly been set right again.

Lauren knew she should have looked away but discovered she couldn't. The scene in front of her was mesmerizing. Although she hardly knew Bethanne, she felt the other woman's joy and relief.

"How did you know where to find me?" Bethanne asked, when she was able.

"I heard you tell Grant this was where you'd be."

"I did?"

"Yes, you did." Max kissed her again, his hands framing her face. He gazed down at her as if being with her was more precious than gold. "I'm here for the family dinner."

"Oh, Max."

For a moment, Lauren feared Bethanne was about to burst into tears.

"Why didn't you answer your phone?"

"I couldn't. I've been on the road all day."

Bethanne hugged her husband closer.

A little embarrassed to be watching, Lauren looked away from the couple. Her gaze drifted to Max's companion. The other man looked as though he was part of a motorcycle gang, complete with a leather vest, bare arms, and tan, bulging muscles. His dark hair was long and tied in a ponytail at the base of his neck, his head covered by a bandanna. His dark glasses made it impossible to see if he was watching her with the same intensity that she was him. He braced his feet apart and crossed his arms while he patiently waited for his friends.

"Hi, Rooster," Casey greeted.

"How's it going, cupcake?" he asked.

Casey laughed at his pet name for her. "I had a terrible day. Bethanne, too."

"It seems matters are looking up for her, though."

"Looks that way," Casey agreed.

His name was Rooster? Interesting, to say the least. Lauren chanced another glance in his direction. If any man was the complete opposite of Todd, it was this one. Not her type, for sure. She hesitated and forced herself to look away. How quickly she'd judged this man she had yet to meet, strictly from appearances.

She'd passed over him with little more than a glimpse. How unfair and judgmental of her. Just that morning she'd told herself it was time to think outside the box, beyond outward appearances. She found herself staring at him, unable to pull her gaze away. Then, to her utter embarrassment, he removed his sunglasses, stared back at her, and smiled.

Chapter Six

*I*t'd been a good long while since Rooster had ridden his bike this hard and this far. He had to admit, it'd been a challenge. He didn't like to think he was getting soft, but that might well be the case. It'd been a year since he'd gone farther than a couple hundred miles on his motorcycle in a single stretch.

Max had been eager to get to Seattle, and they'd ridden practically nonstop. Seeing the greeting Bethanne gave him, Rooster knew Max would consider it worth every minute of discomfort they'd endured on the long ride. The instant the two of them had entered the yarn store, Bethanne's eyes had brightened and she'd practically flown into Max's arms. Witnessing the love the two shared lightened his mood and his day.

Within minutes of their reunion, Bethanne and Max had left the yarn store. Rooster glanced across the street at The French Cafe and his stomach growled, reminding him that it had been hours since they'd briefly stopped for lunch. As he recalled, the croissants at the small deli-style restaurant were buttery and flaky.

He headed across the street and ordered coffee and a croissant to tide him over until dinner. He took the plate outside to a vacant table and sat under an umbrella in order to watch the passersby. He enjoyed people watching and realized that said a lot about him and his personality. Never one to seek the limelight himself, he took pleasure in observing others.

Before they'd left California, Rooster had booked a hotel room for the weekend in downtown Seattle. Max remained conflicted, but Rooster could read the handwriting on the wall when it came to the future of their wine-distribution business. Sooner or later Max, who owned the controlling portion of the partnership, would need to make a decision, and as far as Rooster could see it boiled down to two options—either sell it or move it.

No matter what Max decided, Rooster was tired of living in California. He was ready for a change, so if Max were to decide to relocate, Rooster wouldn't have a problem with the move. He'd spent a fair amount of time in the Seattle area over the years and enjoyed the lush green forests and blue skies.

Rooster was glad he'd arrived at The French Cafe when he did. The small cafe and bakery, which was now open for dinner, did a bustling business, and soon the tables inside started to fill up.

The yarn store closed at six, and he watched Lydia turn the sign over on the door. A couple moments later the woman who'd been knitting with Bethanne left the shop.

Rooster had noticed her right away. Hard not to, with those piercing blue eyes and that dark hair. The combination was striking. She was an eye-catcher for sure—classy, too. Nicely dressed as she was in a pink suit, he guessed she must work in one of the office buildings downtown. He especially liked her choice of jewelry. She wore a cameo with matching earrings. He remembered his mother had a similar one, although he didn't know what had happened to it after she'd died.

He suspected the woman who wore the cameo wasn't married, although the absence of a diamond ring was no guarantee. She had a ring on her left hand, but it was an opal surrounded by diamond chips. Generally, Rooster didn't notice details like this, but she'd caught his eye right away. Fact was, he'd paid attention to just about everything there was to notice about her.

He remembered when Max first met Bethanne. His friend had lost his daughter, and then within a short amount of time, his wife, too. The double whammy had sent Max spiraling emotionally. In an effort to escape the pain, Max had taken to his bike, randomly traveling across the country from one state to the next, with no agenda and no purpose in mind other than to forget and to heal.

Rooster joined him intermittently, mostly to check up on Max and to tell him what was happening with the business, although at the time Max showed little interest in anything to do with their livelihood.

Then while the two of them were on the road, Max had met Bethanne and almost overnight everything had changed. First they'd followed her to Vegas and then to Branson, Missouri. Max had been smitten, big-time. At first Rooster was amused, and later he was grateful. Falling in love with Bethanne had pulled Max out of the deep emotional pit he'd slid into after such devastating losses. She'd given him a reason to move forward, both with life and the business.

Even now Rooster was convinced that if Bethanne had chosen to remarry her ex-husband, Max would have accepted her decision and returned to California to the life he had once known. Love had the power to heal, and Rooster had taken note of that lesson.

Rooster sat up straighter. To his surprise, the woman with the cameo crossed the street and headed directly for The French Cafe. She caught his gaze and smiled politely, acknowledging that she remembered him from the yarn store. She passed him and went inside the small restaurant. Within a few minutes she was back with a cup of coffee. Apparently, all the tables inside were taken, because she came outside and claimed the table on the other side of the entrance away from him. She pulled out the chair and sat so she could look out over the street. She appeared to be waiting for someone, because she glanced anxiously at her wrist and at the people coming and going along the sidewalk.

After a few moments, she hurriedly reached for her purse and brought out her cellphone. She glanced down at it and seemed to be reading a text message.

Rooster watched as she quickly typed out a response. Reading her body language was easy. Her shoulders tensed as she exhaled with what looked like irritation. Rooster guessed whoever she was waiting for was going to be late.

Seeing how busy the cafe was, it seemed a shame that they should each claim an entire table. Having finished the croissant, Rooster discarded the paper plate, reached for his coffee, stood, and approached her.

"Would you mind if I joined you?" he asked. "These tables are becoming a premium."

She glanced up, and a look of surprise came over her before she nodded. "Sure. Why not?"

He pulled out the chair across from her. "Name's Rooster."

"So I heard. I'm Lauren. Lauren Elliott." She held out her hand for him to shake. "Is your name really Rooster?"

"It's what my friends call me." He briefly took her soft hand in his, then leaned back in a relaxed pose and crossed his long legs, propping his ankle on his knee.

Clearly amused, she smiled. "I have to say it's one of the more original names I've heard in a while."

"I'm pretty much used to it. Last name is Wayne." He sipped his coffee. "You're waiting for someone?" He'd deduced that much easily enough.

She glanced at her wrist. "He's already fifteen minutes later than we originally agreed, and then he texted to let me know he was running a few minutes behind. Like I hadn't noticed."

"Not a great way to start off your evening, is it?"

"No, but this is typical of Todd." She didn't sound overly pleased with her date.

Her phone beeped again, and she reached for it. "Now he says he'll be another fifteen minutes." She tossed her phone back in the purse and looked across the table at Rooster. "I'm not waiting." She hesitated and then seemed to reach some decision within herself. "I realize it's last-minute, but how would you like to go to dinner with me?"

"What about your friend?"

She shrugged. "He had his chance. As it happens, he's the one who insisted we meet. I told him earlier we were finished, but he wanted to talk me out of breaking up with him. Fat chance of that happening, especially now, although my mind was already made up."

"Long-term relationship?"

"Too long. Are you interested in dinner?"

"Sure." He didn't want to appear overly eager; the truth was, he could hardly believe his luck. "Do you have someplace in mind?"

"Do you like Thai?"

"Love it."

"Great. I know a small restaurant a couple of blocks over."

This was certainly an interesting development, not that Rooster objected. He just never expected a classy woman like Lauren to be interested in him. Not that she was. Her date had basically stood her up and she didn't want to eat alone, and he was handy. Still, he wasn't going to complain.

Seeing that the place she mentioned was within a short distance, he left his bike parked down the block from the yarn store. They walked side by side, and right away Rooster noticed the curious looks people gave them. It didn't bother him. They did make an odd couple. Him in his motorcycle gear and her, the elegant and stylish business-woman.

"Are you going to let your date know?" he asked.

"Oh, I probably should, but a part of me would like him to arrive and wonder where I went. Although, heaven knows Todd should be able to figure it out on his own." She retrieved her cell, punched out the message, and tucked it back in her purse. "That's one of the things

I dislike about myself. I'm such a good girl, always doing what's right, always following the rules."

"You consider that a flaw?"

"Not a flaw—it's just that I'm so predictable."

Rooster shook his head. "I wouldn't say that. You surprised me by asking me to dinner."

She laughed, and the sound was as pleasant as a melody. "Truth is, I surprised myself. You seem like an interesting man."

"Really?" Rooster didn't view himself that way. Max was the good-looking one. Rooster had never been much of a ladies' man and had always been a bit awkward around the opposite sex, which was probably the reason why at age thirty-nine he remained single. He'd married young and it'd been a mistake, one he'd put behind him a long time ago.

"You're a good person to have as a friend, aren't you?" Lauren asked, glancing toward him as they walked.

Ah, so that was it. She was letting him know she wasn't interested in him romantically. He was being friend zoned.

"What was that?" she asked.

He frowned. "What was what?"

"That look, just now. What's wrong?"

Rooster wasn't aware he'd given any outward indication to what he was thinking. That she found it easy to read him came as a revelation. "It's nothing."

"No, it's not. What did I say?"

She seemed to be mentally reviewing their conversation. "I mentioned that you must be a good person to have as a friend. It isn't everyone who would ride twenty hours, or however long it took you to reach Seattle, with a buddy, especially when you knew that once you arrived you'd be on your own."

"I enjoy long bike rides and it'd been a while since my last road trip," Rooster answered, dismissing her praise.

"You found that comment insulting?"

"No."

"I probably wouldn't have said anything, but being a good friend is a quality I want on my list."

"List?"

"Oh, sorry, it's just a list that I made up of what I think is important."

"In a man?"

"In anyone." She pointed straight ahead. "That's the restaurant I mentioned. The food's wonderful."

From the way she quickly changed the subject, Rooster could see she regretted saying anything about this list she'd compiled.

When Lauren said the restaurant was small, she wasn't kidding. The scent of spices and basil reminded Rooster once more of how long it'd been since he'd had a decent meal. They were seated right away in a booth that required them to remove their shoes and climb into the low seats. Rooster gave Lauren his hand and helped her into the booth before taking his own seat. The petite waitress dressed in traditional Thai garb immediately brought them menus. After discussing the wine options, they chose a bottle of sauvignon blanc.

Lauren's cellphone chirped. She ignored it.

"It's probably your friend," Rooster said.

"Probably," she agreed, "but I'm with you and I consider it impolite to communicate with one man when I'm with another."

Rooster could get to like this woman. "You really are a good girl, aren't you?"

"I told you so. It's downright irritating."

He didn't know if she was joking or not, but he laughed out loud.

A smile lit up her face. "You have a wonderful laugh. Full-bodied and carefree. I like that."

"Is that on your list as well?"

"No, but I'm thinking it should be."

Their meal was delicious, but Rooster thought it could well have been the company more than the peanut sauce. He didn't ask Lauren a lot of getting-to-know-you questions mainly because this was probably going to be the only time he would see her.

She, however, seemed curious about him. Rooster was happy to answer her questions. His one comment was on her jewelry.

"Thank you," she said, fingering the cameo. "I work in a jewelry store and have a small collection of cameos."

"I thought diamonds are a girl's best friend."

"Don't get me wrong, diamonds are beautiful, but I find myself attracted to the subtle art and craftsmanship of the cameos."

When they'd finished, he insisted on paying and left a generous tip in cash. "I'll walk you to your car," he said as he helped her out of the booth.

"I didn't drive. My condo building is just off Blossom Street."

"Then I'll walk you to your building."

"You don't need to do that."

He suspected this was her way of giving him the brushoff, which was fine. They'd had a pleasant evening. Rooster had enjoyed himself and didn't expect anything more. Being with Lauren Elliott was far better than spending the night in his hotel room or killing an hour or two in the lobby bar.

"That is, unless you want to see me to my condo," she added.

"Seeing you home is part of the code of being a gentleman that my father taught me."

"You are a gentleman," she whispered.

"On your list?" he joked.

"As a matter of fact, it is."

They were outside by now, and with daylight savings time in effect it was still light out. "You better tell me about this list," he said, seeing that the subject had come up a number of times in the course of the evening.

"Trust me, you don't want to know."

"Really?"

"It would send most men running for the hills."

"I'm not most men."

"I'm beginning to see that." She straightened slightly as though gathering her resolve. "It's a list of qualities I'm looking for in a . . ."

Rooster strained to hear the last word. Her voiced dipped low, and he hadn't caught it. "In a what?" he asked.

She glanced at him and repeated a bit louder this time. "Husband."

Rooster had never heard of anyone making up a husband list, and it amused him.

"You aren't going to comment?"

"Not really. I'll admit that I hadn't heard of this idea, but it's probably a good one."

Lauren readjusted her purse strap over her shoulder. "I've always been a list maker, and after dealing with Todd for the last several years, I don't want to make the same mistakes I did with him. This way, I have a guide and I can quickly make up my mind."

Rooster couldn't help being curious. "What did you decide about me?" It might be a mistake to ask, but that didn't hold him back.

"I decided to add being a good friend to the list because of you."

"I'm honored."

"You're generous, I noticed."

"How do you know that?"

"I saw the tip you left our waitress."

"She gave us excellent service."

"Thoughtful, too."

"Really?" Rooster had no idea how she'd determined that. Before he could ask, she supplied the answer.

"You asked if you could sit with me to free up a table at The French Cafe."

"Right. And I have my daddy to thank for insisting on walking you home."

"A gentleman."

"I'm batting a thousand."

"Yes, you are," she said, laughing. "I probably shouldn't have told you about the list. If it makes you uncomfortable, I apologize."

"It doesn't." They'd slowed their pace to a near crawl. They continued walking for another block while Rooster sorted through his thoughts, wondering if he had a shot with her. He decided nothing ventured, nothing gained. "Does this mean you'd be willing to see me again?"

Lauren looked over at him and dazzled him with one of her smiles. "I was hoping you'd ask."

Chapter Seven

When you put beads in your knitting, you are really
putting bits of light in your knitting. The gleam and
color-play of beads add a whole other dimension
that could be demure or outrageous, as you please.
Your choice of beads and yarn uniquely expresses
your personality.

—Sivia Harding,
designer and teacher

"Grandma, today was the worst day ever, even worse than Tuesday," Casey said the instant Lydia opened the door to her mother's
small apartment in the assisted-living complex.

Mary Lou Hoffman looked away from the television screen.
"Casey and Margaret. I'm so pleased you've stopped by."

"Grandma," Casey said, getting down on one knee beside the large overstuffed chair where her grandmother sat. "It's Casey and Lydia."

Lydia's mother's forehead winkled with a thick frown. "Of course it is. I knew that."

"It's all right, Mom," Lydia assured her. "I know who I am, and I know who you are, too."

"I'm your mother."

"Exactly."

"I had a really bad day," Casey repeated. "A truly terrible bad day, and I'm not grousing, either."

Lydia's mother focused her attention on Casey. "Remember what I said about bad days. Surely you can think of one good thing that happened."

"Mom tried to get me thinking about the good stuff, too."

"And did you?"

"I did," Casey admitted with some reluctance. "I came up with a couple of things, but it wasn't enough to block out how horrible it was."

"Can you think of just one more good thing to tell me?" Lydia's mother asked. She brushed Casey's hair away from her face and cupped her granddaughter's cheeks with the palms of her hands.

"Something sort of funny happened," Casey admitted after chewing on her lower lip.

"Good. Tell me about that."

Lydia was curious herself, so she scooted out a chair at the kitchen table and sat down.

"I've been volunteering at the After Care Program at the grade school, remember?"

Her mother clearly didn't. "That's good."

"I get extra credit for it in my humanities class if I help," Casey explained.

"So what happened?" Lydia asked, wanting her daughter to get to the story. Brad and Cody were home waiting for them.

"A new boy was there this afternoon," Casey explained. "He's in the second grade, and he said his name is Brian. He's small for his age. I was surprised he wasn't in first grade or even preschool."

"A good name," Mary Lou said. "I once dated a boy named Brian."

"This Brian wore thick glasses and was sort of nerdy-looking."

"The Brian I dated was dreamy," Lydia's mother added.

"Brian told me he'd fallen on his head when he was little and the fall had killed brain cells."

Lydia wondered when the humorous part of this story was coming.

"Oh, dear, the poor boy," Mary Lou offered sympathetically.

"That's what I said," Casey continued. "Then he told me he needed medication."

Lydia was beginning to get a picture of this small child with the thick glasses with a quirky smile who needed attention.

"I took his hand and told him I'd take him over to where the other second-graders were," Casey continued. "But he stopped me. He said there was more, and he looked so serious I stopped and waited."

"More?" Lydia asked.

"Oh, yes. Brian wanted me to know he hadn't taken his medication that morning. He wasn't sure what would happen without his medication."

Lydia smiled, and so did her mother.

"Did you laugh?" Mary Lou said.

"No, but it was a struggle not to," Casey said. "And even without his pills, Brian did fine. He made a friend with Alice, who wears glasses, too, only her glasses aren't as thick as Brian's."

"I'm glad Brian has a friend," Lydia's mother added.

"He said he would be back tomorrow, and he promised to take his medication this time."

"So you had at least one smile for the day," Lydia's mother reminded Casey. "And one smile cancels out three reasons to frown, right?"

"Right."

Lydia stood and checked her purse for her car keys. "I better get home. Dad will pick you up around eight," she reminded her daughter.

Casey nodded.

"I'll save dinner for you."

"If Dad's cooking, it's probably spaghetti."

"Probably." Unfortunately, Brad's doctored bottled sauce wasn't Casey's favorite. She liked spaghetti, especially from her favorite restaurant, but she was picky when it came to sauce, and for Casey the bottled variety didn't measure up to her standards.

"I'll have peanut-butter-and-jelly sandwiches later. Okay?"

"Sure."

"See ya, Mom."

Lydia's mother glanced up. "Margaret, you're leaving so soon?"

"It's Lydia," Casey gently reminded her grandmother, placing her hand over the older woman's.

"Oh, yes, sorry. You already told me that once, didn't you?"

"It's fine, Mom." Lydia bent down and kissed her mother's forehead. Casey looked up and smiled, content and at peace after her truly terrible day. It did Lydia's heart good to see the consternation leave her daughter's face as she sat at her grandmother's side.

"Bring me my knitting," Mary Lou said, as Lydia quietly left the apartment. Her mother rarely knit any longer, and following even the simplest instructions seemed beyond her. While grateful that her mother was alive, Lydia worried about Mary Lou's quality of life. It distressed her to watch her mother's physical and mental health decline. Arthritis made movement difficult, and she spent a good portion of her day in her chair in front of the television. The assisted-living complex scheduled a variety of events to keep the residents' bodies and minds active. When her mother had first moved into the complex she'd participated in a few of the social gatherings, but no longer.

Lydia walked to the elevator and pushed the button. An aide joined her. "You're Mrs. Hoffman's daughter, aren't you?"

"Yes," Lydia responded with an automatic smile. The aide's badge said her name was Marie.

"The one who owns the yarn store."

"Yes," Lydia confirmed.

"I wanted you to know I think it's wonderful what you're doing."

"Thank you." Lydia had a number of charity projects going at A Good Yarn. Early on she'd discovered that knitters were, by nature, generous. With little encouragement on Lydia's part, many of her regular customers volunteered knitted items for a variety of charities. Several knit hats or sweaters for World Vision's Knit for Kids program, and then there were others who contributed knitted squares to Warm Up America! from yarn left over from their projects. And of course there were the tiny caps the shop collected for the area's hospital preemies.

"I found the knitting basket at the bowling alley where my husband is in a league," Marie added.

"The bowling alley?"

"That is you, isn't it?" Marie asked. "The yarn had a sticker that said it was from A Good Yarn shop."

The confusion must have shown on Lydia's face because Marie added, "I had my book group on Tuesday night and my husband is in a league with the guys from work. He drives a Pepsi delivery truck. After the meeting with my book club, I stopped off to see how Les's bowling team was doing, and I found the basket with the yarn and needles."

"Were there instructions?"

"Not really. It was more of an invitation to sit down and knit. I think the note said when the scarf was finished it should be delivered to a homeless shelter or dropped off at your yarn store. You aren't the one doing this?" Marie questioned.

"No."

"I just assumed from the yarn label and instructions that you must be responsible."

"I heard about this just recently. It's a great idea; I wish I could say I'd thought of it, but I didn't."

"No harm done," Marie said, as they stepped into the waiting elevator.

Lydia mulled over the conversation as she drove home. When she walked into the house, the scent of simmering tomatoes with Italian spices confirmed her suspicions. Brad had cooked spaghetti.

"Is that you, sweetheart?" her husband called out. He peeked his head around the opening to the kitchen and grinned when he saw it was Lydia. "Dinner's just about ready. Cody's got the bread and the salad on the table. How's your mother?"

"She thought I was Margaret," Lydia said, as she removed her sweater and tucked away her purse. "The oddest thing has been happening," she said, coming into the kitchen. The pot on the stove boiled furiously. She reached over and turned off the burner while Brad removed the strainer from the lower cupboard and set it in the sink.

"What's that?" he asked, steam rising from the cooked pasta as he carried the boiling pot to the sink and drained off the liquid.

"Someone is leaving baskets with knitting needles and yarn around town with a note asking people to knit for the homeless."

"Really?"

"The yarn is apparently from my shop."

Her husband was preoccupied with mixing the sauce and the noodles together and setting it on the table.

Lydia brought out the silverware. "Will you keep an eye out for one of these knitting baskets?"

Brad looked up at her, paused, and blinked, and Lydia guessed that the entire conversation had gone directly over his head.

"What was that, sweetie?"

"Never mind," she said, grinning. "I'll tell you about it later."

"Cody!" Brad shouted. "Dinner."

This was her life, Lydia mused, and it was good.

Chapter Eight

$\mathcal{M}$ax was exhausted, butt-sore, and ecstatic.

He'd followed Bethanne home from the yarn store on his bike and parked it in the empty slot in her garage. Other than a few items of clothing, he'd packed light. From the trips he'd made to Seattle since their marriage, he kept enough of a wardrobe at Bethanne's not to worry about bringing much with him.

Bethanne waited for him by the garage door that led into her kitchen. Her eyes were all over him as though even now she couldn't believe he was with her. Max's feelings matched hers, although he felt they needed to discuss a number of issues. With this trip, he wanted to settle the matter with her ex-husband once and for all.

While this house was the one Bethanne had once shared with Grant, Max wasn't comfortable with her ex-husband stopping by anytime he pleased. He might be exaggerating, but it seemed Grant found an excuse to connect with Bethanne nearly every day. It had gotten out of hand, and if she didn't recognize it, he did.

"I still can't believe you rode all those hours to be here," Bethanne said, as she stepped into the kitchen and turned off the security alarm.

"I can't, either." He waited until they were inside the house before he brought his wife into his arms and kissed her with both hunger and need. She came warm and willing into his embrace, and his doubts fled. Bethanne loved *him*. She'd chosen to marry *him*.

When the kiss ended, they simply looked at each other.

With her arms looped around his neck, she leaned her head back. "Have you had dinner?"

"No." In his eagerness to reach his wife, Max had barely stopped for anything more than fuel and water. At some point midway through Oregon, Rooster convinced him to pause long enough to eat a sandwich, which he'd done, but that had been hours earlier.

"Me, neither."

"Do you want to go out?" Max felt obliged to ask.

"No. Let me check what I've got here."

Max wasn't eager to head out to a restaurant, either, and was grateful Bethanne felt the same way. As it was, he was half dead on his feet. He followed his wife into the main part of the kitchen. He sat down at the counter while she rummaged through the refrigerator.

"It's either a chicken taco salad—"

"Anything." He wasn't picky. Cocking his head, he enjoyed the view of Bethanne bending over while she sorted through the refrigerator drawers. She had a mighty fine-looking derriere.

"I could make us veggie burgers."

"No, thanks." He was a meat-and-potatoes kind of guy. "I prefer real meat."

"Really." She turned around and braced her hands on her hips. "You ate a veggie burger the last time you were here."

"That was a veggie burger?" Max remembered it distinctly. He'd complimented Bethanne on it. She'd cut up thick slices of tomato and thin slices of onion, added pickled jalapeños along with melted cheese and fried bacon. They'd planned to eat out on the deck, but it'd started to drizzle so they'd stayed in the kitchen. Afterward they'd watched a movie and she'd sat in his lap. All too soon he lost interest in the movie as they got involved in each other. Taking him by the hand, Bethanne had led him up the stairs to the bedroom.

"As I recall, you didn't complain about the veggie burger then."

"You distracted me."

"It seems to me I could easily distract you again," she teased.

"Without hardly trying," Max assured her, chuckling softly.

"Veggie burger or chicken taco salad?"

"Veggie burger," he decided. "Do you want me to slice the tomatoes and onions?"

"Please." Bethanne brought what she needed out of the refrigerator and set it on the countertop while Max got out the cutting board and knife.

He didn't want to start off their time together on a negative note, but this thing with Grant burned in his chest like a hot coal fresh from the fire.

Hoping to casually bring up the subject, he asked, "Have you talked to Grant today?"

"No. What makes you ask?"

The slight edge in her voice didn't escape his notice. "No particular reason."

Bracing her hands against the edge of the kitchen counter, she stared him down. "I don't want you to waste energy on being jealous over Grant when there's no reason."

"I'm not jealous; I'm concerned."

"You don't need to be. I've got this."

The last thing Max wanted was for them to continue the argument that had brought him to Seattle in the first place. "Then I'll leave the matter in your capable hands."

Max saw the tension leave her shoulders.

"Thank you."

Bethanne rewarded him with a probing kiss that he felt all the way to the bottom of his feet. "I'm thinking," he said, still breathless, his eyes closed, "that we might want to delay dinner."

"We have plenty of time for what you're thinking, big boy. You're starving, and so am I."

Max chuckled, and, drawing in a stabilizing breath, he continued with the task at hand.

"Where's Rooster staying?" she asked, as she placed bacon in the frying pan.

"In a hotel somewhere in the downtown area."

"He's a good friend."

Rooster had repeatedly proved his loyalty and friendship. "I know of none better."

She paused and looked to Max. "Why do you think he's never married?"

Max hadn't really given the matter much thought. "Can't really say. His parents are both gone, and he looked after them while in his late twenties and early thirties. The truth is, I think he's a bit shy."

"Rooster?"

"Looking at him, you'd never guess that, would you? I suspect he just hasn't found the right woman; when he does, he'll make his move."

Bethanne sighed, and now that the onions and tomatoes were sliced, Max moved behind her and wrapped his arms around her waist. "What was the sigh about?" he asked, kissing the side of her neck.

"I'm a romantic."

"So I've noticed."

"Max, you're sending chills down my arms."

"Good." He ran his hands down the length of her arms, and continued kissing the side of her neck, savoring this time with her. What a shame they couldn't be together like this every evening, working in the kitchen side by side, listening to music or the news. Simply spending time with each other.

"I'd like to see Rooster married with his own family one day."

Resting his chin on Bethanne's shoulder, Max mulled over her words. "So would I."

"Do you want me to set him up?" she asked. "In my circle of friends I know several single women who—"

"Don't even think about it," Max said, cutting her off. "Rooster isn't the kind of guy who's interested in a blind date. It would be better to leave matters just as they are."

"If you think that's for the best, then I will." She removed the fried bacon from the pan and set it to drain on a paper towel before turning off the burner. "All I want is for Rooster to be happy."

"He'll find his own happiness the same way I did mine," Max assured her.

Together they were assembling the veggie burgers when unexpectedly the front door opened. To the best of Max's knowledge, it had been locked. Bethanne and he had come through the garage and into the house.

"Bethanne?"

Grant.

Max stiffened. Apparently, Grant had a key to the house.

His wife sent Max an apologetic look that did little to quell his irritation. Before now her ex-husband had been aware of Max's comings and goings and had stayed away when he was in town. This evening, however, Grant didn't realize Max was in town.

"I didn't hear back from you about the sunglasses," Grant called from the living room. "Is that bacon I smell? You know I have a weakness for—" He stopped cold when he stepped into the kitchen and found Max with Bethanne.

"Oh, sorry," Grant apologized, slowing his steps. "I didn't realize you had company."

"Max isn't company." Bethanne's voice was chilly enough to freeze standing water. "He's my husband."

"Right."

"I came for the family dinner on Saturday," Max explained. "I understand you're buying." It was sure to tighten his jaw when Grant ended up paying for his meal. Max intended on ordering the most expensive item on the menu simply to add to Grant's misery. It was what the other man deserved.

"Of course. I'm pleased you could make it, Max. Bethanne told me you were tied up with a business dinner."

"I rearranged my schedule."

"So I see." Grant turned his attention to Bethanne. "I take it you didn't happen upon those sunglasses?"

"I would have called if I did."

"Of course."

Grant smiled, but his pleasure was as phony as the man himself.

"Sorry to interrupt your dinner," Grant added. "Let me know if those glasses turn up, would you?"

"I'll be happy to," Max said before Bethanne had the chance to respond. "Looking forward to the dinner Saturday night."

"Good to see you, Max."

The man could deliver his lines like a Shakespearean actor.

Well, so could Max. "You, too, Grant."

Bethanne's ex glared back at him as if to say he was giving Max fair warning. Max read the look in the other man's eyes and held his gaze. Apparently, Grant didn't know his ex-wife nearly as well as he assumed. Bethanne wouldn't cheat on him any more than Max would be unfaithful to her.

He stood frozen until the door had closed after Grant.

"All right, say it," Bethanne murmured stiffly.

"Say what?"

"You're upset."

"I'm not, but I do have one question."

"Okay."

"Can you give me a single reason why Grant still has a key to the house?"

Chapter Nine

*F*irst thing Friday morning, Rooster brought out his computer, logged on, and spent the morning working. A number of times he was forced to refocus as his mind drifted to Lauren. He liked her a great deal, probably far more than he should. It wasn't like him to feel this strongly about a woman after so short an acquaintance. One dinner. Sure, she was easy on the eyes—he'd be blind not to notice—but it was far more than her appearance that attracted him. He enjoyed hearing her laugh. She was intelligent and witty and sensible. Funny how much you could learn about a person after one dinner.

Just before noon, in an effort to clear his head, Rooster took his bike out for a short ride. Still, try as he might, he couldn't stop thinking of Lauren. He found it a bit of an ego boost that she was interested in seeing him again. He was eager to make that happen. Lauren filled his mind, and every time he thought about her "husband list," it caused him to smile. It'd embarrassed her to tell him about it, when in actuality Rooster thought it was a good idea. If he was in the market for a wife, he'd consider compiling a similar one, which left him considering the possibility of marriage. It was time—past time, really, that he considered starting a family. He'd had relationships before, but they had fizzled out, mainly because of the one bad experience, family obligations, and later his commitment to Max and the business. His failed marriage had left him gun-shy and hesitant. He didn't like to dwell on his failure as a husband; clearly, the marriage had been a mistake on both their parts.

Rooster stopped at a barbecue place outside of Kent. He had Lauren's cell number. Although tempted to contact her, he didn't expect her employer would appreciate her taking personal calls while working. A text would be better, but even then he wasn't sure what to say. He was no good at this and was sure to bungle it. Rather than take the risk, he returned his cell to the holder on his belt, angry with himself for being so out of practice when it came to dealing with a woman.

Back in his hotel room, he paced the confines of the room and decided he'd waited long enough. At five he punched out her number, and when she didn't pick up, he left a short message.

"It's Rooster." He didn't figure there was much else to say.

At six his phone chirped. It was Lauren.

"I'm so glad you called," she said, and seemed slightly breathless and troubled.

She was glad, but it wasn't for the reasons he'd hoped. He could hear it in her voice. Something had happened. Right away, Rooster suspected it had something to do with the man who'd stood her up the night before, when they'd gone out instead. "What's up?"

He heard her exhale. "I had a rather unpleasant confrontation with Todd this afternoon."

So he was right. "I'm sorry."

"Yes, so am I. Todd was upset that I'd left the restaurant. He said he'd arrived just minutes after I left with you."

"Really?" That seemed unlikely. "I thought the last text you got said he'd be another fifteen minutes."

"Fifteen minutes *at least*. Since then he apparently changed his story. He wasn't happy when I ignored his phone call, either."

Todd had had his chance. From what little Lauren had said about the other man, being late wasn't something new.

"I'm just getting off work now . . . I'm not usually so forward. You insisted on paying for dinner last night even though I was the one who asked you. Would you allow me to buy your dinner tonight?"

Rooster was stunned, and she seemed to read his hesitation as indecision or a means of putting her off.

"You can always say no."

Rooster had no intention of turning her down.

"Although I hope you don't," she added.

"Okay." He did his best to hide his enthusiasm. "Where would you like to meet?"

"I know a great place down on the waterfront. It's one of my favorite restaurants in the entire city. We might have to wait for a table, but I promise you it'll be worth it."

"You're on."

She gave him a time and the name of the restaurant. "I hope you like seafood."

"I do."

"Then it's settled. I'll see you in a little less than an hour."

"I'll look forward to it."

That gave Rooster enough time to shower and shave. He pulled out a western-style shirt from his saddlebags. It was wrinkled, and after shaking it out several times it didn't look much better. He didn't have time to shop for another shirt, so he got out the hotel iron and ironing board. He wouldn't go through this for just any woman. The shirt looked substantially better when he finished, and he quickly put it on and snapped it closed.

His hotel was only a few blocks from the Seattle waterfront, so he walked down the hill toward Puget Sound, experiencing emotions similar to those he'd had as a teenager on prom night. The last time he'd felt this giddy he'd been in high school.

The restaurant waiting area was crowded when he arrived, but it didn't take him long to spot Lauren. Not for the first time, he realized it would be far too easy to fall for her. One advantage was the fact that he'd be leaving town early Sunday morning, riding back to California. Monday was Memorial Day, and Max and Rooster hoped for a more leisurely ride. If he spent much more time with Lauren, he would surely need to clear his head.

"Hi," he said, coming up behind her.

She turned and dazzled him with a smile. "Hi."

Rooster swore her eyes were warm enough to melt wax.

"Thank you," she whispered.

He should be the one thanking her, although he wasn't about to let her know that. "No problem. I didn't have any other plans for the evening." That was probably the wrong thing to say, even if it was the truth.

"I had a dreadful day."

"Todd?"

"Oh, it's more than that. My employer is going through a rough time with her daughter, and she and her husband can't agree on what to do. They argued, and Elisa left the shop and didn't come back. Garry was upset." She shook her head as if she'd said more than she wanted. "I don't know what it is about you."

Rooster arched his brows. "About me?" he asked, unable to connect the dots. "What do you mean?"

"I tell you things I don't intend to say."

He chuckled.

"I feel comfortable around you."

Probably because she had no intention of ever getting seriously involved with him. "Is being comfortable with someone on your list?"

"No, but it's something else I should consider adding."

Rooster was encouraged to know she'd found him helpful. It was difficult to tell if she was genuinely interested or if he was being relegated to the friend zone. Time would tell. As they waited for their name to be called, Rooster buried the tips of his fingers in his jeans pockets.

The hostess greeted Lauren as if they knew each other and glanced in Rooster's direction without comment.

"Like I said, this is one of my favorite restaurants," Lauren mentioned casually as they followed the hostess. "I've been here quite a few times, enough for them to know my name. It will be worth the wait. You'll notice once we're seated that there isn't any silverware."

"Finger food?"

"Not exactly. With our meal, we'll each be given a wooden board and mallet."

"A mallet? You mean a hammer?"

"Of sorts. That's so we can crack open the crabs ourselves. We'll get plastic bibs, too, but everyone wears them, so you won't look silly or feel out of place."

Over the years, Rooster had heard about these types of restaurants, but he'd never actually been to one. This was sure to be an experience.

"The bib has saved me from dripping butter on myself any number of times."

Rooster found the image of Lauren with melted butter running down her chin strangely appealing. He quickly cast the vision from his mind. "When you think about the restaurant doing away with silverware, it's a rather clever idea. Just think of all the forks they're saving."

"Don't feel you need to order the crab," Lauren assured him. "There's a regular menu as well."

"Will I get a fork?"

She was about to answer when they arrived at their table.

They were seated and handed menus when the attendant filled their glasses with ice water. No sooner had he left when he returned with warm sourdough bread. The scent was heavenly.

"I feel worlds better already," Lauren said, leaning slightly forward. "Thank you, Rooster."

It was on the tip of his tongue to comment, but he stopped when he noticed a well-dressed man walking purposely across the room toward their table. Rooster bristled and guessed this wasn't the restaurant manager.

"Do you know this guy?" he asked Lauren.

As Lauren glanced up from the menu, the color drained from her face. "It's Todd."

Rooster stood up as the other man approached. At six-one, he stood several inches taller than Lauren's friend. "Can I help you?" he asked.

The other man ignored him. "I knew I'd find you here. And who's this . . ." He paused and looked up at Rooster as though he found the mere sight of him comical. "This is a joke, right?" he asked.

"The name is Wayne," Rooster said. "Rooster Wayne."

"Rooster?" Todd repeated as though he found that information highly entertaining.

"Did you honestly think you could make me jealous over *him*?" Todd asked, again as if he found the situation nothing short of amusing.

Lauren nervously glanced around her. "Todd, you're embarrassing me and embarrassing yourself. Would you kindly leave? I've said everything I intend to say to you."

"Not before—"

"I believe you heard the lady," Rooster said.

"You," Todd returned, and bounced his finger against Rooster's chest, "stay out of this."

Rooster clenched his fist. "I've heard enough."

By now their confrontation had attracted the attention of the entire restaurant. The room went quiet, and it seemed everyone collectively held their breath, waiting to find out what would happen next.

Rooster heard a couple of people whisper that this was Todd Hampton from Channel Eight news. Grabbing hold of Todd's upper arm, Rooster half lifted the slighter man from the floor until Todd was obliged to walk on the tips of his feet. Without another word, Rooster dragged him out of the restaurant.

"Take your hands off me." Stretching out his arm, Todd pointed at the hostess. "You're a witness to this. I have witnesses."

This was supposedly said for Rooster's benefit. If Todd thought to intimidate him with a lawsuit, he'd failed. Once outside in the cool night air, Rooster released Lauren's ex.

Todd brushed off the sleeves of his expensive tailored suit. "You're going to regret this," he muttered. His gaze narrowed into thin slits. "I have connections."

"Good for you. So do I. I suggest you heed my warning."

"Fine, whatever." Todd held up his hands as if Rooster had pointed a revolver at him. "You know the only reason she's with you is to make me jealous. She knows I love her; it's only a matter of time before we get back together."

Unwilling to get involved any further in this mess, Rooster turned his back on Todd and returned to the inside of the restaurant. He felt every eye on him as he wove his way around the tables to where Lauren remained seated. Taking out his wallet, he peeled off a twenty-dollar bill and set it on the table. Without another word, he left.

He was outside the restaurant before she caught up with him.

"Rooster, wait. Please," he heard her shout.

He stopped, but he didn't turn around.

"I am so sorry," she breathlessly told him.

"Don't mention it."

"Please don't be upset with me."

As far as Rooster was concerned, he had nothing more to say to Lauren and started walking again.

She trotted along beside him. "I had no idea Todd would do anything like this. I feel dreadful."

"I said don't mention it."

"Why are you so angry . . . I didn't do anything. I was the one embarrassed and mortified. If you want to be annoyed with anyone, it should be Todd, not me."

Rooster stopped in his tracks and stared down hard at Lauren. "You used me."

"I beg your pardon?" She looked stricken by his accusation.

"You used me to make Todd jealous. I don't appreciate being used."

"How can you say that?" she demanded.

"You mentioned me to Todd when you saw him earlier today, didn't you?" he demanded.

"Well, yes, but only in passing. That had nothing to do with my breaking up with him. I'd already made my decision."

"You asked me to dinner."

"Yes, but—"

"You took me to your favorite restaurant. My guess is that you and Todd routinely went there."

"I . . . yes, but—"

"Don't worry about it, Lauren. I served my purpose. Mission accomplished."

He left her then, rooted to the sidewalk, looking crestfallen and confused. Rooster hightailed it back to his hotel, determined to put her out of his mind once and for all.

Chapter Ten

Fair Isle awakens the beauty of the world in color as
you paint with yarn.
—Sheila Joynes,
instructor, designer, and author of
I Can't Believe I'm Fair Isle Knitting,
sheliajoynes on Ravelry

*I*n the wee hours of Saturday morning, Lydia woke from a deep
sleep at the sound of a piercing cry coming from Casey's bedroom.
She bolted upright and tossed aside the covers. Brad leaned up on one
elbow as Lydia turned on the bedside lamp.

"What in the name of heaven is that?" he asked.

"Casey," Lydia said, reaching for her robe.

"Mom? Dad?" Cody cried as he barged into the bedroom. "Something's wrong with Casey."

Lydia was already out of bed. She stuffed her arms into the sleeves of her robe and tucked her feet into her slippers before rushing into Casey's bedroom. Flipping the light switch, Lydia saw that her daughter tossed her head back and forth, writhing as though in horrendous pain.

"Casey, Casey," Lydia said, grabbing hold of her daughter. "Wake up, sweetheart. Wake up."

Casey's eyes flew open, and she released a harsh gasp. Her shoulders heaved as if she'd reached the end of a five-mile run and had pushed herself beyond her physical limits. As soon as she saw Lydia, the young teen started to cry, reached up to grab hold of her mother, and clung to her.

Wrapping Casey in her arms, Lydia sat on the edge of the mattress and gently rocked her daughter. "It was a dream, honey, just a dream."

Casey buried her face in Lydia's neck and silently wept. "I know . . . I know."

Lydia continued to hold Casey close, rocking her for several moments and rubbing her hand up and down the teen's slender spine. "You're safe. No one is going to hurt you."

Casey sobbed once more before she nodded.

After several minutes of sitting in this uncomfortable position, Lydia asked, "Are you okay now?"

Casey shook her head. "Don't go."

"I'm right here." She brushed the tangled hair away from Casey's face and looked into her eyes. "Do you want to talk about the dream?"

"No." Her response was adamant.

"That's okay; you don't need to tell me if you don't want to."

"Stay with me."

"I'm not going anywhere," Lydia assured her, smoothing the back of Casey's head.

Lydia heard footsteps in the hallway outside her daughter's bedroom and looked up to find her husband framed in the open doorway. "Everything all right in here?" Brad asked.

"I think so," Lydia whispered. "Casey wants me to stay with her awhile."

Brad's frown relayed his concern.

"Go back to bed," Lydia told him. "I shouldn't be long."

"You sure she's going to be okay?"

She nodded, and then, because she couldn't see Casey's clock, she asked, "What time is it, anyway?"

"A little after three," her husband told her. This wasn't the way to start their busy weekend.

Brad reluctantly returned to their bedroom.

"Can you lie down with me?" Casey asked with a sniffle.

"Sure."

"Hold me, though."

"I won't let you go," Lydia promised.

Lydia removed her slippers, and Casey scooted over in the narrow bed to make room for her. She would have taken off her robe, but Casey continued to cling to her as if she were the only solid thing in a world that had unexpectedly gone off kilter.

"You won't un-adopt me, will you?"

The question made Lydia want to weep. "Casey, you should know by now that your father and I would never do such a thing. It hurts me that you would even ask."

"I need to be sure."

"You are part of our family now—our daughter—and nothing is going to change that."

Casey sniffled, and as Lydia scooted down in the bed, Casey pressed her head against Lydia's shoulder.

In an effort to comfort her daughter, Lydia softly hummed the hymn "Amazing Grace." Soon Casey's own emotionally wobbly hum joined hers. A couple of times the young teen shuddered a sigh.

It took a long time, but gradually Lydia felt Casey's tight grip on her loosen. Without being able to view the clock, she speculated that it took more than an hour for Casey to return to sleep.

As quietly and gently as she could, Lydia slipped out of bed and returned to her own. She fully expected Brad to be asleep. He wasn't.

He lifted the covers for her to return next to him in their queen-size bed.

Lydia scooted close to her husband, and he wrapped his arm around her middle, bringing her close to his side.

"Is Casey asleep?"

She nodded. "Finally. It took a long time to quiet her. She wouldn't tell me about the dream."

"Can you blame her?" Brad asked, his head close to her ear. "Whatever it was terrified the poor kid. Telling you would be reliving the dream all over again."

"I think it might help her to talk about it—maybe not right away, though, when it's still fresh in her mind. I'll ask her again in the morning." This wasn't the first time Casey had woken them crying out in the night. This nightmare, whatever it was, seemed to be a reoccurring one. When they'd first adopted her at age twelve, Casey had had bad dreams. None seemed as bad as this one, however. It'd taken far longer to comfort her this time than ever before; she'd been terrified and shaking uncontrollably.

"You weren't able to get back to sleep?" Lydia whispered. Saturday was her husband's one day to sleep in, and Casey's nightmare had interrupted that for Brad.

"Adrenaline kicked in when I heard Casey scream. I didn't know what to think."

"It shocked me, too."

"We should have expected this," Brad said, and yawned. He covered his mouth and then stretched.

"The nightmares?"

"That and a whole lot more. The poor girl came to us with a full set of baggage. Abandoned by her birth parents, then living in a series of foster homes. Learning her brother was in jail. By age twelve Casey had seen more drama and heartache than most people do in a lifetime."

Lydia agreed. "She's adjusted so well it's sometimes difficult to remember she's been through so much," she said and sighed. "Even now she's afraid we're going to send her away."

"Did she ask you about it?"

Lydia nodded. "This is the first time in her life that she's had a stable home life, or been part of a family. I suppose we shouldn't be surprised. She's been taken away from every home where she's ever lived." Lydia's one concern for her daughter was linked with her mother. Mary Lou grew weaker physically and mentally every month. Lydia didn't know how much longer they would have her mother. Seeing how close Casey was to her grandmother, Lydia couldn't help worrying what would happen when she died.

"What are you fretting about now?" Brad asked.

Lydia smiled. How well her husband knew her. "Casey and Mom. I don't like to think how Casey will react once we lose her."

"Let's cross that bridge when we get there," her husband wisely advised.

Thankfully, they did manage to fall back asleep. Lydia woke just before eight to find she was alone in bed. Stretching her arms above her head, Lydia smiled as she heard her husband talking to the kids in the kitchen.

Brad had pancakes on the griddle and coffee made by the time Lydia wandered out of the bedroom, yawning. Cody sat at the table, stuffing himself with a large stack swimming in a plate of syrup. Casey sat across from him with a single pancake on her plate but showed little appetite.

"Morning," Lydia said, and kissed Cody's cheek first and then Casey's. "You feel all right this morning?" she asked her daughter, her hands on Casey's shoulders.

Casey shrugged.

"You screamed like a banshee," Cody said. "It scared the living crap out of me."

Casey made a face at her brother. "Get over it."

"Kids, enough," Brad said, cutting off any chance of this exchange developing into a full-blown argument.

Brad had her coffee poured, and Lydia hugged her husband's middle in an effort to thank him. "Have I told you lately how much I love you?"

"And all it took was a single cup of coffee," he teased, and kissed the tip of her nose. "Breakfast?" he asked.

Lydia shook her head. She wasn't one for a big breakfast. Toast and a glass of orange juice were the most she ever ate. Lydia was slight and slender, and had never been a big eater. Two bouts with cancer, the first in her teen years, and the second in her early twenties, might have had something to do with her attitude toward food. Before she was married and a mother, Lydia could easily skip meals simply because she'd forgotten it was mealtime.

Brad set the dirty dishes in the sink. "Come on, Cody, we need to hustle to your game."

Cody wolfed down one last bite of his breakfast and scooted back his chair. He was as tall as Lydia now, and it wouldn't be much longer before he shot past her. "You coming to the game, Mom?"

"You bet." The baseball game started at nine, which gave Lydia just enough time to cheer on her son and get to the yarn store in time to open the shop at ten.

"What about you, Casey?" Cody asked as he reached for his cap and mitt.

"Okay," she said without a lot of enthusiasm.

"Do you have plans for the day?" Lydia asked her daughter.

"Ava and I want to go to the movies. That's all right, isn't it?"

For the next several minutes, Lydia's conversation with her daughter revolved around the movie and Ava. Lydia planned to open the shop but would stay only until noon, when Margaret arrived. Her sister would close the shop. That gave Lydia time to pick up Ava and drop the two of them off at the cinema complex.

By the time Lydia had dressed and finished with her makeup and hair, Casey had cleaned up the kitchen.

"Are you feeling up to this?" Lydia asked, noting that her daughter hadn't shown much enthusiasm for attending Cody's game.

Casey answered with a shrug. "I guess."

"Would you rather stay home?"

"No."

Lydia collected what she needed, mainly her purse and her knitting. Casey joined her, her head down and her shoulders slumped forward.

Lydia waited until they were on their way to the park before she asked, "Would it help if you talked about your dream?"

"No." Casey's quick response left Lydia in no doubt of the teen's feelings on the matter.

Lydia tried another approach. "Would it be easier to talk to someone other than your father or me?"

"Like who? A shrink?"

Lydia hadn't thought this out. "No. The first person who popped into my mind was my mother. The two of you are close and—"

Casey quickly cut her off. "No way."

"It was just a suggestion."

"Can we not talk about my dream?" the teen snapped.

"Sure, if that's what you want. We can pretend it never happened, if that will make you feel better."

"Thank you," Casey returned, less churlish. "I don't want you to mention it ever again, okay?"

"That's your choice. But in case you ever do, I want you to know I'll be ready to listen."

"I said I don't want to talk about it," Casey reiterated in a loud voice. "How many times do I have to repeat it?"

"Okay, message received."

Her daughter remained sullen and silent the rest of the way to the baseball field. As soon as they parked the car, Casey saw a friend and, with only a minimum of conversation, left Lydia.

"Don't go far," Lydia called after her.

Casey whirled around, sent Lydia a dirty look, and then headed in the opposite direction.

Brad had saved a seat on the bleachers next to him, and Lydia scooted past several other parents and grandparents in order to sit next to her husband.

The opposing team was up to bat, and Cody played shortstop. He was bent over, gently swaying back and forth, ever ready to catch the ball if needed.

"Is everything okay with Casey?" Brad asked when Lydia was settled in the seat.

Lydia wasn't sure what to tell him. "She made it clear she doesn't want to discuss the dream." She felt it was probably best not to mention her bad attitude.

"We need to give the kid space to work this out on her own."

Lydia agreed. Glancing around, she didn't catch sight of Janice. "Everything okay with Cody?"

Brad shrugged. "Janice said she'd stop by, but she hasn't shown up yet. Surprise, surprise."

Janice had given birth to Cody and then left Brad and her young son when he was only a few years old. Brad had raised Cody on his own until Lydia had come into their lives and they'd married. One of the happiest days of Lydia's life was when Cody had started to call her Mom. He was her son in every way, the same as Casey was her daughter. Children of her heart if not of her body.

"Will it disappoint Cody if she doesn't show?"

"Probably, but he's been disappointed plenty before. He knows to take Janice's promises with a grain of salt."

It was times like these that Lydia wanted to shake Cody's birth mother for her lackadaisical attitude toward her son.

"What are Casey's plans for the day?" Brad asked, changing the subject.

Lydia knew he was angry on his son's behalf and trying hard to hide his feelings. "Casey will come with me to the shop, and then this afternoon I'm picking up Ava and the two of them are going to the movies."

"You need me to pick them up?"

"If you want. I thought I'd stop off and get groceries from there."

"Okay."

Lydia stayed long enough to see Cody hit a home run. The boy showed athletic skills and genuinely loved sports. When it was time to leave, Lydia found Casey, who appeared to be in a much better mood.

"You ready to go?" she asked.

Casey nodded. She didn't speak again until they were in the car and she'd snapped on her seat belt. "Sorry to be such a pill this morning."

."Apology accepted."

"You're a good mom."

"Thank you, sweetheart. I'm grateful you're my daughter."

Casey glanced over at Lydia and smiled. "And I'm grateful you're my mom."

Chapter Eleven

$\mathcal{M}$ax carried their second cups of coffee to the kitchen table. They'd finished breakfast, and the dishes were in the dishwasher. Bethanne didn't need to be a psychic to notice something was on her husband's mind. No doubt it was related to Grant and their conversation from the night before. They'd talked briefly about Grant, tiptoeing around the subject of her ex-husband. It seemed they were each leery of doing or saying anything that would cause a disagreement. Certainly an argument wouldn't be the best way to start what promised to be a wonderful, celebratory weekend.

Quite honestly, Bethanne had been as surprised as Max to learn Grant had a key to her house. The only explanation she had to give him was that Annie must have given it to her father. Because she was upset, Bethanne hadn't confronted her daughter, but she would in due time. She was sure that Grant had somehow convinced Annie he needed access to the house. Why Grant felt entitled was beyond comprehension.

"As soon as we've finished with our coffee I'll make a run to the hardware store," Max said, setting his mug down on the quilted placemat at the kitchen table.

Her husband had insisted on changing the locks. "I don't think that's necessary—"

He stopped her with a look.

"But if you're determined, then go ahead."

"I'm determined."

"So I see," she said, making light of his insistence. Bethanne had every intention of getting the house key back from Grant. Clearly, that wasn't enough for Max.

"I wanted to talk to you for another reason," Max said as he stared down at his coffee. His hands cupped the mug, and he didn't make eye contact.

"All right." He was so serious, Bethanne hardly knew what to think.

"It isn't a good idea for us to live apart like this."

She agreed.

"You coming to California is hard on you and the business, and for me to fly up here is equally taxing. We each seem to have one foot in Washington and another in California, and frankly, it isn't working."

Bethanne should have seen this coming.

"We need to make a decision. Either you sell your business and move to California or I sell my business and make a fresh start here."

"What about moving your business to Washington State?" she suggested.

"Bethanne, think about it. I have a huge warehouse facility. It isn't like I could pack everything up and transport it a thousand miles. The logistics would be a nightmare. In addition Washington State recently changed its laws so that wine can be obtained outside of a distributor, and you know—"

"Okay, okay," she said, stopping him. "It was just an idea."

"One that doesn't work. It makes far more sense for you to sell your business and move to California and live with me."

Bethanne scooted back her chair, stood, and walked over to the window that looked out over the deck and backyard. The birdfeeder Andrew had built as a Boy Scout hung from a thick branch of the maple tree. "I'd need to sell the house, too." This home contained a patchwork quilt of memories, some good, some bad. Still, it was the home she loved and where she'd forged a new life for herself, stepping out of the role as wife and stay-at-home mother. It was from this house that she'd launched a career and become a savvy businesswoman.

"Whether you decide to keep the house or sell it is completely up to you."

"Why would I keep it to leave it sitting empty?" she asked. The thought of moving away from her children, her home, and her business filled her with a deep sense of loss.

"Like I said, that would be your decision."

Her throat grew thick, and she slowly turned to face him. "Max, do you realize what you're asking me to do?"

His eyes connected with hers, and slowly he nodded. He moved toward her, cupping her shoulders. It took him a couple moments to speak. "It isn't an easy choice for you or for me. If we're going to make a go of this marriage, one of us needs to make the sacrifice."

"I started the party business when Grant left me. I built it from the ground up."

"I know. I built my business from the ground up, too."

Bottom line, Max wanted her with him in California because of Grant's behavior. Even now, more than a year after she'd married Max, Grant had yet to accept the fact that she hadn't chosen to reunite with him.

Her gaze delved into that of her husband. "Now there's going to be a grandbaby."

"Yes," Max said, "and an ever-stronger reason for Grant to invade our marriage."

"Moving to California is cheating me out of the joy of watching this child grow."

"You can visit as often as you want. Andrew and Courtney are welcome to come to us anytime."

Bethanne recalled as a young mother how difficult it was to travel with children. She remembered, soon after Annie had been born, traveling to her parents' home for Thanksgiving. By the time Grant had finished loading up the car and she'd gotten everything they would need for both Andrew and Annie, they'd both felt so exhausted they'd argued. The trip had been a disaster. Annie had come down with the flu and the car had blown a tire. It was the last Thanksgiving they'd spent with her side of the family. Bethanne didn't feel she could ask her son and his wife to make the same sacrifice.

"I'll think on it," she promised.

"Thank you," Max returned, with a grateful smile that told her he understood how difficult this was for her. "I appreciate that you're willing to consider the possibility."

Bethanne's stomach knotted. "Would you consider selling your business?" she asked, thinking of all she would need to relinquish with such a move. "Don't you think Rooster would be interested in buying out your shares?"

"I don't think that's an option."

"Why not?"

"He's pretty much got his finances tied up in the company. We're partners, and this is a decision we'd need to make jointly. I know Rooster is tired of California and would like to live in the Pacific Northwest." He paused when he saw her stricken look. "What's wrong?"

For a moment Bethanne thought she might be sick. "You mean to tell me that Rooster is considering moving to Washington State and you're not?"

Max didn't answer. "It isn't like that. Rooster knows as well as I do that such a move now would wipe us out financially."

"I was hoping you'd consider making an investment in me and my children," she said softly, unable to hide her disappointment. "But because you asked, I'll give the matter of moving serious consideration."

"If you're concerned about selling, then you might want to consider taking the party business to California with you."

"My customer base is here . . . it would be like starting over, but you're right, I could uproot the company." There didn't appear to be any easy answers for either of them, she realized.

Max left shortly afterward for the hardware store. Bethanne waited until he was out of the house before she contacted Annie. Her daughter answered sounding groggy and sleepy.

"Annie, it's Mom."

"Hmm?"

"Are you still sleeping?"

"It's Saturday."

"Can you answer a quick question?" Bethanne asked, doing her best to keep her voice level and unemotional.

"Something come up with one of the parties scheduled for today?" Annie asked.

"No, this is something else. I need to know if you gave your father a key to the house . . . my house," she said determined to get to the end of this matter.

"Yeah. You sound upset. What's the big deal?"

Bethanne ignored the question. "What possible reason would you have to hand over the house key to my ex-husband?"

"He might be your ex-husband," Annie said defiantly, sounding wide awake now, "but he's still my dad."

"Then give him the key to your apartment."

"Mom, you're overreacting. Dad told me he'd left his sunglasses at the house. He said he tried to reach you and couldn't, and—"

"Did he return the key?"

"Well, no. I was out last night, and it's still early—"

"It's after ten," Bethanne interrupted.

"Is that some kind of commentary about me still being in bed?" Annie snapped.

"No, this is about you giving your father something he had no right to have."

"Fine. I'll get it from him this morning and personally return it to you, if that's what you want."

"Don't bother."

"Then why are you being so ugly about this? Are you afraid Dad was going to rob you?"

"He invaded my privacy, and you let him."

"I said I'd get the key back."

"Don't. Max is changing the locks."

Annie groaned. "I suppose this means I won't be getting a key to my own home."

"You have an apartment. This is my home."

"And I'm no longer welcome. Thanks a lot, Mom." With that, Annie abruptly ended the call.

Bethanne was fuming to the point that it was impossible to stand still. She paced the kitchen in an attempt to put order to her thoughts. Annie had stepped way over the line. Still, Bethanne realized there'd been a better way of dealing with the situation. Grant was a smooth talker and capable of talking a hermit crab out of its shell. Annie and her father had always been close, and Annie would be willing to do anything her father asked of her.

Still frustrated, Bethanne vacuumed the entire upstairs and then stuffed a load of laundry into the washing machine. When she heard the front door open, Bethanne assumed it was Max. She swallowed down her regrets over her conversation with Annie and pasted on a smile.

"Is that you, Max?" she asked, coming down the stairs.

"It's me," Andrew called from the kitchen. "I rang the doorbell, but no one answered."

"This is a welcome surprise," Bethanne said, bouncing down the last three steps and standing on her tiptoes to kiss her son's cheek.

"I wanted to check to be sure you were still on for dinner tonight."

"Of course, and Max will be joining us."

"Great."

"How's Courtney feeling?" she asked, and led the way into the kitchen.

Andrew followed her. "The morning sickness is pretty bad just yet, but it's getting better. First thing I do is bring her a couple of sal-tines, which seem to help."

"Coffee?" she asked, gesturing toward the coffeemaker.

Andrew nodded and stepped around the countertop, with his hands tucked in his back pockets. This was a sure sign he was on a mission, and probably one he would prefer to avoid. "Annie called this morning."

That explained it. "We had a bit of a tiff," Bethanne murmured with a regretful sigh.

"So she said."

"She had no business giving your father a key to my house."

"I agree."

Andrew, she knew, would be more apt to see her side of things. "I was upset with her, but I could have handled it a lot better than I did."

Her son got down two mugs from the cupboard.

"I was troubled about more than what Annie did," Bethanne said, the knot returning to her throat. "Max wants me to either sell the party business or move it to California."

Frowning, Andrew turned to face her. "Why can't he move?"

"It's more complicated for him than me."

"It's complicated either way, Mom."

"I know. I'm afraid unless one of us makes a concession that our marriage might not survive."

Her son's frown darkened. "That's crazy. You love Max. I've never known you to be happier, and Max is head-over-heels in love with you."

Afraid if she spoke the tears would leak into her voice, she nodded instead.

"If you're thinking you can't leave because of the baby . . ."

"I don't know what to do," she whispered, and pressed her fingers to her lips.

Right away her son wrapped his arms around her. "Whatever you decide will be fine by Courtney and me. If Annie puts up a fuss, then let her. This is your life and you can't live it for anyone else. You do what makes you the happiest."

"Max makes me happy."

"I know."

A tear slipped from her eye and wove its way down her cheek. Bethanne wiped it away. Her son's vote of confidence was exactly what she needed to hear. "Thank you, Andrew."

"You're welcome." He kissed the top of her head. "Now about tonight . . ."

"I'll call Annie and do what I can to repair any hurt feelings," Bethanne assured him. "I'll make sure there won't be any tension between us for your special dinner."

A car door shut in the distance. "That would be Max," Bethanne said. "He's changing the door locks."

"Can't say I blame him." Andrew glanced at his wrist. "I've got to go. Courtney wants to drag me along to the grocery store this afternoon. I'll say hi to Max and then be on my way."

"Thanks for stopping by." Already Bethanne felt better.

"Anytime," Andrew said on his way out the back door.

Bethanne heard the two men chatting, and a few minutes later Max was in the house.

"Did you find everything you needed?" she asked, looking at the two huge bags Max carried.

Max set them atop the kitchen counter. "And then some. A hardware store is to men what a toy store is to ten-year-olds. I picked up lightbulbs, which were on sale, and a new garden hose, which I left in the garage, and a few other items you may or may not need in the foreseeable future."

"On sale?"

"Naturally."

Men weren't so different than women after all, Bethanne decided.

"It won't take me long to get these locks changed. Rooster called. Would you mind if we met for lunch?"

"No problem. I've got a few errands I need to run myself."

Max nodded, and something in the way he looked told Bethanne this was more than two friends getting together. "Everything okay with Rooster?" she asked.

Max shrugged while he set his purchases out on the kitchen counter. "He's down in the mouth."

"Any particular reason?"

"He didn't say. I've known Rooster for a lot of years, and I don't know that I've ever heard him sound quite like this."

"Quite like what?" Bethanne pressed.

Again, Max seemed to be at a loss for words. "Discouraged, I guess. That's about as close as I can think to describe what was in his voice."

Rooster was probably one of the most positive people Bethanne had ever met. She couldn't imagine what had happened to affect Max's closest friend this way.

Chapter Twelve

Lauren didn't sleep all night. Again and again, her mind reviewed the scene between Todd and Rooster. When Rooster stormed out of the restaurant, he'd been angry, irate, and something else. It'd taken her half the night to identify what that something else was.

Hurt.

Although it had never been her intent, Lauren had angered and hurt Rooster. It went against her nature to inflict pain on anyone, especially someone she happened to like a great deal. They'd known each other briefly, but in that short amount of time, Lauren had come to feel a strong connection to Rooster. She enjoyed his wit and his down-to-earth approach to life. He didn't put on airs or work to impress her. What struck her was how he seemed to concentrate on her instead of focusing on himself and his own accomplishments. The more she dwelled on their one dinner date, the more she wanted to get to know Rooster and spend more time with him.

It would have been easy to simply let this unpleasant episode go, she realized. The incident had left her embarrassed and uncomfortable. Rooster had made it clear that he didn't want to see her again, but Lauren found she simply couldn't leave matters as they were. At the very least, she needed to explain, and apologize.

At eight Saturday morning, when she'd abandoned all hope of sleeping, she tossed aside the covers and sat on the edge of her bed. Her eyes stung as she rubbed her hand across her face.

Her one goal for the day was to find Rooster. It'd been shortsighted of her to choose that particular restaurant for their dinner date. Not once had it occurred to her that Todd would even think to seek her out. And worse, that he'd make a spectacle of himself, her, and Rooster.

The first thing she did was try to phone Rooster. She had his cell number, but he didn't answer. The night before, she'd left a message, but he either chose to ignore it or had deleted it without listening. Unwilling to leave it alone, she decided that if he wouldn't talk to her then she'd personally find him and force him to listen.

That first night, Rooster had said he'd booked a room in a local hotel, but if he'd mentioned the name of the hotel, she had no memory of it. Bethanne Scranton's husband, the woman she'd met at A Good Yarn, was a friend of Rooster's, so the first thing Lauren did when the shop opened at ten was contact Lydia at the yarn store.

"Oh, Lydia, I'm so glad I caught you," Lauren said, when the other woman picked up the phone.

"Lauren, is that you?"

"Yes, yes, it's me. Would you mind giving me Bethanne's phone number?"

Lydia hesitated. "I'm sorry, Lauren. I don't generally give out customers' personal information."

"I wouldn't ask if this wasn't important," she said, and then realized Lydia was right. Elisa and Garry wouldn't want her handing out a customer's phone number, either. "If this goes against store policy, I understand. But would you be willing to contact her on my behalf?"

"Of course."

"Oh, thank you. Would you ask Bethanne to phone me back right away?"

Lydia agreed she would do that first thing. "You sound upset. Is everything all right?"

"No. I need to make amends."

"To Bethanne?"

"No, to the man who came into the shop last Thursday with her husband."

"Rooster?"

So Lydia already knew Rooster. "I appreciate the help. I need to talk to him."

"I'll do my best to reach Bethanne, but no promises."

"Do what you can; that's all I ask. Thanks again, Lydia. I appreciate this more than you know."

While Lauren waited to hear from the other woman, she decided to do her Saturday shopping. She had to keep herself occupied or she'd go stir-crazy sitting around the condo waiting. She tried to knit, but it was useless; her mind leaped in twenty different directions when she needed to concentrate to reacquaint herself with the skill.

Just as she was walking out of the Pike Place Market with its long rows of fresh vegetables, meats, and assortments of specialty foods, her cellphone beeped. In her eagerness to answer, Lauren struggled to hold on to her bag of groceries.

"Hello," she said, hoping against hope that it was her fellow knitter.

"Is this Lauren?" the vaguely familiar voice asked.

"Bethanne?"

"Yes, Lydia got hold of me and said it was important that I contact you. What's going on?"

"It's Rooster," Lauren blurted out. "We had an unfortunate misunderstanding and I need to find him to explain. Can you tell me where he's staying?"

Bethanne hesitated, as if unsure this was the right thing to do. "I'd like to help, but I can't. Rooster didn't mention the name of the hotel."

"Would your husband know?"

"I'm sure Max would, but he isn't here just now."

"Oh." Disappointment echoed in her voice. This was getting more complicated by the moment. "When do you expect him back?"

"He didn't say."

Unwilling to leave it at that, Lauren pressed further. "Could you give me a guesstimate of when you'll see him?"

Bethanne's sigh was audible, as though even now she wasn't sure she should be giving out information. "I can definitely tell you Max will return before six; we're having a family dinner."

"Six," Lauren blurted out. She didn't want to wait that long. If she didn't talk to Rooster soon, it would drive her nuts.

"Why is it so important that you find him?"

"Like I said, we had a misunderstanding," Lauren explained without going into details.

"What kind of misunderstanding?" Bethanne pressed.

Reluctantly, Lauren gave Bethanne a thumbnail sketch of what had happened between Rooster and Todd and then between her and Rooster. She explained that it was particularly embarrassing because Todd was so easily recognizable.

"This is Todd Hampton, from Channel Eight news?" Bethanne sounded incredulous.

"Yes."

"You're dating Todd Hampton?"

"*Was* dating." She placed emphasis on the past tense. "I broke it off, and now it seems Todd believes this is all a ploy to get him to marry me. It isn't. I broke it off and all of a sudden Todd's convinced he can't live without me."

"You like Rooster?"

"Very much. Would you be willing to call Max on his cell?" She should have thought of that first thing.

"I would, but he left it here, charging."

"Oh." Every which way she turned, she hit a dead end. Lauren was fast losing hope. "Can you help me, Bethanne?"

Once more she heard the hesitation in the other woman's voice. "I don't know."

"I feel wretched over what happened. Although we just met, I think given the opportunity we could be more than friends. I'd hate to leave matters the way they are. I can't let him believe that I would use him."

Bethanne paused as if she was giving consideration to Lauren's words. "Max ran an errand this morning and apparently while he was out Rooster contacted him."

"He did?"

"Rooster suggested they meet. He had something he needed to talk out with Max."

Hope sprang up inside Lauren like Old Faithful in Yellowstone National Park. "So Max is currently with Rooster."

"I believe so. Rooster's call is all beginning to add up now that we've talked."

"What do you mean?" Lauren asked.

"Well, it seems to me Rooster appears to have taken a liking to you as well."

So Lauren hadn't been imagining this attraction; it was mutual. Knowing this made her feel worlds better and more determined than ever to set matters straight.

"Do you happen to know where they're having lunch?" Lauren asked.

"I do, but Lauren, this is definitely a guys' place." Bethanne mentioned the name, which was unfamiliar to her. "It wouldn't be a good idea for you to go there on your own."

"I don't care."

"You're going to a lot of trouble."

"It's important."

"Lauren, it's a biker bar."

She swallowed tightly; it could be worse. "Thanks for telling me."

"All right, but don't say I didn't warn you."

"I can't thank you enough, Bethanne."

"You like Rooster this much?"

Lauren didn't hesitate: "Yes."

"Good luck to you, then."

"Thank you."

Feeling better than she had all night, Lauren returned to her condo and hurriedly put away her groceries. As soon as she'd finished, she considered changing clothes but didn't want to waste the time.

Dressed in designer jeans, a pink cashmere and silk sweater, and knee-high boots, she headed out the door, determined to find Rooster Wayne. No doubt she'd stick out in the bar crowd, but she didn't care.

What was important was finding Rooster.

Chapter Thirteen

Rooster cracked open a peanut, chewed down the nuts, and tossed the shell onto the floor. A group of bikers gathered around a pool table in a hotly contested game. Their chatter and shouts echoed around the cavernous room along with the loud honky-tonk music that blared from speakers on the other side of the tavern.

Sitting on a bar stool at the counter with Max, Rooster waited for lunch. Hog's Hideout was known for its grilled Philly sandwich, which he'd ordered for lunch with a side of slaw.

"You haven't said much," Max said, and tossed an empty peanut shell onto the floor.

"Not much to say."

"I thought you were going to look up an old high school buddy while you were in town."

Rooster shrugged. He'd forgotten all about that. "Didn't feel up to it."

Max leaned closer to the bar, paused, and then asked, "So, how'd your dinner date with Lauren go?"

Rooster wasn't up to talking about that, either. "Not so good." Even now he wasn't sure why he'd contacted Max. It'd seemed like a good idea at the time, he supposed. In retrospect, it wasn't. The mistake he'd made was mentioning Lauren in the first place. He'd been taken with her, and had enjoyed their Thai food experience. Max had jumped all over that, reminiscing about his first meeting with Bethanne. Well, Lauren was no Bethanne, and he wasn't Max.

"What happened?" Max pressed.

He should have realized his best friend was going to hound him with questions. If the situation was reversed, he'd do the same. "Nothing much," he said, downplaying the entire ordeal.

"Do you want to talk about it?"

"Not necessarily."

Their order came up, and for the next ten minutes they ate without communicating. When he'd finished, Rooster wiped his mouth clean with a paper napkin. It was the first food he'd tasted in nearly twenty-four hours. He hadn't had the stomach for dinner after leaving Lauren, and he'd skipped breakfast, settling for several cups of coffee instead. He'd grown restless and unsettled, pushing all thoughts of the woman from his mind. It irked him that he'd allowed her to get under his skin and so quickly.

"You mentioned how you felt when you first met Bethanne," he said.

"Yeah. It's been a couple of years now, and that feeling hasn't changed."

Rooster could see the effect Bethanne had on Max every time the two were together. It was like a booster shot of enthusiasm for life. The two of them were good together. Seeing how Max had been willing to love again had inspired him. It'd given him hope that there was someone special for him, too. It'd felt right that first night with Lauren, right and good, but it wasn't meant to be. He should have learned his lesson by now. He wasn't good with relationships with women.

"Did you feel that same kick in your stomach when you met Lauren?"

Rooster shrugged.

"Come on, be honest." Max pushed his empty plate aside. The bartender collected both their plates and refilled their mugs with beer.

"I thought I did," Rooster murmured. "My mistake."

"Any hope of repairing the damage?"

"None." Rooster wasn't interested. Lauren had tried several times to reach him by phone, but he'd ignored her calls. She'd sent him a text, but he hadn't read it. As far as he was concerned, any further communication would be a mistake.

"It isn't all rosebuds and bliss for Bethanne and me," Max said. "Relationships aren't always easy. You, more than anyone, have seen our struggles. Living apart this way has taken a toll."

"I thought you kissed and made up."

"We did," Max said, "and it was good for a while. Neither one of us is comfortable when we're at odds."

"What happened?" Rooster couldn't help being curious. He'd seen the way Bethanne had practically thrown herself into Max's arms the instant they'd entered the yarn store. The entire store had, and it seemed the shop had given a collective sigh of approval.

Max seemed reluctant to explain. "Bethanne and I were having dinner at the house when out of the blue Grant arrived."

"Really?"

"He had a key to the house."

Rooster's brows shot up; no wonder Max was upset. "Bethanne gave it to him?"

"As best Bethanne could figure, Annie did. She said she'd handle it, but I wasn't taking any chances. I wouldn't put it past Grant to have had a spare key made. Bethanne wasn't keen on the idea, but I spent the morning changing the locks."

"I wouldn't trust Grant Hamlin with a dime, let alone my wife."

"You and me both," Max agreed. "Which is why I asked Bethanne to move to California."

It went without saying this would be a difficult decision for her. "How'd that go over?"

Max shrugged. "Like a bucket of cement to the bottom of the Columbia River."

"You're asking a lot," he felt obliged to remind his friend.

"Don't I know it."

"What did Bethanne have to say?"

Max took his time answering, as if weighed down by the question. "Not much. She promised to consider it, and really that's all I can ask for at this point."

"It's a huge decision with lots of ramifications."

Max agreed.

Rooster studied his friend and sympathized. If the situation was reversed, if it was someone he loved as powerfully as Max did Bethanne, then Rooster was convinced he'd feel the same. "This thing with Grant and the house key is what prompted it?"

Max nodded, sullen and silent.

"You want to take her away from her family?" That was the crux of the matter, as far as Rooster could see.

"Not her children," Max snapped back. "Just Grant."

"Because you don't trust Bethanne?" Rooster was willing to ask the hard questions. According to his business partner, Rooster had always been the one Max could trust to dig at the truth. Sometimes it angered his friend, and at other times, like now, Max grew quiet and solemn.

"I trust Bethanne; the one I don't trust is Grant."

"What you're really saying is you aren't sure about Bethanne, then, either."

Max looked ready to argue with him. Rooster was in no mood to get into a verbal exchange with his best friend. "I don't want to bicker over this. Just think about what you're asking of Bethanne," he said, without giving Max time to counter. "What I'm hearing is this—in order for you to feel secure in your marriage, you need to have Bethanne in California. If that's the case, you're saying that you aren't sure about her feelings toward her ex."

Max straightened as if he was prepared to rebut the point and then seemed to change his mind. "Maybe. I hadn't thought of it like that."

"Maybe you should."

Unexpectedly, Max turned his attention away from Rooster and toward the front of the tavern. "Well, I'll be," he muttered, sounding both surprised and amused.

Rooster turned to look at what had aroused his friend's interest and his eyes widened. *Lauren?* It couldn't be her. It didn't seem possible she would accidentally stumble upon him and Max, especially at a place like Hog's Hideout.

For what seemed like several minutes she remained framed in the doorway as if she wasn't sure it was safe to venture inside. Bright light surrounded her as though she was an angelic being. Rooster wasn't the only one who noticed her, either. Every man in the Hideout seemed to have his gaze riveted on her. A muscular biker, who had a cue stick in his hand and was bent over the pool table, froze.

"You see what I see?" Max asked in a low tone.

"Yeah."

"That's Lauren, isn't it?"

"Looks like it." Unwilling to be caught in her spiderweb, Rooster turned away and took a deep swallow of his beer. He was going to need the fortification to withstand the strong emotional pull he felt for her even now, knowing what he did about her.

"Are you going outside to talk to her?" It was more suggestion than question.

"No."

"Any particular reason?"

"A few. She has something to prove to me."

The music, which had been loud and raunchy, seemed to fade to a whisper as Lauren came inside and headed toward the bar. One of the bikers, a big guy with a large belly and an unkempt beard who'd been standing on the outskirts of the pool table, waylaid her.

From the corner of his eye, Rooster watched as Lauren tensed, politely listened, and then shook her head. Reading her lips, he guessed that she was thanking him but declining his invitation. The other man shrugged and returned to where he'd been standing earlier. As soon as he moved away, Lauren hurried to the bar where Rooster sat with Max.

"Hello, Lauren," Max greeted her cheerfully, grinning from ear to ear.

Rooster, who'd turned back to the bar, cradled his mug of beer with both hands. He darted a look at Max and frowned. He didn't understand why Max should look so pleased with himself.

"Hello, Rooster," Lauren said softly, hesitatingly.

He ignored her.

"I hope you don't mind me stopping by like this."

Again he chose to pretend he didn't hear.

She glanced over at Max, who raised his hands as if to say this wasn't his doing.

"I came because I felt wretched over what happened with Todd and dinner. I didn't sleep a wink all night."

She wasn't the only one who'd spent the better portion of the night staring at the ceiling.

"I can't leave matters the way we did . . . I can't."

Max elbowed him with a gentle nudge, and Rooster chose to ignore that, too.

"I came to apologize," Lauren murmured, again with a voice as soft as calf leather.

He nodded, indicating that he was willing to let bygones be bygones. He appreciated that she'd made the effort to find him and apologize, but that was as far as he was willing to go.

"Would you . . ." She hesitated as if unsure she should continue. "I mean, I can see you're still upset . . . I don't blame you. What happened was dreadful and—"

"What happened?" Max quizzed.

Rooster straightened. "That's between me and Lauren," he said, glaring at his friend.

"Okay, fine. I'll stay out of it."

That silly grin of Max's remained firmly in place. He was enjoying this little exchange far too much.

"You were saying," Max said, returning his attention to Lauren.

Lauren focused her attention on Rooster. "I thought . . . I hoped you'd be willing to give me a second chance."

Until this moment, Rooster had resisted her with every ounce of self-control he possessed. Every word she said ripped into the wall of stone he'd erected against her. They fell in a cavalcade and pooled at his feet until he stood vulnerable and exposed before her. That she had this much power over him, in such a short amount of time, left him stunned and speechless.

Rooster turned, and his eyes met hers. Everything about her spoke of sincerity. Her look, her stance, the way she clasped her hands in front of her. The way her beautiful clear blue eyes looked up at him with such honesty was his undoing.

"I mean," she said, and lifted one shoulder, "if you're not interested, I just got another offer."

"Bozo over there is interested," Max said.

Again, Rooster glared at his friend. "I think it's time you got back to Bethanne."

Max chuckled. "I can see I'm no longer wanted or needed here." He slapped Rooster across the back and left cash on the counter for his lunch. He took one last sip of his beer, set the mug down on the bar, and said, "I'll check in with you later."

"Later," Rooster repeated, and while he tried, he couldn't take his eyes off Lauren. He couldn't make himself do it. Silently, she stood before him, waiting for him to speak.

"So Bozo made you an offer," Rooster said with a soft snicker and nodded in the direction of the man with the big belly and the shaggy beard.

"He did," she returned, brightening.

"Anything that might interest you?"

"Maybe."

He could see she was struggling to hold back a smile but with little success. "He told me I could be his woman."

Rooster chuckled. "That sounds too good to be true. Are you sure you aren't making this up?"

"Cross my heart." Taking her index finger, she made a giant X across her heart.

"Then I suggest we leave before the temptation becomes too great." He reached for the tab and paid the bill. When he'd finished, he took Lauren's hand and led her out of Hog's Hideout.

Rooster squinted in the bright light of day and wished he'd thought to grab his sunglasses when he'd left the hotel.

Lauren's phone buzzed. She reached for it and checked caller ID. "It's Bethanne."

"Ah, so that's how you knew where to find me."

She nodded as she pressed the phone to her ear. "Hi, Bethanne."

"Did you find him?" Rooster heard Bethanne ask.

"I did. I can't thank you enough for your help."

"Glad to do it. He's a gem. You couldn't find a better man than Rooster Wayne. He'd never tell you this, but Max would have lost his business and a whole lot more if it hadn't been for Rooster."

Lauren glanced up at Rooster and smiled.

He frowned back. It made him uncomfortable to have Bethanne sing his praises.

Lauren looked to be on the verge of laughing. "I think you might be right. I better go. I'm getting the evil eye from Rooster. Bye, Bethanne."

"Bye. Oh, before I forget, how's the baby blanket coming along?"

Rooster stiffened. *Baby blanket.*

"Okay so far."

"Me, too. I've just finished knitting the border."

Rooster knew about the "husband list," which had intrigued him, but now it seemed Lauren was thinking about getting pregnant . . . unless, of course, she was already in that condition. He swallowed hard. It just might be that he'd bitten off a bigger bite than he'd realized.

With the call ended, Lauren returned the cell to her purse.

"You're knitting a baby blanket?" he asked, hoping he didn't sound as skeptical as he felt.

"Yes. I thought I mentioned that. That's what Bethanne and I were knitting when you and Max showed up at the yarn store."

"Is there any particular reason you're knitting a baby blanket?" he asked, afraid his voice didn't sound quite right. He examined her closely, wondering if he'd missed something earlier.

"Well, yes, for my sister."

"Your sister?" Now he remembered. Learning her younger sister was pregnant was what had prompted this entire desire to create this husband list of hers. The tension left him, and he felt the almost irrepressible urge to laugh.

Lauren paused mid-step. "Rooster? Did you think? You thought . . . I was . . . me, pregnant? Oh, honestly!"

Unable to hold back his amusement, Rooster started to chuckle, and soon Lauren was laughing, too. He stopped when he realized how beautiful she looked in her pretty pink sweater. His gaze wandered to her lips, and he felt his chest tighten with the need to kiss her. It didn't matter that they stood in the middle of the sidewalk in a section of town that was less than desirable. Nothing mattered but bringing Lauren into the protection of his arms.

The laughter drained out of her eyes as she read his intent. It seemed to Rooster that she leaned toward him at the very instant he reached for her. Then his mouth covered hers and his hands tangled in her hair. This was good, better than good. She tasted of mint and springtime as she opened to him and he to her, slanting his mouth over hers in an effort to be close, intimate. She was warm and welcoming, her arms wrapped around his neck. Their bodies fused together, close and tight, as though they were made for this. The disappointment he'd experienced the night before lifted from his shoulders, the irritation and regret wiped out with a single kiss. His heart rate quickly accelerated as the realization hit him that he could easily fall for this woman. The thought frightened him, but not enough to put an end to what was happening between them. Not nearly enough for that.

Someone walked past and bumped into him, and Rooster reluctantly broke off the kiss. "Let's get out of here."

"Okay," Lauren whispered.

He didn't have a single idea where they would go. Not that it mattered, as long as it was a place where he could kiss Lauren again.

Chapter Fourteen

Color is a feeling·for me. I work by feeling!
—Tina,
Freia Handpaint Yarns,
www.freiafibers.com

Sunday morning, Lydia and Brad had barely arrived at church before Casey and Cody shot off in different directions. Casey to the youth group section and Cody to the kid zone. Bible in hand, Lydia started down the center aisle. She liked to sit on the right-hand side about halfway up. Not too close and not too far back. They sat in the same pew nearly every week; it was almost as if they had their own designated row.

After greeting a few friends and getting an update on the Women's Comedy Night, which was scheduled for a week from Friday, Lydia and Brad slipped inside the pew. After Lydia took a moment to be reflective and silent, Brad handed her the church bulletin.

Leaning his head toward her, he whispered. "Jordan's preaching today."

"Oh, good." Jordan Turner served as the youth pastor and gave the sermon once a month. Jordan had married Alix Townsend. That had been a few years earlier, and they now had a toddler named Tommy, who Casey adored. For that matter, so did Lydia. The toddler had the sweetest disposition.

Alix would always be close to Lydia's heart. She'd been a member of the very first knitting class Lydia had taught soon after opening A Good Yarn. At the time Alix had been a young adult and a little rough around the edges—well, actually, more than a little rough. In the beginning, Lydia had been tentative about her attending the knitting class. How wrong she'd been to prejudge the girl.

These days Alix worked as a baker at The French Cafe and was a wife to her fifth-grade sweetheart and a mother to Tommy. Lately Lydia had heard talk about the couple wanting to add to their family.

Not surprisingly, the gritty Alix had turned out to be a talented knitter. Over the years, Lydia had looked on proudly as Alix tackled one complex pattern after another. When it came to yarn and life, Alix Turner was fearless.

It wasn't long before the music started, indicating the service was ready to begin. Looking to the words that showed on the overhead, Lydia and Brad stood with the congregation. Brad reached for her hand as they started to sing.

Jordan wasn't as polished a speaker as the senior pastor; nevertheless, his sermon was uplifting, instructional, and informative. The hour flew by, and soon it was time for the closing song.

Lydia didn't need to worry about finding Casey or Cody; the two would find her and Brad in short order. It pleased Lydia that Casey had fit in so easily with the other teens. She was convinced Alix had had something to do with that.

As they exited the pew the couple exchanged greetings with friends and neighbors. Both Jordan and the senior pastor stood in the narthex at the back of the church. They chatted with each person as the congregation slowly flowed out of the building.

Lydia hadn't always been faithful about attending church services. Not until she'd married Brad and become a mother to Cody did she fully appreciate the need to feed the spiritual part of herself. Often it felt like a hassle to get everyone fed and dressed on a Sunday morning, but she came away feeling empowered and inspired. It was a great way to start the week.

"Lydia."

Hearing her name, Lydia turned to find Alix waving her hand in order to gain her attention. Alix had Tommy on her hip, and the toddler, who seemed ready for his nap, laid his head on his mother's shoulder, his thumb in his mouth.

"Wait up," Alix called.

"Sure."

"I'll get the kids," Brad told her. He was eager to get home to watch the Mariners baseball game on TV.

"I'll meet you at the car," Lydia said, and then to reassure him added, "I won't be long."

He cast her a look that basically said he'd believe that when he saw it. Her husband slowly made his way toward the double-door exit.

Lydia was fairly certain this had to do with Alix's most recent purchase from the shop. The pattern had called for a fingering-weight yarn that she intended to use for a breathtakingly beautiful round lace shawl. It was an heirloom piece that would require weeks if not months of knitting. Lydia knew that with Alix being a young mother plus working thirty to forty hours a week, she didn't have a lot of spare time for knitting. Lydia guessed Alix had run into a problem with the pattern.

The young pastor's wife caught up with her and beamed Lydia a smile. "You're brilliant. You know that, don't you?"

"Well, thank you," Lydia returned. "What did I do for you to come to this foregone conclusion?"

"The new marketing campaign for the yarn store."

The profit margin with the yarn store was minute, allowing for taxes, paying employees, and restocking the shelves with product. Just recently she'd had a heart-to-heart conversation with her husband about how tight everything was financially. At the end of the day Lydia wasn't able to pay herself. Still, she loved her store and her customers. With funds so tight, there simply wasn't enough room in the budget to market the store. This could mean only one thing.

"Are you talking about those knitting baskets left around the neighborhood?" she asked.

"Yes, of course," Alix returned. "I saw one at the roller rink Friday night. Jordan and I took the youth group there, and one of the girls found the basket and brought it to me because she knows I love to knit."

Casey had attended the church-sponsored function but hadn't mentioned anything. But then her daughter only had eyes for a certain boy named Jack who was part of the church group.

Lydia held up her palm. "Sorry, not me."

"You mean to say that wasn't your idea?"

"I wish I could claim it was, but unfortunately, I can't take the credit."

Alix appeared stunned. "It was so clever, too."

"The yarn in the basket was from my shop?"

"The labels had your sticker on them, so naturally that was what I assumed."

"It was in a basket, you said?"

Alix nodded. Tommy whined, and she cupped her son's head and gently bounced him. "It won't be much longer," she promised, and kissed his cheek, and then, looking back to Lydia, explained. "He hasn't been feeling well."

"We can chat later," Lydia offered, although she was more than curious to get Alix's take on these yarn baskets.

"I need to wait for Jordan, anyway," Alix explained. "We're always the last to leave the church."

"Okay, tell me what was in the basket."

"Yarn and needles, plus a few basic instructions."

"Instructions?"

"A note that explained that the yarn was there for anyone who wanted to knit. It also said that the project would be a scarf, and when it was finished it would be donated to a homeless shelter or brought in to the store for distribution. Oh, and it had one of those small spiral notebooks in the basket, too."

"For what?"

"I don't really know, since it was blank. I assumed it was for anyone to make a comment or perhaps to write down their name."

This didn't make a lot of sense to Lydia.

"I started the scarf, cast on the stitches, and knit a few rows myself. Then several of the girls took turns knitting."

"Casey?"

Alix shrugged. "She was too busy chasing Jack around the rink."

Lydia smiled. That figured.

"Did the girls write anything in the notebook?"

"Oh, that was cool," Alix said. "The girls wrote short notes of encouragement."

"To those who would be knitting the scarf?" Lydia asked.

"No, to the homeless person who would receive the scarf. I wasn't sure if that was the original intent, but one of the girls thought of doing that, and it seemed like a good idea. I was sure this whole thing was your mastermind marketing program."

Lydia was all the more perplexed. This was the third time she'd heard of someone finding a yarn basket. "I wish I had thought of it myself."

"Don't look so concerned," Alix told her. "I think it's great and it's sure to generate business. Whoever is doing this clearly buys the yarn from you."

All the way to the parking lot, Lydia mulled over what she'd learned. Brad and the kids were already in the car, and as soon as her husband saw her, he started the engine.

Lydia opened the front passenger door and scooted inside.

"What did Alix want?" Brad asked, and then, without giving her time to reply, asked a second question: "Is she recruiting you for another one of her church projects?"

"As a matter of fact, no."

Brad arched both brows to show his surprise. Alix Turner operated on the theory that if the church needed a task accomplished, she should look to Lydia. As busy as she was, Lydia always seemed to be able to pull a project together.

"Alix mentioned that she saw another one of those knitting baskets at the roller rink on Friday."

"Mom," Casey said, so excited she practically came out of her seat belt. "I forgot to tell you about that."

"I saw one, too," Cody piped in.

Brad twisted around to look at their son. "Where?"

"Charlie's mother showed me one after baseball practice last week. She said it was a really smart thing Mom's doing."

"I wish I was that smart," Lydia whispered.

"Where was it?" Brad asked.

Cody hesitated. "If I tell you, you might get mad."

"I'm not going to be mad," his father assured him.

"McDonald's."

His confession was followed by a short silence.

"Wednesday night? You mean to say you ate a hamburger right before your dinner, young man?" Lydia asked. "No wonder you barely touched your meal."

"I didn't eat a hamburger," Cody murmured. "I ate two, and they were cheeseburgers, not hamburgers."

"Oh, Cody." Lydia remembered that he'd barely touched his dinner, and Cody had insisted he wasn't hungry. Lydia had been concerned he might be coming down with a flu bug. It simply wasn't like Cody, a growing boy, not to be interested in food.

"You said you wouldn't be mad."

"I wish you'd told me earlier."

"I would have, but you don't like it when I eat before meals."

"I wonder why that is," Brad said. "Your mother cooked you a perfectly good dinner that went to waste."

"I know," Cody said, sounding contrite. "But I was hungry and Charlie's mom had a meeting and that was his dinner."

"Yours, too, apparently," Brad added.

Lydia could sympathize. "Honey, next time just let me know, okay?"

"And you won't get upset or anything?"

Lydia was mildly afraid she would break her promise. "I'll do my best, if you do the same. Deal?"

"Deal," Cody echoed.

"Where are we going?" Casey asked, when Brad turned off from the street that led to their house.

"To McDonald's."

"For lunch?" Cody asked excitedly.

"I like Burger King better," Casey piped in.

"Five Guys for me," Brad said.

"Brad?" Lydia asked, keeping her voice low. She didn't have a clue what her husband was up to now.

His gaze momentarily left the road to meet hers. "I think it's time you took a look at one of these knitting baskets, don't you?"

Lydia didn't know why she hadn't thought of that herself. "Yes, it is time."

"It might be gone by now," Casey said. "From what I understand, they don't stick around long."

"Good. Try to get Dad to swing by Burger King," Cody said with a pout.

"We're not buying lunch," Brad said. "If we want to take a family vacation this summer, we need to save our money."

"That sucks," Casey muttered.

"Everything that is worthwhile demands sacrifice of some kind," Lydia reminded their daughter.

"When the time comes, you'll be glad," Brad promised.

"But August is months and months away." Cody didn't seem to agree.

"It'll be here before you know it," Lydia promised.

"I've never been to Oregon or California," Casey said. "I can hardly wait."

"It's not like it's that much different from Seattle," Cody said, sounding like a well-traveled man of the world. "It's just more of the same."

"But in Oregon and California while we're on a family vacation we won't have to eat at home or wash dishes afterward."

"Is my cooking so bad?" Lydia asked, finding her children's conversation less than amusing.

"We're here," Brad said, and pulled into an empty parking space. He was fortunate to find one. The fast-food restaurant was busy.

Bracing his arm along the back of the car seat, Brad turned to face their children. "You kids stay here while Lydia checks out the knitting basket." He pointedly glanced at his wrist, reminding her that the first pitch was less than a half hour away.

"I won't take long," Lydia promised as she rushed inside.

It took her only a few minutes to find the knitting basket. To her surprise, a woman close to her own age sat in a booth in the corner of the restaurant, knitting on the scarf.

"Did you find that here?" Lydia asked.

The woman glanced up and blinked. "Oh, my goodness, did I misunderstand? This is yours? You must think me incredibly rude to pick up your project and start knitting."

"No, no, it's nothing like that. I've been hearing about these baskets, and my son said he saw one here. He said the yarn comes from my store on Blossom Street."

"I found this by the window," the other woman explained. "I assumed it was holding the table, but no one came, so I checked it out," she explained, setting down the needles. "I wandered around, looking for a place to sit, but there weren't any vacant tables except this one. No one seemed to be coming, so I thought whoever was here last must have inadvertently left their knitting behind."

"That's a natural assumption." That made perfect sense to Lydia.

"But when I looked inside, I found an index card that said KNIT

ME." She reached for the basket and dug through it and showed the card to Lydia.

Sure enough, what she'd said was true. "Was there a small tablet inside as well?"

"No, but I didn't do a thorough search. Here," she said, and scooted the basket toward Lydia.

"Excuse me." They were approached by a third woman, carting a tray with her order on it.

Both Lydia and the knitter looked up.

"I couldn't help overhearing your conversation," she said. "I write a human-interest column for the *Seattle Times* newspaper. Would it be all right if I asked you a few questions?"

Chapter Fifteen

$\mathcal{M}$ax looked at his text message from Rooster and couldn't stop grinning. "It looks like love is in the air."

"Oh?" Bethanne stepped into the bedroom fresh from her shower. She wore a silk robe and had a thick towel wrapped around her head.

For a moment, Max couldn't take his eyes off her. "I got a message here from Rooster. He's staying in Seattle until Memorial Day. It seems he wants to take Lauren to the Mariners game later this afternoon."

"And will you extend your visit, too?" Her hands remained on top of her head as she studied him, her eyes wide and hopeful.

This was the biggest problem they faced nearly every week. It was killing him to leave Bethanne and return to his home or to watch her return to Seattle. They belonged together. "I'm no more eager to leave you than Rooster is to leave Lauren."

"That doesn't answer my question," she murmured, holding his gaze. "Is there a reason you need to get back to California? Monday's a holiday."

Rooster had made the decision a simple one. Any way he could spend extra time with Bethanne was worth whatever sacrifice it took. Staying meant he'd be riding back in the same frenzy with which he'd arrived, but he'd gladly do it, although he wouldn't mention his plans to Bethanne. "I can't think of a single thing on my schedule that's more important than being with you."

Bethanne's shoulders sagged with relief, and at the same time a smile lit up her face. "Oh, Max, I can't tell you how much I was dreading watching you go."

Not any more than he dreaded returning. This trip had been good for him and Bethanne. He hadn't known what to expect at this family gathering, celebrating Andrew and Courtney's baby news. Max was prepared to let Grant play the role of Lord Bountiful, and while it had been hard on his ego, he'd let it pass.

Grant chose to sit at the head of the table, raise a toast of champagne to his son, and pay for the dinner at a high-end restaurant. This was Grant's son, and he had a right to be excited and happy. In Max's opinion, Grant had overdone it, but Max let Grant's power play pass without a comment. Bethanne hadn't said anything, but he knew she hadn't been taken in by her ex's display.

Even Andrew had appeared uncomfortable when Grant slapped him across the back and pretended they were the best of buddies. Max knew otherwise, and so did Bethanne.

Annie, however, had eaten it up. She was much closer to her father than Andrew was. The relationship between father and son had been strained ever since Grant left the family. Max was able to ignore Annie's dirty looks that suggested his presence wasn't appreciated. According to his stepdaughter, he was an interloper. Max made it through the evening because he had what was important, and that was Bethanne as his wife. It was early days yet, and he expected that with time Annie would come to accept him; patience was the key.

"I'm so pleased Lauren was able to connect with Rooster," Bethanne said, sitting down on the mattress next to Max.

He wrapped his arm around her shoulders. "Me too, and now seeing that we've got an extra day together, what would you like to do?"

"The truth is, I'd like nothing better than to simply spend time with you. I intended to work in the yard; I know that doesn't sound exciting, but it brings me satisfaction."

"And here I thought you'd spend the day in mourning," he teased. "I pictured you standing in the middle of the street with tears in your eyes as I rode off into the sunset."

"I would have done exactly that, and then I'd go weed my flower beds."

Max grinned. "Would you like some help digging in your garden, my dear wife?"

"I'd love it."

Early on, Max discovered that among her many talents, Bethanne had a green thumb. Flowers blossomed and trees budded with a minimum of care. She had the ability to bring out the best, not only in people, it seemed, but in plants, too. Max enjoyed watching her with her houseplants. She talked to them as she watered and pared away dried leaves. The amazing part was that it was almost as if they could hear her.

Once after an extended trip, he'd watched his wife walk through the house, going from room to room, touching her favorite things and kissing her plants. It helped him understand how dearly she loved her home.

The thought gave him pause. Rooster had asked him an important question the day before. He wanted to know if Max fully comprehended what he was asking of Bethanne when he suggested she move to California. It was more than moving or selling her business; it was leaving this house she loved and all that it symbolized to her.

"I'll cook us a fabulous dinner," Bethanne promised.

"I'll provide the wine."

She smiled, and her shoulders rose slightly with a long sigh. Leaning against him, she tucked her head beneath his chin. "I love these lazy mornings with you."

No more than Max loved spending them with Bethanne. They

were far too few, so he appreciated it all the more when they had these special times with each other.

Bethanne finished dressing, and then they started work outside. Max helped till up an area where she planned to plant a small vegetable garden, while Bethanne fertilized and watered her roses and weeded the flower beds. When they finished, they ate a light lunch.

Relaxing in front of the television, Max turned on the Mariners baseball game.

"I need to make a quick run to the grocery store," Bethanne told him. "Do you need anything?" She had on a sweater, and her purse was draped over her shoulder.

"Not a thing."

"I won't be gone long."

Max set his feet on the ottoman and heard the kitchen door that led to the garage close as Bethanne left. He got a beer out of the refrigerator and watched the first pitch when the door off the kitchen opened again. "Did you forget something?" Max called out.

When he got no response, he got out of the chair to find Annie in the middle of the kitchen. Her gaze narrowed when she saw him.

"What are you doing here?" she demanded.

"I live here," he reminded her.

"Part-time."

"But I'm a full-time husband."

She ignored that. "Where's my mother?"

Bethanne's daughter seemed to be in a rare mood. On second thought, it wasn't so rare. He'd done everything he could think of to win her favor, and finally decided, for Bethanne's sake, that it was enough to simply keep the peace. Often that meant ignoring Annie's verbal jabs and her blatant efforts to engage him in an argument.

"Bethanne is picking up a few groceries."

"What are you still doing here?" She glared at him from halfway across the room. "Mom said you'd be leaving this morning."

"I decided to stay over the holiday."

"I bet you're surprised I'm here," she taunted, "seeing that you made a point of changing the locks and everything. You can try, but you can't keep me out of my own home."

"I wouldn't want to do that." Max was well aware of how she'd gotten into the house. She still had a garage door opener. When she'd left for the store, Bethanne hadn't bothered to lock the door off the kitchen. No reason, seeing that he was in the house.

"But you tried to keep me out."

"It wasn't you Bethanne and I wanted to thwart. It was your father."

"My father—"

"Is your mother's ex-husband. I'm her husband now, and I live here."

They stood like gunfighters in the old west, Max mused, each at one end of the street, waiting for the other to draw and aim the first bullet. "Couldn't we call a truce, Annie?" he asked, hoping he could convince her to accept him, even if begrudgingly.

"No. Way." She gave little doubt to the depth of her dislike of him.

"We both share one thing in common," he reminded her. "We love your mother."

"I do love Mom, but I'll never accept you. I tried. At Andrew and Courtney's wedding when Mom told me she loved you, I tried to let her think I was happy for her. Then later Andrew told me how hard Dad took her decision, and I realized how much he still loved Mom. He would have done anything—"

"You're forgetting Grant is the one who walked out on your mother," Max felt obliged to remind her.

"So? He made a mistake. I bet you've made one or two of those yourself, although I doubt you'd ever admit it."

Max had no intention of arguing with her. "I have, for sure."

"It was a midlife-crisis thing with Dad. All men go through that."

Not all men abandon their wives and children. Again, Max bit his tongue.

"I don't know how you can sleep in this house," she said, spreading out her arms and gesturing about her. "This is where my dad lived. This is where he slept with my mom. Doesn't it bother you that you're sleeping in the same bed as my dad?"

"Actually, it did, which is one reason we purchased a new bedroom set." Max hoped that by agreeing with her, it might take away some of her animosity toward him.

She glared back at him.

"Annie, listen," he said, willing to try again. "You don't have to like me. I realize it's hard for you and your dad to accept that your mother didn't choose to give your father another chance, but—"

"She would have if it wasn't for you."

"Are you sure of that?" Max was unconvinced.

"Yes, I'm sure. Dad is still crazy about Mom. He would have done anything to win her back. He would have stood on his head in the middle of the I-5 corridor if Mom would've given him a second chance. Even now he never dates. All he can think about is Mom and what he lost. It breaks my heart to watch my dad pine after my mother."

"Have you ever had this conversation with your mother?" he asked gently. "The reason I ask is because I did, before we were married. It was important to me that I not tear up this family. Do you know what she told me?"

"No, and I don't care what she said. It was a lie. I'm convinced to the very roots of my being that given time Dad would have been able to convince Mom that they were meant to be together."

Max continued as if she hadn't spoken. "Bethanne told me that it wouldn't have mattered if she'd met me or not. A reconciliation with Grant would never have worked. She isn't the same woman he divorced. She's changed. She told me that after your father moved out, she was close to a nervous breakdown. She was emotionally fragile, and every day was a struggle. It wasn't until she came up with the idea of starting the party business that she was able to face going on."

For the first time since they'd started talking it seemed that Annie was truly listening, and so he continued. "She made new friends."

"And she started knitting," Annie added softly. "After Dad moved out it was awful for all of us. All Mom did was cry . . . She couldn't even make the phone call to sign up for the knitting class. I had to do it for her."

"Then Maverick gave her the start-up money she needed."

"She told you about Maverick?"

Max nodded. "I wish I'd known the old coot. He sounds like he was a wonderful man."

"He was," Annie agreed. She crossed her arms over her chest.

At last Max felt like he was making progress. "I was watching the baseball game. Do you want to come sit with me until your mother gets back?"

Right away, Annie stiffened as if she'd woken from a trance. "No. I meant what I said. You and I are never going to be chummy."

"That's a shame, because I was hoping that someday we could be friends."

"It ain't gonna happen."

He shrugged. "You can dislike me all you want, Annie, but it isn't going to change the fact that I'm married to your mother and I love her. I genuinely love her."

"So does my dad."

"Then your father needs to accept the fact that there are consequences to his actions. Your mother doesn't hold a grudge against him. She forgave him long before I came into the picture, but that doesn't mean she was willing to remarry him."

"You're wrong," she insisted. "I don't care what Mom told you, she would have taken my dad back if it wasn't for you."

Max had heard about all he could take. "Annie, listen, I'm sorry I ruined the perfect picture of the reunited family that you've painted in your mind. I wish we could be friends, but you've made it clear you aren't interested. I can accept that. However, for your mother's sake, I ask that we both make an effort to be civil and get along."

"No, I can't and I won't, because one day Mom is going to wake up and realize what a horrible mistake she made marrying you."

Apparently, Annie held on to the fantasy that her mother would have the same kind of epiphany. The one Grant had had when he realized what a mess he'd made of his life by walking out on Bethanne and their children. Maybe Annie was right, but Max sincerely doubted it.

"You're not thinking of your mother, Annie," he said. "It's all about you, and you're being immature."

The color drained out of Annie's face. "How dare you talk to me like that."

Just then the door opened and Bethanne came into the kitchen, both arms loaded down with groceries. Max immediately went to help her.

"Annie," she said, smiling, genuinely pleased to see her daughter, "this is a surprise."

"I had one myself," Annie returned without a hint of warmth. "Max is still here."

"Annie, please," Bethanne pleaded, her face falling.

"I thought we agreed to disagree," Max inserted, looking pointedly in Annie's direction. He didn't want to drag Bethanne into the middle of their disagreement.

"Not anymore." She returned her attention to her mother. "He said some ugly things to me, Mom."

Frowning, Bethanne looked to Max for confirmation.

"I told her she needed to grow up," he admitted. It was the truth.

"You chose him over me—"

"I chose Max over your father," she corrected.

"Fine. Whatever. But I can't accept it. Max changed the locks to keep me out of the house."

Bethanne didn't so much as blink. "I can see it didn't do much good."

"And you let him," Annie cried, as if she was on the verge of tears.

"We changed the locks to keep Grant out, not you," Bethanne continued. "He no longer lives here, Annie, and you had no business giving him the key to my home."

"So fine, I'm locked out. That's just great, because as long as Max is here, I won't be. I'll only come to the house when I can be assured Max isn't anywhere around."

"Annie, that's ridiculous."

"You made your choice," she snapped. "Max was talking about Dad having to live with the consequences of his actions. That's good, because now you're going to have to live with your own consequences."

Chapter Sixteen

*D*ressed for the Mariners game, Lauren brewed a cup of coffee while she waited for Rooster to arrive. Out of nowhere, she felt a bubble of laughter working its way up her throat. In that moment she realized this was what happiness felt like. It was this irrepressible urge to laugh, this sense of joy that she hadn't experienced in . . . goodness, how long had it been? Too long, she decided; she couldn't remember the last time she'd felt this inner sense of exhilaration.

She'd spent all of Saturday afternoon and evening with Rooster until two that morning. It seemed impossible that the hours had passed so quickly. They'd talked and laughed, gone to a movie and dinner, and then talked some more over coffee in an all-night diner. Even in the wee hours of the morning Lauren had been reluctant to return to her condo. He'd seen her up to her door and kissed her, and the moment had been magical. She'd felt the attraction to him right away—not the physical way she had with other men. This was deeper, stronger, different. She'd been drawn to him as a man, a person with intelligence. When she'd compiled that list of characteristics she wanted in a man it was as if she'd modeled the details after Rooster. It was early yet—they barely knew each other—but nevertheless, Lauren felt it would be very easy to fall in love with him. Unfortunately, their time together would be short.

The thought of Rooster riding with Max back to California in only a few hours left her feeling bereft. It seemed they were just getting to know each other. He didn't want to leave any more than she wanted him to go, and seeing how late it already was, he extended his visit for an extra day. Right away they started making plans, and Rooster had suggested the Mariners game. She was up for anything and was certain whatever he had in mind would be fun.

Her doorbell chimed, and Lauren practically danced across the room to answer it. Rooster was early, which suited her just fine.

Only it wasn't Rooster who was on the other side of the door. Instead, Todd Hampton greeted her with a huge floral bouquet. He flashed her one of his most charming smiles.

"I come in peace." He stretched out his arm to hand her the flowers. "And to show you how sincere I am when I say I don't want to lose you."

Too shocked to respond, Lauren didn't know what to say. Her mouth sagged open and her mind whirled with dismay, fearing Rooster would arrive and find her with Todd.

Lauren hadn't seen or talked to her former boyfriend since that disastrous confrontation Friday evening at the restaurant. Because she didn't know what else to do, she accepted the flowers.

"I wanted to apologize," he said, looking contrite and sincere. "I know you're upset, and I don't blame you. I behaved like a jealous buffoon. I tried to phone several times, but you didn't answer."

"Todd, listen—"

"I've thought about what you said, and you're right—"

"This isn't a good time," she said, her voice gaining strength. "I'm leaving in a few minutes." She hated to be rude, but she really didn't want Rooster to see Todd at her place, not when she'd just gotten matters straight with him after the last time. She took hold of Todd's elbow and steered him back toward the open door.

He frowned. "You don't have time to hear my apology?" He sounded hurt and confused. "I care about you, Lauren. Can't we talk this out?"

"Not today."

"Tomorrow, then?"

She preferred to avoid the question. "Thank you for the flowers, they're lovely and very kind, but unnecessary."

He relaxed, and that oh-so-easy smile of his effortlessly slid into place. It was the same one he used in front of the newsroom camera. "I knew that in time you'd be willing to put this behind us."

Her heart raced like crazy. If she didn't get him out the door soon, Rooster would step off the elevator. "Like I said, I'm on my way out. I'm sorry, Todd, really sorry to put you off, but what I said holds. I don't want to be rude." She didn't have time to argue with him. It was far more important to shuffle him out the door.

Todd looked her up and down, taking in her Mariners baseball cap, jeans, light sweater, and scarf, and frowned. "You're actually going to a baseball game?"

All her dates with Todd had involved pantyhose. "Yes, as a matter of fact, I am."

"I'll be in touch," he said as he backed out of her condo.

Picking up the flowers, she quickly carried them into the bathroom, filled the sink with water, and stuck them inside until she returned that evening. She appreciated the sentiment and that he wanted to apologize, but unfortunately it was too little, too late. Her neighbor down the hall, Mrs. Huizenga, was a widow, and she would enjoy these far more than Lauren would.

Her pulse had yet to return to normal when her doorbell chimed a second time. Drawing in a deep, calming breath, she checked her peephole before opening it . . . thankfully, to Rooster.

His eyes brightened the instant he saw her. "Wow . . . you look great," he said, and held his hands out to her.

"Thank you." She clasped his fingers with her own and brought him inside. As soon as he was in her condo, Rooster took her into his arms and kissed her. His mouth was warm and moist over hers, and her senses went hurtling into the stratosphere. Rooster held her tightly against his body. She felt as though they'd been apart months instead of only a few hours. His chest lifted as he inhaled a deep breath and his grip tightened as they strained against each other. Lauren clung to him, and when they reluctantly broke apart, she offered him a slow, sweet smile, wanting him to know that she needed those kisses, had craved them from the moment he'd left her.

It came to her that as different as they appeared outwardly, they'd connected on a number of levels. Her first impression of Rooster hadn't been wrong. He valued friendship and loyalty, and had been loving toward his parents, especially in the latter stages of their lives.

They kissed again, and when they broke apart his breath came in shoulder-shuddering gasps as he braced his forehead against hers. It was hard to stop, she realized, for him and for her. In all the years she'd been dating, not once had she felt this strongly attracted to a man, especially this quickly. It both thrilled and frightened her.

"Are you ready?" Rooster raised his brows with the question, indicating he was asking more than whether or not she was prepared to walk out the door.

Right away she picked up on his train of thought. The day before, Rooster had given Lauren her first ride on the back of a motorcycle. It'd been quite an experience. At first she'd been terrified, but gradually she'd relaxed and learned to lean with him as he rounded the corners. What she'd enjoyed most was holding on to him, feeling that connection, soaking in his strength and feeling the power of the wind as it whipped past her. "Did you bring the bike?"

"I did. You game for a second go-around?" His look told her he was skeptical.

"You bet I am. I enjoyed my time as a biker babe."

Rooster laughed. "I hate to disappoint you, but it's a short ride to Safeco Field."

"This is a first for me, you know."

"A first?"

"The Mariners game. I've never been to one before."

Surprise flashed in his eyes. "Really? You're the one who lives in Seattle."

"I know, it's ridiculous, isn't it? But . . ." She was about to mention that Todd wasn't into sports, but quickly thought better of it. The less her ex-boyfriend was introduced into the conversation, the better. She would be forever grateful the two men hadn't crossed paths in the condo lobby or at the elevator.

"First time on a motorcycle. First time inside a biker bar, first time to attend a Mariners game. Do you have anything else up your sleeve for this holiday weekend?" Lauren asked.

Rooster chuckled. "Give me a minute and I'll think of something."

No doubt he would. This man was a surprise in every way, and she was completely infatuated.

Although short, the ride to the baseball game was as exciting as her first venture on the motorcycle, though more relaxing and certainly less terrifying. With gray clouds threatening, Rooster parked his bike in a covered lot. Holding hands, they raced across the street to the stadium. He collected their tickets at will-call and then led her to their seats. While close to the field, they were exposed to the elements. Lauren wasn't sure what they would do if it started to rain.

A mist started to fall in the third inning. Lauren was so involved in the game, she barely noticed. Rooster bought her a large bag of peanuts and later a hot dog with plenty of mustard and relish, which was just the way she liked it. Him, too, she learned.

At the seventh-inning stretch, she stood and sang along with the rest of the crowd, swaying left and right. She noticed Rooster didn't join in and glanced his way, surprised.

"I don't sing," he told her.

"Why not?"

"Once you hear me, the answer will be obvious." He wrapped his arm around her waist, kissed the top of her head, and whispered, "You'll need to sing for the both of us."

At the top of the ninth, Rooster got a text from Max. He replaced his phone on his belt and looked to Lauren.

"Everything all right?" she asked.

Rooster grinned and studied her with his gaze. "Max and Bethanne invited us to dinner."

"Would you like that?"

He shrugged. "Up to you."

"Then I say we should go." She liked the idea that Rooster and Max were as close as brothers. When she'd been with Todd, it had always been just the two of them. He had acquaintances but no deep friendships, no one he was especially close with, even from high school. Now that she thought about it, that was understandable. Todd's focus was solely on the demands of his career. Everything else seemed superfluous.

Thankfully, the mist had stopped by the time they left the stadium. "Shouldn't we contribute to the dinner?" she asked, and then realized it would be difficult when they were on the bike.

"I've got that covered," Rooster said, again taking her hand as they crossed the street.

"You do?"

"Yes, my lovely. I never leave home without a bottle of wine."

Naturally.

When they arrived at the colonial-style home, Max opened the front door and welcomed them inside.

Bethanne was busy in the kitchen, cutting vegetables for a salad. She glanced up. "I'm glad you two could join us."

"Me, too," Lauren said. "Thanks for the invite."

Soon Rooster had a beer in his hand and was on the deck with Max, who was busy barbecuing spare ribs.

"Can I do anything to help?" Lauren offered.

"Sit up on the stool and keep me company."

"Glad to."

Bethanne continued to add a variety of ingredients to the green lettuce. She tossed in a few cashews, Chinese noodles, and dried cranberries. "I'm pleased you were able to connect with Rooster and clear up what happened."

"I am, too." And she had Bethanne to thank for that. "I wouldn't have known where to find him without you. I'm grateful."

Bethanne glanced up and smiled. "I was happy to help. What did you think of Hog's Hideout?"

Lauren braced her elbows against the countertop. "It intimidated me at first, and Rooster was no help. He saw me and then immediately looked away, pretending he hadn't, silently letting me know he would rather I went elsewhere."

"But you persisted?"

"I don't know why I found it so important to clear the air. I think the bottom line is that I didn't want him to think badly of me. I couldn't bear for him to believe I would use him, or anyone, for my own selfish purposes. We'd had such a good time; he wasn't anything like I expected." She looked away and feared she might have blushed when she added, "I wanted to see him again in the worst way."

Bethanne smiled again. "So that explains it."

It embarrassed her to relay the details. "In part. I had to explain after Todd caused that dreadful scene in the restaurant. I couldn't let Rooster believe I'd purposely set that up so Todd would find us."

"I don't blame you."

"Rooster practically dragged him outside. I don't know what he said to Todd. I'm not sure I want to know."

"You're probably right." Taking two wooden forks, Bethanne tossed the lettuce and other ingredients for their salad. "I've got the dressing in the refrigerator. Would you mind getting it and then setting it on the table?" she asked.

Lauren slid off the stool and retrieved the dressing. As she set it on the tabletop she looked to this woman she barely knew and asked, keeping her voice low, "Am I missing something?"

Bethanne paused, the wooden salad bowl gripped with both hands. "Say again?"

"Am I missing something?" Lauren repeated.

"What do you mean?"

Lauren was unsure how to put it into words. "Rooster seems too good to be true. He's . . . smart and fun and decent and charming. And, my goodness, he's hot . . . does he have a flaw I haven't seen yet? Is there a dark side to him that comes out when the moon is full?"

Bethanne set the salad in the middle of the table. "Rooster is as genuine as they come. If he has a personality flaw, I have yet to see it."

"Then why isn't he married?"

The other woman mulled over the question before she answered. "That I can't answer with complete certainty. I do know that he took care of his parents until they both died. Then after Max lost his wife and daughter, he covered for him, working crazy hours to keep the business afloat. I think it's simply a matter of opportunity. He might have been stung a time or two, which could explain his reaction to Todd on Friday night."

"True." Lauren half suspected something like that must have set him off.

"But if that's the case, I don't know any of the details."

The door off the deck opened, and Max came inside carrying a plate piled high with ribs. "Are you ready for a feast?"

Dinner proved to be a fun exchange of good-natured teasing and delicious food. The ribs were cooked to perfection. At one point, Rooster leaned over and wiped barbecue sauce from the side of Lauren's mouth with his napkin. His eyes told her he'd rather have kissed it away, and her eyes told him she'd rather he had, too.

"What time do you want to head out in the morning?" Max asked Rooster after they'd finished the meal and lingered over coffee.

"Early. The Kendall-Jackson dinner is rescheduled for Wednesday."

"Right." Max glanced at his watch. "We both better get a good night's sleep, then."

"Agreed."

Lauren insisted on helping Bethanne with cleanup, and she and Rooster left soon afterward. When they got to her building, he parked outside and escorted her to her condo.

"Come in for a few minutes," she invited.

As soon as they were inside, he took her in his arms and she wrapped hers around him, clinging tightly to him. He'd be riding out in the morning, and the thought filled her with dismay.

"I hate that you have to go," she whispered as she kissed the underside of his jaw. He tasted wonderful. He splayed his fingers deep into her dark hair and lifted her head to angle his mouth over hers once more. Their kisses were long, deep, and involved, and when they pulled apart they were both breathless.

"I hate having to leave, too," he whispered, his eyes closed.

She heard the regret in his voice. "We barely know each other, and yet I've never been this strongly attracted—"

His kiss cut off the last of her comment. There was desperation to the kiss, as though he, too, had felt this strong physical pull toward her. It was as though he was afraid once he left her everything between them would fade away and change. It wouldn't. Not on her end.

"Ride carefully," she whispered, and her eyes held his look, intent on making him aware he was important to her.

"I always do."

For several minutes they continued to cling to each other, kissing and touching.

"When will you be back?" she asked, needing to know.

"Can't say."

Lauren pressed her head against his shoulder.

"Soon," he whispered.

"Good." She sighed with relief.

He rubbed his chin over the top of her head. "I have the distinct feeling I'm going to be spending a lot of time in the Seattle area."

"That's even better."

"I'll call."

"Please," she whispered. "Email, too, okay?"

"Should I text and Facebook and tweet you as well?"

She wasn't sure if he was teasing her or not. It didn't matter; she wanted to hear from him in every form of communication available. "Absolutely."

Rooster chuckled and then kissed her again, and this time his kiss was filled with promise.

Chapter Seventeen

*L*auren didn't hear from Rooster until almost midnight Monday.

"Hi," he said. He sounded exhausted.

"Hi. Where are you?" she asked. "Or, more important, how are you?"

"Tired, saddle sore, and I know it sounds silly—we were together less than twenty-four hours ago, but I miss you. It doesn't feel right for us not to be together."

"Oh, Rooster." He wasn't a man who spoke with flowery words, and yet he had the ability to make her heart sing in three-part harmony.

"Because we decided to stay Sunday, Max and I rode straight through. We have a number of meetings this week, and if we'd spent the night on the road the day would have been half gone by the time we got to Santa Rosa."

"I'm just glad you're home safe." Additionally, she was grateful not to know their decision to ride nonstop beforehand. If she had, she would have worried.

"I have to tell you, bed sounds mighty good about now. I'm turning forty this fall, and I'm feeling my age. This many hours in the saddle is no longer my idea of fun."

Lauren grinned. "Just what is your idea of fun?"

Her question seemed to amuse him, because he chuckled. "For starters, watching you enjoy a Mariners baseball game."

Lauren decided she'd been wrong about him. Rooster Wayne was quickly turning into a silver-tongued devil with the ability to sweet-talk her right off her two feet.

"I looked at their schedule, and it just so happens the Mariners have a home game this coming weekend." This was her less-than-subtle way of letting Rooster know that she would welcome his return to Seattle soon.

"Ah, Lauren," he said, sighing with what sounded like regret. "I'm afraid I'm going to need to take a rain check on that."

"Oh." She wasn't able to disguise her disappointment.

"I've got a business trip."

He'd mentioned that he often traveled for business but hadn't said anything about an upcoming trip. "Will you be away long?" she asked.

"Long enough. I'll be in New Zealand."

"New Zealand?" she repeated, and her spirits sank even lower. New Zealand was half a world away; this trip would easily involve a week or two, if not longer. She couldn't help wondering just how much time it'd be before she could see Rooster again.

"Their Marlborough region does an excellent sauvignon blanc," he told her, as if selling her on the reason.

"Isn't that the wine you brought with you to Max and Bethanne's for dinner?"

"I'm impressed you remember."

"I enjoyed the citrus flavor."

"I did, too. The taste reminds me of grapefruit."

"Me, too." The small talk wasn't distracting her from the fact that she might not see him again for several weeks.

"A number of vineyard owners have invited large distributors from around the world to visit their facilities."

"And you're one of them?"

"Yes."

"It's a wonderful opportunity." She forced enthusiasm into her voice, although she wasn't able to hide her disappointment.

"It is," he agreed.

"Then how come I feel like crying?" she whispered, and tried to pass off the comment with a choppy laugh as if she were joking.

"I'd been looking forward to this trip for months, and all at once I'm thinking I'd rather get back on my bike and head straight north instead of this all-expenses-paid trip down under."

"You aren't thinking clearly, remember? You're tired and saddle sore."

"That's the problem. My mind might be too tired to think straight, but my heart is wide awake. I'd rather be wherever you are."

He sounded so sincere, so earnest, that Lauren felt like she could break into sobs. "You say the most beautiful things."

"Don't let Max know; he'll razz me."

"What's happening with us?" she asked, thinking out loud. This was a new experience for her. She wasn't like other women who had a lot of relationships, intense or casual. She didn't fall in and out of love easily. She held on to her heart, and yet within a few days she felt like her head was in the clouds over Rooster. The attraction between them was so intense it felt as if she could barely recognize herself.

"I don't know what's happening, but whatever it is, I don't want it to change. Do you?"

"No," she agreed quickly. "Not for anything. In a matter of days my entire perspective has turned around. I've been attracted to men before, but nothing like this."

"And you claim I say beautiful things?" he asked, chuckling.

"Is it the same with you?" she asked, needing to know.

"In spades."

Lauren was almost giddy to hear it. "Has anything like this happened to you before?"

Rooster hesitated. "Only once, but that was when I was really young. Too long ago to remember. Besides, this is different, way different."

"But not so long to forget."

"Something like that."

"Will you be able to keep in touch while you're in New Zealand?"

"It isn't the end of the earth, Lauren, but I suspect I'll be able to see it from there. I'll be in touch, don't worry."

They spoke for several minutes longer, until they were both ready to fall asleep on the phone.

"Time for bed," she whispered. "Night, Rooster. Dream of me." She was fairly certain he would occupy her dreams.

"Good night, my beautiful, sweet Lauren."

She reluctantly ended their conversation. Although it'd been late, she'd been relieved when Rooster's call came through. He'd told her he'd phone and she'd waited all day, though not anxiously, because instinctively she knew Rooster Wayne was a man of his word. All was well; he was home and safe now.

Tuesday morning, when Lauren arrived at work, Elisa was there. Lauren's employer had spent the weekend with her daughter and Katie's boyfriend in Pullman, Washington.

"You're back," Lauren greeted as she removed her raincoat and hung it in the back room. "How did everything go with Katie and Dietrich?"

"Not good," Elisa responded. "In fact, it went about as bad as it could, and I'm afraid it's all my fault."

"Oh, Elisa, I'm so sorry," Lauren sympathized as she helped her friend set out the window displays.

"Garry didn't want me to go, and he was right. It would've been better if I'd stayed home. It's just the thought of my daughter, so young and pregnant, makes me a little crazy."

"How is Katie?"

Elisa shrugged. "Physically, she seems to be doing fine. Emotionally, she's better off than me. Well, I guess she is, but then it's hard to tell because she's no longer speaking to me."

Mother and daughter generally spoke every day, so this must be devastating to Elisa. Lauren glanced toward her employer, unsure of what to say or how to comfort her friend. A tear rolled down Elisa's cheek, and she quickly brushed it aside as though to hide the fact that she was crying.

"I wish I knew what to say." Lauren felt Elisa's regret and disappointment over the disastrous weekend.

"I insisted on taking Katie to see a doctor," Elisa explained. "Dietrich wanted to come along, but I refused to let him. That set Katie off, but you know how stubborn I can get, and I insisted it was just me and Katie. Now I wish Dietrich had been with us; everything would have gone much better if I hadn't been so stubborn."

"You saw an obstetrician . . . not a clinic, right?" She left the question about forcing Katie into considering an abortion unasked.

Elisa nodded. "I promised Garry I wouldn't pressure her to end the pregnancy. It wasn't easy, but I kept my word." She pulled a tissue from her pocket and blew her nose.

"What did the doctor say?" Lauren asked.

"Nothing new. The home test was accurate. Katie is indeed pregnant."

Lauren pressed her hand over Elisa's and gave her a gentle, reassuring squeeze.

Gathering up her resolve, Elisa squared her shoulders and continued, "My little girl is pregnant, and she's blissfully happy about it. Can you imagine? From all outward appearances she's overjoyed about this baby who's about to ruin her life.

"I don't know, Lauren, I honestly don't know what's happened to my intelligent, beautiful daughter. I swear to you that young man has brainwashed her. She isn't thinking clearly. Katie is no more suited to being a farmer's wife than Donald Trump is to cleaning toilets. I give this relationship another month before Katie wakes up and realizes what a terrible mistake she's making. And by then it will be too late."

Too late to do away with the pregnancy is what Elisa meant.

"You were her age when you found out you were pregnant with her," Lauren reminded her friend.

"This is different."

"Oh?"

"The world has changed since I was her age. Katie has opportunities that weren't available to me, and she's throwing them away. These days it's so much harder to support a family. When Garry and I discovered I was pregnant there were expectations for us to marry. It isn't like that any longer; women no longer feel the need to find a husband when they're still in college. Look at you."

"Me?" Lauren repeated.

"Many women wait to marry until they are thirty or older. If Katie decides to marry Dietrich now, she'll live to regret it. If she wants to have this baby, then fine, come home and we'll raise this child together or put it up for adoption. It would be a kindness to give this baby to a loving home. But Katie marrying Dietrich could well be the biggest mistake of her life."

"Were you able to meet Dietrich's parents?" This was one excuse Elisa had used to convince Garry she should make this trip across the state. Elisa was convinced the Friedmans shared her concern for their son. She had counted on them being reasonable people who would be against Katie and Dietrich marrying as much as she was.

"Just my luck, they were out of town at some onion-growing convention or some rally having to do with growing Walla Walla sweet onions." She looked up at the ceiling, as if calling upon God's assistance in this dreadful situation.

"How did it go with Dietrich?" Lauren asked. Part of Elisa's plan was to "talk sense" into Katie's young man.

"Badly. Even worse than you can imagine."

This entire trip sounded like it had been disastrous.

"Katie refused to let me speak to Dietrich without her being there.

He's a decent enough kid. I don't have anything against him," Elisa said, "well, other than the fact he doesn't seem to understand the concept of birth control. His parents, either, apparently. I learned Dietrich is the oldest boy in a family of eight children. Don't these people realize there's a population problem?"

Now was probably not the best time to remind Elisa that birth control was a shared responsibility. Katie played an equal role in this pregnancy.

"I was polite and kept my cool with Dietrich," Elisa continued evenly. "I simply asked him a few questions, which Katie insisted on answering until Dietrich stopped her. He claims to love Katie, and he loves their baby. He feels the responsible action is for them to marry. That was when I lost it."

Lauren had seen Elisa lose her cool more than once, and it wasn't a pretty sight.

"And now Katie's no longer speaking to you."

"Unfortunately, she took exception to a few of the words I chose to call Dietrich."

"Did you apologize later after you'd had a chance to cool down?" Elisa had a quick trigger, but once she blew off steam she generally had a fast recovery.

"I sent them both a text with a mea culpa."

Lauren knew none of this had been easy for Elisa. "Did you hear back from Katie?"

Her employer reached for a fresh tissue and held it against her eyes. "Katie's due home for the summer in two weeks, and she let me know that she won't be coming back to Seattle."

This explained why Elisa was so upset. "Katie's staying in Pullman? Does she have a job for the summer?"

"She's going home with Dietrich . . . As for a job, I can only assume she'll be working in the fields."

Lauren hugged her friend and let Elisa cry on her shoulder. This entire situation was turning into a huge ordeal. Although she wanted to comfort her, Lauren wished Elisa had listened to Katie and Dietrich instead of trying to make their decision for them. She seemed to think she could steamroll them into doing what she thought best, and clearly that hadn't worked.

"Getting away for a few days will do us both a world of good," Lauren said, hoping that was the truth.

"Away?" Elisa lifted her head from Lauren's shoulder. "We're going away?"

"The gem convention is in a couple weeks, remember?"

"Right. It slipped my mind. You're coming with me."

"I wouldn't miss it."

"I hope your weekend went well," Elisa said, composing herself and changing the subject from the sensitive area of her daughter's situation.

"My weekend was lovely. Rooster and I—"

"Who's Rooster? You've never mentioned him before."

"That's because I just met him."

His name seemed to amuse Elisa. "Doesn't he get teased with a name like Rooster?"

Lauren had wondered the same thing, and she smiled as she recalled his answer. "I asked him and he said, if he was teased, it never happened more than once."

Elisa smiled. "I haven't met this new man in your life, and I like him already."

"I like him, too." *Like,* Lauren mused, was such a weak word. It didn't come anywhere close to expressing how she felt about Rooster.

Elisa's gaze widened. "My goodness, look at you. You're positively glowing. This new guy must really be someone special."

"Rooster is beyond special. I'm in serious danger of falling in love."

"Really? After only a few days? This isn't like you, Lauren."

Elisa was right. This was an entirely new experience for her. "I'm sorry to be so happy when you're so miserable," she told her friend, "but I can't help myself."

"Be happy, please. I'm sure I'll remember what that feels like again, one day, myself."

Lauren's cellphone chirped. Normally when on the job she would ignore it. "Do you mind if I get that?" she asked hurriedly. She hadn't heard from him yet this morning. "It might be Rooster."

"Go ahead. Far be it from me to stand in the way of young love." Then realizing what she'd said, Elisa added, "Young love doesn't mean I'm referring to age."

After four rings, just before her cellphone went to voice mail, Lauren dug it out of her purse and answered. She didn't recognize the number and had to assume it was Rooster phoning from a landline.

"Morning, sweetheart."

It was Todd.

Lauren's heart sank first with disappointment, then frustration. Both emotions warred with each other and she found herself unable to speak for the first few seconds.

"I'm calling from a line at the station. I thought you said you'd be in touch. I waited all day Monday. You're normally so responsible. What's up?"

He'd waited for her? After all the times he'd left her sitting in a restaurant, all the times he'd left her dangling or just plain stood her up.

"What's up?" she repeated. "I told you before, Todd, it's over. This isn't a ploy to get you to marry me, I'm sincere. I'm moving on, and I suggest you do the same."

"You don't mean it," Todd insisted.

"Yes, Todd, I do mean it. Now, please, don't call me again."

She tried to be kind; she wasn't angry, just determined, and all she could do was hope that Todd would believe her and leave matters as they were.

Chapter Eighteen

My knitting changed when I allowed myself to look up from other people's patterns and instead started to watch the work build in my hands stitch by stitch. I stopped worrying about making errors and began wondering "What if . . ." New directions presented themselves.

—Kathryn Alexander,
spinner, knitter, and weaver

*L*ydia knew something was troubling Casey the minute her daughter slumped into her chair at the breakfast table. The teenager, who was by nature a chatterbox, didn't say a word. Even Cody noticed.

"Morning, sweetheart," Lydia said, and served up a bowl of old-fashioned oatmeal she'd cooked with plump raisins. Because the yarn store was closed on Monday for the holiday, she wasn't opening until noon on Tuesday and took more time than usual with breakfast.

"Are you sick?" Cody asked as he dumped sugar and milk over his oatmeal, and when he thought Lydia wasn't looking, he added two additional scoops of the sweetener.

"No," Casey snapped. "Do I look sick?"

"No, you look mad," Cody returned. "What did I do that was so terrible?"

Lydia delivered toast to the table. "Did you get out on the wrong side of the bed?" she asked, and placed her hand on Casey's shoulder.

"What does that mean, anyway?" Casey shrugged off Lydia's hand.

Lydia exchanged looks with Cody. He seemed to be saying he was glad he could escape. The school bus would pick him up in ten minutes, which was one reason he rushed to finish his breakfast.

"What does that mean?" Lydia repeated the question as she sat down across from her daughter. "I don't really know. I never thought about it before. It's something my mother used to say to me. I bet we could find out where it originated online."

"I'll ask Grandma."

"Okay." Actually, it was a curious question. "I know it has to do with being grumpy in the mornings," she said, musing out loud. "From what I remember, it goes back to something from the Middle Ages about getting out on the left side of the bed, but I could be wrong. Mostly it has to do with being cranky."

"I'm not grumpy, and I'm not mad," Casey insisted, raising her voice.

Cody stood, shoved another spoonful of oatmeal into his mouth, grabbed a slice of toast and his backpack, and headed out the door. "What's for dinner?" he asked, pausing in the doorway.

"I haven't given it any thought yet," Lydia asked. "What would you like?"

"Spaghetti," Casey muttered, knowing it was Cody's favorite meal and generally what he requested.

To his credit, Cody pretended not to hear his sister. "Can we have tacos and Spanish rice?"

"That's a switch," Casey said, louder this time.

"That," he said pointedly, "is my *new* favorite dinner."

"I'll take hamburger out of the freezer right now," Lydia told him.

"Thanks, Mom." The screen door slammed as her son hurried to meet the school bus.

Seeing that Casey seemed to be in a bear of a mood, Lydia said nothing, preferring that her daughter reach out to her. She noticed that Casey had barely touched her breakfast. She swirled the spoon around the oatmeal a couple of times but didn't eat. Lydia resisted placing her hand against the girl's forehead to see if the teenager had a fever.

The silence was louder than a shouting match, and when Lydia couldn't bear it any longer, she tried another tactic. "That reporter I met Sunday at McDonald's is stopping by the shop this morning."

Casey perked up slightly. "Will your picture be in the newspaper?"

Lydia couldn't be sure. The reporter had wanted to do the interview right then, but Lydia couldn't. Not with Brad and the kids waiting for her, and so they'd arranged to meet this morning. "I doubt she'll want more than a statement or two."

"Didn't she ask to take your picture or that of the shop?" Casey sounded offended that Lydia hadn't been promised the front-page headline.

"She didn't say anything about a photographer."

"Oh." As though terribly disappointed, Casey's shoulders sagged.

"I'm not even sure why she wants to interview me. I don't have anything to do with those knitting baskets."

"But the yarn is from the shop."

"I know. I'm convinced it's one of my customers." While Lydia recognized the yarn, most of which had been discontinued long ago, she hadn't come up with answers. The wide variety of yarns told her that whoever it was had been a longtime customer. She'd asked several of her friends who frequented the shop but hadn't gotten any help from that end.

Casey looked up. "I think it's a wicked good idea."

"I suppose." It was a wicked good idea, she agreed. However, she wished whoever was responsible had thought to mention it to her.

"Come on, Mom. Everyone is talking about it."

That was true enough. "It's certainly gotten the shop a lot of attention, and we've gotten more business as a result . . . only . . ." She let the rest fade.

"Only what?" Casey pressed.

"Well . . . it's a little embarrassing to have to tell everyone that I'm not involved. Don't get me wrong, I'm grateful, but it would have helped to coordinate with me. In some ways, I feel blindsided."

Casey sat up straighter, and her eyes brightened. "I think I know who it is."

"You know?"

"It's a guess."

"Guess away," Lydia urged. Her daughter could be insightful at times, and there was every possibility that Casey had thought of an angle that had escaped Lydia.

Casey leaned forward slightly, and in a conspiratorial whisper said, "Margaret."

"Margaret?" Lydia repeated, and had to squelch the urge to laugh. "Well, maybe, but I doubt it."

"Trust me. It's Margaret," Casey said, and then advised, "Keep an eye on her. She can be secretive like that. Grandma told me that when Margaret was a teenager she used to sneak out of her bedroom in the middle of the night and meet up with friends."

"Grandma told you that, did she?"

"Yes. She tells me lots of things. You didn't do that because you were the good girl."

She was the sick girl, but Lydia didn't bother to correct her.

"I'll keep a watch over Margaret," she promised, although if it was her sister it would be a complete shock. Margaret was many things, but this publicity ploy wasn't her style. She had an in-your-face kind of personality. Going behind Lydia's back and delivering knitting baskets around the neighborhood didn't sound a bit like her sister.

"Can you drive me to school?" Casey asked after glancing at the time.

"Okay." As it was, her daughter had already missed the bus, and if she was going to get to school anytime close to the bell, it would mean Lydia would need to drive her. "Hurry."

"I will." Casey's mood seemed only slightly more chipper. Any improvement was a plus, though.

Quickly, Lydia cleared the table and stuck the dirty bowls inside the dishwasher. She got the promised hamburger out of the freezer and set it on a plate on the counter and grabbed her raincoat and purse. The sky looked dark and brooding, which sort of matched her daughter's mood.

Lydia was already in the car when Casey joined her. The teenager snapped her seat belt into place and expelled her breath as though she'd greatly exerted herself with the effort.

Taking a risk, Lydia asked, "Did you have another bad dream last night?" She hadn't heard Casey, but then, if she hadn't cried out, Lydia could have slept through it.

"Yeah," Casey admitted.

"Do you want to talk about it?"

"No."

Although this dream had happened several times already, Casey had yet to tell Lydia what it was about.

"Are dreams true?" Casey asked a few minutes later.

Lydia didn't have an answer. Like the question about the phrase "getting out on the wrong side of the bed," dreams weren't something she'd given much thought to before. "I assume there must be different kinds of dreams. From what I've read, certain dreams have meanings."

"Like what?"

"I'm not sure. I remember as a kid I once dreamed about going to school, and when I got there I realized I'd forgotten to get dressed."

For the first time that morning, Casey smiled.

"I must have been feeling vulnerable about something."

"Did you have the dream again and again?" her daughter asked.

"No. Are you having the same dream over and over?" For just a second, Lydia took her eyes off the road.

Casey nodded.

"It's terrifying, whatever it is." Lydia had never seen Casey as emotionally shaken as when she had this nightmare. Whatever it was seemed to upset her feisty daughter unlike anything else.

"I don't want to talk about it, okay?"

"Of course."

"Can I visit Grandma this afternoon?"

"Sure, if that's what you want."

"I'll take the city bus," Casey said, which meant she wouldn't be stopping by the shop or the house first.

Lydia pulled into the circular driveway leading up to the front of the school. She had to wait in a long line of cars with other parents dropping off their tardy children. "Give me a call when you're ready to have me pick you up from Grandma's."

"Okay. Thanks, Mom."

"No problem. I know how much you enjoy visiting your grandmother; she loves it when you stop by."

"I wasn't talking about Grandma," Casey told her. "I meant about not taking it personally when I was cranky this morning."

"Oh?" Lydia still didn't know what she'd done to warrant special appreciation.

"You gave me emotional space."

Emotional space? Lydia couldn't help but wonder where Casey had come up with that phrase. "You're welcome. Have a good day."

"I'll try."

When it was their turn in front of the school, Lydia stopped and Casey leaped out of the vehicle. Even before the car door closed, Lydia could hear a friend call out to Casey. Her daughter waved her arm, and soon the two girls raced toward the entrance just as the school bell rang.

When she arrived at A Good Yarn, Lydia came in through the back entrance, choosing to park in the alley. If customers saw her inside the shop, it would be hard to turn them away.

Whiskers greeted her, and after feeding him and giving him attention she sequestered herself inside her tiny office. Whiskers returned to his spot in the window and curled up for a nap.

Dreading the task before her, Lydia put it off and brewed herself a single cup of coffee. Sitting at her desk, she savored it before she started in on paying bills, a necessary evil.

Business had picked up slightly, but it was difficult to show a profit in a down economy, and they were heading into the summer months, when business generally took a downturn. Lydia had a strict budget she needed to adhere to. Thankfully, she was able to pay her creditors and employees with a small amount left over, which was a nice surprise. It would be helpful to have more than the most rudimentary website, but she wouldn't be able to afford that anytime soon. She was grateful Brad's job supported their family, and he encouraged her efforts with a small business.

A loud knock sounded against the glass at the front door. Lydia glanced at her watch, surprised to find that nearly ninety minutes had passed. It didn't seem possible. Hurrying out of her office, she went to the front of the store and unlocked the door for the *Seattle Times* reporter.

"Hello again," Shannon Kidder greeted.

Lydia had the other woman's business card, and after reading several of Shannon's columns online, she felt the reporter could be trusted to set the right tone for the news piece.

"Come in, please." She opened the door wider to allow the reporter greater access.

Shannon came into the shop, paused, and looked around at the shelves of yarn and the variety of colors Lydia had so carefully organized. Between her and her staff members, several sample projects had been knitted and were artfully displayed around the shop.

"I don't know that I've ever been in a yarn store before," Shannon said, and handed Lydia a second business card.

"Welcome, then. I hope when we're finished that you'll feel free to look around. I thought we could talk at the table in the back." Lydia pointed toward the section of the store where the staff taught classes. The table was used for social knitting as well.

"I appreciate your willingness to chat with me when the shop is technically closed," Shannon said, following Lydia.

"I'm happy to do it."

Shannon pulled out a chair and then removed a tablet from her purse. "Would it be all right for me to record our conversation?"

"Of course." Brad had told her to expect to be recorded. "I went online and read a few of your articles. I like the way you close each with that little play on your name. *And I'm not kidding.*"

"Thanks. I try." Shannon set her cellphone on the tabletop. "Spell your surname for me so I'm sure I have it right."

"Goetz. G-O-E-T-Z."

"Perfect. Thank you. From what I understood when we spoke briefly on Sunday, these baskets with the yarn and needles are as much a surprise to you as anyone."

"Very much so."

"You don't have any idea who is delivering these around the neighborhood?"

Casey had her suspicions, and Brad had mentioned a couple of names, too. "None whatsoever."

Shannon made a quick notation. "But your store is involved in charity knitting?"

"Oh, yes." Lydia felt herself starting to relax as she told the reporter about the preemie-cap program for local hospitals. She brought a few of the most recent donations over for Shannon to inspect.

"We're also involved in Warm Up America! and Knit for Kids, which is a World Vision program."

"And now scarves for the homeless," Shannon added.

"Indirectly." Lydia didn't want the reporter to give her credit when none was due. "Like I said, I'm not the one responsible for these special scarves, although I've certainly knit for each of the charities I mentioned. My customers are the ones with the big hearts. I've discovered that knitters are caring and generous."

"In other words, A Good Yarn provides an outlet for your customers to reach out to help others."

"You could say that, yes." Lydia felt she had the most wonderful, loyal customer base anywhere. Many who routinely shopped at the store had become her dearest friends. Alix for sure; Carol and Elise, who now worked for her part-time; and Bethanne, too. Her mind crowded with names and faces, such dear, dear friends.

This yarn store had also given Lydia a relationship with her sister. Because of her health issues as a teen and young adult, Lydia had never felt close to Margaret. Her sister had deeply resented all the attention Lydia received because of the cancer. It was the yarn store that had brought them together. That and caring for their mother.

The interview didn't take long. By the end of it, Shannon expressed a desire to sign up for the beginning knitting class.

"I hope you do."

"I'm not kidding," she joked as Lydia let her out the front door.

With the interview finished, Lydia returned to her office, looked at the ledger, and realized once more that while she wasn't making money hand over fist, there remained several benefits to owning A Good Yarn. Benefits that far exceeded the balance in her checkbook.

Chapter Nineteen

*B*ethanne noticed that Annie managed to avoid her all week, which was ridiculous. Clearly Annie remained upset with Max, and evidently with Bethanne, too. So be it. It was time her daughter accepted the fact that Bethanne and Max were married and intended to stay that way.

From what Max had told her, Annie's attitude toward him had come to a head Sunday afternoon. Bethanne had the feeling she'd managed to miss the worst of their confrontation, which was probably for the best. Being stuck in the middle between the two of them would have been uncomfortable to say the least.

It was little wonder Max had asked her to uproot and sell the business and move to California if it meant no longer having to deal with her daughter and ex-husband. Who could blame him? Never did Bethanne suspect that her marriage would cause such an upheaval in her relationship with her daughter.

It was true Annie had always felt close to Grant; she was his little girl, and his darling who could do no wrong. Her daughter had taken it especially hard when Grant asked for the divorce. And she'd been the first to champion Grant when it became apparent his marriage to Tiffany was in trouble. The moment the divorce was final, Annie was convinced her parents would eventually reunite. Max had ruined the vision Annie held in her mind of the perfect family.

However, by then Bethanne's eyes were wide open when it came to her ex-husband. Not for an instant did she trust his claims of undying love. Nor was she the same woman Grant had left. Her life was different now, and so was she.

By mid-afternoon on Wednesday Bethanne had had enough with the silent treatment from her daughter. She called Annie's extension and asked her to come to the office.

Fifteen minutes later, Annie arrived. Her bad attitude seemed to radiate off her the instant she walked into the room. She stood in front of Bethanne's desk, looking straight ahead, with her arms folded tightly over her chest. The sour look on her face could curdle milk.

"Sit down, Annie," she said softly.

Reluctantly, her daughter took a seat. Her spine remained rigid, and she seemed completely unwilling to meet Bethanne's gaze.

"Can you give me an update on the Costco employee picnic?" Bethanne asked, deciding to ease into this difficult conversation with a business discussion first.

Annie visibly relaxed and went into a detailed report of the progress of the party plans for the Kirkland, Washington–based company. While Annie spoke, Bethanne stood and walked over to the window, which looked out over the city. While appreciating the view, she listened intently as her daughter gave the report, stopping her once or twice with questions.

When it came to the business side of their relationship, they were on solid ground. Annie had proved to be an asset to the company, taking on the responsibility of handling their corporate clients. Her ideas were good, and she'd proved herself to be more than capable of dealing with these larger accounts.

When she'd finished, Bethanne praised her daughter's efforts. "It sounds like you have everything under control."

"I had excellent training," she said, complimenting Bethanne.

Bethanne walked around to the front of her desk and leaned her backside against the edge. "On a completely different subject—"

"Are you going to berate me about Max? If you are, then I'm leaving right now."

So that was the way it was going to be. "Berating you wasn't my intention. You're an adult and fully capable of making your own decisions. It's highly unlikely anything I say will change your attitude toward Max. It would be foolish of me to try."

"I don't like him, Mom. If you'd heard the horrible, ugly things he said to me, you wouldn't be so quick to defend him."

"I didn't defend him, and I won't defend you to him, either. What happened is between the two of you." If Max had been disrespectful to her daughter, then it went without saying that he'd been provoked. Annie was certainly capable of being argumentative and belligerent.

"He's not a good person, Mom."

Bethanne held up her hand, stopping her. "I believe you've already made your dislike of Max abundantly clear."

"Good," Annie snapped. "Because you need to hear it."

"How you feel toward Max doesn't change my love for him," Bethanne said, and crossed her arms.

Annie's face tightened, and her eyes narrowed with impertinence. "I'll never accept him as my stepfather."

"I'm not asking you to." It was important that Annie understood this. "What I'm asking is that you accept him as my husband."

Annie's eyes flashed first with defiance and then confusion. "What does that mean?"

"It means that Max and I are married. He lives with me when he can, which unfortunately for the time being isn't full-time. We're hoping to change that in the near future."

"Is he moving to Seattle?" Annie demanded, as though this was the worst possible news.

"We don't know yet. It's one option."

It took a moment for the meaning to soak into Annie's stubborn brain. "You're not saying that *you're* moving to California *full-time*?"

"Like I said, I don't know yet. That's another possibility, and one we're thinking through carefully."

As if she'd received an electric shock from the chair, Annie bolted to her feet. "But what about—"

"No decisions have been made, Annie. Max and I are talking, and I wanted you to be aware that there's the possibility that I will either sell the business or move our headquarters to another state."

Her daughter's mouth took on the appearance of a mounted bass. "Have you lost your mind? I can't believe you're actually considering such a thing. You can't leave Seattle. This is our home . . . your home," she amended. "It's ridiculous . . . it's preposterous." Her eyes narrowed. "Max asked you to do this, didn't he?"

"Annie, I'll say it again. Nothing has been decided."

"Mom," she cried, and it almost sounded as if she were close to tears. "You aren't actually considering this, are you?"

"As a matter of fact, I'm giving it serious consideration."

"And you don't understand why I detest Max? Look what he's doing. He's taking you away from all of us . . . from Andrew and Courtney. What about the baby? What about me?"

"Can you blame Max for wanting me in California?" she asked softly. Her chest tightened at the pain she saw in her daughter's eyes. She felt it herself. "Every time he's in Seattle, there's drama."

"Oh, so all this is my fault." How quickly the angry defiance replaced the hurt and worry.

"You aren't the only one, Annie. Your father isn't helping matters any."

"That's because he loves you."

Bethanne disagreed. For a short while, Grant had managed to convince her of his love, but his true colors showed themselves in short order. "I'm sure your father has regrets. He made a mistake, and he's sorry. The real problem is that his ego can't accept the fact that I chose another man over him. He might claim undying love, but the only person Grant really loves is himself."

"How can you say that?" Annie cried. "You don't know what it's been like for Dad since you married Max. I worry about him, Mom. It's like the light has gone out of him. He feels like he's screwed up his life so badly that he'll never be the same again. Dad needs you, and you're turning your back on him."

"Enough, Annie. I sincerely doubt your father is pining his life away because we're no longer married."

"You don't know anything when it comes to the way Dad feels about you."

"Probably not, but the truth is, I really don't care. As far as I'm concerned, our marriage is over and it was years ago. We're both different people now. I wish your father well, I really do, but I'm not going back. If he can't accept that, then it's time he did. Perhaps you're the one who can help him."

Annie glared back at Bethanne as if she couldn't believe what she was hearing. "How can you treat Dad this way? You're cold, Mom. You've got a heart of stone." With that, she fled the office as though running from a burning building.

Releasing the tension with a lengthy sigh, Bethanne walked back to the window and looked out over the Seattle landscape below. Perhaps she was coldhearted when it came to her ex-husband. Max would reassure her that it was a good thing. Grant was no longer part of her life.

The problem was that Grant and Bethanne had children together. They were about to be grandparents for the first time, and there were sure to be additional members coming into the family. She would never be completely free of him.

Less than twenty minutes later, Bethanne's cellphone chirped. Caller ID told her it was Grant. No doubt Annie had immediately contacted her father, hysterical and crying. Oh, that child made for a great drama queen.

Exhaling, Bethanne waited until the third ring before she answered her phone. "Yes, Grant?" Her voice was clipped, making sure he understood that hearing from him was a nuisance.

"Well, good afternoon to you, too."

"What's on your mind?" Might as well get to the point as quickly as possible and be done with it.

"How's your day going?"

"Fine. Do you have a reason for interrupting it?"

"Well, yes," he continued in the same easy tone she was convinced he used with his real-estate clients. "Andrew and Courtney phoned Sunday afternoon to thank me for the dinner. While we were talking, I decided to offer to buy the furnishings for the baby's room."

"That was generous of you."

"I don't want a repeat of what happened with my parents," he said.

Bethanne heard the humor in his voice. Before Andrew was born, they couldn't afford a new crib, and so they'd purchased a second-hand one, which Grant had refinished. When the varnish had dried, Grant hadn't been able to reassemble it. Two of the screws were missing, and he'd nearly blown a gasket putting it back together.

The irony was, his parents were so excited about their first grandchild that they'd purchased a crib to keep at their house for when Grant and Bethanne came to visit. A new crib.

"I was hoping you'd be willing to do a bit of shopping with me," Grant continued. "I don't have any idea what kind of budget to give them. It's been a lot of years since I've even thought about baby furniture. I don't know what cribs and changing stations are going for these days."

"Wouldn't it be just as easy to look online?"

"Of course it would, but I'd feel better if I could see the piece, touch it, test its construction."

"You should take Andrew with you. He knows far more about that sort of thing than I do."

"You're right, I should." He hesitated.

"Annie phoned you, didn't she?" If he wasn't going to say it, she would.

"Yes," he admitted, with some reluctance.

"This whole thing with the baby's crib is a ploy to talk to me about moving to California." It stunned her that Grant believed she was gullible enough to fall for this shopping scheme of his.

"I did want to buy the furniture for the baby," he insisted.

"Like I said, that's generous of you. I'm sure Andrew and Courtney will appreciate it."

"Bethanne, we need to talk." He sounded serious and deeply troubled.

"Frankly, I can't think of a thing you and I have to discuss. I'm busy, Grant. I have a business to run, so unless you have something important to say, I need to go."

Her words seemed to shake him. "Bethanne . . ."

"Goodbye, Grant."

"You're right," he said. "You aren't the same woman any longer."

This shouldn't be news. Without a qualm, Bethanne ended the call.

Just before she left the office, Max phoned. The sound of his voice was like a warm ocean breeze washing over her.

"Your day going okay?" he asked.

"It's going fine," she assured him. She could hear warehouse noises in the background.

"How are matters with Annie?"

"Tense."

"She still upset?"

Bethanne didn't want to drag him into the squabble with her daughter any more than necessary. "I probably didn't help things any when I told her I'm considering moving to California."

The line went silent for an instant. "My guess is that news didn't go over well."

Bethanne laughed. "You could say that, but Annie needs to know in plenty of time so she can make her own plans."

"True."

Because this matter with Annie deeply depressed her, she changed the subject. "I'm grateful you and Rooster are back and safe."

"We are . . . I know you weren't pleased that we decided to drive straight through, but all is well that ends well, right?"

The thought of Max on the road for hours on end shook her. Tired and weary on a motorcycle was a deadly combination. "I'm glad you didn't tell me beforehand."

He chuckled. "I remember not so long ago when I rode twenty hours straight just so I could spend time with you."

"If I'd known what you were doing I would have worried then, too."

"Don't fret, all is well, we're both safe and sound."

Seeing that he was back and in the office, it wouldn't do any good to argue. "Call me when we can talk longer, okay?"

"Sure, honey, but remember I've got that dinner with Kendall-Jackson tonight."

"I know."

"No more fretting over Annie, okay?"

"Okay." Then, because she couldn't help being curious, she asked, "How's Rooster?"

Max chuckled. "I'm afraid he's too lovesick to think straight."

"Is that so?" This was an interesting development.

"I recognize the look because it's the same one I wore after I met you. Any real conversation is beyond him at the moment. I need to repeat nearly everything I say because his head is so high in the clouds it's affected his brain."

"And this was what happened to you?"

"The minute I laid eyes on you I knew I was in trouble. I might as well have given it up because you owned my heart from that moment forward."

"Oh, Max, I do love you so." His words were the balm she needed after this trying day. First it was the conversation with Annie, followed by Grant's efforts to manipulate her.

"We'll muddle through whatever the future holds. I'm sorry about Annie."

Bethanne knew they would both make the right decision. A decision that would affect their lives and their businesses. Perhaps most compelling of all is the impact it would have on her children.

Chapter Twenty

In my knitting world, the most exciting and reward-
ing part is the process of creating a new hand-knit
design. When seated in my Devonshire studio over-
looking the Atlantic Ocean, I am at my happiest and
inspired. My design research, reference books, and
deliciously new Rowan yarns around me—a certain
black-and-white cat contentedly sprawled across a
pile of newly knitted design swatches . . .
　　　　　　　　　—Martin Storey,
　　　　　　　　　designer and author

*L*ydia had been busy at the shop all Thursday morning. Thankfully,
Margaret was available to help. Social knitting would start soon, and
she expected a full house. She'd also been waiting for Evelyn Boyle,
Casey's social worker, to return her call all day, but unfortunately she

was with a customer when the phone rang, so Lydia paused and waited while Margaret picked up the line.

Sure enough, Margaret placed her hand over the receiver and said, "It's Evelyn."

"If you'll excuse me," Lydia said to the customer, who was an accomplished knitter, "I need to take this call."

"Of course," the woman said. "I can finish up here by myself without a problem."

Lydia hurried into her small office and closed the door. Reaching for her desk phone, she sank into the chair.

"Evelyn?" Lydia asked.

"Lydia, I got your voice mail. I'm sorry I wasn't able to phone sooner; it's been a hectic week. What's the problem?"

Now that she had Casey's social worker on the phone, Lydia wasn't sure where to start. "It's just a question," she said, not wanting to make more of this than necessary.

"Apparently, it's an important one. I don't know that I've ever heard you sound more distressed. Tell me what's happening."

"I'm worried about Casey," Lydia whispered, which was probably more than obvious. "She's been having horrible, horrible nightmares recently."

"Tell me about them."

Lydia swallowed tightly. "She wakes up screaming and is so distraught that I have to spend an hour or more with her before she calms down enough to go back to sleep. Evelyn, the poor girl trembles and clings to me with all her might."

"What is the dream about?"

Lydia felt like a terrible failure as a mother. "I don't know; she refuses to talk about it."

"That's not uncommon. Can you tell me when these nightmares started?"

"A while ago now," Lydia answered, thinking back over the last several months. "She had nightmares from the first, but nothing like this. The ones where she wakes up screaming started about a year after we first adopted her."

"About the time Casey hit puberty?"

"Yes." Come to think of it, Lydia recalled that the first nightmare came shortly after Casey had started her period. She woke up the entire house with her screams in the middle of the night, frightening them all half to death.

"Dreams like this often happen with these children," Evelyn explained. "Many of them, and I'm including Casey in this, have gone through more trauma by the time they're five or six years old than you or I will face in a lifetime. Some have experienced unimaginable terror and abuse."

"Casey?" Lydia's voice trembled with the question. The thought of this child she'd come to love with all her heart going through any kind of abuse deeply distressed her.

"I only have sketchy details. All I can say is that her home life was bad enough for the state to permanently remove her from the family. Both Casey and her older brother."

"She was three at the time." Lydia knew only the most basic details of her daughter's early childhood. For the majority of her life, Casey had been a ward of the state of Washington and in the foster-care program.

"In order for these children to emotionally deal with what has happened to them," Evelyn continued to explain, "their minds repress the memories. Then when they're hit with all those surging hormones, it isn't uncommon for memories to resurface. And when they do, it can be traumatic."

"These memories return in dreams?"

"Not always, but that isn't unusual."

"Do you recommend counseling for Casey?" With their budget already tight and with the yarn store struggling, Lydia didn't know where she and Brad would come up with the money to cover this additional expense. However, if Evelyn recommended counseling for Casey, then they'd find a way to help their daughter.

"How frequent are the dreams?"

Lydia didn't have a definitive answer for the social worker. "At first they were just every now and then, but recently . . ."

"They're coming more and more often."

"Yes," Lydia admitted. "Twice this week already. You know what a gutsy girl Casey is, and these dreams simply terrify her. She clings to me and trembles and refuses to let me go." Tears welled up inside of Lydia as she recalled the last dream. Casey had clung so tightly to her that Lydia was left with bruises on her arms.

Evelyn paused. "Would you like me to speak to her?"

It went without saying that her daughter wouldn't be keen on that. "I don't know how Casey will react to that. She completely shuts down whenever we talk about these dreams. It's almost as if she's ashamed that she has them . . . as if she had any control over them." It'd been a while since Evelyn had last stopped by, and Casey had grown somber and silent during the last home visit, as if she expected to be whisked away at any moment.

"Does Casey still come by the shop after school?"

"Not as often now that she's in high school."

"Will she be there this afternoon?"

With social knitting, Casey generally made a point of stopping by the yarn store, following her classes. "I believe so, unless . . ." This brought up another subject that deeply concerned Lydia. "She's close to my mother . . . and Evelyn, I'm worried what's going to happen to Casey once my mother . . ."

"Dies?" Evelyn finished for her.

"Yes," she whispered, and her voice cracked. "Sometimes I think Casey is the one who's keeping Mom alive. I wish you could see the two of them together. They are such a funny pair. My mother's mind drifts and she gets confused, and while I struggle to be patient with her, Casey is as gentle and loving as can be. The two of them spend hours together."

"That's wonderful, and understandable. Your mother gives Casey roots, a sense of family, of belonging. She needs all that and more, especially now."

"But what will happen once my mother . . . you know . . . is gone? By that I don't necessarily mean when she dies. Every week I see her losing more and more of her capacity to function normally."

"Lydia, don't borrow trouble. Let's tackle one issue at a time." Evelyn was the voice of reason, so calm and unruffled. "I'll make a point of stopping by the shop this afternoon. Is social knitting still on Thursday afternoons?"

"Yes, and I'm fairly certain Casey will be here."

"Good, and if not, then you and I can chat."

Seeing that the adoption had been completed three years earlier, Lydia was grateful that Evelyn was willing to listen to her concerns and advise her and Brad.

Sure enough, Casey showed up at the yarn store directly after school, and was her normal cheerful self.

"Hi, Mom," she said as she breezed through the doorway, leaving the bell to jingle in her wake. Whiskers didn't stir but cuddled up among the yarn displayed in the window, mellow as could be.

Lydia watched as Casey tossed her backpack into the same office where she'd so recently spoken to the social worker. "How was school?" she asked.

"Okay. I've got to read *Moby-Dick* for freshman English. Who wants to read an entire book about a whale? Don't teachers know how many pages it has? I bet it's got a million words. Did you have to read it when you were in school?"

"I did," Lydia admitted, and frankly she'd found it a challenge to get through the massive tome, although she wasn't sure it would be a good idea to tell her daughter.

"And did you actually read it from beginning to end?" Casey asked, narrowing her gaze with suspicion.

Lydia hesitated.

"Every single word?" Casey pressured.

Feeling cornered, Lydia decided honesty was the best policy. "Not every single word. I needed to write a paper on it, and so I read as much of it as I could bear and got the essence of the story down."

"What grade did you get?"

"I don't remember."

"Mom. You do, too. I bet Grandma kept your paper. She kept everything having to do with you and Margaret."

Her mother might have saved all her and Margaret's schoolwork, but she didn't have it any longer. It seemed best to let her mother assume that she did rather than to upset her with the fact that a good part of the useless memorabilia that she'd collected through the years had been tossed into the trash.

"I believe I aced it," Lydia finally admitted.

"I knew it," Casey muttered. "I just knew it. Do you realize how much pressure that puts on me?"

"Pressure?" Lydia echoed.

"Yes. I'm your daughter, and now the teachers expect me to be as brilliant as you." She grinned then, just so Lydia would know she was teasing.

Lydia laughed and impulsively hugged Casey. It was hard to believe this was the same teenager who woke terrified from a nightmare so frightening that she was barely able to function in its wake.

At four o'clock the table started to fill up with the group, who enjoyed knitting together twice a week. For whatever reason, the Thursday-afternoon group was larger than the one that met on Tuesday. By four-fifteen every chair was filled and a second table was added.

Bethanne and Lauren sat side by side, and when she had a chance Lydia joined the two.

"How are the baby blankets coming along?" she asked. Bethanne appeared to have made significant progress, whereas it didn't look like Lauren had knit more than a few rows beyond the border stitch.

"So far so good," Bethanne answered.

"I'm only getting started with mine now," Lauren admitted.

Bethanne grinned and seemed to enjoy teasing her newfound friend. "That's because she's been on the phone two and three hours every night this week, talking to Rooster."

Lydia could have sworn Lauren blushed.

"I like Rooster," Casey inserted, joining them with her crochet hook in hand. With Margaret's help, Casey had taken to crocheting, much easier than a pair of knitting needles.

"Lauren likes Rooster, too," Bethanne casually mentioned.

"Okay, I'll admit it. I like him, too, but he's leaving soon, so we're making as much time for each other now as we can."

"Leaving?" Casey quizzed. "He's not orbiting the moon, is he?"

"No, but he's on his way to New Zealand."

"You can still talk every day if you want, you know?" Casey assured her, as if she were an expert on matters of long-distance communication. "I can help you set up an account that will enable you to chat for hours for mere pennies."

"Pennies?"

"Sure. Give me your cell." Casey plopped down next to Lauren and reached for the cell, which Lauren had removed from her purse. The teenager worked her magic and then asked for the phone number where she could reach Rooster. Lauren gave it to her. Right away, Casey punched it in, and within a couple of seconds, Rooster was on the line.

"Lauren?" His voice came over the speaker, and everyone at the table paused to listen in.

"Hi, Rooster, it's Casey."

"Hi. How come you've got Lauren's cellphone?"

"Because I'm showing her how the two of you can communicate via the Internet by phone while you're in New Zealand."

"Oh. Where are you now?"

"A Good Yarn."

"Okay, take the phone off speaker and give it to Lauren, okay?"

"Sure." Casey handed the phone to Lauren.

Lydia was fairly certain Lauren was well aware of how best to stay in touch with Rooster and appreciated the fact that the other woman hadn't squelched the teenager's enthusiasm.

While Lauren was on the phone it pinged, indicating she had a text message. After a whispered farewell to Rooster, Lauren checked her phone. Her reaction told her the text came as a surprise.

"Problems?" Lydia asked, remembering that she'd recently broken off with the television reporter.

"No, it's from my employer's daughter. I didn't know she had my cell number." Lauren set the phone back inside her purse. "I'll answer it later," she said, and then frowned again and looked toward Casey. "Would you happen to know what ACORN means?"

"Sure. That's a texting acronym for A Completely Obsessive Really Nutty Person."

"Got it," Lauren said, grinning now. "I don't think Katie is too far off base with that."

With a jingle, the door opened and Evelyn Boyle walked in. Lydia saw Casey tense as if she fully expected Evelyn to instruct her to pack her bags because she'd be taking her to another home, another family. Leaning next to her daughter, Lydia reached for Casey's hand and gave it a gentle squeeze.

Frowning, Casey looked at Lydia, her eyes round and expectant. "Is she here for yarn?" Casey asked.

Her daughter's hands made a nervous twitch Lydia had never seen them make before, as if she were clawing at some invisible object.

"That's what most people are looking for in a yarn store, silly," Lydia said, making light of Evelyn's visit. She stood to greet the social worker, but Casey, who was normally so outgoing and gregarious, remained at the table, silently looking on with her spine as stiff as a broomstick.

A customer followed Evelyn inside, and Lydia went to assist the newcomer. When she returned, Lydia found Evelyn chatting with Casey. Her daughter, however, looked to be unresponsive and uncommunicative. The broomstick had become a steel plate.

No more than ten minutes after she arrived, Evelyn left. As soon as the social worker was out the door, Casey leaped up like a jack-in-the-box and approached Lydia.

"You told her," she said, her eyes snapping with outrage and accusation.

"Honey, your father and I are worried about you."

"Why would you do that?"

"Because we want to help you," Lydia insisted. She saw that the knitters around the table had stopped and were staring at the two of them. Being the center of attention had always embarrassed Lydia, and now here she was having a personal conversation with her daughter in front of the entire store. "Can we talk about this later?" she asked, silently pleading with Casey to drop the subject for the moment.

"No, we can't. I don't want to talk about it again, ever. Understand?"

When Lydia didn't immediately respond, Casey exploded again.

"Understand?" With a sense of flair and drama, the teenager raced into Lydia's office, grabbed her backpack, and flew out the door.

For several uncomfortable moments, Lydia didn't move. She didn't breathe, either. Having little experience with raising a teenager, she felt at a complete loss. She'd hoped reaching out to Evelyn would help her help Casey. Instead, it seemed it'd done just the opposite.

When she found she could breathe and move again, Lydia returned to the table, took her seat, and reached for her knitting. Her hands trembled slightly as she tugged on the yarn.

"It gets better," Bethanne assured her.

"I certainly hope so," Lydia whispered back.

Chapter Twenty-one

*B*ethanne stared down at the note Annie had left on her desk Monday afternoon while she was out for lunch.

We need to talk. Meet me at The French Cafe at six.

Annie's dislike of Max had seemed to grow much worse since their last confrontation. For nearly two weeks, her daughter had taken delight in making smug remarks about Max. Snipes that were generally said under her breath but hit the mark. In an effort to maintain peace, Bethanne had managed to avoid an angry retort. But the control on her temper was wearing dangerously thin. Bethanne liked to think of herself as even-tempered, and under normal circumstances she was. But Annie's behavior had gotten out of hand, and Bethanne couldn't allow it to continue. It'd come to the point that she'd actually considered asking Grant to speak to their daughter.

It didn't take Bethanne long to realize seeking her ex-husband's help in this awkward situation would be playing right into his hands. If anything, Grant was sure to take delight in knowing Annie had taken such a strong dislike to Max and was making her miserable. She was fairly confident his giant ego would relish the thought.

Annie's attitude was definitely a problem, but one Bethanne would deal with on her own. Other than the note she'd placed on Bethanne's desk, Annie had managed to avoid her the entire day, and frankly, Bethanne was grateful. She had a business to run.

This dinner invitation from Annie was a good sign, she hoped. Perhaps Annie was ready to make peace. All Bethanne wanted was for her daughter to respect Max. It wasn't necessary that they become bosom buddies.

The French Cafe was busy with a rush of loyal customers. Because the weather was overcast and threatened rain, they wouldn't be able to dine alfresco, which Bethanne would have preferred. Well, that couldn't be helped.

After waiting for a few moments, she found a vacant table and ordered the homemade clam chowder served in a bread bowl. Because she knew Annie also enjoyed their clam chowder, she placed a second order for her daughter and then waited for Annie to join her.

At ten after six, Bethanne found herself growing irritated. Annie generally was punctual, and seeing that she was the one who asked for this meeting, the least she could do was arrive on time.

Five minutes later, her order arrived, and rather than let her dinner grow cold, Bethanne reached for her spoon. She'd just swallowed the first bite when the cafe's door opened. Only it wasn't Annie who'd arrived.

Instead of Annie, in stepped Grant.

This apparently was a setup her daughter had concocted to pressure Bethanne into talking to her ex-husband. Automatically, she stiffened, resentful and irritated.

"Sorry I'm late," Grant said, as if this was the plan all along. "Where's Annie?" He glanced around as if searching for their daughter.

Bethanne wasn't fooled. "You don't really expect me to believe you weren't in on this, do you?"

His all-too-easy smile slid like a puzzle piece locking into place.

"Ah, I should have known you'd catch on fast enough." He removed his coat, placed it over the back of his chair, and then sat down. "Clam chowder, my favorite. Thanks for ordering for me."

"I didn't order it for you," she reminded him, half tempted to get up and leave. Then again, perhaps it was best for them to clear the air.

"I know." As congenial as a lover, he reached for his spoon. "You haven't answered any of my calls, emails, or text messages," he said, as though ignoring him had deeply hurt his feelings.

"I've been busy." While that was true, there'd been another reason: Bethanne didn't have anything to say to her ex-husband.

"You left me no choice but to use subterfuge," he said with a contrite look. "I wouldn't have asked for Annie's help if you hadn't forced my hand. I can't let you do this, Bethanne. At least hear me out."

"Is this about me moving to California?"

"It's more than that," he said, his eyes pleading with her. "I realize you're married to Max now and the decision on whether to move is entirely between you and Max."

"Thank you." She hoped to cut him off from any further discussion on the subject.

"But—"

She could have predicted there would be an objection in there somewhere. "Listen, Grant," she said, and held up her hand. "You can stop right now. This is a decision I'm making with my husband. I didn't seek your advice, nor do I want it." Although the words were harsh, she spoke in a matter-of-fact way to let him know this wasn't an emotional response but a practical one.

He blinked as though her words had cut him to the quick. After a moment, he nodded. "I can accept that."

"Good."

He raised his index finger. "Can I say one thing?"

She sighed and hesitated.

"This has to do with Annie."

Exhaling deeply, Bethanne nodded. She could predict what he was about to tell her but decided to let him have his say.

"If you do choose to move to California and take the business with you, Annie has already decided to look for work elsewhere."

It was just as Bethanne suspected. "She told you this herself?"

"Yes. We talk nearly every day."

"No doubt." This was a consequence Bethanne had already considered. "That, of course, is Annie's decision, and it might be for the best all around." Especially if her daughter's current attitude persisted.

"I imagine you've discussed this possibility with Andrew. What did he have to say?" Grant asked, paying attention to his meal once again. He took another bite of the soup and tore off the edge of the bread bowl and munched on that.

"Don't you talk to him, too?" she asked, doing her best not to sound flippant.

"Not as often as I do Annie."

That was because Andrew was onto his father's ways and didn't trust Grant with the same unwavering loyalty as his sister.

"Andrew supports whatever decision I make."

"As do I," Grant assured her.

It was difficult to hold back a laugh. Grant would use whatever means available to him to keep her in Seattle for his own purposes. Bethanne didn't doubt that for a second.

He lowered his head and stirred the soup. "I'd miss you."

Bethanne didn't respond.

"I'll admit it troubles me that you would opt to move to another state and not remain close enough to enjoy our first grandchild."

"I'll visit often." And she would, as often as time allowed. Bethanne had no intention of abandoning her children and grandchildren.

Grant let go of the spoon. "So your mind is already made up. You're moving?"

"As I told Annie earlier, I have yet to make a decision."

He nodded and pushed his meal aside as if he'd lost his appetite. "I appreciate your candor. I wish you and Max the very best." He checked his watch. "I've got a showing this evening," he said as he scooted back his chair and stood.

"I understand the real-estate market is picking up again," she said conversationally.

"It is. I've had a good couple months."

"Congratulations."

Grant hesitated and dragged his fingertips across the tabletop. "It means nothing without you, Bethanne." With that, he turned and walked out of The French Cafe.

Bethanne finished her soup, paid the tab, and then left. She'd deal with Annie for this setup later.

Once she was home, Bethanne changed into comfortable attire and sat on her bed, waiting for Max's phone call. He'd be flying from California Friday afternoon to spend the weekend with her. Although it had been only a week since she'd last seen him, it felt much longer. These separations were difficult on them both.

The call came right when he'd promised. "Hi, sweetheart," he greeted. "How was your day?"

"Busy. Yours?"

"Busy. I heard from Rooster."

"From New Zealand?"

"Yeah, apparently he's pretty miserable."

Bethanne smiled and leaned against the thick decorative pillows piled along the backboard of her bed. "I thought he was looking forward to this trip, taking a few days' vacation and exploring the country."

Max chuckled softly. "That was before he met Lauren."

"Oh, poor Rooster."

Max snickered. "You'd think they'd been torn apart by circumstances beyond his control."

"Hey, hey," Bethanne chided. "If I remember correctly, Rooster traveled with you when you insisted on following me halfway across the country. Don't be so hard on him. He's falling in love, and I, for one, am glad to see it."

"This is different than with you and me."

"Oh?" she teased. "And how's that?"

Max seemed to need a few moments to form a reply. "Okay, you win, it's the same for him as it was for us. Have you talked to Lauren lately?"

"Not since last week at the yarn store, but from what she said, she's missing Rooster, too. She's leaving with her boss for Las Vegas soon."

"Business or pleasure?"

"A little of both, from what she said. Same as Rooster."

"It isn't like Rooster and Lauren aren't talking. From what I understand, despite the time difference, they're spending copious amounts of time on the phone with each other. It's a wonder he's getting any business accomplished whatsoever."

Bethanne was sympathetic toward Max's friend. "One would think you of all people would be a tad more understanding."

"Okay, you're right. I should be, shouldn't I, seeing that it wasn't so long ago that I fell head over heels in love with you?"

"I'm glad to hear it." Definitely very glad, seeing that her own feelings for her husband had intensified tenfold.

"I'm quite enjoying seeing Rooster in love. It seems Lauren is turning his life upside down the same way you did mine."

"From everything I've seen, Lauren feels the same way about him."

Max paused, almost as if he dreaded bringing up the subject. "So, tell me, how did your dinner go with Annie?"

Earlier in the day, Bethanne had sent Max a text telling him about the note. She debated whether she should mention the meeting with Grant and then quickly decided it wasn't a good idea to keep secrets from her husband.

"That bad?" he asked, when she didn't immediately answer.

"It was a setup. Annie wasn't at dinner."

"Let me guess. Grant came instead."

"Yup."

"And what did he have to say?" Max's voice cooled considerably.

"Not much, but not from lack of trying. He wanted to be sure I knew how he felt about me possibly moving to California."

"I imagine he did," he stated in the same chilly tones.

"I didn't give him the opportunity to speak his mind. His opinion doesn't matter, and if Annie chooses to look for work elsewhere, then that's solely her decision."

"Annie's threatening to quit?"

"Yes, but . . ."

"Will she?"

"Probably, but Max, I refuse to let her blackmail me with her threats. At this point, I'm beginning to think her leaving the company might be a good idea."

"No," he burst out immediately. "This isn't what I want for you or Annie. The two of you have worked together from the start. I refuse to be the one responsible for tearing your family apart."

"Annie needs to grow up."

"You're right, she does, but not like this."

"Max . . ."

"Honey, I apologize. I regret ever bringing up the subject of you leaving Washington State. It was a selfish mistake on my part. My only excuse is that I was overly tired from the long ride."

"But what you said . . ."

"I know what I said and I've been kicking myself ever since. The last thing I want is for you to uproot your entire life for me; what we have now isn't perfect, but it's working."

Bethanne felt like crying. "Is it working, Max?" she asked softly. "I'm miserable without you. If we could be together it would be so much better."

"I agree, but that isn't possible for either of us in our current situation. You'll be with me in a few days, and we'll have the entire weekend. Let's concentrate on the time we have together instead of what we don't have."

In other words, concentrate on the positive. "It seems like an eternity since I last saw you."

"It feels like that to me, too."

"And you berate Rooster for being lovesick and missing Lauren."

He chuckled. "Guess you're right. I shouldn't be so judgmental."

Bethanne smiled, loving her husband all the more.

"Now, no more talk about you moving to California, understand?"

"Got it," she confirmed.

They spoke for several additional moments, and by the time they disconnected, Bethanne felt as if she were floating on a cloud. Until Max mentioned it, she hadn't realized how tense she'd been over this potential move. Max had asked it of her, and she took his request to heart, giving the matter serious consideration.

She wasn't sure what she'd tell Annie. Whatever she decided, Bethanne wanted to make it clear that her daughter's threat wasn't a key factor in this sudden turnaround.

"Annie, Annie, Annie," Bethanne whispered, and closed her eyes, seeking wisdom in dealing with her daughter and her daughter's dislike of Max.

Chapter Twenty-two

"*H*i." Rooster's voice came over the line as clear as if he was sitting directly across from her in a restaurant booth. Lauren found it hard to believe that he was still in New Zealand.

"Hi, yourself," she said, sitting on the edge of her bed, her suitcase propped open. "I'm packing for Las Vegas." She was scheduled to be away for only three days. The problem was that she hadn't learned to pack light. Elisa, who was far more seasoned, would get everything inside a carry-on while Lauren struggled to hold it down to two suitcases, which, of course, was ridiculous. "I'm trying to decide what to pack and what not to take. It's an art form." Rooster had been away nearly two weeks, traveling from city to city across New Zealand. "Are you tired of living out of a suitcase yet?" she asked. Rooster, who was accustomed to traveling light, had probably packed everything he needed for two weeks inside a briefcase.

"What I'm tired of is not being able to be with you," he murmured.

Lauren felt the same way. "It seems like you've been away for months." She didn't mean to complain or sound disgruntled. A dozen times a day she thought of things she wanted to share with him; the time they spent on the phone had become the highlight of her days. Rooster made her laugh and her heart sing. This bond, this connection, grew stronger with each conversation.

His being in the South Pacific wasn't so different from his being in California, she supposed. Distance wasn't the concern, being apart was, and now that they'd found each other, it was torture not to be able to be together. Soon, though. Rooster was due back in the States shortly after she returned from Las Vegas. He'd already booked his flight to Seattle; as far as Lauren was concerned, it couldn't come fast enough.

"Your day went well?" she asked, knowing he was playing tourist now, as the main objective of his trip had already been accomplished.

"It was fine; New Zealand is an incredible country." He was on the south island now, and he went on to tell her about visiting the city of Christchurch. "What about your day?" he asked.

Lauren released a deep sigh. "It's Elisa again, and how she's dealing with Katie's pregnancy. We've worked together for a long time now, and she's my friend, a good enough friend for me to speak my mind. Really, I couldn't keep quiet any longer, so I sat her down and we had a heart-to-heart."

"That couldn't have been easy."

"It wasn't, but she's driving her daughter away when Katie needs her mother's love and support more than ever. Her own parents supported her when she told them she was pregnant. It astonishes me that Elisa can't see that. According to her, it's different with Katie; times have changed. While I had to agree that times have changed, the situation hasn't. Katie is nineteen and old enough to make her own decisions without Elisa interfering."

"How'd Elisa take what you had to say?"

For all the times she'd discussed Elisa and Katie, it was as if Rooster knew them personally. He didn't, of course, and, in fact, Elisa had yet to meet him. "I was a bit concerned Elisa wouldn't appreciate my comments, but in the end, I think she did, especially after she learned that I've been texting back and forth with Katie."

Learning that Katie had reached out to Lauren had come as a shock to the girl's mother. "Between mother and daughter, Katie's the one showing maturity. Elisa's an emotional wreck and she's insisting Katie come home for the summer and stay away from Dietrich. Instead of helping, she's driving a huge wedge between them. They've always been close, and it's tearing Elisa apart."

"She sounds like a bit of a control freak."

"When it comes to her children, she is fiercely protective. Her problem is that she views Katie as a child in need of her mother, and while Katie needs her family and their support, she also needs the freedom to make her own decisions."

"You're a good friend."

"I'd like to think so," Lauren said. The conversation hadn't been easy, but she was convinced it'd helped her friend. Afterward, Garry had thanked her.

Lauren ran her hand over the top of the bedspread and lowered her voice to that of a husky whisper. "I dreamed about you last night."

"Was it a good dream?" Rooster sounded amused.

"The best. We were on your bike together, and I was holding on to you with my head pressed against your back. The wind was in my hair and I felt completely at peace, warm and protected."

"I'll take you on another bike ride, if you wish. I've wanted to go up to Mount Rainier sometime. How does that sound to you?"

"Fabulous." In her mind, she pictured a meadow filled with wildflowers and Rooster lying down with his head in her lap, chewing on a long blade of grass. It seemed so peaceful and quiet, so perfect. And so dissimilar from other relationships she'd had through the years.

They spoke for another hour, disregarding the time difference. Even then, it was hard to pull herself away. That night, when she crawled into bed and closed her eyes, her dreams were once again filled with Rooster.

"Are you as exhausted as I am?" Lauren asked Elisa as they opened the door to the hotel room they shared. They'd arrived in Las Vegas late Friday afternoon and checked into the hotel for the gem conference.

Then early Saturday morning they were up before eight, and after breakfast collected their conference badges and attended the show, walking for what seemed like miles. Elisa had set up a series of meetings with key accounts and dealers she and Garry had worked with previously. In addition to selling jewelry, Garry also designed unique pieces, having learned the trade from his father-in-law.

"Remind me to let Garry do this show next year, and I'll be the one to visit Antwerp." In addition to the gem show, which was held twice a year, the couple routinely flew into Antwerp for diamond purchases.

Elisa collapsed in a chair in the mini-suite and propped her legs up on the ottoman. She wiggled her toes as if to test whether there was any feeling left in her feet.

Lauren sat on the edge of the bed and reached inside her purse for her cell to see if she'd missed a call from Rooster. With the noise in the convention center, it would have been difficult to hear her cell, but apparently Rooster was either sleeping or his day had been as busy as hers. Still, Lauren couldn't help being disappointed.

While there wasn't a missed call or voice mail from Rooster, Lauren saw another text from Katie:

Dietrich and I have made our decision. I doubt it's one my mother will approve of, but this is my life.

Lauren could only speculate what that might mean. She liked Katie a great deal, but Elisa was one of her best friends. Fortunately, Katie's relationship with her father remained strong, and the pregnant teenager had kept the lines of communication open with her family.

"You're frowning," Elisa said, studying her.

Lauren continued to study her phone, speculating about what Katie's message meant. At the same time, she wondered if it would be a good idea to mention Katie's message to Elisa or not. Thankfully, the decision was taken away from her when Elisa's cell rang.

Grabbing it out of her purse, Elisa glanced at the readout. "It's Garry." She took the call and said, "Hi, sweetheart. You wouldn't believe the day Lauren and I have had. I swear we've walked ten miles, but it's been worth it. We found the most incredible . . ." She paused. "What?" she demanded. "This is a joke, right?"

Lauren watched as her friend sank onto the edge of the bed as though her legs had gone too weak to hold her upright. All color seemed to drain from her face.

"Did you talk to Dietrich's parents?" Elisa's eyes went to Lauren, and she gestured helplessly. "Certainly they objected. Earlier in the week, they seemed to agree with us."

Lauren knew that Elisa and Garry had been able to connect with Dietrich's parents, who shared their concern over their son and Katie's situation. They, too, felt that Katie should return to her family and deliver the baby, and if Dietrich and Katie continued to feel strongly about each other, they could marry at some future date. It seemed a sensible plan all around. Unfortunately, neither set of parents had taken into account Dietrich and Katie's wishes.

"No, no, no," Elisa cried as she covered her eyes with her hand. It looked as if she were about to break into sobs.

Lauren sat on the ottoman across from her friend, wanting to be supportive and helpful.

"Garry," Elisa said emphatically, "what are we going to do?" A short silence ensued. "I don't know . . . it couldn't possibly be legal, could it? Yes, yes, I know she's of age, but . . ." The rest of what she intended to say faded into thin air.

Lauren released a soft sigh. If she were a betting woman, she'd wager that Dietrich and Katie had taken matters into their own hands and eloped.

"Naturally, Katie would do this when she knew I'd be away," Elisa said, and then sobbed once. "Yes, yes, I agree, we don't want to lose our daughter. I'll book the next flight back to Seattle." Her voice caught as she spoke, and her hand trembled as she ended the call and returned her cell to her purse.

Lauren scooted the ottoman closer to the bed. "What's happened?" she gently asked her friend.

Elisa covered her face with both hands and took a long moment to compose herself. "It's just as I feared. Katie and Dietrich went to Idaho and got married. It's a disaster, I tell you, an unmitigated disaster. They claim they know what they want, and that's being together for the rest of their lives. Despite everything we said and his own parents' advice, they defied us all and took matters into their own hands."

Lauren gently squeezed Elisa's hand. "You're flying back to Seattle?"

"Yes, as soon as I can book a flight. Garry feels we need to go as a family to Pullman and assure Katie of our love and support."

While Lauren didn't approve of what Katie and her young man had done, she agreed with Garry. Now that the deed was done, they needed to work together and not allow this decision to rip apart their family. "Katie seemed to know what she wants."

"The crazy part is," Elisa said as she wiped the moisture from her cheeks, "I did the same thing. Garry and I were so young, and my parents were ready to string him up, and I defied them and married him despite what they wanted."

Lauren wasn't aware of that, but she knew the young couple had lived with Elisa's parents until Katie had been born. Elisa's parents seemed to have had a change of heart; perhaps Elisa would now, too. This certainly was history repeating itself.

"You and Garry made it work," Lauren reminded her.

"We did, and later my father told me he couldn't have chosen a better husband for me even if he'd had the opportunity. He came to love and appreciate Garry. After a few years, when it became clear my brother had no interest in the business, my father willingly brought Garry into the store. It was Garry my father took under his wing."

"Is he as upset about this as you are?" Lauren asked.

Elisa reached for a tissue and dabbed it beneath her nose. "He might be, but for my sake he won't let it show. Katie has always been a strong-willed child. I should have guessed she'd do something like this."

Lauren hid a smile, knowing that the teenager and her mother shared more than one character trait. She agreed that the two college students were young, but she also felt that with strong family support they would do their best to make their marriage work.

"Dietrich's family sounds like they're well-grounded people," Lauren said, hoping that would encourage Elisa.

Her friend nodded as though in a daze. "I'm sorry to leave you," she whispered as she stood and wandered aimlessly around the room, rubbing her palms together as if she needed to generate heat.

"Don't worry about leaving me. I have a good idea what you want to order, and I'll cover the rest of the show."

Elisa dug her suitcase out of the closet and set it up on top of the bed, opening it. She emptied the dresser drawers, dumping clothes into the case without thought or order.

"While you're packing, I'll check flight times," Lauren told her as she brought up the Internet on her cellphone, logging in with the airlines. She scrolled down the different time options. Because Las Vegas was such a popular destination, there were a number of flight choices. She read off the results, and Elisa chose one that left in a little less than three hours. While she finished packing, Lauren called and made the necessary itinerary changes.

"I'm sorry to do this to you," Elisa said when she'd finished.

"I know; don't worry. There's only one day left. I'll follow up on the contacts we made today and catch the early-afternoon flight out on Sunday the way we originally planned."

"I can't believe Katie would do something like this," Elisa moaned again. "Maybe I should have, seeing that her father and I did basically the same thing."

An hour later, Lauren walked down to the lobby with her friend and saw Elisa off in a taxi. She sighed, and then because she was at loose ends she decided to take this opportunity to play a few slot machines. That had been their original plan: dinner and fun afterward.

Although she was tired and had gone without dinner, Lauren thought she would gamble awhile and then order room service rather than dine alone. She put her cellphone on vibrate because it was unlikely she would hear the ring above the ongoing noise and general racket taking place in the casino. It'd been a bit disappointing not to hear from Rooster. She hoped they'd be able to connect soon.

As she sat feeding money into the slot machine, it came to her that Todd had actually done her a favor by delaying their engagement and marriage. She realized now that she'd been fooling herself when she thought she was in love with the newscaster. What she'd been looking for was stability, a husband and children. Her priorities were askew. Instinctively, Todd must have felt it, too, because he certainly didn't seem in any rush to get to the altar—well, not until recently. He'd tried several times to contact her, but she kept her responses cool and to the point. It was over. How thankful she was now that she'd met Rooster.

Her first twenty dollars disappeared so fast it shocked her. After wandering aimlessly though the casino, Lauren found what looked to be another fun machine. She sat down and placed another twenty-dollar bill in the slot and pushed the button. After only a millisecond's hesitation she watched as the figures spun around in a blur. One hit and she won ten dollars. Well, this appeared to be her lucky day.

She'd feel a whole lot luckier if Rooster were to phone about now. With effort, she pushed the thought of him from her mind, remembering something her mother told her years earlier: a watched pot never boils. If she were constantly looking at her phone, it was sure not to ring. Nevertheless, she kept it in her lap in order to feel the vibration.

Twenty minutes later, at about the same time as she was close to losing her second twenty dollars, her cellphone started to quiver. Right away she saw that it was Rooster and her heart raced with excited anticipation.

"Hi," she said, so glad to hear from him that she felt breathless with happiness.

"Hi," Rooster repeated.

Like always, he sounded crystal clear. It was hard to believe he was thousands of miles away.

"How was the convention?" he asked.

"Crowded, busy, nuts."

"Are you exhausted?"

"I was," she told him, but now, after hearing his voice, she felt a thousand times better. "What time is it there?"

He exhaled as though he, too, had gone through a long, hard day. "Late. I don't know. I kept my watch on California time so I'd know when I could call you."

Her heart melted a little. How thoughtful he was; it made her want to cry, missing him so. "Elisa left. Katie and Dietrich decided they didn't care what their parents said. They drove over to Idaho and eloped."

"Without any family?"

"From the little Elisa said, the only ones there were their best friends from school."

"I imagine Elisa is upset."

Lauren grinned. "That is putting it mildly. Garry thought it would be a good idea if the family met with the young couple. They might not agree with their decision to marry so young, but it's more important that they support them now, seeing that the deed is done."

"That's probably for the best."

"I agree," Lauren concurred.

"You're by yourself, then?"

"I am." Although she was in a casino filled with people, rarely had she felt more alone. It was an odd feeling, being disconnected like this from all that was familiar.

"What are you doing? Are those slot machines I hear in the background?"

Lauren laughed softly. "You caught me red-handed."

"Are you winning?"

"Nope. Guess they don't build these huge casinos by giving money away."

"Would it be possible for you to come to the lobby?"

That was an unusual request. "Sure, but why?"

"There's a surprise waiting for you there."

Right away she withdrew the single dollar she had left in the machine and stood. "A surprise?" she asked. "What kind of surprise?"

"Wait and see," he teased. "Stay on the phone, though, because I want to hear your reaction when you see it."

"Okay." She started toward the lobby, her steps lighter than they had been all day. Once she wove her way to the front of the casino, she paused and looked around. The first thing that caught her attention was a huge bouquet of flowers on top of the concierge's desk.

"The flowers?" she asked. The bouquet was huge.

"Yes, but there's more. Go to the desk and tell the man your name."

"Rooster," she said, laughing now, "what have you done?"

"Wait and see."

She kept the phone pressed tightly against her ear. "Should I hang up first and then call you back?"

"No, stay on the line."

"As you wish."

Sure enough, the concierge seemed to be waiting for her. Lauren kept the phone against her ear. "Hello," she greeted cheerfully. "I'm Lauren Elliott. I understand you have something for me here at the desk."

"Ah, yes, Miss Elliott. If you'll wait here, I'll be right back."

He left the desk momentarily, opened the door behind him, and held it open as Rooster Wayne walked out.

Lauren gasped and dropped her phone, and then before she had time to utter a single sound Rooster was around the desk and she literally flew into his arms.

Chapter Twenty-three

*T*he moment Lauren was in his arms, Rooster closed his eyes and exhaled a deep sigh. This was what he'd been waiting for, been longing to do since the moment he'd left Seattle. He'd been in the air more than twenty-four hours, unable to sleep or read or get caught up in an in-flight movie for the simple reason that he knew at the end of this journey he'd be with Lauren again.

In an amazingly short amount of time the warm, generous woman in his arms had won his heart. Holding her close, he felt giddy with a deep sense of rightness. He was dead on his feet, and yet he felt like he could fly. When Max met Bethanne his friend's life had taken a complete turn. Until this very moment, Rooster had never fully understood or appreciated what had happened to his friend. He continued to hold Lauren tightly against his chest, needing these first few moments to deal with the complex mix of emotions assaulting him. The first one he experienced was unmitigated joy, followed by a powerful surge of relief and excitement. Breathing in the light scent of her perfume, he resisted the urge to kiss her senseless right in the middle of the busy hotel lobby.

Lauren spoke first. "I don't understand . . . I thought—"

He didn't allow her to finish. Waiting a single instant longer to kiss her was beyond his control. He lowered his mouth to hers and was gratified to discover that she had tilted her head back, eagerly anticipating his kiss. After weeks of thinking of little else but seeing Lauren again, he lacked restraint. The kiss was urgent and hungry. For just an instant Rooster feared that he'd gone too far, taken too much, and then she grabbed hold of his neck and kissed him back as if she, too, had thought of little else in the weeks they'd been separated.

When the kiss ended, they stared desperately into each other's eyes until Rooster could bear it no longer and squeezed her close. He could feel her heart pound against his chest, beating in unison with his own.

The concierge cleared his throat. Rooster had completely forgotten about the other man. Somewhat annoyed, he glanced over his shoulder.

"Would you like the flowers sent up to the young lady's room?" the man asked.

"Please." Rooster reached inside his pocket and peeled off a bill and handed it to him.

"How is it you're here?" Lauren asked, her eyes delving into his.

He wrapped his arm around her waist, unwilling to be separated from her by more than a few inches. "My obligation was finished, and I couldn't see staying away from you any longer than necessary."

"But you said you'd been planning this vacation for months. How often do you get to New Zealand?"

"Not often," he admitted, and because she tempted him beyond reason, he bent down and kissed her again. "Nothing I could see, no sight, no natural phenomenon was worth being away from you a minute longer." One day he would return to the South Pacific, but when he did he'd make sure Lauren accompanied him.

"Oh, Rooster."

She leaned into him, and he bent down and inhaled the light scent of her hair. He'd dreamed of this moment, held the vision in his mind during the long hours of his flights, and fully intended to savor every second.

"When did you fly back?"

"Today. I came straight here, after changing planes in San Francisco."

"How did you know where I was?" she asked, looking both confused and happy all at once.

"You told me."

"I did? It must have slipped my mind, but I'm so grateful I did."

"Have you eaten?" he asked.

"No. What about you?"

Rooster couldn't remember his last meal. Although meal service was offered on the flight home, he'd turned it down. "I'm famished, but I'm more in the mood for breakfast than dinner."

"I wasn't hungry before, but I am now." Taking his hand in hers, she led the way to the coffee shop, where the hostess escorted them to a table.

Rooster had a difficult time studying the menu when all he really wanted was to look at Lauren. The depth of his feelings for her had caught him in hurricane-force winds, sweeping him up in a whirlwind. Fearing his staring would make her uncomfortable, he decided it would be best to start a conversation. "So, your boss's daughter eloped?"

"Yes. What's ironic is that Elisa and Garry did the same thing when they were in college. Elisa was the same age as Katie is now."

"And the marriage worked."

"Yes. They're a wonderful couple. Katie's a great kid, but I understand Elisa and Garry's concern. If she was my daughter I'd probably feel the same way, though Katie's sensible and mature for her age."

"And the young man?"

"He's the oldest in a family of eight children, and from everything I've heard he's responsible and conscientious. Katie could have made a far worse choice."

"Have they known each other long?"

"Apparently, they met soon after Katie arrived on campus. From what little I know, the attraction was instantaneous. From the moment they met, they were inseparable."

To Rooster's way of thinking, that was how he'd felt about Lauren. Their waitress arrived, and even then it was difficult for Rooster to tear his gaze away from Lauren long enough to give the woman his order.

As soon as the waitress left, Lauren said, "Katie knew the minute she met Dietrich, the same way I knew after—" she stopped abruptly, and her cheeks filled with hot color.

Rooster stared at her long and hard. "Go on," he urged.

Embarrassed, she looked away.

"Are you saying you felt the same way about me as young Katie did about her Dietrich?" he asked, enjoying her discomfort. It made his head spin to know she had experienced the same feelings he had. Rooster had known, too, and the truth of it had been pounded into him these last few weeks while he'd been traveling. Lauren was all he could think about. It was intended as a business trip, but wine had been the last thing on his mind. All that seemed to matter was how long it would be before he could be with Lauren again.

Without meeting his gaze, she nodded. "I've waited for years to meet a man like you," she whispered, and seemed unable to find her normal voice. "You make me feel things I've never experienced before."

He knew exactly what she meant, because it had been the same with him. "I've been waiting for you for years, Lauren, hardly knowing what I was waiting for, never suspecting it would ever happen."

She stretched her hand across the table, and he gripped it tightly with his own.

"We haven't known each other long," she said, as though it was necessary to discount this magnetic attraction.

"Does that matter?" he asked. "Are you going to feel differently a few weeks from now? Is what you feel going to change?"

"No." Her voice was sure, confident. "You?"

He didn't entertain a single doubt. "No."

Their gazes seemed locked together, and Rooster doubted that a fire alarm would have been enough to cause him to break eye contact. His heart pounded hard and strong, and he sensed that this could quite possibly be one of the most important conversations of his life.

Lauren raised her hand to her chest. "I know in my heart what I feel, what I want."

Rooster was almost afraid to ask what she wanted, for fear it wouldn't align with his own desire. It seemed obvious to him that they were meant to be together. "What is it you want?" he asked. As soon as the words left his mouth his heart started to race, his pulse pounding in his ear like a military drum, fearing her feelings didn't match the intensity of his own.

She hesitated and lowered her gaze as though afraid to admit what she was thinking.

"Lauren." He said her name softly. "I didn't realize what I wanted in a wife until I met you."

Her gaze instantly flew back to him. She blinked, and for a moment he thought he saw tears well in her eyes. "Are you . . . asking to marry me?" she asked slowly.

Now wasn't the time to backpedal; it was exactly what he was asking. He'd never considered that it would happen like this in the middle of a coffee shop without a declaration of love or flowery words, but then he wasn't a man who was likely to say the things a woman most wanted to hear. "Yes," he said, being as straightforward as he knew how to be. "Yes, I'm asking you to be my wife, to share the rest of our lives with each other. I'd like us to have children and raise them to be responsible, God-fearing adults, and for the two of us to grow old together."

No doubt about it now, those were tears in her eyes. Her hands flew to cover her mouth. Rooster was instantly concerned, fearing he might have said all the wrong things. He frowned, wondering what he should do now, if anything.

His eyes didn't waver from hers, and he held his breath while he waited for her response. When none came, he realized he'd made a terrible mistake. He could easily blame it on the long sleepless flight.

He'd been up almost thirty hours. "I know it's too soon. I apologize if I—"

"It isn't too soon," she whispered, interrupting him. "I'd like nothing better than to be your wife."

He was stunned speechless. He hadn't known what to expect, hadn't even considered asking her so soon. A lump filled his throat as he struggled to grab hold of his emotions. As soon as he could speak clearly, he asked, "Okay, when?"

Her hands made a restless movement, as if she wasn't sure. "I wouldn't like a long engagement."

"Me, neither."

"Next month?" she asked.

He frowned. Even that seemed far too long to wait. "Next week?"

Her eyes lit up with a bright smile, and she placed her hand over her mouth.

"What?" he asked, seeing that she was all but laughing.

"You're going to think I've lost my mind."

He frowned. "What are you suggesting?"

"What's wrong with tonight?"

He was astounded. "Tonight? You mean . . . today. Now?"

The waitress delivered their meals, which they both ignored.

Lauren nodded. "I'm not giving you a chance to change your mind, Rooster Wayne."

Change his mind? Was she out of hers? If anyone would be susceptible to a change of heart, he would think it would be Lauren. Clearly, after so many hours awake, the drastic time change, and everything else, he wasn't himself . . . wasn't thinking clearly. "My immediate reaction is to do it. But I don't want us to get caught up in some craziness we might later regret, so let's sleep on it."

"I'm not changing my mind, Rooster."

He sincerely doubted he would, either. "It might be hard to arrange at the last minute like this. I'd feel better about it if we waited until tomorrow."

"Agreed," she said.

"And if you feel the same way in the morning . . ."

"I will," she promised.

"So will I," he added. "Then we'll see to the necessary paperwork first thing."

Again, she concurred.

Rooster rubbed his hand over his eyes. He had one other concern. "What about your parents?"

"What about them?"

"Before we continue, I'd like to speak to your father."

"My dad?" She sounded shocked.

"Yes. I want to do this properly, Lauren. I don't want him to think I've coerced you against your will, especially if we're going to rush into this. Have you even mentioned me?"

"I have to my mom and sister, but Dad and I don't talk on the phone that often." She sounded uncertain, as if contacting her father wasn't such a good idea. "Dad can be a bit short-tempered."

"And he might well be, with me stealing away his daughter, but I'll chance it. Why don't I talk to him now?"

"Now?" She was hesitant.

Rooster brought out his cell. "Give me your parents' phone number."

She rattled it off and then bit her lower lip while Rooster waited for the connection.

"Let me talk to him first," Lauren said urgently.

Rooster hesitated before handing her his cell. Her eyes connected with his, and then she relaxed. "Hi, Daddy," she said, sounding chipper and excited. "I wanted to let you know I'm getting married."

Unable to hear the other end of the conversation, Rooster waited impatiently.

"No, it isn't Todd," she said, and cast Rooster an apologetic look. "His name is John. John Wayne." Another brief pause. "Not that John Wayne, Dad. He goes by Rooster. Yes . . . yes, I realize it's an unusual name. Okay, okay, I'll put him on the phone." She placed her hand over the receiver. "He doesn't sound happy about this."

Rooster took the cell out of her hand and winked at her. "Don't worry," he whispered before placing the cell against his ear. "Mr. El-liott, this is Rooster Wayne."

Lauren's father's voice boomed over the other end of the cell. "Bill Elliott. Now, what's this I hear about you wanting to marry my daughter?"

"You heard correctly."

"Do you love her?"

It astonished Rooster to realize he'd asked Lauren to be his wife and not once had he expressed his love to her. "Very much."

"Are you employed?" he demanded. "I won't have my daughter supporting you, so be clear on that."

"No worries there," Rooster assured the other man. "I have a partnership in a California wine-distribution company."

That appeared to satisfy him. "You haven't known Lauren long, have you? The last I heard she had her heart set on that pretty-boy television newscaster. Have to say I never cared much for him."

Rooster grinned. He shared the other man's feelings and sensed that he was going to get along just fine with Lauren's father.

"When do you figure to get married?" the elder Elliott asked.

"We were thinking, seeing we know our minds, that we'd like to make it soon."

"How soon?"

Rooster didn't figure Lauren's father would be keen on his answer. "Very soon. Tomorrow."

The line went silent. "Any particular reason you're in such an all-fired rush?" Bill Elliott demanded.

"Yes. I love Lauren. I'm thirty-nine, and I've been waiting for her my entire life. Having found her, I can't see any reason to delay what we both want."

The line went still, as if Lauren's father wasn't quite sure what to say. "You ever been in jail?"

"Nope. My record is clean. I had a bit of trouble as a teenager, but that was years ago."

"What kind of trouble?"

"Shoplifting. I learned my lesson, and it wasn't the law that gave it to me; it was my dad."

Bill Elliott chuckled. "Ever declared bankruptcy?"

"No. I have a savings account and a retirement investment plan as well."

"Good."

"We'd like your blessing and, if possible, for you and Mrs. Elliott to join us for the ceremony."

"You in Seattle?"

"No, we're in Vegas."

This information was followed by a short pause. "You'll go through with this marriage whether you have our support or not, won't you?" he demanded.

"Yes," Rooster admitted, "but I'd much rather have your approval. I'm sincere. I love Lauren, and I will do everything within my power to be a good husband and to make her happy."

"I have to say you've got guts, young man."

"Your blessing would mean a great deal, sir."

"By heaven, you've got balls. Let me talk to her mother and we'll get back to you about getting to Vegas within the next twenty-four hours."

"Then we have your approval?" Rooster asked.

"Yes, you do, but I want it understood there won't be any wedding until we've done a background check on you."

"Fair enough. I wouldn't expect anything less."

"Let me talk to my daughter," Bill Elliott said.

Rooster gave the phone back to Lauren. She smiled as she took it from him. "Yes, Daddy," she said. "I love him, too. He's a good man, and once you meet him you'll agree with my choice."

They spoke only a moment longer, and then Lauren returned the phone. "He thinks we're both a little nuts."

"Can't say I blame him."

Rooster reached for his dinner.

"Mom is calling my sister, and I think the whole family is planning to show."

"Good."

"Is there anyone you want to invite?" she asked.

The only real family Rooster had was Max. His parents were both gone, and he was an only child. "Max and Bethanne."

Lauren nodded and then giggled as she reached for her fork. "My dad is right, we're both a little nuts, but Rooster, I have to tell you I've never been this happy in my life."

He nearly melted under the strength of her smile. Truth was, he felt the same. It'd been a very long time since he'd been this excited or this content.

Chapter Twenty-four

$\mathcal{B}$ethanne was startled out of a sound sleep by her cellphone. Half sitting up, and leaning on one elbow, she glanced at the digital read-out of the bedside clock. She hadn't been sleeping well for the last several days and, exhausted, had fallen into bed after what had proved to be a troublesome week.

"Hello," she whispered.

"Bethanne, sweetheart, did I wake you?"

Instantly, she was alert. "Max? Is everything all right?" He wouldn't be calling if it wasn't important.

"Yes, it's wonderful."

She rubbed the sleep from her eyes. "It's after midnight."

"I know. Sorry to wake you, love, but what I have to tell you is amazing."

It must be, for him to call this late. "What's going on?"

"A wedding."

"A wedding," she repeated, sitting upright now. "Who's getting married?"

Max chuckled as though highly amused. "Rooster and Lauren."

This made no sense whatsoever. "Hold on a minute, I thought Rooster was in New Zealand."

"So did I. Apparently, he couldn't bear to be away from Lauren and flew back, surprising everyone. He met up with her at some conference she was attending in Las Vegas."

"He flew to Las Vegas?" Bethanne was having a hard time taking in what Max was telling her.

"After Rooster arrived the two decided they were in love and they might as well get married."

Bethanne was shocked. "It's a bit rushed, isn't it?"

"That's what I said, but Rooster isn't about to change his mind, and from what he said, Lauren feels the same. He asked me to be his best man."

"When's the wedding?"

"Sunday afternoon. Lauren's parents and sister are all flying in, and I'm going, too. Can you manage a couple days away? I know it's not good timing for you." This was the first weekend in two months that they hadn't been able to be together. Bethanne knew how busy Max was with Rooster out of the country, and she had her own reasons for begging off. It'd been a dreadful week, and she feared her troubles with Annie would only weigh him down.

"Bethanne?"

"Sorry, I was mentally reviewing my schedule. When do you plan to leave?"

"Seven tomorrow morning. It was the only seat available. Santa Rosa has a small airport, and I didn't want to drive into San Francisco if I could avoid it."

"Do you have a reservation for a room?"

"Yes. I saw to that right away. Can you make it happen?"

Mulling it over, Bethanne leaned back against the thick pillows, sighed, and said, "I'll be there."

"Great." His tone grew serious then. "This has been a lonely weekend without you."

Bethanne felt the same. "I miss you like crazy."

"Me, too."

They chatted only a few minutes longer. Bethanne closed her eyes and sighed. Rooster and Lauren, she mused, and then grinned. She was pleased for her husband's best friend and business partner, and for Lauren as well. It hadn't taken much to realize the two were falling in love. With another couple she might have been concerned, but not with these two. They were both well-grounded, mature adults who knew what they wanted in life. She was happy for them, and neither one came into the marriage with a lot of extra baggage.

Despite this unexpected bit of good news, Bethanne's heart felt heavy. She hadn't seen or heard from Annie all week, nor had she shown up at the office. Her daughter seemed to have taken Bethanne's words to heart and was looking for employment elsewhere, although Annie hadn't bothered to let anyone at the office know of her decision. Bethanne had again been tempted to ask her ex-husband to intercede on her behalf. She'd battled indecision all week, hoping to hear from Annie, but it was not to be.

Annie hadn't called, and Bethanne had stubbornly refused to give in. Bethanne was willing to admit her daughter had come by that obstinate streak naturally.

Awake now, she tossed aside the covers and went downstairs to her computer, logging on to the traveling website she most often used. Thankfully, she was able to book a flight for late Sunday morning with a return early Tuesday. Because she was unsure what time the wedding would take place, this seemed to be the best option.

Once she had the flights booked, she texted Max the information. He seemed excited and happy, but Bethanne doubted that she would be able to hide her misery. If Annie had quit without notice, and that seemed to be the case, then he would find out eventually, anyway.

———

Max met her at the Las Vegas airport at baggage claim. They hugged, and after retrieving her suitcase, he led her toward the parking garage. No sooner had she clicked her seat belt into place when her husband turned toward her.

"Okay, what's wrong?"

She forced a laugh. "What makes you think anything is wrong?"

"Bethanne, please. We might not have been married long, but I know you, and one look told me you're upset about something. I heard it in your voice this week, too."

Tightness gripped her chest, and she looked down at her hands. "It's Annie."

Max sighed. "I should have known."

"She didn't show up for work all week."

"Have you talked to Andrew?"

That had been the first thing she did. "Yes, but he hasn't heard from her, either."

"What about Grant? He must know something."

"I'm sure he does, but I refuse to call him. After that last stunt Annie and Grant pulled, that's exactly what they're looking for me to do. They want me to go running to Grant for help, and I refuse to do that. Eventually, Annie will wake up to the fact that her father is a player."

"Oh, sweetheart, I'm so sorry."

"You did nothing wrong," she rushed to tell him. "If this is what Annie wants, then it's her choice."

Max's face darkened with a thick frown. "I'm flying back to Seattle with you."

"Max, no. This is my problem."

"But—"

"Please." She pressed her hand over his forearm. "Let me handle this my own way."

He looked away and seemed to think long and hard before he responded. "I don't know that I can bear to see you this unhappy, not if it's in my power to make matters right."

"Nothing you say or do will change Annie's opinion of you. For you to even try plays right into her hands. I can't tell you how sorry I am about all this. I've tried to keep you out of it entirely—"

"Which is why we weren't together this weekend. Right?"

She had no option but to agree. "Right."

Max took hold of her hand and brought it to his lips, kissing her knuckles. "We're together now, though," he whispered suggestively.

Bethanne recognized that gleam in his eyes and laughed out loud. "Max Scranton, how can you think about sex at a time like this?"

"How can I not when the woman who owns my heart is sitting right next to me?"

Tipping her head so that it rested against his shoulder, Bethanne felt the weight of the world drift away. "You make me so happy," she told him.

"Good, that's my goal. Don't worry, love, we'll get through this thing with Annie."

"Of course we will."

"But for right now we have a wedding to help plan and an overly anxious groom." Max paused and chuckled. "I don't know when I've seen Rooster more flustered."

"Is he happy?"

"He's giddy."

"What about Lauren?"

Max pulled out of the parking space and followed the signs to the airport exit. "She's at a conference for most of the day. From what Max said, they'd originally planned the wedding for today, until Lauren remembered she had obligations until late in the afternoon."

Bethanne grinned. "Ah, young love."

"Actually, the timing has worked out well. The extra day gives her parents the opportunity to fly in, along with her sister."

"Wonderful." They merged into the freeway traffic. At this point, Bethanne didn't have a clue where Max had booked a room. Not that it mattered.

Max glanced in his side-view mirror before he changed lanes. "As I started to tell you, Rooster is beside himself. He's already booked the chapel, found a minister, and made a reservation for the honeymoon suite." He chuckled. "Want to make a guess which one of the three he took care of first?"

"Max!"

His smile grew bigger. "In addition to everything else, he's dealing with jet lag and is punch-drunk with love."

This was a sight Bethanne was eager to see.

"I've never seen him this happy," Max said, turning serious. "He said you and I inspired him. He'd mostly given up on falling in love, I think. He had a bad experience in his early twenties. He's dated over the years, but never seriously. Shortly after he came onboard with me my life fell apart. I'm grateful he was there when I needed a friend most."

Bethanne pressed her hand over her husband's thigh, knowing that he was referring to the death of his wife and daughter.

"I basically abandoned him and the business," Max continued. "It hasn't been until the last year or so since I've been back that I've come to realize how much responsibility Rooster took upon himself. Not that I would have been much help even if I had been around. He buried himself in work. By all that's right, he deserves Lauren. I couldn't ask for a better friend or partner."

By the time Bethanne was in the room and had unpacked her suitcase, it was noon. She was about to join Max when there was a knock on the door.

When she answered, she found Lauren standing in the hallway.

"Lauren," she cried, excited to see the other woman. "Congratulations."

Her friend flew into the room. "I don't have another meeting for an hour. Bethanne, I'm so grateful you came." She started pacing the confined area. All at once she stopped. "Tell me, honestly, do you think Rooster and I are crazy?"

"No," she responded thoughtfully. "I think you're in love."

"We are," Lauren confirmed, "we really are. I've never felt like this, and Rooster says it's the same with him."

Walking about the room, Lauren couldn't seem to hold still.

"Are you having second thoughts?" Bethanne asked, just to be certain.

"No," she cried, as if this should be a major concern. "That's just it. Shouldn't I? I mean, we barely know each other, but we've talked every day, sometimes for hours and hours. I can't believe we're doing this, but it's what I want, what Rooster wants, too.

"We promised ourselves that if either of us had a change of heart in the morning we'd call the whole thing off. We didn't. If anything, we were more convinced than ever that we belong together.

"I'm overwhelmed with joy, practically squirming with it, and yet if two weeks ago you'd told me I'd seriously be considering marrying a man I barely knew, I wouldn't have believed it possible."

Bethanne understood all too well.

"Shouldn't I be worried?" Lauren demanded. "Shouldn't I be having second thoughts? A rational person would, don't you think? Am I off my rocker?"

"Well . . ." Bethanne wasn't allowed to finish.

"But I don't," Lauren said, and hugged her stomach as she continued on her rapid walk back and forth across the room. "Nothing has felt more right in my entire life."

"Rooster is a good man."

"I know. Do you know what he did?"

Again, Bethanne wasn't given the opportunity to respond.

"Rooster insisted on talking to my father. He asked my dad if he'd be willing to let him marry his daughter . . . me. Really, who does that anymore? I'd mentioned Rooster to my mom and sister, but my dad hadn't heard a word about him, and here was this man my dad didn't know, asking to marry me."

"What did your dad say?" Bethanne asked.

Lauren stopped walking and sighed expressively. "Dad was so taken with Rooster that he basically agreed, but he did mention that he was having a background check done on him."

"I doubt there's anything there that would be cause for alarm." Although she didn't know Rooster as well as Max did, Bethanne was confident she was right.

"Tell me, Bethanne, are we crazy?"

"No," she said softly.

"I'm so grateful you're here. It means the world to me."

"I'm glad I'm here, too; it's important to Max, and to Rooster, too. He's told us often enough we're his family, but now he has you, too."

"You know what?" Lauren said, sitting down on the edge of the bed and gripping her hands together. "I'd begun to doubt that there were men like Rooster left in this world. It's almost as if he's too good to be true."

"I believe Max told me that Rooster said basically the same thing about you."

Lauren's eyes went soft. "My parents and sister will arrive this afternoon, and Mom insisted I buy a new dress . . . I didn't pack anything appropriate for a wedding, but then it isn't like I'd planned to get married this weekend."

"Have you been in touch with Elisa and Garry?"

"Yes." Lauren planted her hands on top of her head. "But I can't tell them. Not right away. Their daughter eloped, and they're headed to eastern Washington to meet with their daughter's husband and his family. I have to be at the store Tuesday afternoon. Is that nuts? Rooster and I aren't going to get any time for a honeymoon; I'm not worried, though. We'll take one later."

"Is Rooster flying back to Seattle with you?"

Lauren nodded. "He has the next several days free, and as soon as Elisa and Garry are back we're going to take off ourselves, just the two of us. My parents mentioned holding a reception in Seattle later in the summer."

"That sounds perfect. Be sure and tell them I'll be happy to help with that."

"Thank you; that's so kind." She bit into her lower lip. "I wish I could tell Elisa, but she's already got so much on her mind with her daughter and her new son-in-law that I don't want to add to it." Lauren checked her watch. "I've got to get back to the convention. I stopped by to let you know how grateful I am that you're going to be here for the wedding."

———

Rooster didn't have much experience with these matters; Bethanne was the expert when it came to weddings and such, being that she was in the business. Still, Rooster was astonished at how well everything had come together. From all outward appearances it looked as if this wedding had been planned weeks in advance.

The hotel's wedding chapel was filled with the most gorgeous arrangements of white flowers. Rooster stood with Lauren under an archway with drooping white and blue wisteria. Amazingly, his bride, along with his future mother-in-law, had found the most beautiful beaded white dress that fit Lauren as if it had been custom-sewn for her. Lauren's sister was at her side as the matron of honor.

Max stood beside him as his best man, and, frankly, Rooster was grateful. Twice during the actual ceremony he went light-headed and feared he was about to pass out. While it could be attributed to exhaustion, the time change, and excitement, he knew otherwise. This was love so intense it threatened to overwhelm him. Ever since he'd lost his parents, he'd drifted, anchorless, basically alone. Lauren had changed that. No longer was he a sole entity. With her in his life, he had hope and a future. Every time he thought about having children with her, he could feel his blood pressure skyrocket. Naturally, he hoped for a son, but he certainly would be pleased with a daughter as well.

When it came time to repeat their vows, he could barely get the words out fast enough. When Lauren repeated her vows, her gaze found his, and tears welled in her eyes as she said the words. Her voice seemed to reverberate around the chapel. To his astonishment, he felt moisture fill his own eyes, which he quickly blinked away.

The room seemed to be filled with happiness. After the ceremony, when the pronouncement was made and he'd kissed Lauren, they were instantly surrounded by family and friends. He saw that many of them had felt the same emotion, the same overwhelming sense that while this marriage might have been arranged quickly, the two of them, Lauren and he, were meant to be together.

Chapter Twenty-five

If you don't like it, it's just not done yet.
—Heidi Dascher,
fiber artist, The Artful Ewe

"Grandma," Casey said, looking down at the Scrabble board and frowning, "P-O-S-E-T isn't a word."

Lydia's mother seemed confused and looked to Lydia for clarification. "It isn't?"

"Check the dictionary," Lydia suggested.

"Okay." Casey reached for her cellphone and concentrated on that.

It was a lazy Tuesday afternoon, and the drizzle and overcast skies prevented Lydia from the yardwork she'd planned on doing. Brad certainly hadn't objected. The Mariners game was being televised, and Cody hated yardwork nearly as much as his father did. Seeing that the men would be involved in baseball for a good portion of the evening, Casey had suggested they visit Grandma.

Lydia was eager to spend time with her daughter. The ongoing saga with Casey's nightmares continued. Just the night before, once again, the teenager had woken the entire household with her screams. Lydia had spent forty-five minutes with her afterward, holding and comforting Casey. These dreams shook Lydia. Because her daughter refused to discuss any aspect of the nightmare, Lydia was left with a feeling of helplessness and frustration.

"Nope, sorry, Grandma," Casey said as she set her phone aside. "*Poset* isn't a real word."

Mary Lou Hoffman looked crestfallen. "I thought for sure that was a good word."

"P-O-E-T-S works," Casey supplied, and shuffled the tiny wooden tiles around, helping her grandmother. "And look, by putting it in this spot it adds up to even more points because you land on a double-point word space."

"I do?"

Lydia continued to carefully watch her mother. It worried her how quickly her mother's mind drifted from the past to the present and to places unknown. At first it was a few noticeable slips, but in the last six months there'd been a dramatic turn. The doctors had taken her off the medication she'd been prescribed that was said to help with memory function. After a certain period of time the prescription lost its effectiveness. That had been a turning point, and the decline had been rapid ever since then.

"Your father used to recite poetry to me when we dated," Mary Lou Hoffman said, looking at Casey.

"He did?"

Lydia noticed how willing Casey was to pretend nothing was amiss. Clearly her mother had Casey confused with her or Margaret.

A wistful look came over the older woman. "Henry Wadsworth Longfellow was one of his favorites."

"We read one of his poems in my English class," Casey said. "It was all right, I guess, but I like Shel Silverstein better."

Even more confused now, her mother looked to Lydia. "Who is that, dear? Should I know him?"

"Shel Silverstein is another poet," Casey explained, without going into detail.

"His poetry has humor," Lydia added. "He's a favorite of Cody's, too." She hoped not to bewilder her mother any more than she already was.

"Your father is a romantic," her mother continued. "He'd never admit to it, of course, but he enjoyed memorizing poetry. He recites it to me in bed. I always loved that. Why, just the other day he read me the most beautiful poem . . . He said it came out of the Bible. I didn't know the Bible had poetry in it, did you?"

"The Psalms do," Casey said softly. "I learned that in Sunday school class."

Lydia's mother looked down on the Scrabble board. "I'm not doing very well, am I?"

"You're doing fine, Mom," Lydia assured her. It was difficult to see her mother's mind wander. Her father had been dead nearly ten years now, and for her mother to speak of him as if he were still alive forced Lydia to accept the fact that her mother was losing mental ground faster than she realized.

"Look, Grandma, you're ahead," Casey said, totaling the game points.

"I am?" The older woman smiled softly and then looked away. "I do miss your father so," she whispered.

"But you talk to him all the time," Casey reminded her.

"I do. He visits often these days. He told me not long ago that I'll be joining him soon."

"Where is Dad?" Lydia asked, forgetting the game and taking her mother's hands in her own.

"I don't know, dear, he won't tell me. He was with me earlier before you arrived, and he said it wouldn't be long now."

Lydia bit into her lower lip and was afraid her mother might be right. It wasn't only her mental capabilities that had fallen of late, but the older woman's health seemed to be declining at an even faster pace.

"What are you talking about?" Casey demanded. "You can't travel, Grandma."

"Travel?" she repeated. "No, I don't suppose I can. I don't have any idea what's happened to my suitcase."

Casey laughed.

Someone knocked on the door, and Casey was on her feet and rushing toward the door before Lydia had a chance to scoot back her chair.

"Oh, hi," Casey said, and stepped aside to let in one of the nurse's aides.

A woman with salt-and-pepper hair and a pink sweater over her uniform of white shirt and pants came into the small apartment. Her name badge identified her as Sylvia. "I hope you don't mind me interrupting."

"Of course not," Lydia assured her.

"I heard you were visiting your mother," she said, directing the comment to Lydia, "and I wondered if it would be all right to give you the scarves."

"The scarves?"

"Yes. I ride the bus into work, and there was a yarn basket at the bus stop. I've been knitting on the scarf almost every afternoon. It's finished now, and a second one as well. I don't get over to Blossom Street that often, and seeing that you're here, I thought I could give them to you now . . . if that's all right?"

"No problem," Lydia said. "I'd be happy to take them with me."

"Great." Sylvia thanked her with a quick smile. "I'll put them down by the reception desk, and you can collect them on your way out."

"Perfect. Thank you." Lydia had lost count of the number of scarves she'd collected from knitters all over the downtown neighborhoods. Baskets had turned up in the most unusual places, and when the projects were finished they were delivered to A Good Yarn.

"We're playing Scrabble," Casey explained to Sylvia.

"I'm ahead," her mother added.

"That's good, Mrs. Hoffman."

"She didn't cheat, either."

"Casey!" Lydia chastised.

Her mother's eyes drifted closed before she caught herself and forced them back open. It was clear the visit and the Scrabble game had worn her out. Sylvia left, and Lydia turned and said to Casey, "I think it's time we go."

"So soon?" the teenager objected.

"Mom's getting tired," Lydia said, lowering her voice.

Her mother looked up, and in that instant Lydia knew that her own mother didn't recognize who she was. "Can I get you anything before we go, *Mom*?" she asked, emphasizing their relationship.

Her mother blinked several times, and then it seemed her mind cleared. "I don't need anything."

Casey started to collect the Scrabble pieces and put them back inside the plastic bag before folding up the game board. Lydia half expected her daughter to protest their leaving before they finished playing. Surprisingly, she didn't. Even Casey couldn't ignore the fact that her grandmother's decline was more and more apparent.

After hugging her mother, Lydia left her mom's small apartment feeling sad and a little depressed. It was time to prepare herself to let go and release this woman who had given her life.

Once they were in the hallway outside the apartment, Casey asked, "Grandma's not going to die, is she?"

The question was heavy on Lydia's mind as well. "We all die sooner or later," she said, being as evasive as she could.

"I mean die *soon*," Casey clarified. "All that talk about her joining Grandpa worries me." She jerked her backpack over her shoulder as if the weight of it had become heavier than she could carry.

"It worries me, too," Lydia whispered.

Casey was silent until they reached the receptionist's desk and collected the knitted scarves.

"That was a stupid idea," the teenager muttered.

"What was?" Lydia asked.

"Whoever thought of those baskets with the yarn. It was stupid."

Lydia realized Casey's negative attitude was a result of the discussion regarding her grandmother. "Actually, whoever thought of it must be a generous, thoughtful person."

"Why would you say that?" Casey asked. "All I ever heard was you complaining about it."

"No, I haven't." Lydia was offended that Casey viewed her concern as complaining.

"Yes, you did," she snapped. "You got all upset about that newspaper lady coming to talk to you."

"I wasn't upset," Lydia explained. "I was worried because she seemed to think I was responsible, and I couldn't take the credit when I didn't have anything to do with it."

Once outside, they quickened their steps to avoid the drizzle.

"I hate the rain," Casey muttered as she reached the parking lot.

"April showers bring May flowers."

"It's June. We should be watching flowers grow instead of dealing with this crap."

"Casey, watch your mouth."

Her daughter climbed into the passenger seat and slumped her shoulders forward as if saying she didn't want to be interrupted. "I still say it's stupid."

"The rain?"

"That, too."

"Are you still hung up on the knitted scarves?"

Casey didn't answer.

"Actually, I think it was a good idea," Lydia said conversationally, ignoring her daughter's ugly mood. "It's certainly brought attention to the shop. Business has increased by more than twenty percent since the knitting baskets started turning up."

Completely uninterested, Casey glared out the side window. "Can I bake cookies when I get home?"

"If you want."

"Gingersnaps, okay?"

Lydia hesitated. "You know those are Cody's least favorite cookie, don't you?"

"I happen to like gingersnaps."

"You like a lot of cookies."

"So now I'm fat."

"Casey, my goodness, what's the matter with you?"

"You just said I was fat."

"I most certainly did not. What I meant to say was that there are any number of cookies you could choose to bake that the entire family would enjoy."

"Why do I always have to cater to what Cody likes? It's because he's Brad's real son and I'm adopted, isn't it?"

Lydia was fast losing her patience. "That isn't it at all. If you want to bake gingersnaps, then go ahead."

"I don't want to bake anything."

"Fine, then don't."

For the remainder of the ride home, the silence in the car was as thick as a concrete block. As soon as Lydia put the vehicle in park, Casey opened the car door and jumped out as if she couldn't get away from Lydia fast enough.

Gathering her patience, Lydia waited for a moment before following her daughter into the house. As soon as she opened the door, Brad looked up from the baseball game and frowned. "What's Casey's problem?"

"What happened now?" she asked.

Brad gestured weakly with his hands. "Don't know. She walked in the door, looked at Cody, and called him a spoiled brat, and then proceeded down the hallway to her room. She nearly knocked the pictures off the wall, she slammed the door so hard."

"Oh, dear."

"What did I do wrong?" Cody asked, joining his parents.

Lydia shrugged. "Casey wanted to bake cookies and suggested gingersnaps."

"I don't like gingersnaps," Cody said.

"Which I told her, and now she's upset."

"Should I tell her I'll eat gingersnaps?" Cody asked, eager to appease his sister.

"No way," Brad insisted. "Let her pout, if that's what she wants."

Lydia put away her purse and removed her sweater before joining her husband in the family area. Brad had the television on, watching the game against the Los Angeles Dodgers. Needing a distraction, she reached for her knitting.

"Casey's worried about her grandmother," Lydia said after a few stitches. "And frankly, so am I."

"Anything new?" Brad reverted his attention from the screen back to Lydia.

"She claims she's talking to my dad again."

"Does Grandma really talk to him?" Cody asked, sitting on the floor and bunching up his knees.

"Of course she doesn't," Brad insisted. "He's been dead since before I knew Lydia."

"What do you think, Mom?" Cody asked.

She hardly knew what to say. "I think my mother misses him so much that in her mind he is still alive."

"Oh." Cody had an odd look as if he was willing to accept what she said even if he didn't understand.

About a half hour later Casey came out of her bedroom. "You can bake gingersnap cookies if you want," Cody called out to her. "I'll eat them."

"I don't feel like baking," Casey said as she slumped down on the sofa.

The phone rang, and Cody waited for a moment before he rushed to answer. Generally, Casey was the one who got to the phone first. "Hello," her son said into the receiver.

"Yes. Hold on a minute, please.

"Mom," he said. "It's the place where Grandma lives. They said it's an emergency."

Chapter Twenty-six

$\mathcal{H}$er first few days back at the shop, Lauren couldn't get out of John Michael Jewelry fast enough. She hadn't officially been married a week, and a good portion of that time had been spent dealing with customers at the store. Elisa and Garry remained in eastern Washington, and Lauren felt responsible for keeping the store open and running smoothly.

Earlier, Rooster had sent her a text saying he'd be waiting for her at The French Cafe just down the street when she was available. As soon as all the diamonds and higher-priced gems were safely tucked inside the safe, Lauren was free to leave.

Although the skies remained overcast, Rooster had chosen a sidewalk table. He stood as she approached. They briefly hugged, and she noticed that he'd ordered her a latte, which was waiting for her. Her heart melted a little; how thoughtful he was.

"Well, how was your day?" Rooster asked, looking relaxed as he sat down and crossed his long legs.

"Frustrating," she admitted. "I couldn't wait to get off so I could be with you. What about you?" she asked.

"Mostly frustrating," he admitted, grinning and then lowering his voice. "I kept calculating how many more hours it would be before I could get you back in bed."

"Rooster!"

He swung his head, and his ponytail bounced against his leather jacket. "What can I say, I'm a healthy red-blooded male who's eager to make love to his wife."

It hadn't surprised her that Rooster had proven to be a thoughtful, gentle lover. It was hard to take in the fact that she was a married woman, although Rooster left her in little doubt of that. For a quickly arranged wedding, it had been wonderful. Lauren was grateful her family had been able to attend, and it'd been a bonus to have Max and Bethanne with them, too. Already, her mother and Bethanne had their heads together working on a reception.

"Did you connect with your boss?" Rooster asked, reaching for his coffee.

Lauren knew he was eager for Elisa and Garry's return so they could have a few days together alone.

"We spoke briefly this afternoon." The conversation had been far too short and, unfortunately, one-sided. Elisa continued to be stressed out over her daughter's future.

"Did they say when they plan to return?"

Her husband had honeymoon plans on his mind, and he wasn't going to like this any better than she did. "I don't expect them to get to town before tomorrow afternoon. More than likely, they won't be in the store until Friday."

Just as she suspected, Rooster frowned at the news. "I'll talk to Max about taking off a few additional days." He reached inside his jacket and pulled out a couple brochures. "I did a bit of walking while waiting for you and came across a travel agency. I was thinking we could get away to Victoria, British Columbia, for a night or two. It isn't far, and we can catch the foot ferry from the Seattle waterfront and stay at the Empress Hotel."

"I've always wanted to spend the night there," Lauren said wistfully. It was a gorgeous hotel built in the early 1900s, with an ivy-covered brick exterior. It had an English flavor, as did the entire business district. Lauren had heard friends claim visiting Victoria was like stepping onto the streets of London.

"Then the Empress is where we'll honeymoon."

"Oh, Rooster, you make me feel so loved." Lauren felt like she wanted to cry. Afraid she was about to embarrass them both, she reached for her latte and raised it to her lips.

"Should I make the reservation?" Rooster asked. "I'll see if they have a honeymoon suite."

Eagerly, she nodded. Rooster had been able to secure a lovely suite for their wedding night, which they had put to good use.

"I didn't get the chance to tell Elisa we're married," she reluctantly explained. Actually, she hadn't been able to say much of anything. Her employer and friend was full of talk about her daughter and Dietrich. Apparently, there was another house on the farm Dietrich's parents owned, and the newlyweds would be living there for the time being. Dietrich required only a few more classes until he had enough credits to graduate. They hoped he'd be able to finish his courses before the baby arrived.

Although Elisa did her best to put on a happy face, Lauren could hear the consternation in her friend's voice. Life on a busy farm wasn't the lifestyle she'd imagined for her only daughter. Besides, the fact that Lauren had married Rooster while they were in Vegas wasn't news she wanted to deliver over the phone.

"Before you talk to your boss, we probably should make some decisions," Rooster suggested.

He was right, of course. They had yet to discuss where they would live. "Do you think you and Max would ever consider moving the business to the Seattle area?" Lauren knew it was a topic that had come up more than once between Bethanne and Max, and it had been a problem with both of them. She didn't want this to be an issue for her and Rooster.

"We've certainly discussed the possibility," Rooster admitted. "It's been hard on Max and Bethanne flying back and forth for weekends." He reached for Lauren's hand and gave it a gentle squeeze. "I know I don't want to spend any more time away from you than necessary."

"I want to be with you, too," she assured him earnestly.

"Max and I have reviewed the costs of such a move a couple times, and I have to tell you, Lauren, it's prohibitive. We can do it, of course, but it'll nearly wipe us out financially."

Lauren was afraid of that. "If that's the case, then we don't really have a choice. I'll give Elisa and Garry my two-week notice and put the condo up for sale." Because she'd purchased it when the market was high, she would probably take a loss on the property.

"I'm sorry, love."

"It is what it is," she returned. It was a small sacrifice to pay in order to be with her husband.

"You enjoy your job, though."

"Another one will turn up that's just as satisfying," she assured him, although she hated to leave her friends. She'd come to love life in Seattle. It would mean giving it all up, moving to a strange town, and starting over again. For a new life together with Rooster, she would do it without question.

Rooster's gaze held hers for an extra-long moment. "I don't intend for you to work long," he told her. "I'd like for us to start a family soon. I suppose we could wait a year or two, but no longer than that."

A smile all but exploded across Lauren's face.

"What?" Rooster asked suspiciously.

"Everything happened so fast," she reminded him.

"Yes, so?"

"So, Mr. Rooster Wayne, I'm not on any form of birth control. I could already be pregnant."

Rooster's eyes widened, and his Adam's apple bobbed. "You could?"

"It wouldn't surprise me in the least."

His grin started to grow until it covered his entire face. "I wouldn't object. In fact, I'd be downright pleased."

"So would I."

They sat, grinning at each other like two cartoon characters, when a dark shadow fell across the table. Rooster looked up first, and Lauren watched as a frown crossed his face.

Todd.

Lauren's heart sank. When they'd been dating she could go a couple of weeks or longer without seeing her ex-boyfriend. Naturally, he always had a plausible reason, and he did keep in touch, usually with quick phone calls or a text now and again, filling her in on his upcoming stories.

Rooster scooted back his chair and stood, looming several inches above Todd.

"Hello, Todd," Lauren said, doing her best to hide her discomfort.

Todd ignored Rooster, turning his back to him. "I stopped by the store but found it closed. I thought you were open later than this."

"John Michael Jewelry has closed at the same time for the last thirty-five years, as far as I know."

Todd didn't appear to have heard her. "I thought I might find you here."

Lauren couldn't imagine why he'd be looking for her; she'd made her position more than clear.

"Todd, please. I've already said everything that needs to be said," she pleaded, not wanting a repeat of what had happened between the two men earlier. Never would she have guessed that Todd was the jealous type.

He continued to ignore Rooster. "I was hoping we could talk . . . privately."

He nodded his head toward Rooster, as if she should ask him to leave for a few minutes so they could speak.

Rooster made a move, but she stretched her arm toward her husband, stopping him. "I'm with someone else at the moment," she said, "but it wouldn't matter if I was or wasn't. There's nothing more the two of us have to discuss."

"Don't be so sure," Todd countered.

"Todd, please. Nothing you have to say is going to change my mind. We're done; actually, we were a long time ago. Can't we just leave it at that?"

"I can't," he insisted. "I love you."

"You heard Lauren," Rooster said, his voice low and cold.

Todd sighed, and rather than speak to Rooster, he continued to talk to Lauren. "Are you going to have your Hells Angels boyfriend drag me outside again?"

Lauren tried to hide her smile. "You're already outside."

"You know what I mean."

"And Rooster isn't my boyfriend." Todd's face relaxed, and he started to smile before she continued, "He's my husband."

For one crazy second it looked as if Todd's eyeballs were about to bulge out of his head. "Your husband," he repeated, and then he said it again as if he found it impossible to believe. "Your husband?"

"Yes. We were married over the weekend."

He shook his head as if to say he didn't believe her. "You were with Elisa in Las Vegas over the weekend."

"Yes, I know. That's where Rooster and I were married."

For the first time since he arrived, Todd turned to look at Rooster and then back at Lauren. "This is a joke, right? It has to be. The two of you don't belong together. Good grief, Lauren, look at this guy. He's . . . he's . . ." He scrambled as if he couldn't find the words to describe the man standing behind him. "He's a . . . grease monkey."

"He isn't, but it wouldn't matter if he was. Rooster Wayne is my husband."

Todd didn't seem to know what to say. "You're not making this up? You really aren't joking?"

"No."

"This can't be true," he said as his gaze dropped to her left hand. "You aren't wearing a wedding band."

"I plan on giving her my mother's ring," Rooster supplied, his voice deep and rich compared to Todd's shocked, high-pitched squeak.

"You are?" Lauren asked, looking to her husband. Like so much else, they had yet to discuss wedding bands.

"You can have it reset if you like," Rooster said, "but it would please me a great deal if you'd wear it."

"Oh, Rooster, of course I will," she whispered.

Todd's gaze went back and forth between them. "You aren't kidding, are you?"

"No." She couldn't understand why Todd kept asking the same question.

Her former boyfriend studied Lauren as if seeing her with fresh eyes. "Were you so desperate?" he demanded. "I would have married you if I'd known that."

"Todd!" She wouldn't allow him to insult Rooster. "I think it's time you left."

"I knew you were serious about wanting to get married, but I never believed you'd lower your standards to this."

"The lady asked you to leave," Rooster said, his voice cold enough to freeze alcohol.

Todd raised both arms. He stepped away from the table and simply shook his head. "I never would have thought you'd do something so out of character . . . this is unworthy of you, Lauren. Okay, so I kept delaying the wedding, but, sweetie, you could have done a lot better than this guy."

She was tempted to tell him that she'd done a whole lot better than if she'd married him, but resisted. No matter what he said, she wouldn't lower herself to his level.

Lauren reached for her coffee. "I believe you've said enough. Goodbye, Todd."

"It's because I wouldn't marry you, isn't it?"

Sadly, she shook her head. "The entire world doesn't revolve around you, Todd, and actually you did us both a favor. We really weren't suited, you know."

"And you're suited with that . . . that Neanderthal?"

"Oh, yes, he suits me just fine." She stretched out her arm to Rooster, who clasped her hand in his own.

"I'd congratulate you, but I don't give this so-called marriage a month." With that, Todd spun around and hurried off.

As Todd faded from view, Rooster sat back down.

"I apologize for Todd," she felt obliged to say. "No matter what he thinks, I'm grateful you're my husband. You're the one I love."

Rooster shrugged as though he remained unaffected by Todd's remarks. "It's hard for me to imagine you ever being hooked up with someone like him."

Lauren had to agree. "I have my man and I'm not letting him go for anything."

"We are different, Lauren."

"Sure we are, and that's the best part."

"The best part?" Rooster challenged. "I can think of other parts that are far better. Parts we're only beginning to explore."

Lauren smiled, too. "So can I."

"See, already we're starting to think alike, just as if we're an old married couple who've been together for fifty years."

"Will you still chase me around the bedroom in fifty years?" she asked.

Rooster chuckled. "I couldn't imagine anything I'd enjoy doing more at ninety years of age."

They relaxed and finished their coffee before walking back to her condo. When she unlatched the door, Rooster surprised her by lifting her off her feet and carrying her over the threshold.

"Rooster," she whispered, smiling up at her husband, "you're far more traditional than I realized."

"No, I'm not," he countered. "I figured if Todd thinks I'm a Neanderthal, then I should play the part."

Lauren tossed back her head and laughed. "Okay, okay, you can put me down now."

"All in good time," he said, and, using his foot, he kicked her front door closed and then, without a word, carried her directly into the bedroom.

Chapter Twenty-seven

$\mathcal{M}$ax wasn't sure how this meeting with Annie would go. Still, he was determined to do everything within his power to remind Bethanne's daughter how much her mother loved her. Before he talked to Annie, however, Max felt he needed Andrew's input. Annie's brother knew her far better than Max did and might be able to offer him valuable insight into Bethanne's daughter.

The two men met over lunch Thursday at a local seafood restaurant on the Seattle waterfront close to Andrew's office.

Max waited for the young man in the restaurant foyer and stood when Andrew joined him. They exchanged handshakes before being escorted to the table and sliding into a booth across from each other. Max had always liked Bethanne's son. He was well grounded and mature for his age. After his father had left, Andrew had taken on the responsibility for the family, helping his mother and looking after his younger sister.

"I know I said it earlier, but I'm pleased and excited for you and

Courtney about the baby. Bethanne's thrilled at the prospect of her first grandchild."

"We're happy ourselves," Andrew said, and briefly glanced at the menu. "They do a great salmon Caesar salad here, if that interests you."

Actually, Max didn't have much of an appetite. This matter with Annie had his stomach tied in knots.

"From what I hear, Annie's being a brat," Andrew said after the waitress had taken their drink orders. He set the menu aside, and Max did as well.

"It's tearing your mother apart," Max admitted. Bethanne had done her best to hide how miserable she was with the rift between her and Annie, but it was impossible. Max had held her in his arms while she wept, and it had nearly ripped his heart out to hear her pain from the way Annie had treated her.

"My sister can be a spoiled brat," Andrew said, and his jaw tightened as if the thought of his immature sister deeply upset him. "I've tried to reason with her, but she's convinced Mother has chosen you over her family."

"But she hasn't."

"That's what I tried to explain," Andrew continued, "not that it's done any good. Annie refuses to accept that Mom and you are together."

The waitress delivered two tall glasses of iced tea with lemon and took their lunch orders. They each chose the salmon Caesar salad.

"The real problem is my father," Andrew continued, holding on to the glass of iced tea with one hand. He didn't make eye contact with Max.

Max had already guessed as much.

"Dad eggs Annie on by claiming he'll never get over losing Mom and how his life is worth nothing without her."

Max looked out over the green waters of Puget Sound and watched the Bremerton ferry glide toward the dock. "Do you think he's sincere?" he asked, although it wouldn't change the fact that he was married to Bethanne and had no intention of stepping aside. They were married and deeply committed to each other. His wife had made her choice, and as far as Max was concerned it was time for Grant to man up and accept his ex-wife's decision.

"It's hard to know my father's motives," Andrew said. "I think one of the biggest surprises of my dad's life was watching my mother come into her own. He walked out, and she was left to find a way to support us and herself. Mom started this party business out of the basement."

Max had heard the story of how everyone loved Bethanne's parties. It was the one thing she felt she did well. From the very first, the business had thrived, until it had grown to the point that Bethanne had been approached about franchising her ideas, a proposal she had later rejected.

"Despite the fact that Mom was left with practically nothing," Andrew continued, "she managed to turn her life around and became a successful businesswoman."

"What did Grant expect her to do?" Max wondered out loud. Up until Grant had left the family, Bethanne had been a stay-at-home mother and a support to Grant. He hadn't appreciated everything his wife had done for him and his career until it was too late. And now Bethanne was married to Max.

In response to his question, Andrew shrugged. "I think he would have felt better if she'd spent the rest of her life pining after him. My mother isn't the kind of person who would allow bitterness to take over her life, although heaven knows she had reason enough. Dad treated her horribly."

And from what Max knew, Grant's attitude toward his two children hadn't been much better, either, although Annie appeared to have conveniently forgotten that.

Andrew picked up his fork and repositioned it on the linen napkin. "Before Mom married you, Dad realized he'd made a big mistake. To his credit, he did his best to rectify that. Before the divorce, my mother's entire life revolved around my dad and Annie and me. Then he was gone and her world fell apart."

"By then your mother was a different woman than the one your father recognized."

"Exactly. Dad was convinced he could win her back. He can be charming when he wants to be, and you know as well as I do how hard he tried to persuade Mom to give him another chance."

This was really the crux of the problem between him and Annie, Max realized. "If I hadn't been in the picture, do you really think your mother might have had a change of heart toward your father?" Max had posed the same question to Bethanne and she'd assured him that wasn't the case. She wouldn't have taken Grant back, no matter how much he'd claimed to have changed. Max believed her. What mattered to him was how Andrew viewed the situation.

"Frankly, I don't know if she would or wouldn't have," Andrew said. "That choice belonged to my mother. As it happens, you did come into the picture, and I, for one, am glad you did."

Max needed to hear this. His fear was that in loving Bethanne he'd brought heartache into her life when she deserved so much better.

"Mom is happier than I can ever remember seeing her. She loves you, Max. What's important is seeing her reap the benefits that she deserves, and one of those is being deeply loved by a good man."

It did Max a world of good to hear this. "I don't know how good I am, but I sincerely love your mother."

"It shows."

The waitress delivered their salads, and for a few minutes they ate in silence. The fresh fish was cooked to perfection, and after a few bites, Max returned to the conversation.

"Do you have any suggestions how I can reach out to Annie?"

Andrew rested his elbows against the tabletop and let his fork dangle over his plate. "I wish I did, and it's going to be harder now that she isn't working with Mom any longer. My sister can be stubborn and unreasonable, and being egged on by my father certainly isn't helping matters."

"Hold on," Max said, a little stunned. "I knew Annie hadn't

shown up at the office. Has she actually left her job with your mother? Without giving any notice?"

"Apparently so. The last I heard, my dad was getting her a job with the real-estate company where he works."

This was discouraging news, and it was sure to upset Bethanne even more than she was already. "Annie's going to work with your dad? Doing what?"

Andrew shrugged. "As a receptionist, I guess."

"That's ridiculous. Does Annie realize she'd be taking a huge cut in salary?"

"Annie's pride won't let her go back and work with Mom."

This situation was worse than Max realized. He'd assumed that Annie's little temper tantrum would run its course and that she'd eventually return to her position, working with her mother. Max had hoped he might be able to speed up the process by talking sense with Annie. He'd hoped to smooth the way, build a bridge between Annie and Bethanne, and give her daughter the opportunity to go back and keep her pride intact.

"Would Annie actually enjoy that kind of work?" Bethanne had trained her daughter as lead in an important division of the business enterprise.

"Annie is hurting right now," Andrew said. "She has this picture of the perfect reunited family in her mind, and she's being completely unreasonable and silly. I told her as much, and she hasn't spoken to me since. If she wants to shut me out, too, then so be it. I don't have time for her games."

To see this wedge driven between Bethanne's children deeply concerned Max. His appetite gone, he set his fork aside and pushed his plate away.

"The thing is, before long my father will disillusion her. At some point Annie is going to wake up and be forced to face reality when it comes to our father. I love my father; I care about him," Andrew said. "It wasn't until my wedding when I saw how broken up he was over Mom that I realized he needed me. A part of me wanted to tell him he got exactly what he deserved, and then there was another part that helped me see that while he wasn't the perfect father, he was still my dad."

Max admired the young man's maturity.

"Annie's attention and dedication are great for Dad's ego," Andrew added. "It upsets me that my sister doesn't see what Dad is doing, but she will eventually."

The question remained how long that would take and what it would do to Bethanne in the meantime. Although Max was probably the last person Annie wanted to see, for his wife's sake as well as his own, Max felt he had to try.

After lunch, the two men parted, and for the next few hours Max conducted what business he could from his computer. His flight back to California was scheduled for that evening. Once again, he'd be forced to leave Bethanne.

He waited until late in the afternoon before he drove over to Annie's place. She lived in an upscale neighborhood in her own condo. Max wondered how long she'd be able to maintain the payments with her much-decreased wages. Pride often came with a steep price.

He jogged up the staircase to the second floor and rang the doorbell. He was about to turn away when he heard activity on the other side, followed by a turn of the lock.

Apparently, Annie had checked to see who it was, because she didn't show any surprise to find him on the other side of the door.

"What do you want?" she demanded, striking a casual pose.

"Could the two of us talk for a few minutes?" he asked, doing his utmost to remain pleasant.

"Fine. Whatever." Still holding on to the doorknob, she stepped aside and let him into her condo.

Max came into the living area, and it was a mess. Discarded clothes littered the carpet, along with magazines and empty fast-food containers.

Annie must have noticed his surprise, because she commented, "I've been busy lately."

"So it seems." Max didn't wait for an invitation to sit down. He cleared a space on her sofa and made himself comfortable.

Annie walked to the other side of the room as if to get as far away from him as possible. "What do you want?" she asked again, and examined a fingernail before putting it in her mouth and chewing on the end.

Rather than watch, Max looked away. "I came because your mother is miserable and it looks as if you are, too."

"Wrong," Annie corrected him. "I'm doing fantastic; sorry to hear Mom's upset, though."

She sounded anything but. Max let the comment slide. "I heard you're looking for another job."

"Found one."

"Oh?" It was tempting to repeat what Andrew had mentioned. Max didn't, because he wanted to keep Annie's brother's confidence.

"I'm going to be working with my father."

Max pretended to be impressed. "Selling real estate?"

She shrugged. "Eventually. Dad's going to train me."

"I'm glad to hear it; I'm sure you'll do well."

Annie sighed as though the conversation bored her.

"Your mother misses you."

"Really. I saw that she tried to call a couple of times."

And Annie had let her mother's call go to voice mail. He wanted to shake the young woman for being so heartless toward her own mother.

"You know I hate you, don't you?" she said as casually as if she were telling him what she'd eaten for lunch.

"I pretty much got that impression." He stretched out his arm along the back of the sofa.

"If it wasn't for you, I'd have my family back."

"Perhaps." Max couldn't see any point in arguing with her.

"Everything would be the way it used to be."

"You're already a family," Max countered.

"Except there's you."

"Yes, there's me. I happen to love your mother very much, Annie."

"So does my dad." She yawned as if to say the conversation bored her. "Why are you here?" she demanded, seeming impatient now.

"To ask you to make peace with your mother."

Annie snorted.

"She loves you, Annie, and having you walk away from her without a word is tearing her apart."

"She made her choice. It's you she loves."

"Yes, she does," he reiterated, "but loving me doesn't mean that she loves you any less. You're part of her, and she is part of you. In the end, I fear the one who will be hurt the most is you."

"I doubt it."

Max studied the young woman across from him and frowned. "You want her to suffer, don't you? You find some twisted sense of rightness knowing you can hurt her."

Annie shrugged, neither confirming nor denying his accusation.

"Be careful, Annie."

"Careful?" she repeated. "What are you talking about? Are you threatening me?"

"No threats. All I'm saying is that the one who is going to end up losing this battle is you."

Her eyes narrowed. "You are threatening me!"

"No," Max said as he stood. "I would never do that."

She pointed her finger at him. "You ruined my life."

Feeling sad and discouraged, Max shook his head. "Actually, I don't think you needed any help. You're doing a perfectly good job of that all on your own." He started toward the door, and then looked over his shoulder. "I hope, Annie, that when the time comes you'll realize how much your mother loves you. If you need anything or need to talk, I want you to know I'm available any time of day or night."

"Like I'd ever reach out to you."

Max thought it was highly unlikely, but he still felt compelled to say so. "Remember what I said," he mentioned again.

"And you remember what I said," she countered.

As he walked toward the staircase, Max heard Annie turn the lock on her door, and it seemed on her heart as well.

Chapter Twenty-eight

Just as she suspected, Lauren didn't see Elisa until Friday morning. Rooster had grown impatient waiting for the owners to return so he could have time together with Lauren before he was forced to return to California. Truth be told, Lauren was as frustrated as her husband. But she wasn't comfortable leaving the shop in the hands of a part-time employee when she knew how much Elisa and Garry counted on her to oversee the business in their absence. It was rare for them both to be away at the same time, but then these were extenuating circumstances.

The bottom line, Lauren realized, was that she hadn't mentioned she'd married Rooster while in Vegas. Even if she had, it was doubtful anything would have changed.

Friday morning, Lauren arrived right on time. Rooster had their suitcases packed and ready for the trip to Victoria. It was short notice, Lauren realized, but once she explained, she was sure Elisa wouldn't have a problem.

Elisa was already at the shop, setting out the jewelry displays, when Lauren let herself in and then relocked the door.

"Welcome back," she greeted warmly.

Elisa expelled a deep sigh. "I can't tell you how good it is to be back."

"Is everything settled?" Lauren asked, knowing Katie's elopement had been difficult for Elisa to accept.

"Pretty much," Elisa murmured, while working to set out the jewelry cases. "Garry and I did what we could for Katie, but I fear it isn't near enough."

"But Katie's happy," Lauren said, doing her best to put a good light on the marriage.

"Blissfully so. Even now, I can't believe Katie would do something like this. I don't know what's happened to my daughter, Lauren, I just don't know."

"But she's only following in your footsteps."

"I know," Elisa murmured, and briefly closed her eyes. "It gives me a far better understanding of what my parents dealt with when I defied them and married Garry. I can't believe I was this stubborn when I was her age. I knew Garry, loved him, and believed with all my heart our love would last a lifetime. It's like seeing myself, but . . ." She hesitated and bit into her lower lip. "But," she continued, her voice trembling, "living on a farm miles from any town of substance is not what I've envisioned for my daughter."

"Katie has her own path to follow."

"I know, I know . . . Garry has reminded me of that any number of times." She rested her hands on top of the display case and shook her head as though dispelling an image of Katie living so far away. "You wouldn't believe the house my daughter is expected to make into a home. I wouldn't let our dog inside there, let alone my daughter. It's a shack, a tumbled-down old shack. Lauren, you can't imagine the condition it was in," Elisa continued. "From what I was told, a foreman who'd worked for the family for years lived there. A bachelor, it seemed. He must have been. I can't believe a woman would ever let her home deteriorate to the condition the place is in now."

"It's outdated?" In her mind, Lauren pictured a small house with faded linoleum floors and checkered curtains hanging over the window by the kitchen sink. Perhaps there was a braided rug or two.

Elisa waved her arms as if to say that wasn't the half of it. "The appliances are from the 1950s."

So she wasn't off by much, Lauren mused, grinning.

"The wallpaper is ghastly. It's so old and worn I could hardly make out the pattern, and when I did I could barely believe my eyes. It was flamingos, and that was in the living room."

Lauren's smile widened despite her determination to remain sympathetic. "I bet Katie wasn't upset about it, was she?"

"Oh, no. You'd think Dietrich had moved her into a castle. She's so excited that she couldn't dig into cleaning it up fast enough. Her father and I refused to let her paint, which is one of the reasons we stayed as long as we did."

From what she knew, both families had worked hard to make the small house livable for the young couple.

"We did what we could for her," Elisa murmured, working as she spoke. "I filled up her cupboards with groceries and . . ." She hesitated, and it seemed as if she was about to break into tears. After a moment, she released what sounded like a pent-up breath and continued. "The thing is, Katie didn't really want us there. She didn't come right out and say it, but trust me, I got the message loud and clear." Tears might not have made it to her eyes, but her voice was full of emotion.

Lauren waited a heartbeat before she said, "As it happens I have a bit of news myself."

"Oh?" Elisa turned to face Lauren, her look expectant.

In retrospect, Lauren wondered if she had a premonition, a sense of foreboding. All at once she found herself hesitant to mention her marriage to Rooster.

"I'm married," she announced.

Elisa extended her chin as if to lean closer . . . as if she wasn't sure she'd heard correctly. "You're *what*?"

"Married," Lauren said, with forced cheerfulness. It'd been easier telling her family than it was her friend.

"You and Todd?" she asked, frowning.

Lauren shook her head. "No, it's over with Todd, you know that."

"Well, yes, but . . ." Then, as if the realization hit her, Elisa's eyes grew as round as Italian meatballs. "Rooster? But you barely know him . . . You mean to say you actually married . . . Rooster?"

Lauren nodded.

Elisa laughed it off. "This isn't funny, Lauren. I'm in no mood for a joke."

"It's no joke. He showed up unexpectedly in Vegas and—"

Elisa held up her hand, stopping her. "I thought you said he was in New Zealand."

"That was his original plan, but he flew back early."

"To marry you?"

"Well, no, that just happened . . . Neither of us planned it."

Elisa shook her head as if unable to assimilate what she was hearing. "People don't accidentally get married, Lauren."

"No, no, it wasn't an accident. He showed up in Vegas after you left, and we realized we wanted to be together. Once we came to that conclusion, we couldn't see any reason to wait. After all, we aren't teenagers."

Elisa reacted as if she'd been slapped, taking a step back.

Lauren was quick to apologize. "I'm sorry, that came out wrong. I didn't mean it like that." She hadn't meant to compare her situation with Elisa's daughter's. Katie was a teenager, although technically an adult. Lauren was mature and well over thirty. Rooster, too.

"I was hoping to take a few days off," Lauren continued, refusing to let her friend's disapproval influence her feelings for Rooster or the choices they'd made.

"A few days?" Elisa repeated, almost as if she were in a trance.

"Yes. We flew back to Seattle together because I knew you needed me here. I've worked all week, waiting for your return. Now Rooster and I would like some time alone before he heads back to California."

This, too, seemed to shake her friend. "Does this marriage mean you'll be moving away now?" she asked, clearly concerned she was about to lose Lauren as an employee.

"I . . . I don't know yet. We haven't had much of an opportunity to decide that."

"You're actually married?" she asked again, and then, as if she suddenly needed to sit down, Elisa lowered herself onto the stool by the diamond-ring counter. Then, making light of the fact, she emitted a short laugh. "It must be something in the water."

"It must be," Lauren said, forcing a smile.

Elisa grew serious once more. "Does Todd know?"

Lauren wasn't sure how her marriage involved Todd, but she answered anyway. "As it happens, Rooster and I ran into him earlier in the week."

"So he knows?"

"Yes, we told him."

"And what did he say?"

It was hard to understand why Elisa remained focused on Todd. This wasn't a conversation Lauren was especially eager to share. "He was surprised."

Elisa snickered. "I bet. My guess is he was as shocked as I am."

That pretty much explained it. Todd, however, being Todd, hadn't been willing to leave it at that. He accused Lauren of being so desperate that she'd married the first man who came along after their breakup. On the outside it might look that way, but in her heart, she knew differently. She loved Rooster, and he loved her. They were right for each other. Right together.

"I've never met him," Elisa reminded her.

"I know . . . we only had that one weekend together before . . . but remember, we talked every day. He's a good man, Elisa, and I love him. I know this seems sudden, especially on the heels of Katie and Dietrich, but I feel Rooster was the right choice for me."

Elisa looked at her as though she didn't recognize the woman standing in front of her.

"He's thoughtful and tender," Lauren continued, wanting to defend Rooster and her decision to marry him.

"You saw him only the one time?"

"No, it was more than that."

"One weekend, then?"

"Yes, but even when he was eight thousand miles away we talked every single day."

"But, Lauren, you can't really know a person after such a short acquaintance."

"I realize how this looks, I really do," she said, and she was sincere. "If it was anyone but Rooster, I'd agree with you, but he's everything I've ever wanted in a husband. We share so much in common. My parents met him—"

"Your family knows?"

"Of course. They flew in for the ceremony. My parents were concerned, too, seeing that we'd only known each other a short while. Dad insisted on having a background check done on Rooster."

This tidbit seemed to rattle Elisa all the more. "And did you read the report?"

"No, there wasn't time. But my father did, and he couldn't find anything about Rooster that raised a red flag."

"What about his family?" Elisa challenged.

Her friend was stretching, looking for something, anything, to prove what a terrible mistake Lauren had made, almost as if she was talking about Katie rather than Lauren. Patiently, not wanting to upset Elisa, Lauren explained, "Rooster is an only child, and both his parents are dead. Bethanne's husband, Max, stood up for him as best man. Max and Bethanne are his family."

Elisa continued to look shaken and unsure.

"Would it be all right if I took the rest of the week off?" Lauren pressed. The shop was due to open in a few minutes; Friday mornings generally had light customer traffic. If Elisa needed to call in someone else, she could.

"Oh, of course. I apologize if I'm being less than gracious over your news."

"I understand; it's a shock."

"What I can't understand is why you didn't mention it much earlier."

It wouldn't do any good to explain. "You and Garry were busy with Katie," she explained, hoping that would suffice.

"But to hit me with it now . . ."

"I'll be away today and Saturday," Lauren repeated, growing impatient. "I still have several days available to use as vacation days."

"Oh sure . . . the time off is no problem."

"Thank you." She reached for her cell and sent Rooster a quick text. She would be ready to leave in a few minutes, and he could pick her up at the jewelry shop.

"Before you leave, would you do me a favor first?" Elisa asked.

"Of course." They'd been good friends for a long time, and Lauren was willing to help in any way she could.

"I don't mean to offend you."

"I know."

"It's just that I'd feel better if you read that background check your father had done on Rooster. Oh, for the love of heaven, doesn't he have another name? I refuse to believe his parents named him after a chicken."

"It's John. John Jerome Wayne. His father's name was Jerome."

"John Wayne," Elisa repeated.

"I believe he picked up the name Rooster after one of the characters John Wayne played in the movies. Rooster Cogburn." In fact, Lauren and Rooster had watched the western featuring John Wayne along with Katharine Hepburn earlier that week. Lauren had loved every minute and made Rooster promise they would never argue the way these two characters had.

"Okay, just promise me one thing."

"I said I would."

"Read that report. Please, Lauren."

"What could it possibly say that would come as a surprise?" she demanded.

"I don't know," Elisa cried. "Do you know how many times he's been married?"

"Yes, once. To me."

"And this story about his family. Isn't that a tad convenient? Everyone is dead and he has no siblings. Doesn't he keep in touch with his aunts and uncles? Surely there's someone?"

"None that he's mentioned."

"That doesn't tell you anything?"

"No. You're starting to sound paranoid. Don't you trust my judgment?" Lauren asked her friend.

"Yes, of course I do, but you know *Dateline* and *48 Hours* are my favorite television shows. It always starts out well in these quick marriages, and then some shocking revelation comes out later."

"Okay, okay, I'll read the report."

"Do it now."

"Now?"

"Yes, before you go away, please."

"Elisa!"

Perhaps her friend was right and she was being foolish and blinded by love. Her father had sent her the file, but if he hadn't seen anything in Rooster's background that alarmed him, then she sincerely doubted that she would, either.

While Elisa opened the store for business, Lauren sat in the back office with her cellphone. It took only a minute or so to bring up the forwarded email from her father.

Lauren breezed through the first few pages of the report. It showed nothing out of the ordinary. Rooster had gotten a number of speeding tickets in his twenties, she noticed. He seemed to have a need to drive fast even now, a habit he was working hard to break.

It wasn't until she reached the second-to-last page that she saw it. Her eyes widened as shock rippled through her.

She needed a few minutes to digest what she'd read.

How was this possible?

How could Rooster not have mentioned something this important? Surely this was information she should know.

In an instant, everything that had felt so beautiful and so wonderfully right seemed terribly, terribly wrong.

"Lauren." Elisa came into the back room.

Lauren looked up and blinked, trying desperately to hide her shock and distress.

"There's a man out front asking for you."

"A man?"

"He looks like he might be a biker or something."

Lauren slid off the chair and stood. It took a couple of minutes before she felt she could speak normally. "I think that might be Rooster . . . my husband."

"Your husband? That's . . . Rooster?" Elisa shook her head several times as if she found the news too shocking for words. "Lauren, no. It can't possibly be. Not him."

Lauren nodded. "Yes, him."

"But . . . the two of you. Lauren, you can't be serious. Can't you see how different the two of you are?" she asked in a pleading tone.

Then Elisa, her closest friend, closed her eyes as if she couldn't bear to watch this train wreck happening right in front of her.

Chapter Twenty-nine

"What's wrong?" Rooster asked, as soon as Lauren was outside John Michael Jewelers.

In order to avoid answering him, she started walking toward the car he'd parked on Blossom Street. "I want to go back to my condo," she said emphatically.

"Did you forget something?"

"No."

"Then why are we going back?" He looked at his watch as if to remind her the ferry to Victoria that he'd booked left within the hour.

"Please, Rooster, I'll explain everything once I'm home." She needed to get someplace private where they could talk undisturbed. Her head buzzed and her mouth felt dry, but not from thirst.

He gave her an odd look and seemed utterly perplexed. Well, he shouldn't be. Lauren was badly shaken. Her nerves were stretched to the breaking point, and her stomach roiled in one huge knot.

They rode in silence so loud it hurt her eardrums.

As he drove, Rooster glanced her way once or twice, as if he was at a complete loss as to what had upset her. He should have known that she'd find out this information about him sooner or later. Elisa was right. She'd been naive and foolish, and stupid. Just plain stupid. She'd been caught up in this romantic fantasy that should be reserved for fairy tales. It took all the restraint she possessed not to press her forehead against the dashboard and close her eyes and pretend none of this was real.

Rooster parked the car in the proper slot in her parking garage. They climbed out and didn't speak until they reached her condo.

They were barely inside the door when Rooster demanded, "Okay, what is it?"

For the longest moment, Lauren couldn't do anything more than stare at him.

"Lauren, tell me!"

"This morning," she started, her voice faltering as she struggled with keeping the anger and disappointment in check. "When I first told Elisa we were married, she was shocked."

"So?"

"So . . . she asked me if I really knew you."

"You know me," he countered.

"Do I, Rooster? Do I really know you?"

"In the biblical sense, I would say you know me pretty darn well."

He might have thought he was funny, but Lauren wasn't the least bit amused.

Rubbing her palms together, she calmly stated, "Elisa asked if I'd read the background report my dad got on you."

"Had you?"

"No, but my father had, so I didn't think it was necessary." What a fool she'd been.

"So you read it this morning after Elisa suggested it might be a good idea? And something in the report badly shook you?" Thankfully, Rooster was good at filling in the blanks. Before she could answer, he added, "You realize those reports aren't always one hundred percent accurate."

She wanted to believe that was the case with this one, but it was unlikely.

"Lauren," he pleaded, "tell me, what did you find that was so horrible that you can barely look me in the eye? Whatever it is, we'll straighten it out."

For just an instant, hope flared that there had been a mistake, and yet, intuitively, she knew that might not be possible.

"Rooster, please don't lie to me. I need the truth." Her words were a plea and a cry.

He blinked hard. "I've never lied to you, Lauren. God as my witness, I've never lied."

"Then tell me. Is this your first marriage?"

He couldn't disguise his surprise. He opened his mouth and then quickly closed it again. "No."

Lauren felt her knees go weak.

"I was married once before," he added. "Years ago." He walked across the condo and looked out the view window before finally turning around and sitting on the sofa.

"So a marriage that took place 'years ago' doesn't count?" she asked, unable to disguise her sarcasm. "Is that what you're saying?"

He gestured weakly, using both hands. "Lauren, get real. I'm nearly forty. Yes, I was married. I don't understand. What's the big deal?"

"The big deal, as you call it, is the fact that you completely forgot to mention this tiny detail about your past."

"So?"

"And so what else has slipped your mind?" she demanded.

"What do you mean?" he asked, losing his patience now.

Interesting, when she called him on this, that he would get defensive. That raised her suspicions all the higher. Elisa wasn't the only one who watched those true-crime series on television.

She had more questions that demanded answers. "What about children, Rooster? Were there children?"

"No." He hesitated, and then reversed himself. "Yes."

"Is it yes or no?"

He exhaled sharply. "Lacey was pregnant when we married and then later miscarried the baby."

"What happened?" she asked.

"How would I know?" he snapped. "Women miscarry babies. It wasn't anything I did, if that's what you're insinuating."

"What happened with the marriage?" she clarified.

He walked away from her and kept his back to her. "You'll have to ask Lacey."

"Unfortunately, she isn't here for me to ask, but you are."

It seemed an eternity before he answered: "We were both young, immature. I had a night job."

"And she got lonely."

He shrugged. "Something like that. Like I said, we married too young, before either one of us was ready to settle down."

"How long were you married?"

"Not long."

The vague answers upset her all the more. "A year? Five years? Ten?"

"A year, maybe."

"Maybe?" she asked incredulously.

"We lived together less than a year and then separated. It took a few months for the divorce to go through, so it might have been more than a year that we were legally married."

"In other words, you weren't together that entire time?"

"No. Come on, Lauren, it happened years ago. I don't remember all the finite details. If you want to make a huge issue out of it, fine. It's a part of my life I'd rather put behind me. You're right, I should have told you. I would have in time."

"Why not before the wedding?" This was the burning question.

"Because I didn't feel it was necessary or important."

"Is there anything else you didn't feel necessary to mention that I should know?"

"No," he all but shouted.

"You're sure about that?" she asked, her voice raised to the same volume as his.

His gaze narrowed. "What did you do? Did you go digging for dirt in my past, is that it?"

"I didn't need to. It was all right there in the background check my father had done on you. My mistake was that I didn't bother to read it."

"What else did you find?" he demanded.

"You told me you were an only child."

His eyes widened, and he looked away. "Okay, you've got me there again. I did have a sister. She died when I was young, too young for me to remember her. So, technically, you're right, I wasn't an only child." He walked into her kitchen and poured himself a glass of water, which he drank down in several large gulps. He set the empty glass down on the countertop and then stepped back.

Lauren didn't know what to say or if she should say anything.

He remained in the kitchen and pressed his hands against the edge of the countertop as he leaned forward. "I'm beginning to get the picture here. You're having second thoughts. Regrets. You're feeling that you might have acted hastily and this marriage wasn't such a great idea after all."

"I . . . I don't know what I'm thinking." Her head reeled. "I'm feeling confused and shaken." Plus a dozen other emotions she had yet to identify that came at her like a boxer's fists.

"You're unsure?"

"Yes," she admitted. "You don't hide the fact that you were married from the woman you're about to marry." The least he could do was apologize, offer a plausible excuse. Anything.

He studied her as though waiting for her to speak.

"Would you have ever told me?" she asked, her voice low now, shaken as she was.

"Of course. You have to admit we rushed into this marriage business."

"We talked every single day, Rooster. Every single day, oftentimes for hours."

"Fine. I'm guilty."

"I've lost faith in you—"

"Faith in *us,* you mean," he clarified.

She didn't respond.

He walked around the counter and stood with the tips of his fingers in his jean pockets. "What do you want to do?"

She didn't know. The truth was, she didn't have a clue what she could or should do. "I can't answer that." For all she knew, she might be completely overreacting. While it was true the news of this brief marriage had stunned her, the fact that he had purposely kept it from her cracked the foundation of trust. It was terribly early in their marriage to be confronted with a lie of omission from her husband.

For the longest time they simply stood and stared at each other as if waiting for the other to make a decision.

"I heard what Elisa said," he admitted after a while.

"When?"

"Just now, while I was in the shop. You might want to know that for future reference."

"Know what?"

"How clearly voices carry from the back office. Out of sight doesn't mean the customer in front can't hear the discussion going on behind the counter area."

Lauren felt the warmth invade her cheeks. So Rooster was privy to Elisa's shock when she realized Rooster was the man Lauren had married. The motorcycle man who looked completely out of place in the high-end jewelry store. Anyone looking at him might assume he wouldn't be able to afford to be shopping in that store.

It deeply embarrassed Lauren that Rooster had heard her friend's comments.

"Do you share your friend's sentiments, Lauren? Is that what this is really about? I don't fit the image of the upscale, corporate ideal Elisa was expecting you to marry?"

"No," she returned quickly, perhaps a shade too quickly.

"Are you sure about that?"

"Yes," she insisted.

The hard look in his eyes challenged her. "Perhaps you should have married Todd."

She shook her head.

An awkward silence followed, and again it was Rooster who broke it. "Okay, now what?"

"I don't know."

"It might be a stretch here, but I'm making the assumption there will be no honeymoon."

Rather than respond verbally, she nodded.

"That's what I figured. So what would you like me to do?"

Again, she was at a loss. "I . . . I don't know."

"Would you like me to go away for a while?"

She swallowed hard. "Perhaps that would be for the best. I need time to think this through."

"How much time?"

She couldn't answer that. "I don't know."

"I'll tell you what," he said with a sarcastic edge. "I'm going to conveniently get out of here and give you all the time and the space you need. Just let me know when you've made up your mind about us."

That seemed the best option.

"I only ask one thing."

She waited.

"I'd appreciate it if you'd let me know, after these last few days," he paused, "if you're pregnant."

She nodded. "I should know within a couple of weeks."

He held her gaze for one long, intense moment and then walked out the door.

It took a few minutes for the shaking to start, and when it did, Lauren collapsed onto her sofa. This wasn't what she wanted, either, but now Rooster was gone and she was even more confused about their future than ever.

Chapter Thirty

Knitting is a series of small steps, lovingly worked one stitch at a time on the path to becoming something tangible and cohesive. At the beginning you may fear that you are doing it wrong, but keep working through that fear. Sometimes the bigger picture isn't apparent until you reach the end of your journey.

—Michelle Miller,
Fickle Knitter

Lydia planned to open the yarn store Saturday morning and stay only a couple hours.

Cody's baseball game was scheduled for one o'clock, and there was a possibility her mother would be able to come home from the nursing facility later in the afternoon after the fall that had broken her arm. Casey was with Mary Lou now, as she had been every day since her grandmother had taken the tumble. It was discovered later that Mary Lou had suffered a minor stroke, resulting in the fall.

Margaret was scheduled to work that afternoon and would close the shop at five-thirty.

Lydia had just turned over the OPEN sign and had started to straighten out the window display when her first customer of the day arrived. It was Evelyn Boyle.

"Morning, Lydia," Evelyn said as she strolled into the shop. Whiskers didn't stir from the front window as the bell chimed. The cat had grown fat and lazy, which wasn't all that different from every other cat Lydia had ever owned.

"Hi," Lydia said, greatly relieved to see the other woman, especially now, when she could talk freely without fear of Casey overhearing the conversation. In fact, it was probably for the best that her daughter knew nothing about Lydia meeting with the social worker.

"I'm circling back to see how everything is going since I last talked to you about Casey," Evelyn stated.

"On your day off?" Lydia teased. Evelyn was like a mother hen looking after her baby chicks. She sincerely cared about the children who were on her caseload and, more impressively, even those who'd been adopted or turned eighteen and were no longer wards of the state.

"I heard about your mother," Evelyn said. "I stopped by earlier in the week while you and Margaret were at the hospital and left you a message."

"I got it, and I meant to get back to you, but it's been a bit hectic this week with Mom in the hospital."

Evelyn's concern was evident in the way her forehead creased with worry lines. "How's your mother doing?"

"Fairly well. Her blood sugars are good, and for a time that was a big concern. The stroke did some damage, but, thankfully, nothing permanent. A few weeks of physical therapy will help. It's amazing how resilient she is. Her left arm is in a cast, and it's cumbersome for her, but she's managing."

"And Casey?" Evelyn asked. The crease lines on her forehead thickened. "How's she doing?"

Lydia's spirits sank as her own worries came front and center. "Not so great, I'm afraid. When we got the news that Mom had fallen, Casey came unglued. I don't know when I've ever seen her more upset. It took Brad and me and Cody to calm her down."

"Is she better now?"

"Yes, but she spends every available moment with my mother at the nursing home. Mom was in the hospital the first couple days and then transferred to the nursing facility," Lydia explained.

"What's happening with the nightmares?"

"They're not improving. If anything, they've gotten worse." Much, much worse, in fact, especially in the last week.

"By *worse* you mean more frequent? Lasting longer?" Evelyn inquired.

"More frequent," Lydia explained. "She's woken us up three times this week, screaming and trembling."

"And she still refuses to tell you about the dream?"

Lydia's heart clenched. "Not a word. If you have any advice, I'd be more than grateful to get it." When it came to Casey and her dreams, the entire family was willing to do whatever was necessary to help the teenager overcome this psychological speed bump.

"Like I explained when you first mentioned it, these dreams aren't unusual for a teenage foster child."

"Casey has been adopted." Casey was no longer a ward of the court. She was an important part of their family.

"Correction. I should have said that for a child who has been part of the foster program and is going through puberty, this isn't uncommon. Many have nightmares in varying degrees of intensity. It sounds like Casey's case might be severe."

This was worse than anything Lydia had ever encountered.

"The best advice I can offer you," Evelyn continued, "is to get Casey into counseling."

Lydia was almost afraid that would be Evelyn's suggestion. "Brad and I have already talked about that."

"I can recommend several excellent counselors."

Lydia nodded. "It's just that when I checked with a couple of the ones our family physician mentioned, the cost was prohibitive for what Brad and I can currently afford."

"I have the names of a few excellent counselors who charge on a sliding scale, according to the family income."

Lydia nodded again. "I'd appreciate getting those names."

Evelyn got out her cellphone and shared the information with Lydia.

"Thank you." She was genuinely appreciative.

Not long after Evelyn left, Lauren Elliott arrived, bringing along the baby blanket she was knitting for her pregnant sister. She'd purchased the yarn weeks earlier but hadn't knit much beyond the border, which was only a few inches. Then over the course of the last two days the new knitter had completed nearly half the blanket. As far as Lydia could tell, Lauren must have spent every available moment with knitting needles in her hands.

"I made a mistake," Lauren said, pulling the project out of the colorful quilted bag.

"Let me take a look," Lydia said, keeping an eye on the door, watching for customers.

Lauren spread the project out on the table and pointed to the error. "The stitch count is off now, too."

"Yes, it would be." Lydia examined the mistake. It wasn't glaring and could be easily overlooked.

"Do I need to rip it out?" Lauren asked.

"You could fudge it." Lydia had done that often enough herself.

"Yes, I suppose, but I'd always know it was there, and it's a gift for my sister, and . . ." she let the rest fade.

Lydia understood. If she could live with the mistake, she let it be, but like Lauren, if the project was a gift, then she took a closer look. "Feeling the way you do, I suggest you frog it."

"Frog it?"

"Rip it, rip it, rip it."

Lauren's smile was only momentary.

Lydia didn't know what had happened in Lauren's personal life, but clearly something had. She'd always known the other woman to be friendly and happy, not in an effervescent way, but polite and sociable. The last couple days, when Lauren had visited the shop, she'd barely said a word. She seemed caught up in her own thoughts and didn't welcome conversation.

Whatever was troubling her seemed to be coming out on the needles as well, Lydia noticed. Her tension was extremely tight, making it almost impossible to move the stitches on the bamboo needles. Just the day before, Lydia had teased Lauren and explained that she needed to relax. She wasn't knitting armor.

"Would you like me to unravel it for you?" Lydia asked, knowing how irksome it could be to undo a project.

"Please."

Lydia pulled out a chair, sat down next to the other woman, and took the blanket off the needles, tugging at the yarn, which was so tight it took effort to slide it free.

"I don't know that I can watch," Lauren said, looking away.

"Don't," Lydia advised. "Frogging hurts, no matter how experienced a knitter you are."

Lauren looked back at her and asked with surprise in her voice, "You mean to say you make knitting errors, too?"

"All the time," Lydia assured her. "I misread a pattern or get distracted. Mistakes happen."

"Don't I know it," Lauren said with feeling.

Lydia looked at her and saw tears form in her eyes. Lauren struggled to hide them, and, not wanting to embarrass the other woman, Lydia pretended not to notice.

After a few minutes, Lydia put the stitches back on the needle and handed the blanket to Lauren. "There you go; it's good as new."

Lauren thanked her and placed the project back inside the quilted bag. "You wouldn't by chance have happened to see Bethanne lately, have you?" she asked.

"No," Lydia explained. "But then, I've been away from the shop a good deal this week. My mother's been in the hospital."

"Oh, I'm sorry. I didn't know. I hope she's doing well."

"She's much better; thanks for asking."

"I should give Bethanne a call," Lauren said, almost as if she were speaking to herself. With that, she left the shop. Watching her go, Lydia felt as if Lauren Elliott must be deeply concerned about something.

Margaret arrived a little before noon, and within a few minutes Lydia was free to leave. She phoned Casey before she left the shop, grateful that her daughter now had her own cellphone.

"How's it going with Grandma?" Lydia asked.

"She's looking much better today."

How cheerful and upbeat Casey sounded. A stark contrast to only a few hours earlier, when she'd woken up screaming in terror.

"I think she might be able to go back to her apartment this afternoon. Would you like to talk to her?" Casey asked.

"Oh, sure." During the last conversation with her mother, Lydia had the disheartening impression her mother didn't have a clue who she was.

"Grandma, Lydia is on the phone."

Lydia heard Casey tell her grandmother, and then the teenager added, lowering her tones, "Lydia is your daughter."

"I know who Lydia is," Mary Lou Hoffman insisted.

A moment later, her mother's voice came over the cellphone. "Hi, honey. I'm feeling much better today."

"You sound great, Mom."

"Are you coming by to visit?"

"I'll be there as soon as Cody's baseball game is over."

"Cody?" her mother repeated.

"That's my brother," Casey whispered in the background.

"Oh, of course, Cody and Brad. You married them."

"You got it, Mom. I'll see you later." She hung up the phone, and, after chatting briefly with her sister, Lydia headed toward the ball field.

When she arrived, she found Brad sitting in the bleachers. He had saved a spot for her next to him. She joined her husband and settled in. The opposing team was up to bat, and Cody played shortstop.

Their son was athletic and enjoyed sports. In the fall, he played on a select soccer team. Having Cody or any child involved in sports was a major commitment for their family, requiring travel to other cities and even other states. To this point, because Lydia often worked weekends, Brad had taken over transporting Cody from one event to the other.

"How'd your morning go?" Brad asked, while keeping his attention focused on the field.

"Evelyn Boyle stopped by."

Brad's gaze momentarily left the game. "Did you mention how bad Casey's nightmares have gotten?"

"I did."

"And what did she say?"

Lydia mentally reviewed the conversation. "Well, it's what you and I came up with originally. We need to get Casey into counseling."

Brad took a couple of moments to digest this. It wasn't an idea they'd overlooked.

"I know what you're thinking," Lydia said, remembering their earlier concerns.

"It isn't the cost, Lydia. Somehow we'll find the money. If Casey needs to talk to a professional, then we'll make it happen, no matter what sacrifice we have to make."

Lydia leaned her head against her husband's shoulder. How she'd been able to marry such a wonderful man she would never know. All she could figure was that God in His goodness had decided to bless her with Brad in an effort to make up for the brain cancer she'd suffered in her youth and then later as a young adult.

"I love you, Brad Goetz."

He chuckled. "Heaven knows I'm crazy about you. I was from the first moment I delivered yarn to the store."

That was how they'd met. Brad had been her UPS delivery man.

"My only concern," Brad continued, "is if Casey won't talk to us about these nightmares, what makes Evelyn think she'd discuss them with a complete stranger?"

He had a point. "I don't know."

"They are professionals," Brad added, as though thinking this through.

"Right. Counselors are trained for just this sort of thing. And . . ." She paused, uncertain how best to mention the change in the yarn store situation.

"Yes?" He glanced her way.

"I have good news."

"Great. Are you going to share it?"

"With pleasure. I was going over the figures for the yarn store in the last month, and business is up substantially." She didn't want to sound overly optimistic. They were heading into summer, when customers didn't think as much about knitting in hot weather as they did during the colder months of the year.

"Really? The shop is doing well financially? Lydia, that's great news."

"It is," she agreed. "And I think it's all due to those yarn baskets someone has set out. All the publicity those baskets have generated has been a huge boost."

"I'm sure that the newspaper article helped, too."

"You're right, it did. Because people are curious, they've made a point of stopping in and asking about charity knitting. Several have purchased yarn. A handful have signed up for beginning knitting classes."

"Sweetheart, that's fabulous."

"I might even be able to help finance Casey's counseling sessions."

Brad took a moment to assimilate the news. "I guess we need to thank the person who came up with this brilliant idea—that is, if we ever find out who is responsible."

Lydia agreed.

Now all Lydia had to do was figure out who'd come up with this plan and find a way to thank them.

Chapter Thirty-one

*B*ethanne sat in her office, but her mind wasn't on the email in front of her or business matters. It'd been almost three weeks since Annie had left. Three long, torturous weeks. Never once did she suspect her daughter would stay away this amount of time.

This had gone on far too long, and over nothing. Despite the fact that Bethanne missed Max and wanted to be with him, she wouldn't be moving to California. On the flip side, it didn't seem likely that he would move to Washington State, either. Bethanne felt as if she were in a no-win situation, complicated by her own daughter.

Reaching out to Annie hadn't helped. She'd already tried that, but her daughter was as stubborn as they come. Andrew had already attempted to reason with his sister, and he, too, had met with no success. Nothing, no logic, no words of persuasion, no heart-to-heart chat, was able to change Annie's mind. She was bound and determined to sever all ties with her mother. Because he loved her, Max had reached out to Annie, too, and met with the same icy reception as everyone else.

It went without saying that Grant bolstered his daughter's resolve. It suited his ego to have Annie stand by his side, no matter what price she had to pay. Although she'd resisted to this point, Bethanne didn't feel she had any other option but to seek out Grant's help, which she suspected was exactly what he wanted.

Using the office phone, she called the office where her ex-husband worked as a real-estate broker.

"Southard Realty." Annie's voice startled Bethanne, although she knew her daughter had taken a job as a receptionist at Grant's workplace.

"Grant Hamlin," she said, as if she didn't recognize her own daughter's voice.

"Mom?"

Bethanne hesitated. "Yes."

"Why do you want to talk to *my* father?" Heavy emphasis fell on the word "my."

"I believe that is *my* business, Annie. Now please put me through."

Annie paused as though debating a course of action. "It's about me, isn't it?"

"Annie, just put me through to *your father.*"

"No."

Bethanne's tempter flared, but she quickly brought it under control. "Don't you think you're being just a little bit ridiculous?"

"Maybe, but I don't care," Annie returned flippantly. "You made your choice, and I've made mine. I want nothing more to do with you. As far as I'm concerned, I only have one parent, and that's my dad."

The words cut like the serrated edge of a knife. Bethanne swallowed hard and did her best to breathe normally, despite the pain. The tension between the two lines was taut, stretched tight as a violin string. Neither spoke, and after a few seconds Annie disconnected the line.

In an effort to hold herself together, Bethanne cupped her hand over her mouth. Once she felt she could think clearly, she punched out Grant's cellphone number. He answered after the first ring, almost as if he'd been waiting for her call.

"Bethanne," he greeted cheerfully, "it's great to hear from you."

She didn't return the compliment. She could picture him in his corner office, smugly leaning back in his chair. He seemed to think he had her exactly where he wanted her, squirming and needing his help.

"How's Annie?" she asked.

He sighed, as if she should already know the answer. "Annie's doing great, and the staff love her working here. It didn't take long before she got the entire office reorganized. I can't tell you what an asset she is."

Bethanne tensed. Grant seemed to enjoy rubbing salt in her wounds.

"It's a joy having her around," he finished.

"No doubt."

"I imagine you must miss her."

More salt. More gloating. It was tempting to lie, but Bethanne didn't. "I miss her dreadfully."

"Annie mentioned that Max stopped by her place. I heard they had a little heart-to-heart, which unfortunately didn't go well."

With this comment, he brought out the entire salt canister. Naturally, Grant made it a question, as if he wanted her to fill in the blanks. What transpired between Annie and Max was their business, and she wasn't about to break confidences. In actuality, Max had said very little about his meeting with Annie. All Bethanne knew was that it had been a wasted effort.

"I know you must be pleased with Annie's unwavering loyalty to you, Grant, but at what cost?"

"What do you mean?"

Apparently, she needed to spell it out for him. "Annie has a business degree; with her experience and background, she could have almost any job she wanted."

"I admit, she's amazing."

"Do you honestly believe she'll be satisfied working as a receptionist for long?"

"Time will tell," he said, seemingly unconcerned.

"Is this what you really want for our daughter?" Bethanne knew her ex-husband could be selfish and self-centered, but not once had she believed he would sink to this level, using their daughter against her.

"I want," Grant said, steel in his voice, "what Annie wants, and at this juncture, it's not being around you. If you must know, she's happy working with me." All pretense was gone. Grant was angry, and he wasn't shy about making sure Bethanne knew to what lengths he was willing to sink.

"Grant, you don't mean that. This is our daughter; don't mess with her future."

"I wouldn't do anything to hurt Annie," he insisted. "Once she gets a feel for the real-estate business, she can get her license, and if she proves herself, she can work for me."

For him, not *with* him; Bethanne caught the subtle difference.

"Now, what can I do for you?" Grant asked, basically telling her that he was a busy man and that she was taking up his valuable time.

Even though she'd suspected it wouldn't do any good to reach out to her ex, Bethanne felt she'd had to try.

"Thank you for your time," she said, and with that she cut off the call.

As far as she could see, the only option left open to her was to wait until Annie became disillusioned with her father. That might take weeks or even months, but in due course it would happen. Grant wouldn't be able to help himself. Eventually, his true self-centered nature would reveal itself. Then, and not before, would Annie be willing to face the truth. Until that time, all Bethanne could do was wait and pray that it wouldn't be long until her relationship with her daughter was restored.

Although she tried, Bethanne's mind wasn't on business. An hour later, when her phone rang, she automatically reached for it.

"This is Bethanne," she said.

"Hi, it's Lauren."

Bethanne sat up straighter. Max had been deeply concerned about Rooster. Something had happened between the newlyweds that had caused them to split. From what Max had said, Rooster refused to discuss it. Concerned for his friend, Max had asked Bethanne if she'd had a chance to speak to Lauren. She hadn't. After some thought and discussion, they decided to wait until Lauren reached out to Bethanne. This was the first time she'd heard from the other woman.

"Lauren, it's good to hear from you."

"Can we meet for coffee?" Lauren asked.

"Of course. When?"

"Is this afternoon too soon?"

"Not at all." Bethanne knew Max would be relieved.

They set a time, after work, and agreed to link up at The French Cafe. As soon as she was off the phone, Bethanne reached for her cell and sent Max a text.

Meeting Lauren this afternoon.

It didn't take long to get a reply: Excellent.

The rest of the day passed quickly, and Bethanne and Lauren arrived at the cafe at about the same time. They each ordered coffee and sat at a table in the corner that offered them privacy.

Bethanne studied her friend. Lauren looked sad and beaten down. Rather than make eye contact, she stared down at her coffee as if she were reading tea leaves broadcasting her future. Bethanne waited for Lauren to speak; after all, she was the one who had asked for this meeting.

It took a few moments before Lauren asked, "Have you talked to Rooster lately?"

"No," Bethanne told her. "Have you?"

"No."

Which was the crux of the matter, Bethanne knew, and she boldly asked, "Why not?"

Lauren's thin shoulder lifted with a shrug. "Most everyone tells me I made a terrible mistake rushing into this marriage."

"Is that what you feel?"

She shook her head. "I don't know what I feel any longer. I'm confused and miserable. I feel like I've made a terrible mess of my life."

"From what Max tells me, Rooster shares your misery."

Her head came up, and it looked for an instant as if Lauren was about to break into tears. Sadness radiated off her like summer heat off asphalt.

"Whatever it is, it'll work itself out," Bethanne assured her, and at the same time realized she was speaking to herself as much as her friend.

"Did you know Rooster had been married before?" Lauren asked, sitting up straighter now.

"No." This was news to Bethanne. Not that it mattered one way or the other. "That upsets you?" she asked, wanting to be clear.

"Not in itself . . . It's just that Rooster never told me. I don't know that I can be married to a man who keeps secrets like that. It makes me wonder what else he might be hiding."

Bethanne took the first sip of her coffee while she gave this matter some thought.

"What does that say about our future together?" Lauren asked her. "What else might he choose not to tell me down the road? On the outside it might seem like a small thing, but my fear is that this could be indicative of his nature . . . and I can't deal with that."

Bethanne's hands cupped her mug. "I can't tell you why Rooster chose not to tell you. The marriage must have been years ago. Max has known Rooster for a long time and never mentioned it."

"He said he was young and immature," Lauren volunteered.

"Did he give you a reason for not telling you?"

"Not really . . . and he didn't seem to have any regrets about keeping it a secret. He did admit that he probably should have told me— but he didn't offer an apology."

"Isn't this something the two of you can work out?" Bethanne pressed. From what Max had said, the newlyweds hadn't spoken in almost two weeks. More and more, this situation reminded her of what was happening between her and Annie.

"I'd like to square matters between us," Lauren agreed, "but . . . it's more than not knowing about his first marriage."

"Oh?"

"People who have met the two of us claim that Rooster is all wrong for me. That we're too different, and while the attraction might be there now, it will wear off in time."

Unable to hold back her amusement, Bethanne smiled. "Oh, Lauren, I heard all those negative voices, too. Look at Max and me. When we first met he was riding his motorcycle aimlessly across the country and I was on a road trip with family. As far as I knew, he didn't have steady employment, and from all outside appearances, he was nothing more than a drifter."

Frowning, Lauren studied her closely.

"And here I was," Bethanne continued, "falling hopelessly in love with him. Max followed me to a couple of cities. At the time, I was trying to decide if I should get back together with my ex-husband. Well, you can imagine what my family and friends thought about Max."

"But he's partners with Rooster in the wine-distribution company," Lauren said.

"Yes, but at the time I didn't know it."

Lauren didn't say anything for a long time. Nor had she tasted her coffee. "I know I sound pathetic and silly to listen to what anyone else has to say about Rooster and me."

"What does your heart tell you?" Bethanne asked.

A look of sheer misery came over her. "I don't know what my heart wants. I thought I knew . . . I was so certain marrying Rooster was the right thing, and then all these doubts came at me like a major-league pitcher in the last game of the World Series."

Bethanne grinned at the mental image. "I know how you're feeling, Lauren, I do, because I went through many of the same emotions you're feeling now."

"But you weren't already married to Max."

"You're right, I wasn't. Still, I had a major decision to make, and I chose to marry Max despite what my daughter felt, despite Grant's desperate attempts to win me back, despite what my friends told me. I had to listen to my heart." She paused long enough to press her hand over her chest. "I married Max, and not once, for even an instant, have I regretted that decision."

Again, Lauren grew silent. "I wish I could say the same thing."

Regrets so soon? It broke Bethanne's heart to see Lauren filled with these doubts. "I will tell you that while I haven't known Rooster for a long time, I have always known him to be decent, and honorable and fair. I've never known him to lie."

"He lied to me . . . a lie of omission."

"Perhaps," she agreed. "Let me tell you about my first introduction to Rooster Wayne."

"Okay." She glanced up and looked eager to hear the story.

"As I mentioned earlier, I was traveling across the country with my ex-mother-in-law and Annie. We were somewhere in Nevada and stopped at a diner for lunch. The owner was beside herself. Her staff had all come down with the flu, so she was the only one there, cooking, serving, cleaning off the tables. She was completely stressed out because the diner was on the bus route.

"An entire busload of travelers was about to descend on the restaurant, and she would be forced to do everything on her own. When we heard her predicament, the three of us decided to help. I was appointed waitress because I'd had a job waiting on tables when I was in high school. Can you picture the scene?"

Lauren smiled and reached for her coffee. "Like a movie."

"Then four guys rode up to the diner on their motorcycles. They'd been on the road several days, and they looked like it. Dressed in leather, road weary, and hungry."

"Max and Rooster?"

"Plus a couple of their friends." Bethanne smiled at the memory. "I didn't know what to think. I was nervous and wary." She'd actually trembled when she approached the table to take their orders.

"I can imagine," Lauren murmured.

"I took their orders, and then the bus arrived and in a matter of minutes the place was packed. The four of us were running about, doing the best that we could. I got the order of a man who took up an entire booth on his own. He could have sat at the counter, but instead he chose to sit in a booth."

"That says a lot all on its own."

"Exactly," Bethanne concurred. "From the moment I approached him, he was rude, arrogant, and demanding. His coffee wasn't hot enough, and when I brought him another cup he had complaints about that, too. Nothing I did satisfied him."

"So what happened?"

A warm feeling came over her. "Rooster happened."

"Rooster?"

"Yes. He slid out of the booth, walked over to where that trouble-maker sat, and leaned against the tabletop until his face was mere inches from the other man's. Then he looked this pipsqueak in the eye and told him his demands were delaying his lunch. Then Rooster said when he got overly hungry, he got *real* cranky."

Lauren smiled for the first time since they'd met that afternoon. "Did that shut the troublemaker up?"

"Oh, big-time. Rooster was several inches taller, and he looked mean enough to rip the guy a new face. I didn't hear a word of complaint from that moment forward."

"I bet you didn't," Lauren said.

Bethanne reached across the space and placed her hand on Lauren's. "Eventually, you're going to need to make up your own mind when it comes to Rooster and your marriage," Bethanne said gently. "The best advice I can give you is to stop listening to everyone else and listen to yourself."

"I wish it was that easy," Lauren whispered.

"But it is, it really is," Bethanne promised. "You'll know. Do your best to drown out all those other voices and tune in to what your head and your heart are trying to tell you. Can you do that?"

Lauren was quiet for a moment and then nodded. "I'm certainly going to try."

Chapter Thirty-two

*T*alking to Bethanne had helped Lauren immensely. Her friend was right. She had to stop listening to anyone else and follow her instincts when it came to her relationship with Rooster.

Lauren woke up Saturday morning with a bad case of cramps. While a pregnancy would certainly have been an added complication, she found herself deeply disappointed. A baby would have given her a legitimate excuse to reach out to Rooster, to seek a resolution to this impasse.

Even though she wasn't feeling well, she was scheduled to work a half-day on Saturday from noon to closing. Sitting at the breakfast table, she sipped her morning coffee and checked her cellphone.

Her heart clenched when she saw a text message from Rooster. It was only a few words, but it spoke volumes.

R U pregnant?

The message had come in at three a.m., which told her he'd been awake, wondering, thinking of her. She'd spent many a sleepless night herself in the last two miserable weeks. She found it embarrassingly comforting to know this hadn't been an easy time for him, either.

How long she sat debating on her response, Lauren didn't know. In the end she decided on one word.

No.

Even as she pushed the "send" button, she was left to speculate whether he'd feel the same mix of emotions she had. Would he be relieved or be filled with a deep sense of disappointment the way she had?

For several minutes she waited for a response, but none came.

As she showered and readied for work, Lauren was filled with doubts and misgivings over her text to Rooster. She feared she might have sounded abrupt and dismissive. The problem was that she hadn't known what else to say.

What she should have done, she realized in retrospect, was reach out and talk to him. She had toyed with the idea and then decided against it because he'd asked her to contact him once she'd made a decision. If she had phoned, what would there have been to say? Lauren simply had nothing more to tell him . . . not yet, at any rate.

For all she knew, Rooster could have written her off as another mistake. If he had feelings for her, if he genuinely loved her, it made sense that he would contact her and offer reassurances. He hadn't. By the same token, she hadn't reached out to him, either.

Follow her instincts. Listen to her heart. But the messages coming from her heart were mixed with doubts and fears. One minute she was convinced she couldn't live without Rooster, and the next she was sure the marriage had been a complete blunder on both their parts.

It would help if she'd felt like she could discuss this dilemma with her parents, get their advice. But she hadn't reached out to either her mother or her father. The only person she'd told was Bethanne. Lauren was too embarrassed to admit that she might have one of the shortest marriages in their entire family history. Her parents and her sister didn't have a clue what she was going through, and for now that was what she wanted.

Once at John Michael Jewelers, Lauren was swamped with customers. She didn't have time to think about Rooster. Saturday afternoons were often their busiest time of the week. A good portion of
the early part of the afternoon was spent with a young couple who
came in to look at engagement rings.

Lauren noticed how they had eyes only for each other. At one time
it'd been like that with her and Rooster, too. As she helped them with
their selection, she learned Jason was home on leave from Fort Lewis
and would be shipping out soon for Afghanistan. Shelly, the young
woman who would be his wife, looked at him with such love and
tenderness that Lauren could barely concentrate.

As she showed the couple a selection of rings in their price range,
the answer she'd been seeking came to Lauren. Beyond a doubt and
without question, she knew her husband loved her and that she loved
him. It was in that instant when her heart spoke and she was able to
listen. She belonged with Rooster. Instantly, a sense of joy and freedom came over her. Her doubts fled, and her fears evaporated.

As Lauren rang up Jason and Shelly's purchase, she knew what she
had to do. No matter what it took, she would go to Rooster and insist
they talk. Then, together, they would find a way to make their marriage one that would last a lifetime.

Not long after the engaged couple left, another customer arrived.
Todd.

"Hello, Todd," Lauren said, when he stepped up to the counter
directly in front of her.

"Hi, Lauren." His eyes held on to her for an extra few moments.
"I heard from Elisa."

Lauren glanced over her shoulder. She couldn't imagine what her
friend would have to say to Todd.

"What did she tell you?" she asked, frankly curious. Elisa had
never been a fan of the newscaster. It shocked Lauren that Elisa would
reach out to Todd.

"Elisa didn't want to break your confidence, but she implied that
matters haven't gone smoothly between you and Rooster."

A chill went down Lauren's spine.

"I won't talk about my personal life while on the job," she said pointedly. "If you're interested in making a purchase, then I'll be happy to help you, but if not, then I suggest you wait for a more appropriate time."

Elisa sent her a frantic, apologetic look. Lauren couldn't believe the woman she considered her best friend would betray her like this. She stiffened and looked away. This was a matter she'd bring up with Elisa later.

"As it happens, I am interested in buying something," Todd told her, and glanced down at the display of engagement and wedding bands. "My inheritance came through, and I'm in a better financial position."

Lauren would gladly have turned him over to another of the sales associates, but they were all busy with other customers.

"What would you like to see?" she asked, doing her best to keep all emotion out of her voice and sound professional. She trained her gaze at a point directly behind Todd and avoided eye contact.

"A diamond ring," Todd said.

"For a man or a woman?" she asked, thinking she must sound akin to a robot.

"A woman's diamond ring. A beautiful one. The best you've got."

Unable to stop herself, Lauren's gaze shot to him. "A woman's?"

"Yes." He sat on the plush upholstered stool reserved for customers and stared down at the diamond rings on display.

"What price range?" she asked, doing her best to hide her surprise.

"Twenty thousand."

A high-end diamond. Interesting, to say the least. "You should be able to find a lovely ring for that price," she continued, in the same robotlike tone.

Todd scanned the wide selection of engagement and wedding rings, taking his time, giving each ring serious consideration.

"Would the young lady prefer white gold?" Lauren asked.

He glanced up. "Yes, I believe she would."

Lauren was growing more confused by the moment. Had Todd

come into the store to gloat? Their breakup had taken place only a few weeks earlier, so it didn't seem that he'd found someone else this quickly. But then, she had, so it was a possibility. Apparently, it was true, which only verified what she'd told him at the time of their breakup. If Todd had genuinely loved her, they would have married long ago. It seemed he'd found that woman, and, frankly, she was pleased for him.

Afraid to ask too many questions, Lauren brought out a second tray of diamond rings for him to review.

"What do you think?" he asked, looking up at her, his gaze warm and gentle.

"Think?" she asked, perplexed.

"Well, yes, seeing that I'm buying the diamond engagement ring for you, I'd like your input."

Lauren gasped and slapped her hand against her chest. "Me?"

"Yes, my love, the diamond ring is for you. I made the biggest mistake of my life letting you go. You know how I feel about you. I was a fool. You made a mistake, too. It's time we set all these mistakes right. I'm asking you to marry me."

For one wild, impulsive moment Lauren had the nearly overwhelming notion to flee. It took every bit of restraint she possessed not to grab her purse and run for all she was worth. While her mind had her racing out the front door, her feet refused to budge. Her mouth had instantly gone dry, and all she seemed capable of doing was staring at Todd in utter incredulity.

"I'm married."

"We can fix that, Lauren. We both know you married that . . . that Neanderthal to get back at me. You needed to do something drastic in order to wake me up, and, darling, it worked. The minute I heard the news you'd married Rooster, I went into shock. Then Elisa said things hadn't worked out as you'd planned, and I realized I'd been given a second chance. I wasn't about to let this opportunity to set matters straight slip by."

"I love Rooster," she said, more convinced than ever of what her heart had been trying to tell her for two long weeks.

Todd shook his head, denying her statement. "No, you don't. You used him to teach me a lesson. Well, Lauren, I'm an A-plus student. We'll get the legal stuff dealt with; I have friends who will help with the annulment, and . . ."

Lauren could barely believe what she was hearing. "Todd, please, stop. Just stop."

Frowning, he stared back at her.

It was hard to take in what he was saying. Once she had his full attention, she continued. "Do you honestly believe that I would use another human being in such a despicable way? Do you seriously think I married Rooster in order to get your attention?"

He blinked at her as if she was speaking in a foreign language.

"You seem to believe I married Rooster for my own selfish purposes. What kind of person do you take me for?" she asked, both sad and angry. "That only goes to show you don't really know me at all."

"I didn't mean it like that," Todd said, doing his best to back-pedal.

By then they'd garnered the attention of nearly everyone else in the store. Elisa looked concerned, as well she should. Lauren wasn't someone who had a quick trigger, but she was fast reaching the point where she was about to explode.

"I'm not interested in being a bigamist," she said, and she took the tray of diamond rings and quickly inserted it back into the display case and locked it. "Todd, I appreciate what you're trying to do, but it's too late. In your eyes Rooster might be a Neanderthal, but I see him in a completely different light and I happen to be completely and totally in love with him. I'm sorry, and I genuinely mean it, but your proposal is too little, too late." With that, Lauren retreated into the back room and started pacing, so frustrated and upset that she could barely think clearly.

Five minutes might have passed, or it could have been ten or twenty, she wasn't sure. All Lauren knew was that she needed to walk off this anger. Pacing, she would have worn down the carpet, had there been one.

Elisa joined her, and Lauren shot her friend a look hot enough to melt iron.

Before she could speak, Elisa held up her hands, imploring her, "I was wrong, and I apologize."

"You called Todd?" Even now, Lauren couldn't believe her friend, her dearest friend, would turn on her like this.

"Yes. It was stupid of me, and I've regretted it every minute since. I had no idea Todd would do anything like this."

"What were you thinking?" Lauren demanded.

"I don't know," Elisa admitted, shaking her head. "It was right after we got back from being with Katie and Dietrich and you told me you'd married Rooster. It was one shock after another, and when I met him, it was like seeing my daughter with that onion farmer. Instinctively, I felt the marriage was all wrong."

"Katie's marriage wasn't a mistake, and mine isn't, either. I happen to love my husband."

"I know that now," Elisa said, and tears filled her eyes. "I was wrong about you and Rooster. I've watched you these last two weeks, and I've seen how miserable you are. You honestly love him."

Lauren bit her lower lip. "I do, I really do."

"It shows, Lauren, and when he came into the shop and asked for you I could see how much he loved you, too. He's crazy about you. He could hardly wait to take you away, and maybe, just maybe . . . I've asked myself this a dozen times. Maybe I was afraid you would move to California and I would lose you, both as an employee and a friend. I couldn't bear that, and so I selfishly made you doubt yourself."

"It was more than the questions you made me face," she whispered. Elisa didn't know about Rooster's first marriage.

Although she'd already made her decision, Lauren had yet to tell Elisa her plans. "I'm going to Rooster. I'm going to California."

"Yes, go," Elisa urged. "I can't bear to see you this miserable. I'm your boss, but I'm also your friend, and as your friend I want you to be happy. If that means you leaving Seattle, then so be it. Go, and be happy, Lauren."

They hugged and then cried together. Lauren couldn't wait until she had a private moment. As soon as she was sure no one could listen in on her conversation, she tried to contact Rooster. His phone immediately went to voice mail. Waiting a half hour between calls, she kept trying, but each time he didn't pick up. Unwilling to be thwarted, Lauren returned to her condo and called the airlines.

She retrieved her suitcase from beneath the bed and tossed a few items into it. After several more fruitless tries, she decided either Rooster was purposely not responding or his cellphone wasn't with him. It didn't matter; she was going to him.

To be on the safe side, not wanting to make a complete idiot of herself, she phoned Bethanne.

"You told me to listen to my heart," she said, without bothering with the exchange of niceties.

"Lauren?"

"Yes, it's me, and I've decided I need to be with Rooster."

The line went silent for a few seconds before Bethanne burst out enthusiastically, "That's wonderful."

"I love him."

"And I know he feels the same way about you. Lauren, if only you knew."

"Knew what?"

"Knew what Rooster's been going through. Max said that in all the years he's known Rooster, he's never seen him like this. He isn't eating, he isn't sleeping. He looks dreadful. Max said there's no talking to him."

Her stomach clenched. "If that's the case, then why won't he answer my calls? I've tried to reach him again and again, but he isn't picking up."

Silence followed, and then Bethanne said, "That's odd."

"I thought the same thing. It doesn't matter. I've booked the next flight to Santa Rosa . . . I leave first thing in the morning."

"Oh, Lauren, I'm so glad. Rooster is a good man, and he loves you so much."

Lauren felt like she wanted to cry, and at the same time a sense of exhilaration filled her. She felt jubilant, as if she could walk on water. Her top priority was to reach Rooster and find her way back into his arms. When she rolled over in bed at night she wanted the security of him at her side. And, God willing, one day to have a family with him.

All night Lauren tossed and turned while she waited for Rooster to return her calls, voice messages, and texts. It seemed she woke every hour in order to check her cell to see if she might have inadvertently missed a reply. The silence was torture.

Undeterred, she caught a taxi to the airport and boarded the flight to Santa Rosa Sunday morning. The flight was miserable, but thankfully short.

It was still morning when she landed, and to her surprise she found Max at baggage claim waiting for her. Immediately, her heart went into overdrive. The only reason she could think that Rooster's best friend would meet her was if something bad had happened to her husband. Had she been so obtuse not to think of this sooner? Not once had she considered that Rooster might have been in an accident or hurt.

By the time she reached Max, her heart was beating so fast it sounded like a race-car engine in her ears. "What's happened to Rooster?" she begged, grabbing hold of Max's arm.

"Nothing. At least nothing that I know of, anyway."

Her relief was instantaneous. She closed her eyes and whispered, "Thank God." Then another thought came to her. "Then why are you here?"

He shrugged. "Because Rooster isn't."

That, too, was a possibility she hadn't taken into consideration. "Then where is he?"

Max frowned. "I wish I knew. He took off on his motorcycle."

"He didn't tell you where he was headed?"

"No. All he said was that he needed time away in order to clear his head. He rode out of here like the hounds of hell were nipping at his heels."

"He didn't take his cellphone with him?"

"Apparently not."

"When will he be back?" She fired the questions at him like a Gatling gun.

"I can't tell you that, either. What would you like to do?"

"Do?" she repeated. She didn't have a choice, not really. She would do what any wife would. "I'll wait for him," she said.

Max nodded approvingly and reached for her suitcase. "Then I'll take you to his place."

Chapter Thirty-three

Life is too short to knit with ugly yarn.
—Jennifer Vancalcar,
owner and dyer, Holiday Yarns

"We're going out to dinner?" Casey asked, her dark eyes narrowing with suspicion as she stood in the hallway outside Lydia's bathroom. "*Just* the three of us?"

Lydia looked away from the mirror, the eye-shadow applicator in her hand. "Cody's spending the night with Jaxon."

"Yeah, but I heard you talking to Jaxon's mom," Casey said as she leaned against the doorjamb, "and you *asked* if Cody could spend the night."

"I did," Lydia concurred.

"It's not my birthday," Casey reminded her.

"Yes, honey, I know."

Casey straightened, left momentarily, and then just as quickly returned. "Are you mad at me about something?"

"No. Your father and I wouldn't be taking you to dinner if we were upset about something, would we?"

Casey frowned with uncertainty. "Ah . . . I guess not."

"My girls ready?" Brad called out from the living room. He'd been dressed and prepared to leave ten minutes earlier.

"Give me another second," Lydia called back.

"I'm ready . . . I think," Casey added. She walked out of the bedroom and came back a second time. "This dinner is about Grandma, isn't it?"

"Casey, relax." Lydia should have known her daughter would be apprehensive. She wished now that she'd explained matters earlier. "Yes, your father and I want to talk to you, but it isn't anything bad."

"I know Grandma's getting worse," Casey said, with a slight edge to her voice. "She sometimes can't remember who I am now . . . and she forgets to eat."

Her mother remained a major concern for Lydia. Earlier in the week Margaret and she had met with the director of the assisted-living complex regarding her mother's return from the hospital. Since Mary Lou's fall and stroke, her physical and mental health had rapidly deteriorated. Before the end of the meeting, Mrs. Wilson had recommended that Lydia's mother be transferred to a memory-care facility.

Lydia hated the thought of bringing her mother into a completely new environment. While in the hospital and nursing home, she'd looked small and lost and afraid. Like everyone, her mother was most comfortable with what was familiar. And while she didn't participate in many of the social activities at the retirement facility, her mother had settled nicely into her own small apartment.

"Margaret and I are thinking about moving Mom," Lydia explained.

Casey was instantly concerned. "Moving her? Where?"

"We don't know yet. We've just started looking."

Anxiety tightened Casey's sweet face. "She'll still be close by, won't she? You aren't taking her out of the city, are you?"

"Casey, I don't know. Now, let's get going; your father's made reservations."

Brad was already in the car by the time Lydia and Casey joined him. Casey climbed into the backseat, and, after snapping the seat belt in place, she tightly crossed her arms.

"Hey, what's going on?" Brad asked, looking at Casey from the rearview mirror.

"Mom's moving Grandma."

"We really don't have any choice, Casey," Lydia explained with a tired sigh. "I don't like it any better than you do." This was a difficult decision and Lydia and her sister took their responsibility for their mother seriously.

"Grandma needs us," Casey insisted.

"Which is what this is all about," Lydia said, doing the best she could to explain. "Moving Mom to a memory-care facility is taking care of her the best way we know how."

"Will I still be able to visit?"

"Of course."

"What if this new place isn't on a bus route?"

"Margaret and I will take that into consideration when we check out the facilities." The closeness between the two was an asset to her mother's health. Casey's attention and devotion had helped Mary Lou tremendously, and, for that matter, Casey, too.

"Promise you'll do your best to keep Grandma close so I can visit her?"

"Promise," Lydia echoed.

"Is all that settled now?" Brad asked. He still hadn't backed out of the driveway.

"I guess," Casey muttered with a pout. "But I don't like the idea of Grandma moving."

"I don't think anyone wants this," Brad assured her, "but, like your mother said, it's necessary."

"Whatever."

Brad had made reservations at a fun Italian restaurant in the downtown Seattle area that specialized in spaghetti. The atmosphere was homey, and the food was good and relatively inexpensive. It was one of Casey's favorites places to eat. Cody's, too.

The hostess escorted them to a booth, and Casey sat across from Brad and Lydia. Brad ordered two glasses of Chianti Classico for Lydia and himself. Casey kept her gaze focused on them both after the server took their drink orders.

"Whatever it is you want to talk about must really be bad," she muttered, studying her menu as if it were the final test for getting her driver's license.

"Bad?" Brad asked. "What makes you say that?"

"I know stuff," Casey said, leaning back in the polished wooden booth. Her eyes narrowed. "You don't live in as many homes as I have without picking up on things."

"Really?" Brad leaned forward, highly interested, it seemed. "And what have you learned?"

"First off, I could always tell when a family had decided to pass me off to someone else. They reacted one of two ways. Either they completely ignored me as if I was already out the door. Or they started doing all kinds of nice things for me."

"Like what?" Brad asked. "Taking you out to dinner in an Italian restaurant?"

"Not anything that big. Little things, like buying me a new pair of shoes or getting my hair cut or something like that."

"You don't think your father and I are going to pass you off to another family, do you?" Lydia asked. This had been a keen concern of Casey's earlier. Lydia hoped that by now Casey had come to understand that she was their daughter, a part of their family, and a big part of their hearts and their lives.

"No, no," Casey assured them. "It's not that."

"So what are you thinking?" Brad asked.

The server returned with the two glasses of wine and Casey's favorite soda. "Are you ready to order?" he asked.

They each decided on something different. Lydia enjoyed the eggplant Parmesan, Brad asked for spaghetti and meatballs, and Casey wanted lasagna. After writing down their requests, the server left.

Brad waited until the young man was gone before he said, "Getting back to your answer to my question." He gestured for Casey to continue with her explanation. "You think something's up because your mother and I are taking you to dinner."

"Without Cody," Casey added pointedly, "who you made sure was someplace else this evening."

"Without Cody," Brad said, and reached for his wineglass.

Her husband, Lydia noticed, seemed to be enjoying this.

She wasn't. Already, her stomach was in knots, and she wondered if she'd even be able to taste her dinner.

"I figure you and Mom want to tell me something," Casey continued, "only I don't know what it is."

"We aren't sending you away," Lydia reiterated.

"Well, duh. If you were going to do that you would have done it long before now. I'm not the easiest kid."

Brad chuckled. Sensing her nervousness, he reached for Lydia's hand and gave it a gentle squeeze. "Come on, Casey, you aren't so bad."

"My grades were good." Casey was proud of her final school report, and well she should be. She'd scored As and Bs in every subject. When she'd first come to them, her grades had been below average and she'd struggled in reading and math skills.

"Your grades weren't just good; they were great. Even in math," Lydia added. The subject had been her daughter's weakest. It was because Casey needed to attend a summer-school course in math that she'd originally come to live with them.

"You're taking me to dinner because you wanted to tell me about Grandma?" Her voice elevated with the question as though she was afraid of what they had to say.

"Not really," Lydia said, "although that's part of it."

Casey shifted uncomfortably. "It's the nightmares, then, isn't it?"

"Indirectly."

"You're afraid what's going to happen to me if Grandma dies."

"It has us worried, honey," Lydia agreed. "And it isn't if Grandma dies, it's when."

Casey brushed off their concern. "I'll be okay."

"What about the nightmares?" Brad asked.

"They'll go away eventually," Casey answered, as if these horrific dreams were a small thing.

"They've been happening more frequently lately."

Casey lowered her eyes and nodded. "I know, but it'll get better soon."

All evidence pointed to exactly the opposite.

"I've had these dreams before, and they come and go," she mentioned casually. "Really, it's no big deal."

Brad looked over at their daughter, and his words were low and serious. "Casey, these dreams terrify you; we want to help."

Their daughter looked up again and blinked several times. "You want me to tell you about the dream, don't you? That's why you brought me to dinner."

"No, sweetheart, we don't need you to tell us, especially since you feel strongly about it. You haven't wanted to talk about what the dream involves, and that's fine."

"It is?" A look of relief came over her as her shoulders relaxed against the back of the booth.

"But you need someone who can help you."

Right away, Casey tensed again and adamantly shook her head. "I don't need anyone."

"Casey . . ."

"I'll outgrow it."

"Sweetheart, listen," Lydia said gently, and leaned forward, stretching her arm across the table, "we aren't doing this because we're angry or upset. We want to help you get over whatever it is that is causing you to have these nightmares."

"I don't want to know what's causing them," she said, her voice growing stronger now. The people in the booth across from them glanced over, and right away Casey lowered her voice. "I'll be okay . . . I won't have the dream anymore."

"You're being unrealistic. Sooner or later you'll need to confront whatever is behind this."

"No, I won't," Casey insisted, in complete denial.

"All we're asking," Brad said in gentle, encouraging tones, "is that you talk to someone trained in this area who will help explain why this is happening. And then they can give you a means of dealing with it."

"Like who am I supposed to talk to?" That suspicious edge was back in full force.

"A trained professional."

Casey flattened her hands on the tabletop and half rose from the bench seat. "Are you going to send me to the loony bin?"

"Loony bin?" Lydia said, unable to hold back a smile. "Where in heaven's name did you ever hear that expression?"

"From Grandma."

"Of course," Lydia whispered. It should have been obvious.

"To answer your question, your mother and I aren't sending you anywhere. You're staying with us."

Casey took a long drink of her soda through the straw. "That's a relief."

"But we want you to talk to someone."

"Who?" Casey's eyes narrowed.

"A counselor."

Even before the word was completely out of Brad's mouth, Casey started to shake her head. "No way."

"Casey, please listen."

"It's not going to happen."

The waiter delivered their dinners, but they barely noticed. Casey sat with her back as stiff as a corpse, determination written on every part of her body.

"Besides, we can't afford for me to talk to anyone. I heard you and Dad discussing this a few months back. When Dad found out how expensive seeing a counselor was, he said there was no way the family could fit it into the budget."

"But I also said," Brad interrupted, "that we would find a way, because that's what families do. You need help, and as your parents, we are determined to see that you get it."

"A counselor costs lots of money," Casey reminded them, looking smug.

"The thing is," Lydia said, gripping her daughter's hand, "we have already made an appointment with a counselor. Evelyn Boyle recommended one who is willing to charge us on a sliding scale."

"A what?" Casey asked with a frown.

"We'll be charged according to our income level," Brad explained.

"And because of the boom in sales at the yarn store, we're able to do this. I need to thank whoever it was who put out those baskets."

"The yarn baskets?" Casey echoed, her frown darkening.

"I don't know who is behind this, but I owe them a huge debt of appreciation. My business has gone way up due to all the publicity. I've been able to give Margaret extra hours and make some improvements I'd been putting off due to finances. And now we can get you the help you need, too."

"Whoever thought of that idea did your mother a huge favor," Brad added.

Her daughter lowered her head, but not before Lydia noticed a huge smile come into place. "Casey?"

"It was Grandma and me. Oh, and Ava helped me, too."

"Excuse me?" Lydia was sure she hadn't heard correctly.

Casey looked up. "It was Grandma and me," she repeated, louder this time. "I heard you and Dad talking about how the yarn store is barely surviving financially. I told Grandma, and we decided we should do something to help."

"You seem to listen in on other people's conversations a lot," Brad noticed.

Casey shrugged. "It's a habit I picked up in foster homes. It was the only way I knew what was happening."

"Go on," Lydia said, anxious now to hear about her mother and Casey's scheme.

Excitedly, Casey reached for her fork and waved it about. "Like I said, I heard you tell Dad that the yarn store wasn't doing so great. Then I told Grandma. Together we came up with the idea of putting baskets with yarn around for people to knit."

"Who thought of it?"

Casey shrugged. "Grandma, sort of. She said whenever she saw a basket with yarn in it she wanted to sit down and knit a few rows. That got me to thinking that maybe other people might feel the same way."

"But, my goodness, where did you get all those baskets?"

"From Grandma."

Mary Lou had several such baskets, but Lydia specifically remembered clearing them out of the house when they moved their mother. "Margaret and I gave those baskets to charity."

"You tried, you mean," Casey said, her smile huge now. "Grandma took them out of the pile and had them placed in a box in her storage unit at the assisted-living place."

"She remembered the baskets in a storage unit?" Amazing, seeing that half the time her mother didn't recognize Lydia any longer.

"And she had lots of yarn there, too."

"So you're the one who took those baskets around town?" Brad asked, and sounded shocked and amazed.

"Yup. And Ava helped deliver them, too." She waved her fork at them. "Don't let your dinner get cold. This is really good. My favorite."

"About the counselor."

Casey's shoulders sagged. "Okay, okay, I'll go talk to her. It is a woman, isn't it?"

"Yes," Lydia assured her.

"I'll go."

"Thank you," Brad told her.

Casey frowned again. "Only because you want me to, but I'm not going to like it, and I'm not promising to tell her the dream, either."

"All we're asking is that you be open and willing."

Casey sighed as if a huge demand had been made of her. "I'll try."

"Thank you, sweetheart," Lydia said.

Brad dug into his spaghetti and meatballs, took one bite, and looked up. "Hey, this *is* good."

Chapter Thirty-four

Max climbed the stairs to Annie's condo and knocked on her front door. He figured he had a good chance of catching her at home at ten o'clock on a Sunday morning. It wasn't likely to be a pleasant meeting, but he felt obliged to make one last attempt to reason with Bethanne's daughter.

He rang the doorbell, and then, planting the tips of his fingers in his back jean pockets, he waited, his heart pounding, praying what he had to tell her would make a difference.

To Max's surprise, it wasn't Annie who answered the door. Instead, it was Grant Hamlin, her father. This meeting was going to be even worse than he'd expected.

"Max!" Grant sounded just as shocked to see him.

"Annie home?" Max asked.

"No," he said starkly. "You just missed her."

"Do you know when she'll be back?"

Grant shrugged. "I can't say."

Max nodded but didn't budge.

"She knows how much I like Starbucks coffee. You know Annie. She loves her dad, so she volunteered to run down to the corner to pick me up a cup."

"She's a thoughtful daughter."

Grant stared at him hard. "She is that, all right."

"Can I wait here for her?"

"By all means."

Max hesitated. He didn't like the look in Grant's eyes, and he wasn't sure he should trust the other man. "You don't mind my waiting?"

"Not at all. It might do us good to talk man to man, just the two of us."

"I agree."

Grant stepped aside and held the door open for Max. "Make yourself at home," he said, and gestured toward the sofa. Bethanne's ex-husband claimed the chair, and for an awkward moment all they did was stare at each other.

"What's your business with Annie?" Grant asked.

Max sat close to the edge of the sofa cushion. "Bethanne mentioned that you've taken her under your wing at the real-estate office." It bothered him as much as it did Bethanne that Annie worked as a receptionist when she was vastly overqualified for the position.

"My Annie's got the same organizational skills as her mother."

"How does she like working for you?" Although he asked, Max didn't expect the truth.

Grant shrugged. "So far so good. She's getting a little antsy to get her Realtor license. All in due course. I'll let her know when she's ready to start training."

Max decided to let the comment slide rather than point out the obvious. With Annie's business acumen and attention to detail, she was more than ready. Max found it difficult to understand why her father would want her in a lesser position.

"You didn't mention why you stopped by," Grant prodded.

Mainly because Max hadn't been given the opportunity. "I wanted to tell Annie that I've decided to move my wine-distribution business to Washington State."

Grant seemed unable to hide his surprise. His eyes widened a fraction, and for a moment it seemed he didn't know what to say. "Really?"

"It wasn't an easy decision."

"From what I heard, the cost of moving a business such as yours is prohibitive."

It was going to hurt financially—that was certain—but in the long run it should work out well. "It isn't about the money."

Grant shook his head in disbelief. "It's always about the money. I'm surprised you haven't figured that out before now."

"For some that might be the case," Max agreed, resisting adding anything more.

Grant crossed his arms. "I suppose you're making this gallant sacrifice for Bethanne's sake."

"Yes." And for Annie and Andrew and Courtney and Bethanne's first grandchild, but Max felt it was better not to mention his reasons.

"You love her that much?" Grant asked, as if even now he found the move unbelievable. Drastic, even.

"More, and because I love Bethanne, I love her children, too."

"My children," Grant said forcefully.

"Your children," Max agreed. "You're their father. Nothing's going to change that, and I wouldn't want it to. When Bethanne and I decided to marry, I fully intended to love her children."

"Right noble of you," Grant muttered sarcastically. "So you're moving to Seattle."

"Yes."

"When?"

"It'll take a few months, I suspect. Rooster and I talked about it quite a bit before he left."

"Rooster left? Another business trip?"

"In a manner of speaking." Max wasn't going to let Grant sidetrack him with questions about his partner.

"In other words, you're going to be around Seattle on a permanent basis?"

"Yes." That was sure to upset Grant.

The other man went silent for several seconds. "Your being here could get downright *uncomfortable for you*," Grant suggested. The last few words hung in the air between them like a wire walker suspended above Niagara Falls.

"What are you suggesting?" Max asked, confronting Grant head-on. He didn't like the sound of this threat.

"I'm saying such a move might mean trouble for you in the future," Grant murmured. "I have Annie on my side, and we both know how miserable Bethanne is without her daughter. Annie's a bit of a drain on me, but she serves her purpose. I could change things and coax her to reunite with her mother."

This situation with her daughter had torn Bethanne apart. Grant knew it and used Annie against his ex-wife for his own selfish purposes.

"Spell out exactly what you mean," Max demanded.

Grant laughed as though Max's anger amused him. "I have the power to make you and my ex miserable."

"And you'd use Annie to do it?"

"Without a qualm, but," he said, and raised his index finger, "I have a solution."

Max brought his hands together and clenched them into tight fists. The hairs on the back of his head stood up, and even before Grant spoke, Max knew he wasn't going to like what the other man had to say.

"A solution?" he repeated.

"Yes." Grant relaxed in the chair, looking smug and confident. "Like I said, I could convince Annie to make amends with her mother or I could make sure Bethanne paid the price for dumping me when she did."

Grant seemed to conveniently forget that he was the one who'd walked out on their family. He'd been involved in an affair long before he'd divorced his wife.

"Is there a *but* in this as well?" Max asked. "You know, *but* something could change your mind?"

Grant shrugged. "This hasn't been a great year for real estate," he commented.

Max had heard the market was picking up. That didn't appear to be the case with Grant, however. Bethanne had told him this was the third or fourth brokerage firm her ex-husband had been with since their divorce.

"Finances are tight for me at the moment," Grant admitted. "It's a temporary situation that should be rectified soon, but at the moment I'm low on funds."

Outraged, Max bolted to his feet. "You want me to pay you to persuade Annie to mend fences with her mother?"

Again, Grant's answer came in the form of a nonchalant shrug.

"That's blackmail."

"Call it what you will, but I'd prefer to think of it as a business proposition. I do something for you and you do something for me. You know what I mean. You scratch my back and I'll scratch yours."

Max was so angry he was afraid he was about to do something he would later regret.

"I'm sure we could come to amicable terms."

"I don't think so," Max said between gritted teeth.

Grant sighed as though disappointed. "It's a pity." He glanced at his watch. "I can't imagine what's taking Annie so long, but you can bet when she arrives you won't get a warm welcome."

"Actually, Dad, I'm here," Annie said, stepping out from the hallway and into the living room.

"Sweetheart," Grant said, and rose to hug his daughter. "I was just telling Max—"

"I heard what you had to say to Max," she said, and glared at her father. She braced her hands against her hips, and her face was red with anger. "I'm a bit of a drain, am I? You want to hurt Mom? And this conversation with Max isn't the only one I heard. I came back while you were on the phone with Monica."

Grant's eyes rounded with surprise before he recovered. "Honey, you only heard one side of the conversation—"

"It was enough," she said. "More than enough, actually. All this talk about Mom breaking your heart and how you'll never be able to love again was nothing more than a bunch of bull."

Max could see his presence wasn't needed or appreciated. This was between Annie and her father. "I'll go. Can we talk later, Annie?"

She nodded. "And thank you," she said, as she cast him an apologetic look.

As he walked out the door, a smile came over him as he heard Grant try to explain away the proposal Annie had heard. He wasn't privy to Annie's response, but from the little he did hear, Bethanne's daughter was having none of it.

Max's steps were lighter than they had been in a long while as he returned to his wife. He parked in the garage and whistled as he let himself into the house.

"I'm home," he called out as he stepped into the kitchen.

"I'm out here." Bethanne was on the back patio, planting flowers in the wooden boxes he'd installed along the top of the railing. She wore garden gloves and a big straw hat. Max joined her and slipped his arms around her waist from behind, kissing the side of her neck.

"This is a warm welcome. Where'd you go?" she asked.

"Out."

She made a dismissive sound. "I know that tone of voice. You've been up to something, Max Scranton."

"Could be. Need any help here?" he asked, resting his chin on her shoulder, admiring his wife's amazing green thumb.

"Are you volunteering?" she asked.

"Not really, but I felt I should ask."

She laughed softly. "That's what I thought. Say, how about a motorcycle ride this afternoon?"

Max released her. "I don't think that's a good idea."

His wife twisted around so that she faced him and frowned, her gaze full of questions. It wasn't like Max to refuse to ride. "What's up?"

Bethanne had a smudge of dirt on her cheek, and, using his index finger, Max wiped it off. "Have I told you recently that I'm the luckiest man in the world to be married to you?"

"No, but I'll accept the compliment. However, I feel that I'm the lucky one. I still can't believe you're moving to Seattle for me."

"For us."

Bethanne braced her forehead against his chest, and it looked as if she was about to cry again. When he'd first told her of his decision, his wife had been so overwhelmed she'd been unable to speak.

Now that it looked hopeful that Rooster and Lauren would get back together, moving the wine-distribution company to the Puget Sound area made even more sense.

The doorbell chimed, and Bethanne and Max broke apart. "Will you get that?" his wife asked, wiping the tears from her eyes with the back of her gloved hand.

Max shook his head. "I have a feeling you're going to want to answer this yourself."

Bethanne frowned, and when the doorbell sounded again, she hurried into the house and to the front door. After a couple moments, Max wandered back into the kitchen in time to see Bethanne and her daughter hugging each other.

"I'm so sorry, Mom, so sorry. I've been an idiot about you and Max. Can you both forgive me?"

Bethanne sobbed and clung to her daughter.

They continued to hold each other for a long time. Max walked over to the corner of the kitchen counter and pulled out a box of tissues. Bethanne's gaze caught his, and she smiled through her tears.

"Dad lied to me," Annie said as the two women came into the kitchen arm in arm. "And then he tried to lie his way out of it."

Max handed both women a fresh tissue. Then, to his surprise, Annie broke away from her mother and hugged him. "I need to apologize to you, too. I'm sorry for the horrible things I said to you, Max. You love my mom, you honestly love her."

"I do, and I care deeply for you, too, Annie. You're part of Bethanne, and I love those she loves."

"I've been such a brat."

"You won't get an argument from me," Max said and chuckled.

"What happened?" Bethanne asked after dabbing the moisture out of her eyes.

Annie's gaze went from her mother to Max and then back again. "Dad stopped by this morning, and he complained about my brand of coffee. He's really picky when it comes to coffee, so I volunteered to get him a cup from the Starbucks on the corner."

From what Max knew of the other man, Grant was picky about a lot of things other than a certain brand of coffee.

"I left," Annie continued, "and realized it was cooler out than I had expected, so I came back into the condo for a sweater."

Max suspected it had been something like this.

"Dad didn't hear me come in. He was in the kitchen on his cell with his back to me, talking to a woman named Monica. It was clear he was involved with her romantically, which I sort of knew, because she calls the office three and four times a day, always with a convenient excuse.

"I tried to ignore what Dad was saying, but it was pretty graphic as he described what he intended to do to her physically."

Bethanne shook her head and held up her hand. "I get the point."

"I went into my bedroom and then the doorbell rang and it was Max. Dad answered the door, and I was stuck in the hallway. I didn't want Dad to know I'd been listening in on his conversation, and at the same time I couldn't very well walk out the front door." She glanced over at Max. "Do you want to tell Mom what my father proposed?"

"No, it isn't necessary. Your mother already knows what kind of man your father is."

"And now I know, too. I can't believe I was so blind; I can't tell you how sorry I am."

"We all do foolish things," Bethanne said in a comforting way, eager to forgive her daughter.

"Can I have my old job back?" Annie pleaded.

"Yes, oh, yes. I've missed you so much . . . everyone has."

"I've missed you, too."

Mother and daughter hugged again, and then, to his amazement, Annie let one arm loose and stretched it out toward Max.

knitting the baby blanket for her sister, and then, in a spirit of confidence, knit another for her and Rooster's child if she were ever to become pregnant.

"He hasn't been in touch with anyone?"

Silly question. "No."

"Not even with Max?"

"No." Lauren had to believe Max wouldn't keep anything from her. If Rooster had been in contact and Max had lied about it, then he was a good actor. He seemed as concerned about his friend as Lauren was.

"Surely Rooster won't stay away much longer."

That certainly was Lauren's wish. "Who can say? Max told me after he lost his wife and daughter he took off on his motorcycle for something like three years."

"Three years? You don't think Rooster will be gone that long, do you?"

"I . . . I don't know." All Lauren could do was hope and pray that he would feel her love and that would draw him back. Each night she lay in bed, sleepless and filled with anxiety, willing Rooster to head home. Home to her. Home to the life they would build together.

Lauren had so much she wanted to say. So much she longed to tell him. First and foremost, it was important that he know how much she loved him and wanted to make their marriage work. It'd taken her this long to find a man she wanted to spend her life with, and she refused to give up without giving their relationship every opportunity to succeed.

Elisa hesitated. "I hate to ask this, I really do, but Garry and I need to know how long you intend to wait for Rooster. Will you remain in California and find work there? Basically, I'm asking if Garry and I should hire another sales associate."

Lauren wished she had an answer, but she simply didn't know.

Elisa must have sensed her uncertainty, because she added, "If you decide you'll remain in Santa Rosa another week or so, Garry and I will hold your position."

Chapter Thirty-five

*L*auren's phone chirped, and even knowing Rooster had left his cell behind, she grabbed it, hoping, praying it was her husband. Hope did indeed spring eternal.

"Hello?" She made her greeting a question, a plea, desperately wanting to hear from Rooster.

"Lauren, it's Elisa."

Her optimism was dashed against the sharp-edged rocks of reality. "Oh, hi," she said, doing her best to recover and hide her disappointment.

"I take it you haven't heard from Rooster."

"Not a peep."

"You've been waiting for him how long now?"

"A week today." Although it felt like a year. Each day dragged by with a slowness that was nothing short of cruel. Lauren had done everything she could think to keep busy. She'd cleaned his house, rearranged furniture, baked cookies, shopped for groceries, finished

"Another week?" Lauren felt incapable of making a simple decision.

"I don't want to sway you one way or the other," Elisa added. "I've learned my lesson, and I apologize again for not keeping my opinions to myself."

"You're my friend, Elisa, and friends speak their minds."

"Perhaps, but with you and with Katie, I really blew it."

Hearing her friend's humble apology boosted Lauren's spirits.

"All Garry and I need is some guidance regarding your plans."

Lauren knew she couldn't continue to stay in California. Eventually, she would need to return to Seattle. She had financial responsibilities, and she needed her job to meet those obligations. "I'll talk to Max and get back to you."

"Okay, I'll wait for your call." Elisa and Garry had been more than patient. It would be a disservice to them to keep them dangling much longer.

Monday morning, when Lauren knew Max would be at work, she took Rooster's car and visited her husband's best friend. They'd touched base a couple of times over the last seven days, but Max claimed he had nothing to tell her. Lauren believed him. Max was concerned, too.

His assistant, a grandmotherly woman, showed her into Max's office. He was staring at his computer screen and frowning when she came into the room. He glanced up, saw her, and blinked.

"Lauren." He stood, walked around his desk, and gave her a brief hug. "Have you heard from Rooster?"

"No. You?"

Max shook his head. "I don't think we need to worry. Not yet."

"I came because I need your advice."

"Sit down." Max gestured toward the chair for her to take a seat. Still standing, he leaned his backside against the edge of his desk, stretched out his legs, and crossed his ankles. "Now, what can I do for you?"

"My boss needs to know what my plans are, if she should hold my job or not."

Max appeared as unsure as she felt.

"I'd like to stay and wait for Rooster," she admitted, "but I can't remain in California indefinitely."

"To stay or to leave? That's a good question." He rang his assistant and asked her to bring in coffee, which she did. It seemed Max needed the caffeine to help him think this through. After a bit, he returned to his desk chair and asked, "How are you holding up?"

She shrugged. "Okay, I guess. I just wish Rooster would let one of us know where he is."

"I know. I was hoping . . ." He left the rest unsaid.

"Does he do this sort of thing often?"

"No, never." Max appeared as perplexed by his partner's behavior as she was.

"Why wouldn't he take his cellphone?" she pleaded. This was the most frustrating thing about Rooster's disappearance. At least then she'd be able to text him. That way he would know that she loved him and wanted to take whatever steps were necessary to make their marriage viable.

"I suspect he either forgot it or simply chose not to be bothered."

"By me?"

"By anyone," Max clarified.

"What if he's been in an accident? What if he never comes back? What if a gang jumps him and leaves him for dead? What if he decides he wants nothing more to do with me? What if—"

"Lauren, Lauren . . ." Max stopped her, holding up his hand. "I don't have any answers for you. I wish I did. I will tell you that Rooster can take care of himself, so you shouldn't worry on that account. He needs to clear his head, and once he does, he'll be back. How long that will take is anyone's guess."

Cupping the foam coffee cup, Lauren let his words sink in. All at once she felt clarity and knew what she needed to do. "I'm going back to Seattle. I'll give Rooster the rest of this week before I book my airfare. I'll tell Elisa and Garry I'll return to work . . . I don't know what else to do." And really there were only a few options available to her.

Max nodded. "I can't say I blame you. If I hear anything from Rooster, you'll be the first person I contact."

"Thank you," she whispered. Not wanting to take up any more of his time, she left.

The rest of the day dragged, as did Tuesday and Wednesday. The key, Lauren realized, was keeping herself busy. It was either that or go stir-crazy with worry. The what-ifs continued to plague her like pesky mosquitoes on a muggy summer night. Once a question came into her mind, it was a painful itch that was hard to ignore and a constant nuisance. She did her best to swat down the doubts, but with little success.

Wednesday night she was sitting up in bed reading when she thought she heard the faint sound of a motorcycle in the distance. As the harsh engine noise grew closer, she was convinced it had to be Rooster.

Right away her heart started to pound hard and fast. Certain now that it must be Rooster, Lauren leaped out of bed and ran a complete circle around the room before she could think clearly. Once she did, she grabbed a hairbrush and jerked it through her hair. Then she reached for her favorite cologne. In her rush, she sprayed her face instead of the pulse points in her neck and then was forced to blink several times as her eyes filled with tears from the irritation.

Rather than turn on the lights, she hurried downstairs and stood in the middle of the living room in her long white nightgown, clenching her hands in front of her, waiting to surprise her husband.

Sure enough, a few minutes later the door off the garage opened and Rooster stepped into the house. His boots made clunking sounds against the hardwood floor as he walked into the darkness. He had a side table just off the kitchen that Lauren had moved when she rearranged the living room furniture. When he went to drop his keys where he normally did, they crashed onto the floor.

"What the . . ." he muttered and switched on the lights. Instantly, a yellow softness flooded the area.

She wanted to say something, but her heart was in her throat as excitement and joy filled her. Her first glance at him nearly took her breath away. He looked tired and road weary, as if he'd been on his bike for days without end. His shoulders were slouched slightly forward as if he was deeply depressed.

Lauren wasn't sure when he saw her or even if he did. "Hello, Rooster," she whispered.

He stood half a room away and froze, glaring at her as if she were an apparition, as if he wasn't sure he should believe it was her.

In her mind, Lauren had fantasized about their reunion. Being a die-hard romantic, she had envisioned him rushing to take her in his arms, kissing her senseless.

Instead, Rooster stared at her as if she was the last person on earth he wanted to see. She waited for him to comment, to say something, but he remained stubbornly silent.

"I moved a few things around," she said, motioning toward the table. Her voice sounded odd even to herself. "Actually, I sort of rearranged the entire living room."

His gaze left hers as he glanced around, and as his eyes scanned the room, his frown deepened. It went without saying that he didn't like what she'd done.

Lauren felt she should explain. "While I was waiting for you . . . I read a book on feng shui and decided to put a few of the basic principles into practice." She wanted to explain more of what she'd learned but hesitated. He still hadn't said a word, didn't give her even the slightest indication that he was pleased to find her in his home.

He certainly didn't seemed impressed with her efforts. "What else did you do?" he asked . . . demanded.

She made flopping motions with her hands. "I baked oatmeal-raisin cookies."

"I hate oatmeal."

His words felt like an accusation, as if she'd purposely set out to bake something he would dislike. "They're in the freezer . . ."

"The freezer?"

"I tend to eat when I'm upset, and so I removed the temptation."

He hadn't moved one step closer to her. Lauren had waited for this moment for days, her heart in her hand, and nothing was turning out the way she'd hoped . . . the glorious reunion she'd envisioned.

"What are you doing here?" he asked next, and again it was more demand than question.

The lump in her throat made it impossible for her to speak. Apparently, she'd made a huge mistake, and Rooster wasn't willing to give them another chance. While he'd been away, he'd cleared more than his head; he'd cleared his heart of her as well.

Rather than even attempt an answer, she swallowed hard and nodded, letting him know that she received his message loud and clear and she would leave. Tears clouded her eyes. They both remained stock-still.

"You want me to leave, don't you?"

He didn't answer.

His action told her that was exactly what he wanted, but his eyes claimed just the opposite. His gaze remained intently focused on her, as if he couldn't make himself look away.

It was that small encouragement that she clung to, that tiny hope that all wasn't lost.

"I won't do it," she whispered, doing her best to keep the trembling out of her voice. "I'm not going away." Ignoring the hard set of his mouth and the unwelcome in his stance, she moved toward him, not stopping until she stood directly in front of him. Right away she noticed that he couldn't look at her. He closed his eyes as if some great battle was taking place inside of him.

Standing on tiptoes, she brushed her mouth over his. Her lips were soft, light, and gentle.

Rooster remained frozen, unyielding.

Refusing to be thwarted, she kissed him again, this time with more feeling, slanting her mouth over his, letting him know she wasn't going without a fight.

She felt him weakening, opening to her, but it lasted only a moment before he jerked his head away. He took a step back, putting some distance between the two of them.

"What are you doing here?" Rooster asked again.

Lauren rocked back on her bare feet, accepting now that it simply might be too late and she might have already lost him. Tears pooled in her eyes and she bit her lower lip.

All at once Rooster swore under his breath. Within the space of a single heartbeat he came to her, taking hold of her by the shoulders, half lifting her from the floor. "I don't care . . . I don't care why you came . . . It doesn't matter . . . I'm just glad you're here." He held her tightly against his upper body as though to absorb her right through his clothes and into his skin.

Lauren looped her arms around his neck and clung to him. And then he was kissing her as if he was a starving man who'd stumbled upon a Thanksgiving feast, as if he couldn't taste enough of her fast enough. With her hands framing his face, she kissed him with the same hunger, with the same intensity, until they were both panting, nearly oxygen deprived.

When he finally broke away, Lauren swayed off balance. His hands on the curve of her shoulders were all that kept her upright. His own shoulders heaved as he held her at arm's length.

After several moments, he seemed to regain his breath. "I need a shower and a shave." He paused long enough to kiss her and added, "Then we can talk."

"I'll make coffee."

Rooster nodded, and Lauren started to turn away, but her husband caught her hand and stopped her and raised her fingers to his lips, kissing the back of her hand.

As though it pained him to be away from her longer than necessary, he headed into the bedroom while Lauren went into the kitchen. She had just pulled out the coffeemaker when she heard Rooster call her name.

"For the love of heaven, woman, what did you do with my underwear?" he called out.

Hearing him opening and closing drawers, Lauren rushed into the bedroom. "Sorry, I forgot to tell you I changed a few things around in here as well."

"So I noticed." He looked about the room and shook his head. The bed was on the opposite wall and the dresser was where the bed had once been.

"You moved the bedroom furniture around on your own?" he asked with a frown.

She nodded. "I had a lot of energy to burn off, and, according to what I learned in the feng shui book, there was no balance in the room."

Rooster simply shook his head.

"You'll find your things in the middle shelf in the bathroom." It made sense to Lauren, as that was where they should be.

"And towels?"

"Hall closet."

"Anything else I should know?"

"Just one thing," she whispered. "I'm crazy over you."

Rooster reached for her, his large hand at the base of her neck as he pulled her mouth to his. The kiss was deep and filled with weeks of longing. When he broke it off, he braced his forehead against hers. "I won't be long."

"Okay."

Ten minutes later he came into the kitchen dressed in a freshly washed pair of jeans and a shirt. His hair was wet and his face clean shaved. Lauren had two cups of coffee on the kitchen table. "Are you hungry?" she asked. He looked as if he was several pounds lighter and desperately tired.

"I'm fine."

They sat across from each other. Rooster reached for her hand, clenching it tightly in his own.

"Why did you take off?" she asked, the first question that came to mind, needing answers.

He didn't meet her gaze. "I'd pinned my hopes on the fact that you might be pregnant, and when I learned you weren't it felt as if our marriage was a lost cause."

"Oh, Rooster, I was disappointed, too."

"I thought if we had a baby you might be willing to give me another chance. When you weren't, I had to get away and lick my wounds. From the look of things," he said, and glanced into the living room, "you've been here awhile."

She nodded. "Ten days. I apologize for the changes, but I needed to keep busy, and this helped me feel closer to you."

Rooster kissed her fingertips. "I'm sorry, Lauren. I was a fool not to tell you about Lacey and me . . . Even now I don't know why I didn't. You deserved to know everything."

"I don't ever want there to be secrets between us."

"That's a promise I won't have trouble keeping."

"Where did you go?" she asked. It seemed as if he'd been away forever.

"The crazy part is, I can't really tell you. I simply rode. Max did something similar to deal with his grief. Getting away seemed to help him, and I thought it might help me."

"Did it?"

"No," he admitted. "I couldn't stop thinking about you. After a while I accepted the fact that I'd lost you by my own stupidity. I assumed we were about to have one of the shortest marriages in history. I did everything I could to put you out of my mind."

"Did it work?" she asked, needing to know.

"No, but I tried," he admitted.

"Why were you so cold when you first walked in the house?" she asked. Perhaps one day she'd tell him that he'd ruined her end-of-the-movie fantasy of their reunion.

Rooster set down his coffee. "I thought at first the house had been burglarized while I was away."

"Yeah, sorry about that."

"And then you were there, like a vision, a figment of my imagination, and I was stunned. I'd made the decision to do everything within my power to put you out of my life and move forward."

"I intend to make that impossible, so you'd better get used to seeing me every day for the rest of your life."

"I think I'll be able to deal with that."

"Good thing," she said, smiling, unbelievably happy.

"You'll notice it didn't take me long to change my mind," Rooster reminded her.

"Long enough." She didn't know if her heart could have taken it if he had sent her away.

Rooster sipped his coffee and seemed to sway in his chair.

"When was the last time you slept?" she asked, immediately concerned.

He looked up at her as if he was unable to answer the question. "I don't remember."

"That's what I thought." She stood, took her coffee and his, and carried their cups to the sink. "We'll talk more in the morning, but for right now, we're going to bed."

"If I can find it," Rooster teased as he stood, a little uneasy on his feet.

"You'll find it," she assured him, and slipped her arm around his waist.

"You'd better not plan on sleeping," he told her, his eyes dark and serious. "At least not right away."

"We'll see," she said, cajoling him.

But Rooster proved to be right. It was a good long time before either of them fell into a deep slumber.

Epilogue

"Oh, Bethanne," Lauren whispered as she stepped into the reception hall, viewing it for the first time. The room was beautifully decorated for her and Rooster's wedding reception. The round tables were adorned with baskets of flowers in pale green and lavender. The chairs were covered in white linen, with large lavender-and-white silk bows tied in the back. Her friend had seen to every detail.

"Does this meet with your feng shui requirements?" Rooster teased her.

"You're not going to let me live that down, are you?"

His answer was a warm smile that washed over her like sunshine. "You can rearrange the furniture any way you want. Only next time you might want to mention it, especially if you decide to move the bed again."

Lauren struggled to hold back a smile. The feng shui book had made a strong impression, and ever since reading it, she routinely moved the furniture around. Rooster rarely noticed until he went to sit on a chair that was no longer where he assumed and instead landed on his backside on the carpet. It'd become something of a joke between them.

"This is the same place where Andrew and Courtney had their wedding reception," Bethanne explained.

"And where Bethanne agreed to be my bride," Max said, his arm around his wife's trim waist.

They shared a long look as though the memory of that reception lingered in their minds. Lauren hadn't known Bethanne or Max back then, but she wished she had. Over the last several months she'd come to consider Bethanne a good friend, and Max, too. Her hope was that her marriage to Rooster would be as strong and secure as that of her two friends.

"It won't be long before the room is filled with family and friends who want nothing more than to wish you every happiness."

"I am happy," Lauren said, looking up at her husband, "so very happy." Her eyes locked with Rooster's. Even now, three months after their Vegas wedding, it was hard to believe they were actually married. What they'd done had been completely illogical, and yet it had been so very right. Rational people didn't get married on a whim. They'd both taken a tremendous risk; thankfully, it had all worked out. Lauren fell more in love with her husband every day. She'd blindly walked into this marriage; they both had. Yet, in retrospect, she'd do it again in a heartbeat. In fact, Lauren wouldn't change a thing . . . then again, maybe she would. She'd cheated herself out of a honeymoon, but they'd been making up for that lost time ever since Rooster returned from his sojourn.

Their life together had been a whirlwind of activity. Max and Rooster had been working long hours to put everything into place in order to move the company. All the necessary paperwork was in motion. The wine-distribution company had located a warehouse in an industrial area in South Seattle, and Max had negotiated the lease. In time, Max and Rooster hoped to build their own warehouse.

Rooster traveled between the two states as often as possible. Every minute they were apart was agony. Lauren didn't know how Bethanne and Max had managed over the last sixteen months. Thankfully, it would be only a matter of time before the two couples would live full-time in the same city and they could do away with the long commute. Frankly, Lauren couldn't wait, and for more reasons than Rooster even knew.

"You did a wonderful job with the decorations," Lauren told her friend. "I hardly know how to thank you."

"Seeing how happy you've made Rooster is appreciation enough. But you need to thank Annie. She's the one who did the majority of the organization."

"I will."

"She'll be here with Tony."

"Tony?" Max asked. "I thought she was dating a guy named Bill."

"That is so last week," Bethanne teased her husband.

"Everything's worked out between Annie and her mom?" Rooster asked.

Lauren nodded. "Working for her dad for those few weeks woke Annie up when it came to her father. From what Bethanne told me, it all worked out for the best."

"For us, too," Rooster murmured.

"Oh, yes." Lauren looked up at her husband and noticed that his eyes flared briefly. For a moment she thought he might lean down and kiss her, but to her disappointment, he restrained himself.

"How many guests should we expect?" Rooster asked as he worked his finger around the collar of his dress shirt. He'd agreed to wear a suit for the reception, and she had to admit he made for a fine figure, but this wasn't his normal attire.

"We got over a hundred RSVPs," Lauren answered, but there was only one guest's name she felt she should mention. "Todd's coming, along with a friend." He was dating an intern from the station, and the two seemed to have hit it off nicely.

Rooster frowned. "You invited Todd?"

"Yes. We talked about it, remember?"

He eyed her suspiciously. "I vaguely remember, but, as I recall, you distracted me."

Lauren did her best to hide her amusement. "As I recall, you can be very easily distracted." Then, turning serious, she asked, "You don't mind, do you?"

"Not in the least," he assured her.

The door opened, and all eyes turned in that direction as Katie and Dietrich arrived. Katie paused and looked around. "Oh, my, are we the first ones to arrive?" Glancing at her watch, she looked up. "We're way early, aren't we?"

"It's not a problem," Lauren was quick to tell her. "Let me introduce you to my husband and friends." She made the introductions, and greetings were exchanged.

"When are you due?" Bethanne asked, apparently noticing the small bulge in Katie's tummy.

"December."

Dietrich stood behind Katie with his hands on top of her shoulders.

"Everything is good between you and your mom?" Lauren asked. She suspected it was. Elisa seemed to have adjusted to the fact that her daughter was her own person and fully capable of making her own life decisions. While the circumstances weren't ideal, the young couple was making it work. According to Elisa, Katie had done wonders with the small house on Dietrich's parents' farm. Dietrich had finished his studies and had taken over the everyday management.

"My parents have been great," Katie told her. "Mom went a bit crazy in the beginning, but that's understandable, and it's in the past. She's already going way overboard when it comes to buying things for the baby. It's a little girl; I don't know if she told you."

"She did." Lauren had watched the quick turnaround her friend had made and was proud of her. Elisa and Katie talked nearly every day, and Elisa made trips to the Walla Walla area at least once a month. Already Lauren could see that her friend was going to be a wonderful grandmother.

Katie glanced at her wrist. "Mom and Dad should be here any time."

A man came over and spoke briefly to Bethanne. After he left, she explained, "That was the deejay. He wants to test the sound system."

"Perhaps we should check out the dance floor," Max suggested, reaching for Bethanne's hand.

Rooster tensed and leaned forward to whisper in Lauren's ear, "I'm not much good at this."

"Don't worry," she said as she followed the two other couples toward the dance floor. "Just hold me and shuffle your feet a bit, okay?"

Katie and Dietrich stepped onto the polished oak dance floor and the music started. Right away, Dietrich took Katie in his arms. Bethanne and Max followed. Rooster released a sigh and wrapped his arms around Lauren. For someone who assumed he lacked the dancing gene, Rooster did amazingly well.

Lauren closed her eyes, and Rooster pressed his chin to the side of her head. "Thank you," he whispered.

"For what?"

"For your husband list, for loving me, for hiding my clothes and moving my furniture around. Mostly, thank you for completing me. You're my family now, Lauren, and hopefully we'll add to that family in due course."

"You might have your wish sooner than you realize."

In a flash, he lifted his head. "What did you say?"

"I'm late," she told him.

"What does that mean?" he demanded.

"It means I'm late, but I never am, and so I bought a home test kit."

"And?"

"And the stick turned blue."

"Blue?"

"Positive, in other words."

He went completely still. "You're pregnant?"

"It looks that way."

"Hey, look," Max said as he passed by them, Bethanne in his arms. "Three brides all together. Blossom Street brides."

"Max," Rooster called out excitedly. "We're pregnant."

Max's face broke into a huge grin. "Congratulations. I figured you two were up to something."

Lauren's husband tightened his embrace and heaved a lengthy sigh. "I don't know that a body can take in this much happiness all in one fell swoop."

"Brides and babies," Max said, laughing and shaking his head at the same time.

"It seems like a pretty wonderful combination to me," Bethanne chided.

Elisa and Garry stepped into the hall. Elisa looked around. "I thought we were early, but it looks like the party has already started."

"We're testing out the sound system," Katie explained to her mother. "Come on, join in."

Garry immediately swept Elisa into his arms and whirled her around the room.

Lauren noticed that Rooster seemed unable to take his eyes off the couple.

"They took ballroom dancing classes," she told him.

"Wow, they're good."

"You want to take a few dance classes?" she asked.

Rooster snorted. "No way."

"You might like it. Garry balked at first, but he came to really enjoy it." Several times while at the store Lauren found her employer practicing his footwork, dancing with an imaginary partner.

Rooster hesitated. "I can't see me ever taking dance classes, but then I never really saw myself as a husband much, either, and now I'm a husband and I'm going to be a father." He shook his head as if even now it was more than he could assimilate.

"I don't suppose I ever mentioned that twins run in the family."

Rooster's eyes went wide.

Alix and Jordan arrived and waved at Rooster and Lauren.

"Join the party," Bethanne called out. "It's just getting started."

It wasn't long before the reception hall was filled with guests. Lydia, Brad, Casey, and Cody arrived, along with Todd and his date, who he proudly introduced. Todd looked happy, and when he caught Lauren's attention, he winked.

"I saw that," Rooster muttered.

"Are you jealous?" she teased.

"Can't see any reason why I should be." He kissed the side of her head, his breath fanning the small hair by her ear. "Brides and babies," Rooster whispered as they mingled with their guests, greeting each one. "This is better than the best motorcycle ride I ever took."

"You silver-tongued devil," she chided, and laughed. "You know exactly what to say to sweep a girl off her feet."

Beginner's Scarf

Designed by Sandy Payne for "Beginning Knitting" classes held at Debbie Macomber's A Good Yarn Shop.

Materials: Debbie Macomber's Blossom Street Collection, Wild Meadow. Worsted Weight, 253 yards (250 meters), 3.5 ounces (100 grams)
Needles: US #8 (5.00 mm)
Gauge: 20 stitches to 4 inches (10 cm)

Cast on 27 stitches

Garter stitch
Rows 1 through 10—knit

Stockinette stitch
Row 11—purl
Row 12—knit
Row 13—purl

Row 14—knit

Row 15—purl

Row 16—knit

Row 17—purl

Row 18—knit

Row 19—purl

Row 20—knit

Repeat rows 1 through 20, 13 more times, or desired length

Knit 10 more rows

Bind off

Weave in ends

Optional: apply fringe

ABOUT THE AUTHOR

DEBBIE MACOMBER, the author of *Blossom Street Brides,*
Starry Night, Rose Harbor in Bloom, Starting Now, Angels
at the Table, The Inn at Rose Harbor, and *A Turn in the*
Road, is a leading voice in women's fiction. Eight of her
novels have hit #1 on the *New York Times* bestseller list,
with three debuting at #1 on the *New York Times, USA*
Today, and *Publishers Weekly* lists. In 2009 and 2010, *Mrs.*
Miracle and *Call Me Mrs. Miracle* were Hallmark Chan
nel's top-watched movies for the year. Debbie Macomber
has more than 170 million copies of her books in print
worldwide.

www.debbiemacomber.com

ABOUT THE TYPE

This book was set in Sabon, a typeface designed by the well-known German typographer Jan Tschichold (1902–74). Sabon's design is based upon the original letter forms of sixteenth-century French type designer Claude Garamond and was created specifically to be used for three sources: foundry type for hand composition, Linotype, and Monotype. Tschichold named his typeface for the famous Frankfurt typefounder Jacques Sabon (c. 1520–80).

World Vision®

Building a better world for children

Knit for Kids

As a bestselling author and an avid knitter
with a big heart,

DEBBIE MACOMBER

proudly serves as the International Spokesperson
for World Vision's Knit for Kids.

Join Debbie and our nationwide family of
28,000 volunteer knitters to help fight poverty
with your knitting needles! You can give warmth
and comfort to children in need, across the
nation and around the world.

Visit **worldvision.org/knitforkids**
to download a pattern and start knitting today!

Visit **worldvision.org**
to see what else we're doing for children
around the world.